The Blind Light

ALSO BY STUART EVERS

Your Father Sends His Love
If This Is Home
Ten Stories About Smoking

The
Blind
Light

STUART EVERS

PICADOR

First published 2020 by Picador
an imprint of Pan Macmillan
The Smithson, 6 Briset Street, London ECIM 5NR
Associated companies throughout the world
www.panmacmillan.com

ISBN 978-1-5290-3097-6

1 3 5 7 9 8 6 4 2

A CIP catalogue record for this book is available from the British Library.

Typeset by Palimpsest Book Production Ltd, Falkirk, Stirlingshire
Printed and bound by CPI Group (UK) Ltd, Croydon, CR0 4YY

L.I.B, C.V.E, M.L.E

Wildboarclough

2019

Saturday 17 August

They were at their most together there, at their most together then. This he thought, or something like it, sitting in the field between the farmhouse and his neighbour's property. It had been a seventies summer, one of the hot ones, and in much the same spot as he now sat, he and his elder sister had perched on a black plastic silo, sharing a pair of binoculars to spy on the Carters. It was the perfect vantage; the ideal elevation to see into their garden, their trampoline and fishpond, their rockery and patio. They did not comment on what they saw, there were no arguments as to how long they could hold the binoculars. They just sat and watched, Nate's legs sticking to the plastic sheeting; his sister's heels beating the compacted grass beneath.

He remembered what they'd seen. What he'd seen at least. The father smoke-blown at a tiny Hibachi grill; the mother carrying a large bowl of salad; the shirtless boy and summer-dressed girl, sun-blonde both, setting the table. Uncle Jim, Auntie Daph, Tommy and Tasha.

Busked by flies, they'd thought themselves secret agents, covert operatives watching the Carters conduct their foreign customs. Nate would have been about eight, so Anneka twelve or thirteen. Her in a brown dress, long hair like burned wheat, an elastic band on her wrist for luck; him with a scab on his knee, an imaginary island eroded through picking. He remembered this as he held the same pair of binoculars. The dress. The scab. The magnified garden, the magnified family. The coveting of Tommy's Dunlop tennis racquet.

How tall the silo had felt, how high, and it was not so high, just that he was so small. Small then, and slight. Ha ha. To think that. So small and his father's voice so big, so hoarse and so loud, shouting at them from the farmhouse.

'Get down from up on there, you two!' their father had shouted. 'What have I told you about the silos?'

Nate had put down the binoculars and looked to his sister.

'Hand them over,' Anneka had said.

'But Dad—'

'Hand them over, Nate,' she'd said.

And so he'd passed her the binoculars and later they'd both been in trouble. But at least they'd been in trouble together: equally miscreant, equally punished.

He held the same binoculars now; it was late in the day; the heat of the afternoon clinging still. He picked up the binoculars and focused them on the Carters' garden. A recent interest, this: one started when the casual rentals began a few years before. On weekends and school holidays he watched families and friends, small children and teenagers, hen parties and stag dos, sometimes catching a furtive glimpse of breast or buttock. The Carters had installed a hot tub where the old patio had been and Nate liked to see the trunkless men and bikini-stripped women hopping in and out of the water, lamp-lit at night, sun-blushed in the day. Once he'd seen some sex. Some oral too. He'd meant to put down the binoculars, but hadn't.

The garden was hoed and manicured, better appointed; a wood-burning oven where the Hibachi had once been; an eight-seater table on a grey slate patio; blue-matted sun-loungers stacked beside the hot tub. There were two cars parked out front, but no one in the garden. They'd come outside soon, though, before the sun downed, he was sure of that. He wanted to see Carter and Tommy first; wanted to see them before Anneka arrived. Brotherly, that.

He checked his phone and it was fully charged and fully barred; there were no missed calls and no messages. From the sack at his feet, he took a can of beer and offered it up in toast to the dusking sun.

'I remember,' Nate said, 'when all this was nought but fields.'

It was Carter's joke. Carter now, Uncle Jim then. His big hands on Nate's slope shoulders; Carter's laugh booming like a story-book giant. Nought but fields, ha!

Just two fields, in fact; the land divided by a dirt track and a parched hedge of hawthorn and blackthorn. The Carters' land on one side, his on the other. Down the hill, the grass on his side – thistle turf and clod, tinder dry – led to a tree-crowded dell. He'd not been down there in years. A check with the binoculars. Nothing. No car coming through the leaves. No sign of Anneka. Not there, nor by the cowsheds that huddled close to the farmhouse.

He drank from the can and the beer was cool. He checked the phone, replaced it in the cup-holder. Anneka had never called him, not once. He no longer knew her voice. When he called her number, it rang out until the call was caught by another woman's voice, one owned by a telephone network. At first he left messages; later, he simply rang off as the once-real woman answered his call.

Hers was one of many voices he could no longer remember. In his head, when Anneka said, 'Hand them over,' he didn't hear her voice, just something generically female, generically young. Same with lovers, school-friends, teachers: they all sounded underwater and muted. He remembered his father's voice though. The dead have insistent voices; they cut and jab. His father's especially.

He checked his phone, still fully barred, still fully charged, and picked up the binoculars. As though this a new idea; one just alighted upon.

There was no movement in the garden save for the drowse of the tarp on the hot tub, the shiver of olive tree fronds. Inside though, there was the suggestion of occupancy: shadows in the windows; figures behind the glass. He watched them gather, then the outside lights came on, casting bright over the patio, the French doors; the doors opened by a woman he didn't recognize. The woman was followed outside by Tommy. Certainly Tommy. So close through the lenses he could spit and reach him.

They walked out onto the patio, Tommy pointing, the woman, his new wife, Nate assumed, following the line of his arm. Nate watched them sit at the table, drink from tumblers, talk, laugh, clasp hands, kiss. No one joined them. He watched Tommy and his wife stand and take in the view, loosely linked by arms, smiling, their tumblers abandoned on the table as they walked back inside.

The first time he remembered seeing the Carter house he was four or so. They'd driven for what had felt like the whole day and it was not quite dark, but all the windows burned bright, burned in golds and silvers. They pulled up outside the gabled facade, the date 1848 carved into a white stone surrounded by umber brickwork, the ground-floor windows framed with lush red velvet curtains; the bedroom windows sashed with blue gingham. The size of the door and its lionhead knocker; the smoothness of the parquet on entering; the size of the room he was to sleep in, the hugeness of the bath, the glitter of chandeliers as they ate, none of it he could quite believe existed.

'Am I dreaming?' he'd asked Anneka.

'No,' she'd said, 'It's real.'

A few years later, when his father told them they were moving north, Nate had assumed they would live with the Carters. That he would become part of the household, share Tommy's toys, run riot through the garden. He'd tried not to look disappointed when they were shown to a stone cottage not much bigger than their house back home. It was cold and austere, a look of furious utilitarianism, but with a stout front door that seemed loaned from a medieval keep. When the lights were on, it would be fine. When the fire was lit, it would be home. And it was. Remained so.

He finished his can, crushed it under his shoe, folded up the chair. Dark had come, fleet as rabbits, and he used the phone's torch to guide him up to the farmhouse, its kitchen window now unlit, though he knew he'd left the lights on. Bulb gone. Fuse blown, most likely. The electrics were shot and had been for years, another chore he'd left to fester.

In the bulb-blown kitchen he opened doors and cupboards looking for candles. In the third drawer down he found them, along with some matches. He lit one, let the wax drip onto a saucer and set it down. The light haloed, a golden caul. He went to light another candle and saw something reflected in the window. A glass half full, an open bottle of wine. He didn't turn, but looked into the window, the glass and bottle in the candlelight, blurred and sketched in the pitch. He heard the sound of water from upstairs, the sound of feet on the stairs, saw the light of a phone dance through the open doors, then stop as it entered the kitchen.

'Hello, Nate,' she said.

What to say to that. How to speak, how to form words. Forty years or so, and her voice again. Her face again. What to say to that.

'I assumed this was for my benefit –' she pointed to the wine – 'I know I should've waited, but it's been such a long drive. And then the lights went out. Almost as soon as I poured it.'

A smile in the window pane. To turn now. First thing to do. To turn. And he turned, but pinned himself to the lip of the counter. Wanted to say hello but could not say anything. Fuses blown up and down the body.

'What's wrong?' she said. 'Cows got your tongue?'

She laughed and it was her laugh, immediately her laugh. Same laugh at the same joke she used to make. A private joke. Something he'd said once, getting the idiom all wrong, and her never letting him forget it.

'Sorry about the lights,' he said. 'I need to look at the fuses.'

'I like the candles,' she said. 'Look at the fuses later.'

He nodded. She sat down and sipped the wine.

She looked changed and unchanged: the same thin nose and cleft chin, but sharper around the cheekbones, lined at her seaboard eyes. Hair the same muddy brown, but dusted with ash

7

and tin, cut short and boyish; her hands blue-veined now, thin-skinned. The same sprung vigilance to her posture, though; like she was ready to dodge an oncoming hazard.

'How did you get in?' he said. 'All the doors were locked.'

He remembered her shrug – Where's my ball? *Shrug.* Have you seen my jacket? *Shrug.* When are you coming back? *Shrug* – a slight movement, little more; not quite disdain and not quite not.

'The spare key,' Anneka said, holding up a Yale. 'All those years and you keep it in the same place. Lax security, Nate. Very lax.'

She wagged her finger, an old impersonation. Their father warning of something, a danger or a threat.

'I didn't see your car,' he said.

'I parked it around the back,' she said. 'Didn't want to announce my presence too soon.'

The times he'd imagined it, this reunion: where it would happen, how. Sometimes hugging her in a house she owned; sometimes sitting beside her in a cafe or bar; sometimes here, in the kitchen, slapping her across the cheek. All the rehearsals, their drama and their intrigue, and her now here, in their childhood home, as he asked her about door keys and car parking.

Her face clenched, then softened, her eyes inching over his face, something invasive about it, as though forty years would be revealed in a few seconds' staring.

'Are you not going to hug me?' she said, approaching him, her arms slightly splayed, inviting without encouragement. Nate held her limply, like he was transporting a body or an imbecile. Anneka kept her arms by her sides at first, then tightened them around him. She smelled of nothing. Not a thing. Like the scent of fresh water, the scent of cold.

'You haven't changed,' he said, whispering into her ear. 'Not at all.'

Anneka pulled back and put her hands on his biceps, kissed him on the cheek, faint lips grazing his beard.

'I wouldn't have recognized you,' she said. 'I could've walked past you a hundred times and I'd never have known it was you. Maybe I did once. Imagine that.'

She studied his face, seeking him out beneath the broken nose, the weather-etched skin, the sag beneath his jaw.

'Time moves different when you're up with the dawn,' he said. 'It beats at you. That's what Dad always said.'

'You don't look like him,' she said. 'I thought you'd grow into him. I thought I'd open the door and see him here as clear as you are now.'

She left him by the sink and sat at table, taking their father's seat. Straight to it without thinking. He wondered whether she remembered or not.

'You don't look like Mam either,' she said, picking up her glass. 'You ever consider you were adopted?'

They both laughed. Another old joke, one Nate had forgotten until then. She seemed to know exactly what to say, when to say it, when to run through the old routines.

'Sometimes,' he said, taking his own seat at the table, 'I feel like I'm standing just like him. Saying the same things as him. The exact same things. Does that happen to you?'

She sipped her wine. Her face clenched again. The softness of the light, the gutter of the flame, softened nothing, cosied nothing.

'Let's not talk of him, Nate,' she said. 'Please let's not.'

She looked to where the clock had once been, an old ticker that had given out years before, never to be replaced.

'This house stinks, you know that?' she said. 'I noticed it as soon as I came through the door. The stink. Like something rotten.'

Her thin-skinned hands, the blue veins. Hands like their mother's, delicately fingered, resting on the table as though ready to play piano.

'I thought maybe you were dead. You know' – she made a pistol with her right hand and put it to her temple – 'bang, bang to the head. Farmers do that a lot, so I've heard. I read about it once. It's an epidemic, apparently.'

'It's a farm,' he said. 'Things stink.'

She shook her head.

'But that's just it. It doesn't smell of farm. I was prepared for the smell of shit, but this . . . this just stinks.'

'It smells the same as it ever did,' he said. 'You've just forgotten.'

'I haven't forgotten anything, Nate,' she said. 'Not a thing.'

She looked back towards the missing clock.

'Or maybe I have,' she said.

Her eyes lit for a moment. Something suddenly recalled.

'I remember spying on the Carters,' she said. 'You remember that? We'd take the binoculars and sit on the silos, thinking we were secret agents.'

She was smiling, encouraging a response, an engagement, something confederate in her eyes. It felt cruel. Why that of all things? No accident, no accident at all. Like she'd been snooping, like she could pluck his most recent thoughts from his head. He felt her there, kicking around, looking at junk, sifting through rubbish.

'Secret agents?' he said.

'You must remember,' she said. 'We used to sit on the silos and watch the Carters eat dinner and play in the garden. You wanted their paddling pool and you wanted their tennis racquets even though you couldn't play. You don't remember?'

'Maybe,' he said. 'It sounds like something we might have done at least.'

She looked at the walls, the stone flags, the stove, drank her wine. After four decades, you are a different body; different cells, different biology, let alone different character. And yet Anneka was so much the same; the same slight judder as she inhaled, the same skittishness as the weeks before her A-levels. Welcome home, Anneka. You have been missed. Hated sometimes, but always missed.

'You cooked?' she said, pointing to the pan on the hob.

'I thought you might be hungry.'

Anneka carried her wine glass to the oven and stirred the pot, held up the spoon and let the liquor fall, the sauce slapping as it hit the surface.

'You know,' she said, 'I've not eaten meat in twenty years.'

'Really?'

She looked back at him from the stove, as though cooking there a long-standing chore.

'No,' she said. 'But it's possible, isn't it? You should have done a ratatouille or something.'

'I don't think I've ever had ratatouille, let alone made it.'

'I don't care for it much myself,' she said. 'I've never liked aubergines. Don't think I'd even seen one before we had that moussaka at the Carters.'

'That I remember,' he said. 'Mam gave us that face that meant we had to eat whatever it was on our plates. And you looked up all innocent, and said, "What's all this purple stuff?"'

'They had a good old laugh at us, didn't they?'

'Yes,' he said. 'A good old laugh.'

Nate lit the gas ring under the casserole and took the wooden spoon from Anneka. The two of them, side by side, her getting down bowls from the shelf above the stove, placing them on the table, like they did this every Friday night. Once hot enough, he brought the pan to the table, set it on a trivet, got them a ladle. Anneka filled the bowls; Nate cut them slices of bread.

Steam from the bowls, from the casserole, and all the things to say and nothing right to say. She could not quite look at him; he could not quite look at her. He picked up a slice of bread and buttered it to the very edge of the crust, dipped it into the sauce. She did not move and did not eat; the clock did not tick.

'They're here, you know,' he said at last, looking down into his bowl. 'They're both here. Carter and Tommy.'

'You've seen them?'

'Yes. I saw them out in the garden. Tommy at least.'

They looked at each other then, met eyes across the table, and suddenly so much to say and still unsure as to how to start.

'We don't have to do this, you know,' he said.

She shook her head.

'We have a deal,' she said. 'You agreed. I have the emails to prove it.'

'But—'

'No buts, Nate.'

He looked at his sister, his sister older than he could have ever imagined, still the girl with the lucky elastic band.

'You agreed too,' he said eventually, going back to his bowl. 'Mum's looking forward to seeing you tomorrow. You promised, so no welching.'

She put down her spoon.

'You sounded like him then,' she said. 'Such a Dad word, welching.'

Nate smiled. A big chip-tooth smile.

'As soon as the words were out of my mouth, I knew you'd say that.'

He put his hand across the table, and she accepted it, squeezed it.

Her there, definitely her. In that face, looking back. He smiled and drained his wine glass. She did the same and Nate passed her the bottle. Anneka poured for them both. At their most together there, at their most together then.

Doom Town and the One

1959

January

I

Floodlights pool at the western edge of the civil defence base; their beams hazed with low-lying fog. They are lit but are usually dark in the mornings, no matter how bad the visibility. From the stoop of a Nissen hut, Drummond watches his former comrades dance the last steps to the parade ground; the waiting transports idling there, ready to take them to railway stations and bus depots. They are a ragtag rush of men, youths really; like him all just shy of majority, all reacquainting themselves with the lightness of shoes, the thinness of suits. He hears their chatter, their whoops and hollers, their fetterless joy. It is the joy of men who are alive. The joy of men who have survived. The joy of those who have earned their liberation. No joy like it, that joy. The fools that they are.

Two years of enclosure; two years and now no longer prisoner or protectorate. He is free to leave. Expected to leave. To take a wagon with the lads, board a southbound train, ride a Tube carriage, walk the last stretch to home, open the door to backslaps from his grandpa, kisses from his great-aunt, something rustled up in the kitchen, never mind the hour. He looks at his wristwatch – a quarter to eleven – and calculates the distance, the time it would take to reach home. From Cumbria to Essex. North-west to south-east. Home for midnight. Midnight latest.

A transport drives off, another quickly follows it. The grind of tyre on pebbledash, the hammer of accelerating engines, the cheers of men, the opening of a gate, the closing of a gate, and then nothing. No voices, no bootsteps, no shouted orders. The windows of the surrounding Nissen huts are unlit; the study block, the mess room, the kitchens are similarly dark. Drum stands, the last man alive. That's how it feels, upright in the chill wind: the only survivor, kit bag in hand, alone in a deserted coastal town.

He could leave. He could stay. He has, for once, options. Two years of being told, of being instructed, of obeyance, and now expected to make a decision alone. Sometimes it's better just to be told; it's easier that way. Heard it's the same with criminals. His Uncle Nudge, the black sheep never out of prison for long before being sent back, said he preferred it inside. 'Four square and a bed every night, no one mithering,' he'd say. 'Who's going to argue with that?'

Drum walks towards the parade ground, eyes left, distracted by the floodlights on the training ground, their beams glinting from wire and strut and mesh. There are no exercises planned – all men are to be off site by midday – so why the floodlights? No such light was ever afforded the servicemen ordered there; they were never even given torches. Must be for the benefit of others. Ministry men, government officials, field marshals. Likes of them. Dignitaries given a short tour of the civil defence training ground: its reconstruction of a town in the aftermath of an atomic strike. Look! The bombed-out houses. Look! The stricken roads. Look! The fallen church. A slow shuffle around, floodlights picking out authentic touches. A shoe burned into a floorboard. A dead-body dummy behind the wheel of a Ford Anglia. The melted keys of a Remington typewriter.

Or perhaps this is when they add those details, when the sergeants and staff add more provocations, more images to harrow, more smashed glass to the asphalt streets. Maybe this happens every time the men leave, Drum never noticing because usually he'd be prepping dinner in the kitchens by now. Perhaps that, yes. Preparations for the next show.

The lights are a distraction, one welcomed, open-armed. His eyes are on the floodlights as he makes his way towards the parade ground. A walk to Millom. A walk to Gwen. Walked it many times, takes no longer than half an hour. Or wait for another transport.

Cadge a lift to the railway station. One of two things. To stay or to go. A binary option. He looks at the lights. There's time enough to make a decision. Plenty of time. No rush. He can go to Doom Town for a final time, take a last look, to fix it fast in the memory. He has the time to do that.

The pathway between the study block and the mess hall is cinder and stone; it scuffs boots, let alone shoes. He's wearing his good shoes, the oxblood brogues, the pair Carter bought him. He does not look down to the damage done; he does not want to be reminded of Carter. In the hospital, in the infirmary, Carter. Not to think of him. Nor think of Gwen. Concentrate on the lights instead.

Between the main campus of the base and the civil defence training ground, an open stretch of scrub and turf; an untended no-man's-land. He walks across it and does not think of Carter or of Gwen, of staying or leaving. He does not mine the past, though it weighs on him; does not consider the present, though it is pressing; does not look to the future, though he knows he might glimpse it. He concentrates only on walking; the eating up of time and of distance, the distant light.

At school he was told if he found himself stuck on a question he should move on to another. His mind, without him realizing, would still be working on a solution, and on revisiting the problem, he'd be more likely to know the answer. A kindly tip from his mathematics teacher, but one that sat uneasy. How can you trust yourself if the mind works without your consent?

Reaching the outskirts of the town, the first ghost houses behind the fence, he remembers something from a book Carter lent him, a poetry collection: the words *grimly gay*. His face, he imagines, is that: *grimly gay*. He says the words as he walks – *grimly gay grimly gay grimly gay* – until they are white noise and companionable gibberish.

The gate to the training ground is open; its padlock and chain coiled inside the fence. The roofless houses and brick-strewn streets are boldly lit despite the fog. On his unauthorized visits, so many of them over the last three months, he's seen it only by torchlight, by thin sunlight at dawn. The lamps make it seem stage-set, ready for cameras; actors waiting somewhere for their scene. It is no less terrifying for that. No less real. No less choking.

On the street, close enough to kick, amongst the masonry and glass, he spies a rusted washboard, its frame cracked, but still recognizable as a washboard. He does not think of Gwen, of Carter. Instead he is reminded of a washboard strummed percussively; a skiffle band from back home playing a song in a room underneath a pub. The sweat on the washboardist's brow, the tubthump in the heat, the rolled shirtsleeves, the loose strings of the guitars. In the silence, he hears the song they played. 'The Rock Island Line'. You're gonna miss me when I'm gone.

2

The pub has a thick-beamed door and three solid locks; it is a job to open: the bolts requiring guile and power; the mortice an unhurried coaxing. Gwen is practised, but it still takes longer than she'd like. Once it is unlocked, she sets her mouth, touches her hair, checks the clock. On the stroke of eleven, a half-hour earlier than most other pubs, she opens the door, its gaoler clank, its whine and scrape. Always on the stroke. Pride herself on it.

She opens up onto pale winter light, sky a shade of cinderblock; so dull an illumination. So dull and no one there to darken it. She fastens the door to the latch and someone is swiftly behind her, his smell familiar.

'Morning, Nick,' she says, turning around. Old Nick smiles between demented side-whiskers, below hood-lipped eyes. He shakes his head and from the hip pocket of his tattered herring-bone jacket takes out a fob watch.

'Late this morning, my dear,' he says.

'No,' she says, hands across the door, barring his entry. 'On the stroke, as always.'

'No,' he says. 'Late. Late by five minutes . . . six now.' He taps the dial. 'I wound it this morning and set it to the pips.'

He smiles, gently forgiving, a pastoral look; an aged, reverend face.

'I'm sorry,' she says, accusing eyes on the smug clock.

She releases her arm and he walks into the bar, a ream of paper under his arm. He brings his smell gusting inside: clothes half-laundered; cooling sweat, woodsy almost. He hangs his overcoat on the hatstand, drapes his white-fringed scarf on top: just so.

Eleven in the morning and his cheeks red from rambling hills, from the salt-spite of the coastal pathways. Always mud on his boots, always mud on his trousers. Like he's missing a dog. Like he's lost one out in the fields.

Gwen lifts the hatch and starts pouring his black and tan, layering stout on pale. Old Nick sits at his table, the biggest of the barroom, closest to the fire, and organizes his work into three neat stacks.

With a pencil, he scores through a line of text. He licks the pencil tip afterwards, quickly, as though tasting his words. The pumps gutter beneath Gwen's feet; Nick's black and tan settles, the stout floating, still miraculous. With care, she carries it to his table and sets the jug down on the beer mat. Same as every day. Exactly the same.

She remains there, but he does not look up; one hand on the page, the other absently filling his pipe. Such thin and filthy fingers, long nails luned with tar and dirt. He says he can't work without slag under his nails, without earth on his palms. It's never looked like work to her.

'There you go,' she says.

'Ta,' he says. She looks down at his pages; he covers them with his arm. He glances up and there is a cold blue in his eyes, like the gas burner on full blast.

'Let me finish with this,' he says. 'And then we'll talk. I think that's best, don't you?'

3

The frosted turf on either side of the path gives way to the beginnings of the terrace. The first house he comes to he enters; its front gashed open, like a wrecking ball has been taken to it. The houses are like those on the estate on which he grew up; smaller, but similarly proportioned. The kind of properties everyone lives in, familiar to all.

Entering the town that first time, three months before, he noticed the church most of all, its absent spire, a small flock of seagulls on its still-standing archway. Ordered in through the gate on the south side of town, and there it was in front of them. Deliberate, this. To remind them that the bomb respects no god, no society, no man or ideal. A true leveller. They were made to stand to attention, to look straight ahead, to take it all in. The exploded terraces, the paneless windows, the motor-car husks, the church. The town smelled of smoke and something malty, a brewery stink. The sergeant walked behind them for a time, then marched them to the makeshift field hospital for instructions.

The inside of the house is typical: dust and brick and reminders of the lives once lived there. The upstairs is obliterated, there is no roof or ceiling. In what once was the kitchen, a stove is partially melted. Above it, on the last remaining plasterwork, somebody has scored their name. *Chazzer*. Underneath, somebody has added *Spud*. Underneath that, just three letters, *b-o-n*; the graffito unfinished, its author clearly interrupted.

★

At Ford's they'd called him Tin; at Ford's they'd called him Kettle. Sometimes they'd called him Kit; sometimes Bass. So many names for the same Drum: so many names for the tall young man with the chestnut-coloured curls who riveted doors in silent shifts, who always kept pace with production line speed, who listened and nodded and never complained when the men went out on strike. Unassuming, shy, but a good bloke. Agreed by all. Told that all the time. A good lad. A good worker. Two good years at Ford's; two good years of being a good comrade, of being called Roll, or Stick, or Oil. Then service. Where they called him Horse.

The first morning of his initial training, at the National Service base in Shropshire, they were called to the shower block. The first time he had been seen naked by anyone since boyhood. The other servicemen saw his cock. They did all but point. Even in the cold, so much bigger than everyone else's. He looked down and it appeared grotesque. Animal. He hid himself. It did not matter. From then on he was Horse. Even to the sergeants.

Newly named, he undertook the first days of training, days of blade-sharp trouser creases; boots shining like fresh paint on bonnets; sergeants' voices loud and close. Nissen hut and drill ground, Nissen hut and mess hall. At night there was light bullying: some lads mocked for prayers; some for wanking once the lights were out; some for quietly crying. At dawn, the sergeant banged a copper kettle to hasten them from bed. *Wakey, wakey, girls!*

He talked only when spoken to, same as when he'd started at the factory, advice from his grandpa. Listen as much as you can, say as little as you can muster. There were other factory lads there; they seemed to take to it easier than the others. Understood routine. Understood to do what was necessary and no more. He wrote to his grandpa and told him he was taking his advice. That he was showing no fear, and all was well.

Before lights out on the fourth night, a card school opened at the end of their hut, a small group involved, the rest of the thirty watching. Drum saw the con by the fifth hand, had seen the same scam at the factory: new lads taken for their first pay packet. There were six in, four skates and a pair of marks. The posh lad was called Carter, was up by a lot. He would be dealt an enticing hand, one almost unbeatable, then be soundly beaten.

Over his cards, Carter looked up to the assembled servicemen. A small, satisfied smile. Drum could have watched him lose; could have looked away, could have quietly predicted the hand Carter would be given as incitement. But their eyes met and Drum tipped him the slightest of winks. A suggestion of a wink, nothing more. Enough though. Enough for Carter to go back to his cards, study them again as the skates hurried him up. After reconsidering his cards two or three times, Carter folded. He took his winnings as the skates cleaned out the other mark. Factory smarts. Always have someone else to fleece.

The following night, Carter stopped Drum midway between Nissen hut and mess hall.

'Not tonight, Josephine,' Carter said. 'Tonight we eat with the officers. My treat.'

'You're an officer?' Drum said.

Carter smiled. Drum had never seen a smile like it. A smile of intense pleasure, one derived from providing something another man could not.

'No,' Carter said. 'But tonight we'll eat as officers. My way of thanks.'

In the officers' mess, they were sat at a table for two. Drum looked around, expecting to be turned out, sprung from the room; something that seemed to amuse Carter.

'Don't worry, we're all friends here,' Carter said. 'Thank you for bailing me out last night. That showed some guts.'

It hadn't felt like courage. It hadn't felt like valour. It felt like a dumb risk, stupidly taken.

'That's all right,' Drum said. 'Thanks for all this.'

'You are more than welcome. More than welcome.'

Carter nodded, bringing his thanks to an end as a bottle of wine arrived at their table, two plates of meat in sauce and potatoes with it.

Carter poured the wine and picked up his glass. Drum did the same. They chinked glasses and Drum tasted the first wine of his life, thin and sour on his lips. He looked down to his food and began to eat, the meal appreciably better than in the mess. He ate and he drank and he listened. Listened perhaps most of all.

Unbidden, Carter began his grandstand and spiel, the stories of his short life. How he'd been sent down from Oxford; how his 'rather important and powerful' father had insisted he take his National Service; his erotic adventures undertaken in foreign climes. His tales came at speed: exaggerated, tall, and without restraint in language or imagination. Drum had met men like him at Ford's, full of themselves and full of shit; but no one who seemed to believe it quite the way Carter did.

At the conclusion of an almost certainly untrue story of a gypsy woman who'd loved him but given him the clap, Carter put his hands on the table. He didn't say anything, didn't eat anything, didn't reach for the wine; just looked at Drum from a series of angles, as though what he saw might quickly change.

'You don't say much, do you?' Carter said. 'I thought cockneys all talked twenty to the dozen.'

'I'm not a cockney,' Drum said. 'I'm miles from being a cockney.'

'But still,' he said. 'You've said no more than ten words all night, and I've given you chapter and verse on yours truly. So, your turn. Tell me about you, Moore.'

To be called Moore was already a kindness. It was appreciated. More than the wine and the food. The consideration of that.

'There's nothing to tell,' Drum said.

'You have a girl?'

'No.'

'We'll have to fix that. Especially since . . .'

Carter lowered his eyes to Drummond's crotch, then quickly back to his reddening face.

'Come now,' Carter said. 'Tell me something you've never told anyone before. I told you the gypsy woman story, after all. Fair's fair.'

He leaned in to Drummond, rested himself on his elbows. The

intimacy of it, the proximity of his face: there was no chance of saying nothing now. Not with a wine-loosed tongue and a sense of owing; the keen of Carter's face, his elbows on the table. The closeness of him.

'There's nothing to tell,' Drum said.

'Indulge me.' Carter said. 'If we're to be friends, we need to share our stories, do we not?'

Drum looked down, closed his eyes. No chance to demure. No chance of escape.

'I almost killed a man,' Drum said.

That face. That face looking back.

'Go on,' Carter said.

'We were at a dance,' Drum said. 'A skiffle group was playing and this bloke said something to a girl I liked. He touched her. He said things to her. And something just went snap. I don't know. Something just snapped inside of me. Barry and Danny had to hold me back. If they hadn't, I swear I'd have kicked his head clean off.'

The effect he'd expected. Carter's face glowing, a locus between horror and deep admiration. The same look he'd seen on the faces in the canteen at Ford's as O'Driscoll had told the same story. That rushed disbelief, the sweet nip of the violence, the quickening of the pulse.

'Well, well,' Carter said. 'Still waters and all that. Still waters indeed. I think you'll be a very useful friend to have, Moore.'

A useful friend. Yes. Useful.

★

Drum walks through the blasted house, out of its open back rooms, into a collapsed ginnel. The cobblestones are rucked, displaced, skittled around like shot. The three cobbles he arranged into a pyramid on his last visit are still there. They are approaching permanence now; surviving intact for over a month. Three stones, laid and placed, ready to be kicked.

4

Nick works in silence, kitten licks of the pencil, kitten sips of beer. He is a published poet, a memoirist, playwright, professional wildsman, approved of by London society, a society he disdains. Once a year he goes there, providing him with a year's worth of reasons never to leave home again. He claims to have never spent more than one single night away from his flat in the town, and all of those under sufferance.

In a letter, stowed inside a loaned copy of *Women in Love*, Nick once asked Gwen what it was like to be raised in a public house. She never replied to his letters or his questions – casual enquiries amongst digressions on birds, on the turning of the seasons – but this one had troubled her time.

'There is, I believe,' the letter said, 'a certain kinship between those who live above places of business, as I have these last sixty-odd years. The divided kingdom: the public space below; the private realm above. The stairwell a kind of *purgatorio*, a portal between our exterior selves and our interior existence. I wonder, though, whether this is different in a tavern. A shop is a space of quick interaction, of expedited process; an inn, on the other hand, is a place of contemplation: an intermediary between private and public. How does that affect one, I wonder? What happens to the public space when the last patron has ambled from the fire and the doors have been bolted on the world?'

Over the course of that week, she mentally drafted and redrafted a response. Point is. (She would start.) The thing is. When you think about it. What you don't understand is. What it comes down to is. She would meander this course, wishing her brother were back from Service, wishing her mother were back from the dead, both around to add some pepper to the pot. Her father was no use; if she asked about the past, he embarked solely upon his own fool nostalgia, stories that were never her own.

Point is, the bar was forbidden when we were young. Mam and Da would be downstairs, but might as well have been in Barrow or Berlin. We always had breakfast with them before school, the two of them walking us to the gates when we were young; doing the dishes and kissing us goodbye when we were older.

The thing is, the pub was just home, nothing more. John and I used to fight a bit, him being the younger and things to prove and all that, but we were close. We all were. Mam smelled wonderful; Da did too. Mam like a fairground; Da like new shoes. Tea every night in the kitchen, watching Mam putting on her make-up, Da combing his hair. At just before six, even when we were of age, we'd kiss them goodnight and watch them walk down the stairs together, their clothes starched and their hands together, ready for the night ahead.

When you think of it, pub hours are good for kids. Mam and Da would take us out after school walking, rambling in the afternoons, no matter the weather. We'd look for birds' eggs and rabbits, walk the dog. Out in the fields, we'd talk Welsh, scare pigeons and magpies. Gill and Patty, they never saw their das. My da was always around when you needed him. Just don't go down to the bar. That was the only rule.

What you don't understand is that we were a little frightened of the bar. Just enough. When I was little, I used to hear singing coming up from the saloon. Men off to war, those coming back, those who became names on the plaque behind the pumps. I thought singing in the pub only happened when people had died or were going off to die. I hated to hear Da sing downstairs. I thought maybe he was going to war too.

What it comes down to is that the pub is less of a home now. Da rots upstairs, not long for the world, or so he says. John will be home in a few months to take his true position behind the bar. He will play Da to a T. His wife, that shrew of a woman, will be a hire-purchase Mam. And what shall I do, Nick? What will become of me? What shall I now call home?

This well before she met Drum, but those last thoughts – what shall I now call home? – coming back strong over recent weeks. Is this merely expedience? Would it have mattered who it was, so long as they could offer a home far from here? These the thoughts too tender to press for too long, so she lets them settle like the stout on the pale. Do not agitate. Just pour the drinks, just tend the bar, just wait until Jessie comes to relieve you. Just another hand-over, just another change of shift.

5

It is easier being in Doom Town than outside it. Over the months, he has come to believe this. When walking the blasted streets, you become inured to it, you take in the destruction, kick at things on the pavements, and it's a salve, it's safe. It has happened, these are the facts. This he needs to feel once more, the surprising coddle of it, the specificity of it. Away from the town, the details become amorphous, a swim of memories roiling around, confusing themselves, a kind of *holistic* terror (Carter's words). He is determined to remember correctly. To look as a camera, to imprint the town exactly as is, not as he might later reassemble it.

He turns back from the ginnel, back through the house and out onto the street. The next three houses he skips, but enters the fourth, one that has the shell of a television set in the sitting room, charred scraps of playing cards on the floorboards. Behind the TV, he notices a dead-body dummy, one unfound by the last teams, or recently added. It is a child dummy. It has a face. Crosses for eyes, a running stitch for a mouth.

★

On the fifth day of initial training in Shropshire they were marched to the parade ground. On the nearby lawn, sack-men dangled from a series of wooden gallows. The sergeant gave the servicemen their instructions. Approach. Stick. Twist. Remove. Drum charged his sack-man. Approach. Stick. Twist. Remove. He paced back and saw blood on his hands. Blood on his boots and on his tunic. Fine spray and huge gouts. He charged the sack-man again. Approach.

Stick. Twist. Remove. The blade inside the sacking. The blade inside the man.

That night, he slept covered in blood; that night, he slept with offal spilling from his guts; that night, he slept seeing all the men he would kill, their faces, flanks and sternums; that night, he slept as a murderer, as a soldier, and thought of his father. His smile. The photograph of him and Drum's mother holding their infant boy, neither to reach the age of twenty-five.

At the end of the two weeks of initial training, they received their postings, the places they would serve. Some off to Korea, Ireland, Cyprus; others stuck back home, made useful for the remainder of their tariff. Drummond had expressed a preference for the Royal Engineers but was given the Catering Corps: the Catering Corps on the training base at which he was already stationed. He came out of the assignment meeting and Carter was there, smiling his wolf's smile.

'You can thank me later,' he said.

Carter had organized it. Or more specifically, Carter Snr had organized it, along with a cushy two-man berth over the quiet side of the base. When Drum moved in that afternoon, their small billet had already been furnished with Carter's gramophone and wireless.

'In my village, there's a church,' Carter said that night as Drum polished boots and Carter drank beer. 'As you walk in, there's a plaque that reads, "This church was built in thanks by the Earl of Derbyshire, on the safe arrival of his three sons back from the Boer War." Imagine. Three sons and not a single scratch! No wonder he thanked the Lord with land and stone. He built the church as he would a mausoleum, no expense spared.'

Carter sat down in the armchair. Drum picked up another boot, began to buff it, hands black as factory.

'And that's why we're here, Drum. Had I fought and died, that plaque would have chafed my father every Sunday. To have been so careless as to lose one boy when three of Derbyshire's all made it home! It'd chafe him every day of his life. It'd chafe him so much I'm almost annoyed it isn't going to happen.'

As he started on Carter's boots, Drum thought of where he could have been stationed; the countries he might have seen, the places he might have been slaughtered. All the countries of the world where he could have met his end. All the people he could have met, all the sights he could have seen.

'I've never been abroad,' Drum said. 'Part of me wishes they'd sent me off like Curwin.'

'Plenty of time for all that afterwards,' Carter said. 'And without people shooting at you. And without Curwin. I'd rather be shot at than have to bunk with that.'

Carter laughed, picked up a book, began to read. The sound of the brush on the boot, the sound of pages turning. Drum looked up every now and again, saw Carter cross and recross his legs at the ankle. It was the certainty Drum could not quite grasp, the certainty and the fluidity. Carter was sure of himself in all situations, but slippery: different with officers than with the men; different when on the parade ground than when in the mess; different with Drum than with all others; and yet always himself, always surely, certainly Carter.

With his friends at home, the ones made at school, the ones made at Ford's, each of them knew their place: who was the joker, who was the fighter, who was the dreamer. Carter would know his place immediately amongst Drum's friends at the plant. Would ingratiate himself, hold his own with Mikey and Don and Pat and Teddy and Jack. They would ask him more questions in an afternoon than they'd ever asked Drum. He could see them all in the pub after shift, Carter at their centre, telling a story, Drum on the outside of the group, listening in as everyone laughed.

The weeks passed. In the kitchens from morning until night; potatoes drowning in metal vats, the curve of their peel, the dog-whiff of bully beef. The patterns of shift were familiar, the jobs repetitive, the noise surprising, the results often edible. It was blank work, undreaming work; each day starting and ending the same as the day before.

They began to talk of Leave; of what they might do. Drum wanted to see his grandpa, his great-aunt Vi, meet up with the factory lads, but Carter had other plans. A fishing trip, an hour or so's drive south, down to a place he knew in Wales. A bivouac to share, an abundance of carp, eating like kings over a fire he said he knew how to build.

'It will be pure gravy,' Carter said. 'You and me and the fish on the fire.'

Drum wrote a difficult letter to his grandpa. His grandpa wrote back that he understood and to have fun, to be safe. Always to keep himself safe.

A week before Leave, Carter was called to the telephone. He returned to the billet and got out the Scotch, poured one for Drum, just the one, at least initially.

'I'm not cancelling, you understand,' Carter said, handing Drum the glass. 'Just postponing. Next time, I promise.'

Drum shouldn't have been surprised, shouldn't have felt slighted. He looked down at the Scotch, did not trust the face he'd show his friend.

'Daphne's back from Switzerland, you see, and has demanded my presence. Nothing I can do.'

'Daphne?' Drum said. 'Is that your mother?'

'My mother's name is Phyllis,' Carter said. 'And since when do people call their parents by their first name? Daphne's my fiancée, Drum. Do keep up.'

In all the stories, all the chatter, Drum was sure he'd never heard the name Daphne. Carter looked at him like he was stupid; Drum tried to look apologetic rather than betrayed. Failed, sure of that.

'I don't recall you ever—'

'I've told you about her several times, Moore,' he said. 'Just last week I told you about her old bag of a mother, and then I told you about that time we went to Manchester and how we had to

32

pretend to be married to stay at some flea-trap hotel. Do you forget everything I tell you? Does it just go in one ear and out the other?'

Carter was smiling, but it didn't seem like a joke. Had the delivery of a joke, but not the intent.

'I remember now,' Drum said. 'I'm sorry, mind like a sieve. Daphne, of course.'

'Daphne,' he said. 'Yes. Daphne. Poor girl. Stuck with me forever. Makes you wonder what she did in a past life.'

Carter smiled and took the easy chair, began to pull off his boots, then stopped.

'You know I'd rather be fishing with you,' Carter said. 'Any day of the week.'

That weekend, Carter said his goodbyes and Drum stayed behind at the base, sleeping mainly. In the evenings, he drank the brown ale left in the crate and wrote letters to his grandfather, telling him of the wonderful time he was having. How good it felt to cook carp over a woodfire, to have fish skin under his finger-nails; how good it felt to be out in the fresh country air.

*

Drum picks up the sacking-child, its footless legs, its handless arms, and carries him out of the house. He lays him gently down outside on the pavement, neatly by the kerb. He assumes it is a boy child, it looks like a boy to Drum. Someone will find him. Someone will come. Sleep now, boy. Sleep well.

EARLY MORNING OPENING

I have never been one for taverns and bars; but over the last few years, I have found myself rising early, walking through the town to the coastal pathways and back again, trampling grass and pasture, graveyards and industrial estates, down ginnels and snickets, ending, eventually, at an inn which has become the last staging post of my morning ritual.

You will, perhaps, have read the essay by Orwell in which he describes the Moon Under Water, his gentle, teasing description of the ideal English pub: its three bars and liver-sausage sandwiches, its stuffed bull's head over the mantle. The inn in which I reside most late mornings to read through poems and work on this town portrait (much of which has been revised with a pint of black and tan beside me in the barroom), would, I fear, fulfil few of Orwell's essentials.

The Crown is a well-proportioned single room, with seating for some thirty or so patrons. The flooring is dark lacquered parquet, the colour of the landlord's slick-oiled hair, and the tables are as dark, most of them (save the one at which I work) rickety and prone to wobble. The windows are mottled, shellacked with tobacco grease, uncleaned in all the years I have been a regular. Above the mantle, a triptych of pictures, watercolours of local scenes, is perfect for moments when the muse has vanished, and I am left, wandering-eyed, looking for some pinprick of inspiration.

They serve a decent pint at the Crown; some men will even cross town to sample its beer. It was not ever thus. I am old enough to remember when the inn was exclusively known as Taff's Gaff, and the subject of a boycott by older townsmen.

The rumours are – and rumours are currency here; a commodity as abundant as iron ore once was – that the landlord won the pub in a frenzied game of three-card brag. This would have been between the wars, when the Welsh and the Cornish were depleting in number, but suspicion and not a little hostility remained towards them. So, Taff's Gaff. Frequented by the Welsh, the sons of the Welsh, and those who did not see the need to walk a mile for good beer.

Few now know it as Taff's Gaff; most do not know that the landlord is a true Welshman – his accent is soft, and he wears his heritage lightly. Above-stairs, according to his daughter, he speaks his own guttural, impenetrable language; but in the bar he is a welcoming sight: a tall, big-boned, huge-hearted kind of man, one whose company is sought and who has that barman talent for sympathetic listening: nodding his head with factory communists; shaking his head with Tory farmers; sighing with the old over the state of the young; laughing with the young over the stupidity of the old.

In recent times, after Taff's wife – a barmaid of the old-fashioned sort, a provider of love and pet and darling, a sultry wink, a charged chuckle – was taken by God, their daughter has minded the pub, her brother set to take it from her on his return from National Service. She does not resemble her mother or her father, though she somehow combines elements of them both; as though, like the pub they ran, their progeny is a fifty–fifty enterprise.

Her eyes are her father's: catlike and wide, blue as the brook in summer. Her hair is jet, a shining lustrous black she wears up on her head, scaffolded in a modern version of her mother's *coiffure*. Her carriage is upright, almost masculine; her mouth is wide, red-lipsticked, always. There is a touch of the Snow Whites about her; she is what one might describe as striking rather than beautiful; though with a sad cast to her eye that speaks of her mother's death and her father's retreat above-stairs.

Over time, we have developed a relationship of sorts. At the opening of the inn at eleven, she serves me my black and tan, and at some point after I have finished my pages, we discuss books. Readers in London and the South may feel this an unlikely turn of events, but the reading of books is more common here than one might think: the library in the town is always busy, and not just for those escaping inclement weather.

One morning, I noticed her reading Agatha Christie. The next day she was on James Hadley Chase. The following morning another Agatha Christie. When next I saw her, she began another James Hadley Chase and I could take it no more – to have such voracity, and to spend it in the arms of such lumber, such dead wood! – and so I hurried home, drink untouched, and returned with a copy of *Northanger Abbey*.

'Try this,' I said, perhaps a trifle pompously, though I hope I presented myself more as a concerned bystander. 'One should read good books or none at all.'

Her face went from shock, to perplexity, then settled

on amusement. It has settled there ever since, even now after we have discussed some fifty books, and her literary appreciation has deepened. Towns such as ours are full of such surprises: our community is more than just farmers farming, miners mining, or barmaids tending bar.

Nicholas Oldman, *The Regional Forecast*
(Castell & Castell, 1961)

7

Each house displays a different kind of devastation; in each there is something unique: a baby's dummy, a dog's leash, the innards of a transistor radio. Over these last months, the more time he has spent here, the more Drum has noticed the attention to detail, the little touches that convince. The house he's crossed the road for has a splintered bookcase, spines of the odd volume surviving, bits of leather he has touched, scraps that have crumbled in his hands.

*

Once a week at the Shropshire base a package would arrive at their billet, a selection of books from the Carter family library, or a delivery from a local bookseller. All the men Drum knew were readers. Those that could read, at least. At the plant, at home, they read their Marx, their Engels, their pamphlets and manifestos, translated speeches, articles from brothers in Algeria, in Kiev. At the factory, Clifton kept a well-stocked library of left-wing publications, paid for by union dues, and ran a reading group on lunch breaks. No one Drum knew owned books though; books were things only ever on loan.

Aside from Mannering, who was never without a cowboy novel, and Norm, who had a thing for spy thrillers, Drum didn't know any men who read fiction. Fiction was childish, fiction was feminine. It was apolitical. Seeing Carter that first night in the billet take out a novel – even if it was written by a Russian – made him nervous. Pansy, perhaps. Didn't know him. Not really. And now in a shared billet. He took out the copy of Marx his grandpa had bought him as a farewell gift, the only book he'd never needed to return, and started again at the beginning.

'So you're a communist, are you?' Carter said, quickly over to Drum's cot, taking the book from him, pinching it between fingers like it was stinking out the billet.

'A union man,' Drum said, taking it back. 'There's a difference.'

'Sounds like the same thing to me,' Carter said. 'It's all Bolshiness in the end, isn't it? Funny, I've come to expect Reds under the bed, but not in the cot beside me.'

They were drinking brown ale, the base quiet and the gramophone on low.

'Do you ever take anything seriously?' Drum said. 'All you ever do is make light.'

Carter stood up and poured the dregs of the ale into his glass.

'This world is too serious to take it any other way,' he said.

He spun the antique globe on the small dresser. Spun it and with a finger stopped it somewhere in Africa. He shrugged and spun again.

'There's really no point in being serious, my commie friend,' he said. 'Everything is set. Nothing changes. Not really. Things only change when people like my father say so. They set the conditions for change, and they decide how far it'll go. We can sit here and argue about commies and Tories and the rights of man, but we're all just shitting in the wind. Your mates out on the strike at Ford's? Good luck to 'em. Good luck to 'em all. But they'll only get what's already been decided. And they'll go back on the lines and be grateful for it. A little battle won, but the war lost before they've even entered the fray.'

It sounded rehearsed, this argument, honed perhaps at university, designed to prick the bubble of his political friends, designed to draw a line under discussions that had begun to bore him.

'You're wrong,' Drummond said. 'Things *are* changing. Look at us sitting here. A posh bastard talking politics with a skate like me. You think that's an accident? This is the first time in history there's ever been peacetime conscription in this country. First time ever, and it was Labour who brought that in. You know why? It's a quiet revolution. Throwing everyone together to see what happens. Giving men trades, showing them the world, opening their minds. National Service is just the start. The old orders, your father included, they're coming down.'

He was pointing, pointing the way Clifton had pointed when he'd said much the same thing in the pub after Drum's last shift at Ford's.

'Do you honestly believe that?' Carter said. 'Or are you just parroting one of your shop stewards? I hope it's the latter. If not, you're deluded. I hope you're better at riveting doors than you are at understanding the class system.'

'When the revolution comes,' Drum said. 'You'll be first against the wall, you know that?'

Carter laughed.

'We own the walls,' he said. 'Don't forget we own the walls. The pavements and streets too.'

'For now, yes,' Drum said. 'Not for long, mind.'

Carter set his head to one side, weighing up an idea, something to consider. He finished his beer and went to get another, but thought better, instead going to the small pile of books on his nightstand. He threw over a leather-bound copy of *Great Expectations*.

'I'll swap you,' he said. 'A Dickens for your Marx.'

Drum shook his head.

'Don't be soft,' he said. 'I can't read that.'

'You can read complex political philosophy, but not Dickens?'

'It's not that,' Drum said. 'There's just no point in it. You learn nothing. It's just words.'

'You learn nothing? How would you know if you don't read it?'

'It's bourgeois,' he said. A word he usually mispronounced, a word that sounded stupid as soon as he said it.

'It's Dickens,' Carter said. 'Nothing *bourgeois* about it.'

He said it differently, as though a French word in a French accent.

'Humour me,' Carter said. 'We have all the time in the world to kill, haven't we? Why not give it a go? And you never know, you might convince me about old Marx. Maybe you'll turn me red.'

He laughed and clicked his fingers, insistent like Drum was an elderly waiter. Drum handed him the Marx and took up the Dickens, determined to find fault on every page. Failing, mostly.

Over the next week, Drum was perplexed by Dickens's old-fashioned spellings, the words he did not recognize. But he kept reading, for himself and for Carter. In Joe Gargery he saw something of his grandpa, in Magwitch so many men from Ford's. He saw Carter in everyone, even Miss Havisham. He saw Carter in all the books he read from then on, in Flaubert, in Trollope, in Daniel Defoe. Carter ghosting about in all the characters, in the things they said, the decisions they made.

★

Drum looks into the next windowless shell. On the wind, he can hear something. Perhaps a gate banging; perhaps some masonry crumbling. A clink or clank of some kind. He closes his eyes and listens. He opens his eyes and scans the room, the way one might an exhibit. By what was once a kitchen table he sees something blackly welded to the floor. A child's doll perhaps. Set there, no doubt to break him. He has not noticed it before.

8

The barroom clock chimes half eleven, and Nick has not even put his lips to his black and tan. They only open early for him; it's rare anyone comes in before midday. And he sits and does not drink. Just works the pages, lets the black and tan drift. After the toll she hears her father upstairs shuffling from sitting room to kitchen. The tea will be cool in the pot, but he'd rather drink that than make his own. *Mae'n well yn oer.*

★

At their mother's wake, her brother John, back from Service, played father for the mourners, their da unable to show himself. Back-claps and thanks-for-comings and have another drink, won't yous? Garrulous, almost; a fine mimicking. John worked the barroom and Gwen served the drinks until there was no one left, and she and John were in the bar alone, glasses teetering on every surface, silted with beer, sticky with gin. That the start of her working behind the bar; the start of her father's gradual retreat upstairs.

'You spend so long in darkness, you become a nocturne,' her father said after John had gone back to Service. This when her father still addressed her in English, when he still came down for the evening shift. Not long after the funeral, no more than a couple of weeks. It had been a packed bar, a rush at eight, a swell at last orders. Wesley from the pit had played his banjo; her father had not sung, though punters had begged him to give them an air. He now sat at the bar, gin in hand, talking as though he had the attention of an audience.

'I wasn't sure you'd take to it. It takes a sort. And look at you now! A nocturne, just like your mother.'

His frame was already losing heft; his face already creased as slag. He raised his glass to her, the way he had to cricket captains and baritones, to policemen and fiancés, a slight stammer, a shake to the gin.

'You should take more water with it,' she said, nodding to his glass. 'You're making as much sense as Old Nick.'

His laughter and then a miner's cough, though he'd never been deeper than to change a barrel.

'Your mother used to say there was no light here, just different shades of dark. You see that now, don't you?'

When helping on a shift, he sometimes draped an arm over her, the way he had with her mother. He sometimes called her darling the way he'd called her mother darling; called her sweetheart the way he'd called her mother sweetheart.

'She would have been proud,' he said. 'Minding the place the way you do.'

Gwen took a packet of cigarettes from the pocket in her apron, struck a match and closed her eyes on his disapproval.

'And when John's back?' she said. 'What then? Won't be needing me with him and Barbara around.'

Gwen sat down at Old Nick's table, cloth marks ghosting the blistered wood, the fire dying in the grate.

'Always need good barmaids. No point in a pub otherwise. He'll do you right, you'll see. I'll make sure of that.'

He finished the gin, placed a kiss on her forehead and said good-night. The public bar no longer public, its lamps no longer lit. A nocturne, aye.

★

She looks at her watch, not trusting clocks now, but time seeming right, just after 11.30. In an hour Jessie will come to relieve her. A special favour. How many times she's asked Jessie to do this; how many times Gwen has paid her out of the till and not told Da. Too many. Jessie glad of the money; glad also to be party to some solid, if unspectacular, scandal. Glad for that the most, Gwen suspects. Still, Jessie has kept her confidence thus far. Gwen has not suffered any knowing looks at least.

Jessie is to relieve her, then Gwen will meet Drum at the town square, under the clock. Her idea. Drum suggested meeting at the pub, but Gwen wanted to have a moment in the light with him, to stand in the grey sunshine and kiss him and steel themselves for what they were about to do. She imagines the clock striking the hour, him kissing her, and then walking under cold blue skies to her father's sanctuary.

She hears Drum ask the question, ask for *her hand*, and hears Da tell him to speak in Welsh. Gwen is prepared for this and has coached Drum phonetically as to what to say. She hears Da say in English, no daughter of mine. I will not allow it. I forbid it. She sees Drum's calm and honest eyes looking into her father's. She hears Drum tell her father that he loves her. That he wants to keep her safe, provide for her. Wants to make her happy. She sees Da smile. This is how it will go. She knows this. She is sure.

And yet the whole thing feels transactional. Though there are promises and entreaties instead of dowries, it's still a horse-trade. What do you offer for my daughter? Da will not stop her, but he is sure to kick and mewl. He will tell her that he will die without her. He will say that she can go when he goes. She will tell him that it's time to leave. That others will look after him. John and his wife. She will tell him it is time for her to leave. She will tell him that it's time for him to let her go.

Old Nick turns a page. He looks up and smiles at Gwen. He drains half of his beer in one draught. He knows already. She can tell. He has something about him, of important information ready for discussion. He disappears back to his work, he is lost to it, gone deep inside his papers. She would like to escape there, too. Better there. Safer between the sheets.

9

The high street extends for almost a mile and he walks it like he's window shopping. Inside the once-grocer's are twisted wire baskets, rusted cans, a cash register; inside the once-chemist's the shelves are no more than kindling. He imagines lives bustling through here, populates it with people from home. The soft face of the butcher, Mr Dutton (Mutton to everyone; everyone a comedian), Trisha from the bakery with the painted-on eyebrows, Harold the fishmonger, pout like a bloater. He sees his great-aunt Vi stopping to gossip; men from Ford's coming out of the bookies. All the stories of their lives, all of them taken in a single flash.

★

There were always stories at the Shropshire base, stories written, but more often told. There were new conscripts every two weeks, a new audience every fortnight, all of them hungry for tales of real soldiering, real action, and Carter happy to provide them. In the bar of the NAAFI, a crowd would gather, and he would recount his war stories, the missions he and Drum had undertaken, the dangers they had survived before falling on their feet in the Catering Corps.

Carter did most of the talking, but Drum contributed colour and detail to their fictive exploits. There was a multitude of them, embroidered over months, honed and tightly composed. They had seen a bewildering array of action. They had performed at every theatre of war. Carter had an appendectomy scar that became a gut shot from a sniper, a stab from a cutlass, shrapnel from a mine. No one questioned it. No one disbelieved him. The books helped

Drum to lie. They made his stories clearer, they had more suspense. The younger men hung on his words too.

In almost every story, Carter was saved by Drum at the last moment; Drum always arriving in the nick of time with an impossible intervention. At the end, the men would look at Drum differently. Respect accorded, deference even.

As a coda, Carter would gather the men in a close huddle.

'Be lucky, all of you,' Carter would say. 'And if you can't be lucky, make sure someone has your back.'

Drum wondered sometimes if that was it, whether Carter considered him as a kind of lucky charm, found like a four-leaf clover. They never did go fishing on their Leave; Carter never mentioned it again. Leave was tricky. The worst time. The journey long to home, but quicker for Carter. Carter talked of Daphne, how much she and Drum might get along, but there was never an invitation to meet her.

Carter showed him photographs of Daphne. A thin, willowy woman, expensively dressed, laughing into the camera.

'She looks lovely,' Drum said.

'Yes, that's how she looks,' he said. 'Exactly that.'

Going home, Drum did not look changed, act changed, speak differently, Drum was careful not to; but he imagined Carter doing things, hearing things, being things Drum could not fathom. Drum resented the telephone. The knocks on the billet when Daphne or Carter's mother were on the line for him; the touch on the back of Carter's whites if they called during shift. Sometimes Drum would go into the vestibule and watch Carter speak into the Bakelite mouthpiece, twisting the flex around his fingers as he spoke.

Carter's father called just once that Drum knew of. Called with news that he was transferring Carter to a civil defence base for the last three months of his Service. A specialist course, a selected group, to learn the rules of post-nuclear engagement.

'He's building a shelter,' Carter said as some kind of explanation. 'My father, the mad old trout, is actually building a huge atomic bomb shelter under the family pile. Says he's been planning it since Sputnik. State of the art, it is, apparently. "No point surviving the bomb and not knowing how to live afterwards," he said to me. Thinks I'll get an insight. An instinct for how to cope once the big show starts. Get us ahead of the game.'

Carter spun the globe.

'I tried to get you on the course, too,' he said. 'I tried, I promise. But best I could do was a transfer.'

With a finger, he stopped the globe, somewhere over Russia.

'You did say you wanted to see the world,' Carter said. 'Some people get to see Korea, you'll get to see Cumbria!'

Carter laughed that laugh. Drum looked around the billet, the boots by the door, the turned-down beds, the gramophone playing be-bop.

'I always thought the Far East sounded too hot,' Drum said. 'I'll get on fine with Cumbria.'

'So you'll come?' he said. 'I did hope you'd say yes.'

'Yes,' Drum said. 'What else am I going to do?'

He didn't want to make it sound angry, didn't know if he had or had not. Carter wasn't really listening anyway, he was already taking books from the bookcase, stacking them into a box. Drum followed his lead, packing up his kit bag, quickly, easily done.

Afterwards, they opened brown ale and Carter proposed a toast.

'To real war,' he said.

'To real war,' Drum replied.

Within a week, they were at the Civil Defence Training Base in Haverigg, ready to join the two-week course usually undertaken by men in the last fortnight of their service. It had been decided that Carter and Drummond would complete the training in their first two weeks, after which Carter would join his course-mates and Drum would go into the kitchens.

They were split into different billets, thirty men to a hut. Bunking with others again presented challenges. He was careful in the showers. The men were lighter of mood than the ones he was used to, these men so close to their One, the longed-for last day of Service. Drum saw Carter around the base, often in the company of the CO, a man called Jerrick, a close friend of Carter's father; but Drum and Carter did not speak for almost a week. Back to silence. Back to talking only when spoken to.

They did not take it seriously, his fellow servicemen, or so it seemed to Drum. Perhaps they saw it for what it was: grown men playing war on a two-square-mile playground. They slept well, did not dream of the destruction, thought only of demob and their One. Of heading home, of the lives they would now lead. That's how it seemed. How it seemed as he envied their snores.

In the mornings there were field exercises in what they all called Doom Town; in the afternoons, short lectures in which they learned of blast radiuses, fallout drift, Hiroshima and Nagasaki. 'Essential preparations,' Jerrick said as he put on a radiation suit and mask, the men invited in groups of ten to try them out. Carter was in the first group; Drummond was called towards the end. He breathed heavily in the suit's interior silence; walked and felt the sensation of wading through deep water; heard his own heartbeat, terrifying fast.

Eventually, in the second week of training, Carter and Drum were paired on rescue detail. They'd been allocated the east side of town, each building to be searched, any dead-body dummies to be stacked and left kerbside; the living, as played by their fellow servicemen, to be assisted if found. Mainly dummies, though.

Inside the bakery, Drum saw flour in the dust, spelt on the floor-boards, crusts in the debris. Underneath the oven's rusted door, someone had arranged an oversized dummy and a long, blackened peel. A point (Drum). A shrug (Carter). A nod (Drum). His turn. Drum dragged the baker, fat even in mock death, to the threshold, his straw lining shedding over the cold stone flags.

When Drum returned, Carter was working the peel in the oven, fishing for imagined loaves.

'Yesterday, I was in the pub,' Carter said, the peel moving deep inside the oven.

'Lucky,' Drum said.

From his tunic, Carter took a cigarette; from his trouser pocket a box of matches. The flare and smoke in the gloom against explicit orders. He leaned against the oven, hawk nose pinked from cold; cheek-stubble blading despite a first-light shave. Fringe grown out and brushing his eyebrows. Six foot and muscled now, meat on his once-lean frame, man-shaped and man-sized. Face not. Not the defiant confidence of the parade ground, but a little-boy face; whiskers from calling for Mummy.

'I swear I could smell the beer,' he said. 'Like they were still serving. Just for a moment I could see Bobby from the Wolf. The smallest hands you've ever seen, Bobby's. Like a child's. I saw those hands and I cried for him. The rescue detail came and they were carrying me on a stretcher, and I was crying for Bobby, and for Johnson, Dirty Mac, Syd . . . Imagine crying for that bunch of skates.'

Carter shook his head; Drum looked beyond him to the oven, its dead and empty mouth.

'You see all this,' Carter said, 'and you just know. The scale of it, the absolute violence of it, the terror of it all. You see it and it's no longer an exercise. What was it that Collins used to say? "Enough to make your shit shiver." That. Exactly that. They want to make us shit ourselves with fear. It's what they want.'

Drum looked away, wondered if his fear was coming through his pores, through his skin. When he closed his eyes, he saw the glass on the street, the maws where once there were walls. He saw his grandpa and his great-aunt melted into fat, a slick outside the fishmonger's window.

'Maybe,' Drum said. 'But I think we're also supposed to feel hopeful. That we can survive all this.'

'And do you feel hopeful, Moore?'

'I feel sick,' he said. 'Like I could puke out my whole stomach.'

Carter threw his cigarette into the oven. There was a moment's glow and then nothing, the black insides black again. Two piped lines from his nose, smoke folding, wicking away. His smile. That smile.

'Tonight we go out,' Carter said. 'Get the stink off. No more talk of it.'

'Cocktails at the Savoy, is it?' Drum said. 'Or pink gins at the Palais?'

Carter shook his head, the dramatic way he did, full force of perceived disappointment.

'There's a pub. Not too far. Beer's good apparently.'

'And there's a way out?'

'There's always a way out.'

They heard voices, loud callings for survivors. A nod (Carter). A nod (Drum).

'And there's girls,' Carter said. 'I met one last night. Jerrick was good enough to drive me to town after dinner. She has a friend. We're meeting at eight.'

'What about Daph—'

'We're at war,' he said. 'Things are different. You need to realize that.'

As if he didn't. As if only Carter saw what he saw. Carter looked up and down.

'And for God's sake,' Carter said, 'wear the good suit. The one I bought you.'

*

He lingers in every shop, picks up cans and tins, sees rats scurry over char and burn. Carter is somewhere. Gwen is somewhere. They are breathing, walking, thinking, and he is here, with the rats; with the cracked bricks and bloated wood. Marking time, letting it run. If Doom Town says anything, it says there are consequences. That decisions have implications. He could go home and it would be safe. It would be safe to take up the old life, for nothing to change. What does he know of love anyway? Better to go home alone than to promise a better life he will be unable to deliver.

Nick has been warned not to set down his pipe on the beer towel, but he does it anyway. She pours his second black and tan and places the jug beside his briar. He looks around the empty saloon, checking for company. His gust has turned to stink.

'I saw you with your serviceman last night,' he says.

And so to it. *Remember, Old Nick is watching.* Nick lives in a simple apartment above the milliner's; his study, a dormer on the top storey, views out over the whole of town. Those with something to hide know the streets to avoid, the secluded areas beyond his purview; the lovers' lanes and cobbled ginnels. You could end up in one of his books or poems or plays if not careful. Best to play safe. For two months, she and Drum have played safe. Each morning she's poured the black and tan and waited for Nick to say something. About having spotted her heading out to the Queen's Head, or getting into a car with an unrecognized man. At first Drum thought Gwen must have a jealous boyfriend, a violent ex-lover, such was her care and diligence. She always blamed it on her father.

'You must be mistaken,' Gwen says to Nick. 'I don't have a serviceman.'

'I'm certain it was you,' Nick says, eyes wide for guilt or shame. 'You were on the way to the Queen's, by the look. Eight thirty or thereabouts.'

'He's not my serviceman,' she says. 'Even if I was there, which I wasn't.'

Nick takes a sip of his beer, delight beneath the hoods of his eyes.

'Well you weren't here,' he says. 'I popped in for some matches and Jessie was behind the bar.'

'I was probably upstairs with Da,' she says. Should have known he would stop by one night. Just to be sure, just to get his facts in order.

'If you say so,' he says. 'Though this was far from the first such sighting. What you might call a pattern emerging.'

'A pattern?'

'You were observed with him as he got into a taxi on Albert Street. Near midnight. Wednesday week. Spotted with him three times since then. Like I said, a pattern.'

The magistrate eyes, resting his prosecution. Albert supposedly safe. Binoculars or telescope the only explanation.

'He's not my serviceman,' she says.

'I suppose the men come and go so quickly they never belong to anyone,' Nick says.

He sits on the barstool, the way he often does before discussing the book he's lent her. He smiles like a hunter baiting traps, already anticipating the rabbit in his stew. He strikes a match. She blows it out before he can light his pipe.

All service is performance. Her father told her this. Always remember you're playing a part in which you know your lines, but the punter does not. On her first shift, she applied bright-red lipstick though she usually went for more muted shades, and has done so every shift since. A mask of sorts. In the company of Nick, however, its colour seems to have faded. Over time she has revealed herself, and she can no longer rebuild the walls he has broached and vaulted.

'A handsome enough fellow from what I could tell,' Nick says, striking another match and lighting his pipe. 'Though my eyesight is not what it once was, and streetlight can be so forgiving, don't you find?'

She knows her anger is visible, despite her laughter, despite the quick peal of it, despite it being met by Nick's low dirty chuckle.

Hot at the cheeks, the first sign, a tensing of the hands, a tendency to look too hard in the eyes. And it is rage she feels; rage rather than just ire or anger; rage, full-blooded and bold-pulsed, a feeling of tightness across the chest and at the base of her neck.

She pours herself a soda water from the syphon, loses some of his words in its hiss and rush.

'. . . his face and I thought, aye, this is a Londoner. One can always tell a Londoner. Something about the mouth, a kind of slackness. In London they all look like that, you know. You see them on the buses, on the Underground, on the filthy streets, they all look the same.'

She has asked Drum about London. She has imagined walking its streets with him. The small house they will share, the bed in which they will sleep. The library she can see herself working, no longer a nocturne.

'He's not from London,' she says.

'From the South, though?' Nick says.

'He is a long way from home, yes.'

'And you,' he says, 'are comforting him for homesickness?'

She should end it here. End it with a quick *now, now* and a matronly wag of finger. His eyes are eager, his lips slightly parted. She should say nothing.

'Patty's in love with his friend,' she says. 'I'm merely being polite.'

She begins to wipe the bar down, though it needs no wiping. She does not look in his direction. He will not let the last word go to her; words are his master after all.

'An attitude which does you great credit,' he says. 'I am sure he appreciates your attentions.'

'Mr Oldman,' she says. 'There are no attentions for him to appreciate.'

He nods and smiles, looks to the triptych above the mantle. He takes a long pull from his pint and puts down his pipe.

'I think the young believe their mating rituals are a mystery to the old,' he says. 'But let me tell you, the dances may look different, but the steps remain the same.'

He chuckles to himself, carries his drink back to his table. He takes out his battered copy of Wordsworth that's always to hand, and everything is as it should be, if things were the way they should be.

She watches him read, the way he turns the pages, waiting for her to go to him. He exerts a pull as well as a stench. He sips his drink. Is he even reading the words? Even following the lines?

If someone comes in, she will not go to him. If someone comes through the door, she will serve them and smile. No one comes through the door. She watches him make a note in the book with his pencil. He looks up from his book and to her.

'Now, come on, tell me what's to do,' he says. 'Come here and sit for a time. We share things, do we not? Our little secrets?'

'I fear you will be jealous,' she says, across the bar.

He laughs.

'I fear you may be right, my dear.'

In the town library, one of the few buildings to have both walls and a roof, the chair and table he set right have been moved, upended again, and put back in the same position he'd found them. An overzealous serviceman looking for dummies, perhaps; or maybe the rooms are swept every so often, rearranged according to a detailed schema. He heaves the table up again, scorched but usable, puts the chair under it, sits at the desk, checks his watch.

There is a space where a clock once hung on the wall, its glass is shattered over the floor. Some of the books have been spared. Not many, but a few. They are encyclopedias. A boon for any survivor.

★

Gwen told him she dreamed of working in a library. The light of the lamps, the stamp in the books, shushing those who talked. The first time they met, she told him that. In the bar of the large hotel, Drum surprised at such an opulent, if slightly faded, accommodation being situated in a place like Millom.

A boom town once, she told him. Iron ore discovered years back, the largest deposits found in Europe, maybe even the world. Her family were Welsh, they'd come in dribs and drabs over the latter half of the last century, them and the Cornish the only ones with the skills to tease out the bounty. She spoke and he listened, and heard the pun. Doom. Boom. Wondered if that was deliberate too. A joke for those in the know.

There had been women before. A posh friend of Carter's who'd enjoyed a bit of rough; a couple of girls in Shropshire, accents sounding Welsh, excited by his difference to the local lads. They had not lasted. Without Carter, he found himself stuck for things to say, save for things Carter had already said. The girls liked his silence at first, but soon tired of the increasingly uncomfortable exchanges. When they first met, Gwen did not appear to care for him either, whether in quiet or in conversation.

Carter's girl Patty looked like she might work in the typing pool at Ford's: carefully made-up, knowing of what men said to one another, clever at keeping them just at a distance. Gwen wasn't like anyone he knew from home. She smoked and sipped her gin and her mouth was wide, and so red-painted, her hair piled high, her eyes kohled and bored. He could not imagine her in Dagenham, could not imagine her in Millom either. Like she would pass through any place she found herself.

He asked Gwen the usual questions – Where from? Where do you work? How was your day? – and she answered him shortly. There were other places she could be. Clear that. He thought she'd give it two drinks before making her excuses.

'You know,' she said. 'You sound like you're from Australia.'

Drum laughed but she remained serious, had not laughed at even the most tried and tested of Carter's routines. Yet there was something in the way she said it, an interest beneath her cool. There was a response to this, something expected, though he had no idea what it was. And then the moment passed and Patty was telling them a story about a friend who'd once stolen a brooch from her, then denied it, while actually wearing the piece in question. Not listening, having clearly heard the story several times, Gwen picked up her handbag and rummaged through it for something. The bag gaped and she took a book from it, set it down on the table. *Saturday Night and Sunday Morning.*

'I've read that,' Drum said. 'Carter bought it for my birthday.'

She found her cigarettes, lit one and put the pack down on the table.

'Did you like it?' she said. Eyes no longer bored. Surprised, not bored.

★

In the wrecked library, he thinks of that moment. Of her face, the way she was surprised, interested or bored, often almost at the same time. He liked that expression. He liked the conversation they went on to have, the way she talked about books, the way she talked about one day working in a library as if that were something people like them could do. He liked that she put her hand on his arm when he said he never knew his parents, that they'd died in the war. He liked listening to her talk of her father; the way she bit her lip when she mentioned her mother. He liked it when she said he could see her again. He liked it when she kissed him.

There is the clanking noise, the clinking noise again. He looks around the room, to see if the noise is coming from inside the library but there is no obvious cause. He checks his watch again. She will be on her way to meet him soon. He should leave now.

12

Patty loved Tony, but Tony loved Glenda. Gill loved Harry, but not as much as Harry loved Gill. Richard loved Gwen, but Gwen didn't really love him back.

Patty loved Tony, but Tony married Glenda. Gill loved Harry, but Harry got a girl, name unknown, in the family way, so Gill tried to love Frank. Richard stopped loving Gwen, but Gwen did not pay it any mind.

Patty no longer loved Tony, but did not permanently transfer her love elsewhere. Gill still loved Harry, but loved Frank enough, and their daughter above all else. The reverend took an interest in Gwen, but Gwen was not interested.

Patty loved Gwen, but no longer loved Gill, for she disapproved and talked only of baby. Gill loved Gwen, but pitied Patty and talked only of her baby. Gwen missed her mother and her brother.

Patty loved a serviceman called Carter. Patty was sure that Gwen would love a serviceman called Drum. Patty asked Gwen to meet with him at the hotel bar that night.

Gill called in on Gwen the same afternoon. Gill invited Gwen for tea because her handsome brother-in-law was staying with them for a time.

Gwen decided to go to the hotel bar. Gill could not cook and her brother-in-law was Scottish.

This the backstory. Most of which she won't tell Nick.

13

This is what she tells Nick:

'Patty met a serviceman at the Queen's. Posh lad, she said, sweet but a bit of the devil in him. I could tell she was smitten. Always is. Anyway, she asked me to go along with her to the Grand to meet him and his mate. "Looks like Montgomery Clift," she said. "At least according to *James* . . ." It was Jessie's night on so I was free. I could have just stayed home, but why not? I'm allowed to have fun, aren't I?'

Nick nods. 'But of course, my dear. Of course you are.'

'So we met up and he looked a little bit like Montgomery Clift, I suppose. If you squinted. Patty's bloke looked like Marlow, you know, who lives in Haverigg? The one who drives that sports car? Posh and full of himself. He didn't shut up. Thinks himself a bit of a comedian. His friend hardly said anything though. He asked me where I'm from and all that, but you could tell he was just going through the motions.

'He had this accent. He sounded Australian to me. I said that and he sort of laughed at me, with his eyes more than anything. And I thought we'd be done after two drinks. Thanks for the drinks and home. Shame, because he was nice-looking. Had nice manners when he wasn't vacant.'

'So what happened?' Nick says. 'I take it there were more than two drinks.'

'I blame you, Nick,' she says. 'It's your fault entirely. I opened my handbag to get cigarettes and he saw the book inside. The one you lent me. He saw it in my bag and said, "Carter bought me that for my birthday."'

'Which book?' Nick says. She ignores him. Makes him work it out himself.

'I asked him if he'd enjoyed it. "I'm not sure enjoying it's the word," he said. "Sometimes I feel as if I'm living it. Carter thinks it's exotic. He keeps asking me if it's authentic. I told him the author got the boredom right."'

She pulls in closer to Nick.

'It was like I saw him, or he saw me. Or we saw each other. I don't know. Not love at first sight, nothing as trite as that, but this deep kind of . . . I don't know. Not connection, not empathy, but something more dramatic, and more ordinary than that.

'You told me once about how you met your wife, Nick. And I love that story, I really do. And the way you described it, that's the way it felt. "Like blind light glimpsed / on a shared horizon / no one else lit / but only we two." You understand?'

Nick nods, feeds the bowl of his pipe.

'He took the book from me then, and he flicked to a passage he liked, the same way you do when you're excited about something. He found it and his fingers were below the line "Whatever people say that I am, that's what I'm not." He read it to me. And so I said to him, "And what do people say that you are?" And he said, "I don't know. I have no idea who I am."'

Nick takes a long sip of his black and tan.

'And what did you say?' he says.

Say it. Shock him. Give him what he wants. What he's been after. Do it for him. A last thing before you go. Perhaps, if you say it you'll have to go. Say it. Shock him.

'I didn't say anything, Nick,' she says. 'But I wanted to. What I thought, Nick, what I was going to say to him was: "If I fuck you, you'll know who you are."'

That face. Oh worth it for that face.

'Go on,' Nick says. 'Tell me more.'

THE COSMOLOGY OF THE BOMB

At the civil defence training base where I was stationed between 1957 and 1962, the most comprehensive nuclear library in the country, if not Europe, was assembled. Books arrived daily, volumes with any passing connection to the subject, from vast scientific tomes to works of premonition and prophecy, were unpacked and shelved under one of three subject headings: technical, cultural and esoterica. It was not off-limits to the servicemen, but few to my knowledge ever set foot inside.

Though the library was dank, it did have two comfortable armchairs arranged around a gas fire and a table on which to set a bottle. Not long after arriving, I claimed it as something of a personal sanctuary. I read the technical and scientific journals. I read the speculative fiction. I drank and I warmed myself at the fire. Most of all, I sat and I communed with the bomb.

Some years after being stationed, I took a bottle of brandy, as was my custom, to the library. The door was open, the lights on, and there was a glow from the gas fire. Inside, two servicemen were engaged in deep conversation. One of them I knew, the other I didn't.

They were talking about what the base meant, and how much of it was planned. It sounded like a conversation they had had many times already, a familiarity in their discussion, one that neither believed could ever be concluded. I'd heard the same arguments before, and they were both half right. But it was not their theories that interested me, more the conversation that followed.

After a brief silence, the man of my acquaintance asked about a woman with whom his friend was involved. I can clearly recall his reply.

'I think I'm in love with her,' he said. 'But I don't know if it's just because of here. Because of this place. Maybe I'm being provoked into loving her because of the bomb.'

All the books I have read on the subject of thermonuclear war, and it is this conversation that, to me, gets to the true heart of the matter. It made me think what the doomed town actually *meant* to those who viewed it. It made me think about the effect the bomb has on us all, on all our decisions, even down to the people we choose as lovers.

At these times of heightened tension, it is both a boon and a necessary distraction to look beyond the obvious and the presented. It is our duty to delve beneath what we are told and uncover the truth. There is what I like to think of as a cosmology of the bomb, a systemic underpinning of its influence on the world. There is a netherworld over which the bomb has dominion. It is not enough to 'protect and survive'; one must understand the powers at work, the control the bomb exerts. And through this understanding come to halt those powers. Halt them, take back control, and find ourselves in a new age. An age of wonder, of clarity, of hope, and of love.

Bryan Jerrick, *My Cold Wars* (Underworld Press, 2001)

15

Nick clearly wants to know more, but she does not wish to reveal the length of the relationship, the length of her deception. It would raise too many questions. She wants to make it feel fleeting, some heyday in the blood, something dangerous and passionate. She wants to make it more dramatic than it is.

She could tell him more. She could tell him of the walks they have taken, the drinks they have had, the alleyway kisses they've snatched. She could tell him of discovering Drum's parents were both killed in the war, young people both, and how he was brought up by his grandparents. She could tell him of the longing she felt when not with him, how she resented the base for taking him from her. She could tell him of the night in the hunters' lodge, the thrill of waking next to his body. She could tell him all of this. None of this he would want to hear.

Nick looks excitedly up from his black and tan. She wishes she'd not said that word, the word he likes to drop into conversation to see her colour. *It's only fuck, my dear. It's just a word.* She wanted to make him blush, but the blood has clearly gone another way.

'You remember Richard?' she says. 'This is nothing like Richard. It was sweet, the way he loved me. But there's nothing sweet about this. I blame you. You and the books.'

Nick picks up his jug, takes a small sip and puts it back down.

'You intend to elope with him?' he asks. 'Run off into the dark, dark smog? Is that the plan?'

'Perhaps,' she says. 'I don't know.'

Nick nods and puts his pipe back in his mouth, puffs away until the bowl needs relighting.

'Have I ever told you of my sister Ethel?' he says, holding the open box of matches. 'Quite the catch in her day. All the boys loved her. They used to bribe me with sweets so I'd deliver her messages. A glorious girl, she was. Had her head turned in the first war though. Met some tiresome cockney and that was that. Left home and never came back. He beat her, of course . . .'

How true this? How much invented? From his look, impossible to say.

'I love him, Nick,' she says. 'He loves me too.'

They have said this to each other. She has not told anyone else. What does that say?

'Oh, how foolish that sounds,' Nick says. 'How very girlish and green. You love him? He loves you? You want to run away? How old *are* you, my dear? Have you not learned? Have the books we've read been wasted upon you? You love this gurning ape and so you're going to leave, be his skivvy and chambermaid? You're more than that, Gwendoline. You were always more than that. Anyone can see that, my dear.'

There is salt-spite back on his cheeks, the wattle under his chin has inflamed like that of a turkey. Once he was probably handsome. Still has something to his eyes. Something livid in them.

'You said I might be jealous,' he says, 'and I am. I am jealous of your youth. I am jealous of your days to come. But I pity you for it, too. I pity you because I would change nothing of my life. Not one thing. A rare gift, that. Hindsight that nods approvingly.

'I've loved one woman. We courted, we married, we lived, she died. You want my wisdom? My advice is stay here. My advice is wait. My advice is that this will prove ephemeral, and before you know it, you'll be my sister Ethel, dragging kids around dirty streets, dreaming of home. You are a fine woman. Don't let some man take that from you.'

He downs the last of the black and tan, puts his Wordsworth in his pocket.

'The comforts of home,' he says, 'are worth ten of the big

dreams. And you can still have them here –' he taps his head – 'you don't need to go running off to find them.'

He is flush as he gets up from the table, stinking more as he puts on his coat, winds his scarf around his chicken neck.

'Told you you'd be jealous,' she says.

16

Outside the library he looks up and down the high street. There is nothing there, nothing moving, just the fog sitting low against the rubble. No clanking or clinking. He checks his watch again.

Gwen will be happier here. Safer here. She will find another here. One better suited. Yes. To go all that way south, to leave her family, and for what? How many years before they're ash and soot, before they're holding a dead child, or hiding in basements and cellars? So much safer here, so much better here, with the fields and the brooks and the sea lapping at the bluffs. Let her live. Be in peace. Marry a vicar, a plumber, a librarian. Let them give her the love she is due. Allow her to go on, forget him except for low days when she wonders what might have been. How her life might have panned out hundreds of miles from her father and her brother. The bomb could drop and she would still be safe.

But she is happy to go. She wants to go. She has been planning it. If not him, another will come, another up from the base, a child unplanned and up the aisle before it starts to show. No safe places anyway, this learned in the study rooms. Safety an illusion: the only defence is preparation, is knowing the drills. She would be safer with him. Loved by him. Protected by him. He has survived the two years of Service; there must be a reason for that. To be so safe, and then to come here, to be safe again. Reason in that, surely. Come the bomb or no, he will be there to save her. Be there to hold her against the blast. Yes.

The wind rattles down the high street. The wind and the fog and the bomb and him. And the clank again. A tapping sound, like leaking pipes.

17

The bar remains empty until the midday crowd arrives. Six or seven of the regulars. They all have names and she greets them individually, and individually they tell her to give them a smile or tell her to cheer up. That it might never happen. She smiles and pours their drinks as normal.

Where is Nick? Gone straight home, or at angry march across the town, appalled at her naivety, disgusted with the ease of her affections, muttering to himself like Lear? Right, to think that of her. Right, of course, all the things he's seen. Madness to ignore his wisdom. Madness to listen to it, too.

She didn't tell him enough. Had she told him more, he would have understood. He would have liked the stories. He would have enjoyed them.

She should have told him about when she knew. Knew properly. That would have convinced. Not the moment with the book, but later, in the countryside, far from the town, the two of them in an old hunters' lodge belonging to a discreet friend of Carter's. He would have seen it then.

*

The boys had Leave owing and Carter drove Patty, Drum and Gwen in a big car to somewhere up in the Lakes. The girls sat in back, supposedly on their way to visit an old school friend in Barrow; the boys up front, talking and giggling, fiddling with the radio. Patty was too excited to talk, just squeezed Gwen's arm, believing this the weekend her serviceman would propose, and nothing Gwen could say would disabuse her of the notion.

They arrived at a stately place, too stately for the likes of them, and at the groundsman's entrance, Carter gave their names as Mr and Mrs Price and Mr and Mrs Jones. An unnecessary deception, the groundskeeper barely containing his disgust at Carter and his accomplices; this clearly far from the first time he'd used the same aliases.

The hunters' lodge was a semi-detached cottage with two front doors, one red, one black. Carter went to the black door; Drum, like a dutiful husband, took Gwen's small suitcase to the red door. Patty said goodbye to Gwen, kissed her by the car, then followed Carter into their lodge, disappointment and upset no doubt close behind.

Inside, under the watchful glass eyes of a Canadian moose, Drum kissed Gwen. They made love in a four-poster bed with duck-down pillows and thick cotton sheets. Afterwards Gwen smoked cigarettes and laughed as the sunshine crept through the open windows. That the moment. The sunlight and the smell of Drum, the play of sheets against her legs. That the moment. The one she should have told Nick about. The burr in the air between them, the very ordinariness of it. The absolute humdrum of it.

She knew it when he got up from the bed. She knew how it would go. Was sure of it, more certain even than Patty.

He went to the bathroom. She heard taps turned on and the sound of running water. She knew what she wanted and did not want; both of them possible, both of them alluring in their own way.

He closed the door on the bathroom, naked and muscled. He knelt down at the side of the bed and apologized for not having a ring, or any clothes on, or a house to call his own, but that he would like to share these absences with her forever.

In the light, he looked just like Montgomery Clift. In the light, she said yes. She said yes, but to keep it a secret, even from Carter. Not to tell him until she was ready. In return, she would not tell

Patty. Not that Patty would ever want to hear it anyway. To this he agreed. In the light, like Montgomery Clift.

*

She can still feel the softness of the bedclothes. She can still feel the sense of completion, of a stage conquered, of something final. She can still imagine a world in which she did not go to the lodge, in which she did not make love to Drum, and did not, in the after-swell of lovemaking, see her life entwined with the man relieving himself behind the noise of running taps. She does not much care for that world.

Jessie comes into the bar in a cloud of perfume, hair styled high and blonde, the kind of woman who is described, by herself and others, as brassy. She's an exceptional barmaid and does shifts whenever needed across town. She rarely works the same bar two nights in a row and always turns down the offer of full time. She likes to say she is free.

'All right, love?' Jessie says. She opens the hatch and slips behind the bar. She takes off her coat and the regulars' eyes dart towards her chest, better to see the kind of blouse she's wearing.

'Thanks for this, Jessie,' Gwen says, embracing her. 'You're a lifesaver.'

'You're welcome, love,' Jessie says, then whispers. 'Now go and give him one from me.'

He waits to hear the pipe noise again. There is silence. He thinks of pipes leaking. Of water in pipes, water pouring through them. He thinks of the hunters' lodge. The decision to be made and him needing to shit.

He ran water from the tap as he spattered the bowl; watched the taps flow into the basin and down to the sewers. He saw the water then himself. An older him, in the wreckage of a town, crying upon seeing a rusted tap. Crying at all the water he'd once had and had let drain away.

He turned off the tap and made the decision. He was certain at that moment, the sex still in his blood, the intensity of sharing a bed with a woman.

A life is choices, a running sum of them; this something Drummond had never considered before. Carter had made decisions over the course of his life, and they radiated with consideration, with gut reaction or deep thought: they were consequential, burdened with expectation. Drummond had a choice of two suits; three ties. These the decisions he had made. No one to notice whether he'd agonized over them, or simply picked the nearest clean item. Two suits, three ties.

He hears the pipe noise again; the clank, the clink. Unsure whether further away or closer now. He checks his watch. He will be late, but one last stop. A final place of decision.

Upstairs, she checks in on her father. He is in his chair facing the window, looking out towards Haverigg,

'How you feeling, Da?' she says.

'*Dim saesneg!*'

He coughs, a gunnel of spit running from the corner of his mouth. There is a maritime whiff about him, like unwashed groin. He's half dressed, as far as a shirt, but still in the flannel pyjama trousers, a shawl over his shoulders, face glowing orange from the three-bar fire.

'*Dwi'n aros i farw.*'

'Same as usual, then,' she says. 'You want tea?'

He grunts and points to the china cup on the footstool beside him.

'You need to go though, Da, before you have any tea.'

'*Na.*'

'Need to do it, Da.'

She helps him up, his slack skin and sparrow bones, and shifts him to the commode. He pulls down his trousers, slips his penis under the lip so he won't spray the carpet. She waits until piss dribbles against the pan; there are breaths of flatus but no movements of the bowel. She hears a feeble spray. Another. She waits for five such, then passes him some toilet paper.

'*Urddas,*' he says. He wipes but pisses at the same time, wetting his hands and thighs, this last spray more vital than the preceding, positively a stream.

'I'll get a bowl of water,' she says.

The water takes an age to warm, the time calming, no need for shout or stamp. She takes the bowl through and washes his hands and thighs, the smell of carbolic and piss, the gentleness of her dabs. His pubic hair is steely, his penis thin, his legs constrained by a muddle of pyjama bottoms. She dries his legs and hands, a small stirring at his crotch, something tightening. He pulls up the pants and the bottoms, shuffles himself back into his chair.

'Fy nocturne. Fy nghariad,' he says. 'Dwi'n aros i farw.'

'You're not dying yet, Da. Though if you wet the carpet again, I'll kill you myself.'

In the kitchen she tidies away his lunch plate, boils the kettle, thinks of scalding him. She sees herself pouring hot water on his arms. The inflammation, the flesh turning flush, then milky white. On the counter, surrounded by crumbs and crusts, there's a serrated knife. The softness of the gut as the keen blade enters; the thin incisions on a wrist, the red smile below an earlobe. The surprise on his face. The horror of that. She picks up the knife and quickly closes the drawer on it.

The kettle whistles, and she makes the tea, takes through the pot. He is asleep in his chair. No point in waking him. To sleep now. He will understand. When he wakes, he'll understand. John will be back soon. Barbara's a registered nurse and only too happy to call him Da, wipe him down, make his lunch. He'll understand. It will be better this way.

20

The spire of the church is canted and riven. Drum looks along the high street, down towards the town square, the war memorial scythed through its middle. The clinking, clanking continues, getting closer. No voices though, no call-outs. Perhaps a street sign flapping in the breeze, tapping against stone. Something like that. Something along those lines.

He takes a right at two old Fords, burned out and yet clearly Anglias, such a waste of fine motors; should have got junkers, not things people could drive. The first time he saw them, he'd had to pause, stand by them, look inside to see if they were genuine. The odometers were melted into the dash, the number reels spun black.

The pathway banks down, away from the high street. In the centre of the road, a pub sign, like the mast of a ship, blocks the way; its wooden plinth soot black and the paintwork blistered, the pub name obscured. He stops and hears the clinking again. Louder, the clinking. Coming for him. Into the pub, inside to be safe. Always safe there.

Drum visits the pub most often, even more than the library. The walls are still intact, even one of the windows. There is something in the way the pumps remain at half mast, still at pour; something in the way the cash register rings a permanent sale, charred notes and coins blackly inside; something in the way glass scatters the bar, in the way the jug handles still hang above. It is almost soothing, the barroom; it's the closest thing he knows to hope.

The pubs he and Carter have drunk in. All those pubs and taverns. The conversations had, the confidences exchanged, the lies traded. And when it comes to it, it is his One and he is alone. He should be going home. He should be on his way to Gwen's. Instead he is sitting on a stool, at a table that would collapse if he put his elbows upon it.

The clinking. The clanking. Closer now. Loud in the dark. Familiar, the closer it comes. A tap and a chink and a clank. Closer and louder and coming towards the pub, coming towards the door. Louder and more familiar. Glass on glass, glass inside a bag.

The door is stout, it has withstood every blast and fire, and it opens with a slow whine. There are pit clouds of smoke and the orange coal of a cigarette. Behind them, Carter stands in the doorway, clean white bandages over his busted arm, a white bandage over his head, blood on the bandage.

Drum stands, as though a lady is present, a commanding officer. Carter limps towards him, bids him sit, sets down a bag of bottles on the table that does not fold under its weight.

'Jerrick told me he'd seen you,' Carter says, standing over him, looking down on him. He smokes his cigarette, looks for an ashtray and throws the cigarette to the floor.

'I thought you'd be here,' he says. 'You can't escape me, Drum. I'm like the bad penny. I always turn up.'

From the bookshelf, Gwen takes the *Atlas of the British Isles* and searches out Dagenham, finding it by the Thames, close to the estuary, a few miles from Southend-on-Sea and Foulness Island. She puts the book back on the shelf. She decides to wear the blue shift with white polkas. Both her father and Drum have complimented her on it.

She dresses in her bedroom, makes up her face. So long a distance. So far away. Are you sure, my love, are you sure, *cariad*? She looks at herself in the mirror and sees no change. The same face and the same eyes. The mirrors will be different there. She will see a different woman. No longer a nocturne.

It is quarter to one. It will take her ten minutes to walk to the clock tower. She wants to be there first. She wants Drum to see her first. She wants him to know all is well. She will greet him with the widest of smiles, with delirious kisses. Is that not what happens in books?

In one of their war stories, Carter described a moment they realized they were in trouble.

Something in the angle of the light, something in the air, like fat frying, a low hum like a radio that's on but with the sound turned right down. It's hard to explain, but when you're there you recognize it. You see the whole picture, the whole of what is about to happen.

A lie, but well crafted. And that's how it feels. Sitting in the pub, Carter across from him, pouring drinks. Like waiting for the report. Waiting for the bullets to fly.

'I couldn't find the whisky,' Carter says, handing him over a glass. 'So it's brown ale, I'm afraid.'

'You should be in hospital,' Drum says.

'People keep telling me that,' he says. 'But I didn't want to let you down, did I? Didn't want to leave you alone on our very last day, did I?'

He raises his glass.

'To the One,' he says.

'To the One,' Drum replies.

★

On the last Thursday of their Civil Defence Training, the servicemen would make it off base, head into Millom to celebrate the eve of their One. The next day, Drum would see the aftermath: the black eyes and broken arms of Friday morning, the missing teeth. The other nine men on Carter's course mostly left the base on those Thursdays, got as far away as possible, Carter often with them.

The course changed Carter. Drum doubted whether Daphne or Carter's parents would have noticed anything materially different in him, but it was the depth of his silence when he didn't speak, the vacancy of his eyes in that quiet, which suggested otherwise. For the first time there was equivocation, a lack of certainty when they were together. Drum no longer even knew if they would see in their One together. They had secrets from each other now; they talked less, and when they did, Carter slipped back on his surety, wore it like a fine coat. As though nothing had changed.

Yesterday, the last Thursday of their service, they met at the library after early dinner. It was there amongst the stuffed shelves they usually met for quiet drinks on base. A morbid, quiet place, but always warm.

'So we're going, then,' Carter said.

'If you want to,' Drum said.

'We made it to the end,' Carter said. 'We need to celebrate.'

Drum couldn't say no. Wanted to, but couldn't. Couldn't tell him about the engagement, either; Gwen still disallowing that. Anyway, better to have a reason to write. To tell him the good news. Better that. Better than spoiling their One. No, not spoiling it. The wrong word. Better than *disrespecting* it.

Carter and Drummond rode down to Millom in a wagon with men they did not know, some already drunk. A clutch of motorcycles, pillion riders on each, boys whooping bandit shrieks, tore up in front of them; servicemen thinking themselves the first to have absconded *en masse*, the first to throw bottles at cows and sheep, the first to dream of fingers inside the knickers of local girls.

'Stick close to me tonight,' Carter said as the wagon dropped them at the edge of town. 'You promise me that?'

'It'll be just like Oman,' Drummond said. 'Or like that stand-off in Belfast. I'll be right behind you.'

'I'm serious,' he said. 'No fucking jokes. You stick close to me tonight.'

They took the first pub they came to, the whole company, the saloon and public bar both. Talk only of what would happen after their One. The girls back home. The jobs. The things they would do. Swim. Sleep all day. Eat fish and chips. Go to the football. Watch their hair grow. Never eat bully beef again. Joy on the faces, beer in their guts.

'What're you going to do, Carter?' one of them asked.

'I'm going to live, boys,' he said. 'I'm going to live.'

Carter took a hip flask from his pocket, drank from it, handed it to Drum.

'After what we saw in Cyprus, we're both going to live, right, Moore?'

'Amen to that,' Drum said, holding up the flask. A present from Daphne, a quote in Latin etched in its silver.

Carter began the Cyprus abduction routine – the dark shadows and rushing footsteps, the bags over heads, the occult accuracy of Drummond's thrown knife that disabled their captors. It was perhaps Carter's favourite, the one he told most often, certainly; something in the descriptions of the heat and the peril that felt a touch more picaresque than the other fictions. It was probably why he talked over Drummond's asides, did not ask Drum for corroboration. This last time, just for Carter.

'And all of that,' Carter said, 'I'd do a hundred times over rather than spend one more minute with my future mother-in-law.'

Carter shivered, exaggerated, as though someone had walked over his grave. 'Ugly?' he said. 'If they gave her a facelift they'd drop it.'

The men laughed and banged tables as Carter shifted smoothly from soldier raconteur to the end of the pier. After each gag, Carter banged the table, boom, boom. A gag about Daphne, boom, boom. Another gag about her mother, boom, boom. Carter laughed loudly, hugely, neck jutting out over the pints-heavy table, pointing at the men – he knows what I mean! – and the men leaning back in their chairs, tears, actual tears, of laughter at Carter's bile. Boom, boom. My mother-in-law. Boom, boom. Take my wife.

In a lull, a collective getting back of breath, Carter turned to Drum. He pointed at him, right at his face.

'I don't know if you know Moore, here,' he said to the crowd. 'I've known him since the first week of Service. And he's a diamond, is Moore. A real diamond. Do you know what they called him back at base?'

Drummond had no idea how he looked, what face he was stuck with, how the men saw him. Narrowed eyes maybe. A pleading look. Something weak. Something desperate, most likely. Please don't.

'Back at base, everyone called him Horse,' Carter said. 'They called him Horse because Moore's hung like a horse. Hung like a fucking *shire* horse, he is. It's like a baby's arm holding a hand grenade, like a third leg it is. The officers, they called him Tripod. Did you know that, Horse? That they called you Tripod?'

The men laughed and pointed, more of them now, standing around the table.

'Come on, Horse,' Carter said. 'Show them. Show them all. Get. It. Out.'

The men chanted with Carter, fists stomping the table. Get. It. Out. More joined in, the noise and the heat and Carter's face red, hair brushing his eyes, smiling that wolf smile. Get. It. Out.

'Enough,' Drum said. The tattoo diminished, the voices lowered.

'I would,' Drum said, 'but I'm afraid I'd have your eyes out with it.'

Huge applause. More laughter. More banging of tables. Carter clapped him on the back, hard, and the men roared and cheered. Carter handed him the hip flask. Drum didn't take it.

'Can't you take a joke, soldier?' Carter said. 'Can't you take a fucking joke now, boy?'

More drinks arrived, more pints. Drum didn't take his from the table. No one noticed. Carter was deep in another story as Drum moved through the bar. He got to the door and no one noticed. The freedom of that. To open the door, which he did; to push through it, which he did; to walk onto the silent, unpeopled street, which he did; to walk towards Gwen's place, which he did. The freedom to see her, drink a quiet pint, share a kiss before tomorrow. The freedom of that.

Slowly he took the incline up towards the rise, the fury acid in Drum's stomach, the rage tight in his jaw. He should have seen it. The eventual humiliation, the punchline to a joke that had run so long even Drummond had forgotten the set-up. The One. The fucking One. A reckoning, the One. Should have seen it. Two years. Two years and come the One, all over. An unnecessary employee; a shiftless worker; a batman. Watch the posh, his grandpa had said. They'll bugger you whichever way they want.

He stopped at the war memorial and sat down on the bench to calm himself, dead flowers within kicking distance. He stayed there for some time, imagining punching Carter. Smashing him with fists. More than kissing Gwen, killing Carter. Time spent with that. His punches and kicks.

The clock tower tolled, and down the hill he heard voices; the uniforms spilling out of the pub. He watched them walk into town, then saw the door open again, a small knot of servicemen involved in an altercation with some locals, Carter at its centre. Carter was shouting at a local, then at four or five of them. Drum couldn't work out what he was saying, but could see the tendons in his neck even from that distance.

Two men attacked Carter. The uniforms were held back by the other locals, forced to watch. The two men took turns, alternating foot and fist. Drum watched the kicking, watched the punches. Counted them like breaths as he walked towards them. Carter slumped down to the pavement, but the men didn't stop. Stopped only when Drum launched himself against them, knocking them down like pins. The men fled, uniforms and locals both, running off leftwards, rightwards. Just Carter and Drum. Drum and Carter, Carter's blood on the asphalt, on the brickwork of the pub.

Drummond got his arm around Carter's shoulder, pulled him up, lugged him up the road, towards the war memorial.

'I'm sorry,' Drum said as he dragged him. 'I'm so sorry, James. I'm so sorry.'

Drum put Carter down on the bench, held his head, tried to keep his head from lolling. Carter moved to say something, then puked down the front of his tunic.

Stick close to me. Stick close. Until the ambulance comes, stick close.

★

In the light streaming through the pub window, Carter looks almost dead. Were it not for the alarming dance of his eyes, Drum would think he was dead. But it's clear to Drum that something is abroad, something has happened. Carter knows the truth of the previous night. He has been told the full story. That Drum could have done something much sooner. That Drum let the beating happen. That Drum is a coward, deserter, turncoat. Drum could not take a joke. Drum could not give his friend the benefit. Drum made a promise and did not keep it.

'I'm sorry,' Drum says. 'I should have—'

'What should you have done, Drum?'

Carter leans in to Drum. A smell of cigarettes, of dried blood. He looks unhinged, glass-eyed, still drunk, or drunk again.

'You said stick close—'

'That's what I said, yes. I said stick close, no matter what.'

Carter drinks his drink and smokes his smoke.

'And did you?' he says.

There is a feeling of test, as though he is being examined. It's difficult to know whether he is about to be set upon by Carter, or embraced. Drum would accept the hiding. He is deserving of it. Part of him wants it. That part of the mind to which he has no access.

'Of course you did, Drum. Even after everything, you kept your promise,' Carter says. 'What I said . . . that was unforgivable. But you stuck by me. I knew you'd save me. I was sure of it.'

Carter raises his glass.

'To sticking together,' Carter says.

Drum wants to tell him. Wants to say that he did not stick close. That he saw what was happening and he let them have their punches, their kicks. An accident, Drum being close. Just an accident.

'Anyway,' Carter says. 'Now tell me. You're not really going to marry that girl, are you?'

23

Under the clock tower, people milling past, errands to run, quick in the chill. She looks at the minute hand turn. Past one o'clock now. To be expected, not to make it out on time. She will give him an hour. She will give him a minute or so longer. She waits until the clock tower tolls again, then sets off home.

Home now, but not home. Abandoned once, abandoned forever. She is seething rage. She feels the sparks of it, the spits from the fire, her heels clack like she is crushing bones. She passes closed pubs and locked shops, factory workers returning home from the early shift. Outside the old milliner's she stops. She stops and rings the bell for the upstairs flat. The door opens and there is Nick, wild-haired, woken from post-pub nap.

'Hello, my dear,' he says.

'You were right,' she says. 'Of course, you were right.'

'Come on in,' he says. 'Do, please, come in.'

He closes the door behind her. A stout door with locks. She follows him up the stairs. Perhaps here to stay. Perhaps here she will be safe. Yes, perhaps here.

24

Drum holds his glass in front of him, out still in toast, unsure whether to deny or confirm. There is a clock, its face cracked, its hands halted at just before ten o'clock. He looks at his watch. It is just after one. He is late. Should be there now with her. Under the clock tower, taking her arm.

'How did you know we were engaged?'

Carter opens out his arms wide. 'I didn't, but I could tell. All that furtiveness. The *need* on your face. There wasn't anything else it could have been. But you're not really going through with it, are you?'

'Yes,' Drum says. 'Yes, I'm going through with it.'

'Is she up the stick?' he says.

'No,' Drum says. 'No, nothing like that.'

Carter stands and walks the glass-danced floor, kicks at a stool that disintegrates beneath his shoe.

'Oh, Moore, you poor old skate. Why would you do such a thing? You're young. You can do anything, go anywhere! Christ, if I had your freedom, I wouldn't be throwing it away on some barmaid from sheep-shagging country.'

'You're getting married,' Drum says. 'You've been engaged this whole time!'

'And that's my cross, Drum. I can no more stop that from happening than I can stop the bomb. Daphne and I will get married and there'll be kids and there'll be a house and a job, all the rest of it. But I am going to live, do you understand me? But I'll only be able to do that in the shadows. You? You can do it in the light! I'm stuck with this. You're not.'

Believed this, clearly. The ire in the eyes and the tapping of the foot. Another test, of sorts. Convince Carter, make him see. Because you love Gwen, and whatever doubts you've had before, you know that. Know that, somehow. Why else be here and not on a transport home?

'I love her, James.' How weak that sounding, so hopelessly wet. Carter kicks another stool, a more resilient one that scuttles across the floor.

'You hardly know the girl, you daft old sod. She's not even bloody pregnant! Look around you, Drum. Look at this place. You know what it all means. You know what this place is telling you. It's telling you to live. All those places you've never been? You can go there now. You've got the world to go at!'

Drum laughs. For the first time, he wants to call him out. Call him a bastard. Tell him how ridiculous he really is.

'With what?' Drum says. 'With what, exactly? Fresh air and the savings from Service?'

Carter sits back down across from Drum, puts out his hands, as though wanting to take Drum's in his.

'You only have to ask,' Carter says. 'A job. Whatever you want, I can get it for you. I can organize something, put in a word for you. You only have to ask. You know that. All you have to do is ask. Anywhere you want to go, anything you want to do. Just ask. I owe you that. He could have killed me, that bloke. Any one of them—'

'You don't owe me anything,' Drum says. 'It's not all balances and accounts, debits and credits.'

'That's quite naive,' Carter says. 'Noble, but naive.'

He could ask for anything. At that moment, it's clear that's what is on the table. He can ask him for a job. Ask him to take him from factories and fumes and industrial actions. Only have to say. Only have to form the words.

'I just want to go home, James,' Drum says. 'I just want to marry Gwen and go home.'

And put like that it sounds mealy, put like that it sounds petty and small. He doesn't know Gwen. He doesn't want to go back to Ford's, to the estate, to the pub on a Friday, a fish and chip supper afterwards. Carter is right. Carter doesn't know what he is talking about.

'I offer you the world,' Carter says, 'and you choose Dagenham.'

Carter refreshes the drinks, looks around the barroom, as though there are pretty girls waiting for him to romance. He smiles.

'It was worth a try,' he says. 'At least now I'm sure. You looked like you might hit me for a moment; just for a split second I saw that boy who almost kicked a man's head clean off. Congratulations, Moore. May you be eternally happy.'

A toast, silent, save for the clank. He will smell of ale when he meets his future father-in-law. Something Gwen will notice for sure.

'I need to go,' Drum says. 'I'm meeting Gwen.'

'Oh no,' Carter says. 'No, that isn't the plan. I have the car out front. It's still our One, for Christ's sake. I've got it all planned. I've booked us a hotel in the Lakes. Fishing and champagne. Doing it in style. My treat.'

'I've got to meet Gwen,' he says. 'I promised.'

'We'll call her from the base. She'll understand.'

'No,' he says.

And meaning no. Saying no. He can buy mints to freshen his breath. He could buy flowers for Gwen. Saying no and meaning no. Never once has Carter mentioned fishing on their One, never mentioned it before. Saying no and meaning no.

'What difference does a day make?' Carter said. 'What's one day going to hurt? Call her and tell her there's been complications and you'll be with her tomorrow. I'll drop you back myself. Easy as pie.'

Carter raises his glass, expectantly. Just a day. When put like that, what difference a day? Gwen sure to understand. And a little white lie. Two years should not just be forgotten with a snap of the fingers. And when will he see Carter again? A lifetime to be with Gwen: how long left with Carter? They never did make it fishing. They never did catch those carp.

'I'll need to call her,' he says. 'She'll be waiting. I'm already late.'

'Of course,' he says. 'We'll stop in at the office on the way. It'll all be fine. Trust me.'

They get up from the table and open the door, the town bright under the floodlights. On the way up the high street, past the ruins and the beached machinery, they talk about Ireland and the shoot-out they narrowly won; Korea and the masked assassin; Cyprus and the uprising. They pass the library, the church, the fishmonger's and bakery, their bitten brickwork and open roofs. They walk and they share a bottle between them, the brown ale glinting in the artificial glow.

The Stars Shine Down from Heaven

1962

Friday 26 – Sunday 28 October

I

The chances are he helped build his car; the odds good his fingerprints are beneath its paintwork. So many chassis, so many doors,
and his dabs on them all. As a young man, he took pride in that,
took pride in seeing Fords out on the road; offered a mental salute
towards their chrome and steel. *I made you. You came along the line,
and I made you.* Hubris perhaps, but he still sometimes feels that
same creeping joy: on seeing two lovers in a Ford Anglia, all smiles
and sex; or on passing a day-tripping family, four heads mutely
singing behind steamed-up windows. Scant and fleeting, but still
there: a reminder of what the working week is for.

'Remember, they're not just machines,' an old hand on the line
said, not long after he'd started at Ford's. 'The cunts are dreams
too.' A wink then. Pursed eyes, red-tinged from fume.

'Henry Ford told me that himself.' A laugh, close followed by
cough. His name was Curtis. Talk to me of dreams, Curtis.

Chances are he helped to build his car; the odds good he riveted
the door of the car that will not start. His first attempt was met
with silence; the second with a dying low; the third, full out with
choke, a further failure. In the stone-cold weather, a little hesitancy
to be expected, no need for panic.

'Not today,' he says. 'Not today.'

A fifth attempt, a *come on* of encouragement, a threat of vengeance, and the engine catches: a roar as he pumps the accelerator;
a mewling as his foot pulls back. Never in doubt. The surprised
heater blows hard against the fogged windscreen as he places a
tender, thankful hand on the dashboard.

Eyes down, closed and then open: a pair of wet size-nine prints on the rubber mat beneath the pedals. A vandalism that. Grandpa has recently cleaned the interior: it is spick, span, Bristol fashion. Grandpa words. Must have done so as they were packing. The footwells and seats have been swept; the dash buffed with beeswax polish. Grandpa drives twice a year but valets the car as though he chauffeurs royals to the races. For them – for him – a clean car and a spare tyre; a glove compartment stacked with roadmaps. All for them – for him – though it is Grandpa's car too. Fifty–fifty, at least in name; half the money his. The roll of peppermints in the door's compartment, a couple removed and the paper twisted to a fine point, all Grandpa's though. His, but happy to share. Happy to share with anyone.

He wipes the condensation from the inside of the windscreen. Hazardous, Grandpa warned him, in this weather, unsafe such a long trip.

'The weather's changing, Gramps,' Drum said.

'Not what I hear,' Grandpa said.

They were standing in the sitting room of his great-aunt's house, of late his grandfather's house too, though there was nothing of him there save for a picture of his wife on the mantle. The plum-and-milk sofa had antimacassars; there were pastoral prints hanging in gaudy frames; the room smelled of lilac and baking. In silence, Drum embraced his grandpa, surprising him: the old man unwilling at first, then accepting his arms, beating his palms on Drum's back, manly like.

'We'll be back soon,' Drum said. 'You take care, now.'

The old man laughed, big laugh on him, stoop shoulders rocking inside a beige cardigan.

'Take care? It's not me who's pricking on up north in this weather,' he said.

Vi came through from the kitchen with tea on a tray, a plate laid with just-cooled biscuits. Drum kissed her goodbye, held her close enough to claim a smudge of flour from her cheek.

'Sorry, Vi,' he said, walking to the front door. 'No time for tea. Must rush.'

He paused at the door, hand on the lock. He wanted to fix them at that moment: their biscuits dipped in their tea, saying their crumb-mouthed farewells. Enough.

A photograph of them, along with other snaps, is in an album buried in the stuffed boot. Drum and Gwen haven't been away for a weekend since Anneka was born, and his suggestion they should pack for all eventualities went unquestioned. They divided the tasks: Gwen filling a suitcase for her and little Annie; Drum responsible for the rest. Bags are strewn across the back seats, a space left beside them for the too-small carrycot in which they hope Annie will sleep. Inside the house, Gwen is getting Annie off to sleep as Drum warms the car, opens out the maps, plots again the route; a thin finger tracing the hours ahead. Six hours. Six hours maybe more.

North of St Albans, west of Bedford, the map dampens. A single teardrop falling on Hertfordshire, dissolving the county. The others he catches, hands quick to his eyes, the tears making tracers: strafes of yellow, glitches of red. He beats his fists against the steering wheel; enough just to smart, enough just to heat them through. The roll of peppermints rattles in the door, almost rhythmic. How long it lasts.

Quiet now, still and quiet now; staring at the Ford logo at the centre of the steering wheel. How he would like to sound the horn. How he would like to hold it down and yowl in its wake. He grips the wheel; knuckles white as lard. He stays like that for time: straight-backed and shallow-breathed, heart slowing, the tightness of his chest unclenching, not sounding the horn. Looking down at the map, not sounding the horn. Listening to the idle of the engine, not sounding the horn. Eyes straight ahead, watching the street, ten white knuckles not sounding the horn.

From the paper roll, he loosens a peppermint and sets it on his tongue, holds it there like communion wafer. He makes an O with his mouth and his inward breath freezes with mint, ices his teeth. He takes the map from the dash, Hertfordshire remaining damp and obscured.

He follows the roads they will take. Six hours at least. *Better to travel than arrive.* A laugh at that. A poster at the plant, an illustration of a Ford Edsel, a family inside: American, unmistakably. In the canteen, framed on the wall. One of many. So many posters. So many advertisements. Better to travel than arrive. *The cunts are dreams too.* Talk to me of dreams, Curtis.

2

Anneka went down easily, her afternoon nap the only time she was sure to sleep. Twenty months old and still at night never more than four hours straight. Waking in the dark, hungry mouth for breast, open mouth for scream, lately now articulating short sentences, but *Mama*, mostly. Loud in the silent, night-time house – *Mama*. Shuffling from bed, Gwen moving light-footed, dodging creaking floorboards, into her daughter's room – *Mama*. Anneka standing with her fists gripping the bars of the cot – *Mama*. Gwen hoisting her up and carrying her to the single bed – *Mama*. Gwen out with her breast, then the sound of jaw. Lying there all hours of night, feeding her daughter's sucking mouth; her biting, mischievous mouth. A different girl in the light and day. A nocturne, aye.

At the kitchen table Gwen smokes a cigarette. In front of her are cheese sandwiches wrapped in greaseproof paper, a hand of bananas, a thermos of tea, milk in a bottle; beside them a list of items not to forget, its entries scored and ticked, double-entry certain. Annie is in the carrycot in the sitting room. Four maybe five hours ahead in the boxy car. How many to be filled with scream; how many with Annie under her coat, suckling for want of entertainment? Her own fault. Should have weaned by now. Not even a radio in the car. Just talk and tea and the look as Gwen lights a cigarette; Drum cracking the window, the brief pleasure hardly worth the silent reproach. Four, maybe five hours. Jesus wept.

Another week, another day even, she would have refused him. There were enough reasons against: Annie's cold and cough, the weather, the distance, the company at journey's end. All good excuses, all solid, practical objections. Another week, aye.

'Oh, I forgot to say,' Drummond said over Wednesday's chops. 'I got a letter from Carter this morning. They've finally fixed up the house and wondered if we wanted to visit this weekend.'

He'd already accepted; she saw that in the glance up from his dinner. She wanted to say it was short notice, but didn't. That what she'd have been expected to say. She instead cut the fat from the lamb, forked it to the side of her plate.

'It'll be fun!' he said, perhaps hearing her unvoiced response and pushing through with whatever he'd already prepared. 'A little playmate for Annie, good food, nice walks. It'll be good to get away. Forget about things for a time.'

'Things?' she said.

'Yes,' he said. 'Things.'

So light, and so casual. Just *things*. What things to forget; what things to winnow away from. *Things* hiding a myriad; *things* hiding a multitude. She knew what he meant. The strikes at work. The second child they were not yet expecting. Him muttering to himself as he lit the fire of a morning. Him unable to concentrate on his library book of an evening. Him sitting in the small chair in Annie's room, watching the two of them sleep. Things, these. *Things*.

And enough, these things. Making sense, these things. No reason to say no. No real reason. No reason other than she would rather do anything else. But no reason to disappoint. No reason to drag it out the evening.

'Won't you be needed on the picket?'

This cruel.

'They won't miss me,' he said. 'Won't even know I'm gone.'

This a lie. A straightforward tell, the scratching of the throat, one she'd come to know since the move to Dagenham.

'Anyway,' he said. 'I can picket the morning, and then we can drive up in the afternoon while Annie sleeps.'

She looked down at her fatless chop.

'Okay,' she said. And that face. Delighted boy-child face. Lifting his eyes, scrambling his features, erasing days and weeks from his forehead. That face.

'Are you sure?' he said.

'You're right, it'll be good to get away,' she said. 'I'll do us some sandwiches. We can eat while Annie sleeps. Be nice to see Carter and Daphne again. It'll be fun.'

It would not be fun. It would be a backward glance, a respooling. The two boys drinking whisky, telling their imagined war stories; Gwen making slow going of any common ground with Daphne. Would that Carter had married Patty. The fun that would have been. Patty married now, a kid now, moved up to Scotland with a man called Peter. Peter and Patty, their child called Paul. So far away, Gwen wrote her in a letter, you might as well be on Mars.

She'd first met Daphne at her own wedding; the second time at Daphne's more opulent celebrations. They have exchanged little more than a hundred words with each other, most of which in the course of one stolen moment in a rose garden at the back of Daphne's parents' house, the two of them sharing a cigarette, faces flushed from champagne, momentarily separated from their partners at the Carters' wedding.

'So,' Daphne said, 'it's done then.'

'Yes,' Gwen said. 'Ring's on now, no taking it off.'

Daphne sat on a cast-iron bench, flicked ash into the flower bed.

'You're happy?' Daphne said. 'You think you made the right decision?'

'Ask me in twenty years.'

Daphne motioned to her to sit down next to her. She smelled of sweat and the roses, expensive cigarettes, champagne halitosis.

'You could ask me now, and I'd probably say I've not done the right thing,' Daphne said. 'But it is the right thing, isn't it?'

What to say to that. How to respond. To say, you could do better. Not to know if that were the case.

'You two make a good couple,' Daphne said. 'Hale and hearty, the two of you. You stand well together. That's what my mother said is the most important thing. The way you stand together is the way you'll stay together.'

At that she'd laughed, high and fluted the laugh, and then Drum and Carter were back, whiskies in hand, wondering where they'd got to. Gwen stood and positioned herself next to Drum, wondered how they looked side by side; how they looked to the assembled wedding guests. Hale and hearty. Staying together.

Thinking of that as she agreed, as she cleared the plates, as she checked on Annie once more, thinking of that as they went to bed. Sex that night. Their usual night for it, Wednesday. He tried to touch her breasts, but she moved his hands away. Sex with a certain abandon, without pressure. No thoughts of baby, coming or present. She told him to do what she liked him to do and he did it without giving up early. Afterwards, he let her smoke in the bed. He didn't even complain when she asked him to fetch an ashtray.

She looks at the clock. She smokes. In her handbag there is the letter from her father, read so much its paper has begun to shine. That, perhaps, more the reason. A part of the reason. Count to ten, tell the truth. Most of the reason. Honesty the best policy. Without the letter from her father, there would have been no longing for field and pasture, no yearn for frosted hikes and deep country air, no yen for dung and starry skies. For Drum, yes. For him, yes. But not without the letter. The letter more than the strike. The letter more than his deep silences and stuttering lips.

*

Slim amongst Tuesday's second-post bills, the envelope and her father's careless scrawl surprising. Letter sent because she had not called; letter sent because she could not face the short, cold walk to phone box; letter sent as last resort; resentment, she imagined, in the price and lick of a stamp.

With a butter knife, she opened the envelope. Inside, a sheet of paper crowded with crooked, tight-spaced words. For him a long letter, two whole sides, the sum of which the usual complaints: you never call; send photographs of Annie; you must visit soon. Then, at its end: Nicholas Oldman has passed.

In the warm of the small kitchen, Old Nick dead. Taken sudden, his heart just giving out. Found dead in his study, pen in hand, slumped over desk and papers. Died the Monday and buried the Saturday. Too much of a fuss for Da: *Old Nick would not have wanted all that*. The funeral a town carnival: streets lined with silent, hatless men; silent, weeping women. The cortege led by horse and carriage, hooves louder than engines, the town's most famous son, its own poet, boxed and scattered with wildflower and moor-heather. A long, rambling route taken from undertaker's to church; men and women spilling into the churchyard, clotting around the open door. And then laid to rest.

They all went: Da, John, Barbara and their boy Jack. *A beautiful service*. Afterwards, in the pub, an informal wake that lasted the night and nudged the early hours. The take good that week. *Best for years*. A few days later, a headstone carved and erected. Below date of birth and death, the stonemason's letters: *'I thank God for this town and its people'*.

Annie was asleep, so Gwen cried. Gwen's tears caused Anneka distress, the same as sharp words or the fights and thumps from next door. *A sensitive soul*, Great-Aunt Vi's one-time diagnosis, at which Gwen had laughed. *Take my nipples, know what sensitive means*. Gwen cried, a heave of weeping, an unexpected sensation in the sternum, gagging on breath, some words said, the usual kind, the oh-nos and the oh-my-Gods and the low, simple nos.

He'd stayed in touch since her leaving. His idea, and his letters. Three in three years; a poem composed on the occasion of her wedding day. Simple, gilded words she'd kept in her vanity case and not shown to anyone, not even Drum. For no one else, those words. His florid copperplate, beautiful on watermarked paper, just for her. *No one pours a black and tan like you / It is a different drink in different hands / a half-light memory bid adieu.*

There had been a reading, six months before, at some hall or somewhere, right in the heart of the city; an invitation extended she'd declined without discussion with Drum. To go, indecent. Unsure why. Why that word. But indecent, yes. Had she mentioned it, Drum would have insisted she attend. Insisted he accompany her. Of this she was sure. He would have got Vi to stay with Annie and they would have made a night of it: taken the Underground, the racketing carriages fast through the suburbs, then into the deepening dark; a drink in some small, gas-lit boozer beforehand and then to the hall, their clothes plain amongst the formal wear. The applause for Old Nick at the mahogany lectern, accent thicker the further south he came, and as he read, that face of Drum's: the factory face, projected attention but lost somewhere else, halfway to sleep.

'Sorry,' Gwen wrote, 'but we have plans. Perhaps next time give me more notice.'

Of late, she'd not much thought of him; not Nicholas Oldman, not the pub, not the town, not the coast, not the fields, not even her brother or father. The odd dream to take her back, but no homesick wobbles in the day, no itchy feet for gorse, for kicking sand against waves, no family hankering. Her calls home are a courtesy and chore; her father asking when she's planning on coming back, telling her he won't last the week without his daughter. Each entreaty met with *soon*, and *soon* being enough. Barbara was taking good enough care of him, so he said when they spoke, and the pub was busier than ever. John born to be a barman, born a landlord: this another constant. When she heard this, she'd say she was glad it'd worked out so well for everyone. So well for everyone but Nick. Everyone but him.

In the kitchen sink she washed her face and looked at the clock. An hour and the girl would wake; an hour and it would start all over again. Outside the rain had eased. She looked into the hallway, tiptoed past Annie and lightly took the stairs. In her vanity case, she found Nick's letters, a touch of pipe-smoke still to the pages, carried them downstairs and slipped them into her handbag.

Five doors down, she knocked at Vi's place. Vi opened the door, big Vi with her big yellow hair and small yellow teeth.

'Would you mind taking her?' Gwen said, pushing the pram inside. 'Just for an hour or so?'

Vi's face: practised sympathy, brought out often for cancer, death, lost babies, divorces and affairs. Multipurpose, warmly meant and knowingly useless.

'Everything all right, love?' she said.

'Fine. I just need to call my da. A mate of his died.'

'Oh, I'm sorry to hear that, love,' she said. 'Annie'll be fine here. You go call your dad.'

Rain hit the black petals of the umbrella. She closed the door and set off with quick steps, the distance punctuated with things she'd forgotten to do, things that Annie would need when she woke.

On entering the Oak Bar of the Eastbrook, the men looked at her, maybe twenty of them. They sized her up, then turned away. Behind the pumps, the barmaid, fierce with make-up, poured a pint for a man in overalls.

'Black and tan, ta,' Gwen said.

The barmaid looked calculatingly at the taps.

'A pint is fine,' Gwen said.

The barmaid poured the pale and then the stout. A good job. It would have pleased Nick well enough. Gwen carried the drink to a table by the window and took the letters from her handbag. She read them twice; the poem three times. Dabbed at her eyes when she was sure no one was looking.

She wanted to tell Nick he'd been wrong about Drum. She wanted to tell him she was happy. She wanted to tell Nick, as she had been unable to do in life, that without him there would be no Drum, there would be no Annie, no reading books of an evening, no rigour of thought.

'Ah, that's all on you,' she heard him say, 'don't go blaming me for all that.'

But she did blame him, her Old Nick. The man who had let her say no; the man who the following day congratulated her when she told him there had been a delay to Drum's demob, a message waiting for her on her return to the pub. Drum en route now to be with her. No look of disappointment on his face. She wanted to thank him for that.

Goodbye, Nick, you old skate. Goodbye, Nick, dead now and heavenward, reunited with your wife and walking an endless moor, God in every gorse and grouse. She raised her glass to him. On her lips, a line from the poem: *You do not just go, you disappear.*

In the held glass, a man's face appeared: a cloud in the black and tan. It broke and the man was standing in front of her, shadows cast from his flat cap and ferret-lean body.

'Listen, love,' the man said. 'I've been all over the world and let me tell you this. I've seen it all. But I've never, *never* seen a woman drink a pint before. Never. Not once in all my days.'

She looked at the drink, then up at the man, once-kind eyes in a battered, pugilistic face. She smiled and hoped it would repel, that he would not take it as licence to sit. A moment of terror, there. How long before she could escape? How long before he said she was being unfriendly or impolite?

No power this side of the bar. No dominion. Just a woman alone with an unprecedented pint, its two-tone hue coquettish perhaps; maybe a code for something. He stood looking at her. She had no words, no quick lip to scold him. No longer a nocturne. Aye, not her father's nocturne, at least.

The man smiled. Perfect teeth. Denture perfect. She felt his eyes on her chest. On her arms and on her face. He shook his head. He walked back to his table and his companion.

'You believe that?' he said to the man at his table. 'You ever seen the like?'

The line between pale and stout strayed as she held the glass.

She set it down on a beer mat and the Watney's logo darkened. She packed up the letters and held the bag against her chest. She wanted to drink the black and tan, but could not; not even for Nick. She got up and left the bar, deliberately and slowly, out into the rain-lashed streets. Not a look at the men, not a glance behind.

*

She has packed the letters, the ones from Nick and the one from her father. She will smoke the cigarette and will gather Annie up and she will be cheerful on the journey. She will sleep and then she will be refreshed, and then she will be good. She will be pleasant no matter what. For Drum, yes. For herself, too.

3

In the warming car, waiting for the front door to open, he looks down the street. It is empty of people, the rain harrowing the pavements. For the fifth time in as many minutes he gives thanks to shop steward Francis; a fine union man, a man of rare conviction, sacked for convening what Ford's considered an illegal meeting. In solidarity, the factory was all out on strike; in solidarity, the plant was at a standstill. All thanks to one man and his meeting. Front-page news for a time. Thank you, Brother Francis. Thank you, St Francis of Dagenham. Without you, brother, my family surely dead.

*

The front page of the *Daily Mirror* was dominated by the strike for almost a week. On the bus to the picket, Drum would read about their own lives while others talked of the stewards preparing for war, of the militants puffed up and proud, of tactics, of revolution. Hard not to think of Carter in the billet, telling him, we own the streets, the walls too. Wanting to believe the union men and knowing Carter was probably laughing about it over his breakfast. When asked, Drum said the right things. He turned up for all pickets, was counted when there were votes. But Carter was there, in the back of the canteen, in the barrack-room noise, in the smoke-sweat and stewed tea, in the mob of men and women from Paint, Trim and Assembly laughing at their seriousness.

On the third, maybe fourth day of strike action, Ford's was still the main story in the *Mirror*, but tensions in Cuba made a small sidebar on the bottom right. Drum read all he could, though the information was scant, perhaps a storm in a teacup. The next day, the stories had reached parity, the day after, the strike at Ford's was shunted to the side, the stand-off between Kennedy and Khrushchev the main headline. Then no mention of Ford's at all. Just Cuba dominating the front page. That on the Wednesday.

On the bus to the picket that morning, no one talked of Cuba. Drum never heard it mentioned once. The strike the only topic, and once that exhausted, the usual conversations of men. Malkin and Brown discussing how much they hated the singer Adam Faith, but would love to slip a length to Dilys Watling, the guest star on Faith's show. Nott telling Fraser he was on a promise with this bird from the Coronet and Fraser saying in his dreams. Talk of Spurs, West Ham, the Arsenal, Chelsea. Not one of them afraid, not one of them seeing what was to come.

Drummond went back to his paper and read again about the situation and stand-off, saw again what he saw. He saw the escalation, the intransigence, no one willing to lose face. A bald man and a vain man: this how the world ends, two men unwilling to show fear. Drum saw it all, the radiation gusts skidding the Atlantic, the North Sea; the tactical deployments, the readying of the missiles, the way they erected slowly on their launch pads, the cradle of them in the aircrafts' bellies, the fingers on buttons; how the buttons looked, not simply functional, but ceremonial.

And he saw Carter's bomb shelter. The way it had been described in his letters, the vastness of it. State of the art. Envisioned by his father, but finished by Carter after his father's death and the house coming into Carter's possession. How safe they would be. How safe they would all be. When he got to the picket, he sloped off to call Carter from the payphone at work. On the way home he sent him a telegram, called him again from the phone box at the end of the road. He did not receive an answer. It didn't matter. He was owed. Carter had been clear on that. Whatever he wanted. Whenever it was needed.

On the production lines, men dream their way through shifts, their hands and eyes keeping time, working to a pre-ordained tempo. Muscles work staccato bursts in din and dust, unmoored from thought; minds off somewhere other: wandering and lost. Only way. Without dreams you rot from the inside. And so dreams. Hours of Cup Final-winning goals; of the seduction of women; of Pools wins and flash motors. Hours of reeling in a monster perch; of a son or daughter winning a place at the grammar; of money enough at the end of the week to spend on beer and a fish supper. Hours of Eden, then home on the bus, to kids and bills and a wife whose dreams you can't imagine.

These dreams, yes; but others, too. Darker and more appealing in the rut of work. The arguments you win with ease. The punch you land on your no-good son. The bullets you fire as you declare a workers' takeover of production. All the world's ills corrected. A private realm in which you're always right and always land the killer blow.

These see you through the first years. Ire and spite, joy and luck. Beyond that, though, these finely sculpted worlds feel bloodless. Their perfection riles. They need tension. The two entwine then; the vicious and the victorious. The break-leg challenge in the Cup Final that ends your career; the woman who runs off with your best mate; the burning through of your fortune and no pot to piss in. More complex worlds, wider in scope. Your utopian revolutionary state turns dictatorial and murderous, denouncing you as a reactionary. The kid gets into the grammar and comes home hating your common accent and piggish table manners. You lose your Pools coupon and spend your life rifling bins. These the dreams that take hold; these the dreams with legs.

Drum has his bomb dream. It begins with the sounding of an alarm at the factory. Only he knows what it really means and is home in miraculous time. There he ushers Gwen and Annie into the basement, the cellar they thought boarded up and desolate, in fact a well-stocked shelter: a radio set, tanks of water, tins of meat and fish and fruit and vegetables, two cot beds already made up with blankets, a locked cabinet housing a shotgun and revolver, boxes of ammunition. Safe there the three of them.

Except not safe, never safe. The bombs hit too close, blown off course from London. They survive the blast but the radiation gets them. Scavengers find them months later, rob their food, skull Annie and take Gwen. A bullet in Drum's head, his murderer laughing as he pulls the trigger.

*

When Gwen opens their front door, he imagines himself shot and about to die. He watches her struggle with the door. The carrycot is between her legs, skimming the carpet. He jumps from the driver's seat and takes the cot from her. His daughter is heavy, fat from mother's milk. Thief and sunlight both. Gwen opens the car's back door and he slides the cot onto the seat, just enough room with enough of a shove.

'You mind if I sleep while she does?' Gwen says as she skirts the vehicle. 'Wake me when she starts to scream.'

'Just got to call Carter first,' he says. 'Let him know we're on our way.'

She takes off her coat and balls it up for a pillow as Drum puts the car into gear and pulls away. At the end of the road, he stops at the callbox, gets out of the car and dials Carter's number. It rings out. He dials again and it rings out again, the same as it has the whole week. He pretends to put the coin in the slot – a canny French Drop – then speaks over the dial tone.

'We're on our way,' he says. 'Get out the Scotch.'

He puts down the receiver and looks to the car: inside, his sleeping wife and sleeping daughter. No one to even observe the deception. How he would like to sleep so quick. Six hours. Seven possibly. Jesus wept.

4

Stiff-necked, Gwen wakes, hot under her pullover. The windscreen wipers jive, bored and busy; the heater hums a low, sour breath. Drum hunches in the driving seat, his head inches above the wheel, the better to see through the driving rain. She watches his rapt attention, hopes he can see through the downpour.

Before Anneka, they'd take the car out for a drive on a Sunday. Places of beauty. The coast. The Epping Forest. On Saturdays, they'd ride the Underground into the city, the sights to see, the museums to visit. They'd alight at Victoria or Embankment and though there were buses, they walked the streets in cold and shine, saw the new and the old, the burning lights and shadowed nooks. A loose ring on her finger, her arm in his, standing in front of a Titian, an Egyptian mummy, a dinosaur's bones, the dome of St Paul's. The bridling joy of those walks. The sheer abundance of them.

The last time she and Drum went into the city Gwen was five months gone; slow walking, a bus offered, a taxi; both of which she refused.

'Is it far?' she asked.

'It's not far,' he said. 'But I know you can't walk like you used to.'

'I'm not a cripple,' she said. 'I can still walk.'

Her ankles and thighs ached the short stretch of road up to the Monument, the gilded urn atop the Doric column. Standing in the quiet, September-warm street, they held hands and watched as a short man in a pork-pie hat took a photograph.

'I should have taken you here before,' he said. 'We could have gone up to the top.'

'We can still go to the top,' she said.

'There's more than three hundred steps, love.'

She felt something in her stomach, the old one-two; winced with the shock of it, snatched his hand, placed it on her belly. The feet or fists shifting under her skin.

'He's cast his vote, then,' Drum said.

'She's not in favour.'

'I wonder where he'd like to go,' he said. 'Fella, would you like to see the Palace? Tap once for yes, two for no.'

The baby kicked twice.

'She's clearly not a royalist,' Gwen said.

They ended up touring the National Gallery; a decision reach-ed without consulting the foetus. Inside, in the stately cool, they saw the creation of the world and its destruction; sex and death; landscapes and portraits. Outside, they ate sandwiches, looking up to the statue of Nelson, his one good arm resting on his sword.

'She's going to be so lucky to have all this,' Gwen said. 'On her doorstep. All of this.'

'He's going to be so lucky to have *you*,' he said. 'Whatever happens, he's got you.'

She'd once heard a story of a woman who had birthed a pulsating mass of eyes. Someone from the town had a kid with two rows of teeth and the forceps' pads permanently dented into his skull. Tina Boyle went mad after her girl was born, tried to drown herself or the girl, one of the two.

Drum put his arm around her and they stayed there for a time, watching the pigeons in the fountains, the children throwing seed, the hawkers doling out their little bags. On the way home, she fell asleep on Drum's shoulder, him waking her, gently, softly, as they pulled into their station stop. As she woke, she knew they would not do this again.

Though she does not think of that moment as she watches Drum at the wheel, the sensation is the same. A touch of witchy intuition, inherited from her mother's side, the sense that something has changed though impossible to finger exactly what.

'Thought the weather was going to change,' she says, looking through the windscreen. There are a few other cars; all slow, all tentative, all mindful of the deluge and the shortening visibility.

'It *has* changed,' he says. 'It's better than it was.'

She roots down inside the footwell and takes out the thermos.

'Tea?' she says.

'Yes,' he says, not looking from the windscreen. 'Please.'

She pours the tea and hands it to him, looking at the cup and his hand, not the windscreen, as he has taught her.

'She's not stirred,' he says. 'Out for the count.'

Gwen looks over her back, Annie curled in on herself, coiled in the blue-starred blanket.

'We'll pay for that later,' she says. 'No chance of her sleeping tonight.'

'Never sleeps the night anyway,' he says.

She takes an apple from the bag, passes it to him. Usually he would shine it on his sleeve before eating, but at the wheel he just takes a bite, loud and greedy.

'I dreamed we crashed,' she says. 'That a big lorry smashed into us.'

'Just now?' he says.

'Huge thing it was. It almost wiped us out.'

'Almost?'

'It was a miracle really. We should have been flattened, but we were fine. Not even a scratch.'

She puts a hand on the dash.

'The superior engineering of the Ford to the rescue again,' she says.

'Well, they do call them the cars of your dreams.'

'I thank God Henry Ford doesn't know about *my* dreams.'

'He'd be shocked.'

'Not as shocked as you.'

Together they laugh, low and conspiratorial, aware of waking Annie, and Drum turns his eyes from the road just for a moment to catch Gwen's. He looks happy, she thinks, schoolboy-before-the-holidays happy, the same face as when she cooks steak or kisses his neck without warning. She thinks she must look happy too.

Her happiness, the ease of it, has been puzzling. She expected it not at all. Nick's premonitions of disaster a low ringing; memories of her friends' shifting tone when discussing their husbands: at first giddy in love, later in mystified vexation. So common this, she felt she must be delusional. When asked about him by other factory wives in the pub, she made the same noises they did. She complained of his flatulence, his indifference to the house, the way he never made the tea. None of which was true.

She did not say he washed the dishes of an evening, changed the nappies on weekends, brought her flowers without reason, fetched her water in the night. To do so was to risk chiding, knowing looks between women. Better to say nothing and in saying nothing, avoid a hex. People only ever say they're happy before it's taken from them. Do not invite that in. Never to say that. Instead, say it with a hand on the leg. A kiss before breakfast. A whispered I love you at the most surprising time. Lips on his stomach, telling him her dreams, the things she saw there.

'This was a good idea,' she says. 'To get away.'

He swings the wheel and the car changes lane. They pass a red car driving even slower than them. She looks back at Annie sleeping, still soft breath, still under.

'I feel a bit guilty, if I'm honest,' he says. 'Boys out on the picket and us up on holiday. Years ago, I'd have cut me dead when I got back.'

'If you want, we can sing "The Red Flag".'

'Maybe later,' he says. 'After a sandwich perhaps?'

She unwraps the sandwiches and passes one to him. She watches him eat, watches him strain his eyes on the road. She thinks, briefly, of the Carter wedding, the way the two of them clung to the walls, faced it down like an ordeal, before heading back to the inn where they were staying, drunk and exhausted, laughing at how sore-thumbed they looked.

She imagines the house where they will stay, the size of the beds and the towels, the vastness of the kitchens, and a room, just one big room, full of books. She eats her sandwich. She smiles at her husband. Her baby does not wake and no lorry ploughs into them. She thinks about her cigarette. The one she will smoke after her sandwich. She thinks about the strike of the match and the crack of the window.

5

The Midlands come in lightening rain and brighter skies, busier roads and smoking chimneys, miles of sprawl he has never explored, never known except from behind a windscreen. Four hours now. Maybe less. No panic now. No panic. Plans to be made. Planning what men did best. Contingencies. A range of them. Main thing, they are safe. Whatever happens, safe.

At first, as Gwen and Annie slept, he felt anything but safe. He saw cars bonnets-up and steaming at the roadside, men changing tyres, operating jacks. Vigilance needed, constant vigilance. A police car went past in a blue wash of sirens; an ambulance attended a crash site. Two cars fused. A new fear: the ironic death. At the pearling gates to heaven, St Peter raising a deified eyebrow and saying, 'Ah, yes, Drummond, just in time to beat the rush. And I see you brought your family too.'

He was grateful for the silence, for his sleeping family, the distraction of the roads. Feeling sure he could reach the Carters before they woke, the roads shortening, the wind blowing them a tempest to the north.

In the silence of the car, neither girl making a noise more than breath, he approached the problem as though in a divisional meeting of the union. He liked the combative nature of it. The men ripping his arguments apart, pulling them back together. Those telling him to go home. To abandon the action. Him shaking his head, the way the stewards did: pitying and disdainful.

I have made calls to Carter. And yes, they have not been answered, but I have sent a telegram. He will be expecting us.

Why did he not telegram you back? Why not take your calls?

So many reasons, none of which are important. Why would he telegram back? He knows I'm on my way.

You can't trust someone like that. One rule for us, another for them.

He is a man of his word. He made a promise.

Piss-poor planning, if you ask me. What if they're not in? What if they're on holiday?

If they're on holiday, I'll force the window or something.

And say what? How will you explain to Gwen?

I have a note. Written in his hand. Saying they've been called away and will be back the next day.

And if they're in and never got the message?

Carter will cover for me. Best liar I know. Can think on his feet.

Assuming he wants to help you. Brothers, would you help this coward bastard?

Worst comes to worst, I have money. We check in at the Wolf.

Good luck explaining that one, Brother Moore.

6

She lights her cigarette and he cracks the window, she cracks hers too, and the rain blows in from both sides, spangles the sleeve of her cardigan. He puts a peppermint in his mouth. As soon as she's thrown the dog-end out the window, he will offer her one from the roll: the last act of the dance. He turns up the heater. He hums to himself.

'I should wake her,' she says.

'No,' he says, 'let her sleep.'

'She'll be murder if we let her sleep past four.'

'Be murder anyway.'

'I'll finish this, then I'll wake her.'

'I said not to,' he says. 'Just let the girl sleep.'

She holds the cigarette out of the window.

'It'll be fine for you. You'll be drinking with Carter. It'll be me up to the small hours with a bitten tit.'

She likes to cuss at him, moments like that. Exasperate him; confuse his ire.

'Another half-hour'll make no difference.'

'Not to you, no.'

'I don't think you realize the stress of driving in these conditions. I can barely bloody see out the windscreen.'

'I knew this was a bad idea,' she says.

'You just said it was a *good* idea.'

'I was trying to make you feel better! Who would want to travel in this weather? To see Carter and Daphne of all people . . .'

'Now look—'

The car takes a hit to the left wing, whatever striking it bouncing up onto the passenger-side window. Drum instinctively swerves to the left, onto the roadside, the tyres crunching stone and shingle. He slams on the brake and clutch, the car sliding down a narrow gulley, half on the road, half off. They careen, Drum turning the wheel, getting the car off road. She closes her eyes, braces for impact. The wheels feel like they are on glass, then beach, then glass again. She bows her head and keeps her eyes closed. Glass and shingle, glass and shingle, then thrown forward at the end, hands on the dash, stopping herself from heading through the window.

'Gwen,' he says. 'Gwen, you all right, Gwen?'

Hands on her, and she looks up and there is no blood and there is pain in her neck but the pain soon goes, and he is breathless. The engine ticks and steam rises from the bonnet.

'I'm not hurt,' she says, 'I'm not hurt.'

He looks to her, and she looks behind to the carrycot. It has shrugged down into the footwell. Annie is scrunched down, her face against the back of the driver's seat.

'Annie,' she says and grabs her from the pile of blankets, holds her to her breast.

'Oh, my girl. Oh, Annie love. You're safe, Annie. You're safe, Annie, my darling one.'

Red cheeks then and eyes open and Annie screams. Gwen shushes and sorries, runs her hands over the bones, the legs and arms, and Annie screams and screams, and Gwen pulls down her top and offers her breast, the only sure way to calm her. Drum tries to hold any part of his daughter, her bobby-socked feet, her chunky legs, but Gwen pushes him away.

'My girl,' she says, 'Annie-moo, you're safe, little girl, you're safe now.'

Annie opens her eyes and pauses her screams, screams again louder if that were possible. Gwen struggles a nipple into the infant mouth. She feels the milk flood from her into her child, feels the shake and chill of her baby, holds Annie as close as she can, wishing her skin could envelop her.

'It's not safe,' Gwen hears Drum say. 'We need to get out. It's not safe.'

'No,' she says. 'We're staying here. Aren't we, Annie? We're staying right here.'

7

He leans against a five-bar gate, kicking mud from his wet boots. Hands shake, cold and shock. He can hear traffic and the occasional scream from Annie. He does not turn. Fear that he will see himself in the wing mirrors, his reflection in the driver-side window. All this and for what. And for what now? Four hours from Carter's. More than four, surely. Stuck now at the roadside, perhaps to get the best views of the coming bombs, their rainbows blooming in the damp.

They remain inside the car, his wife and child. His. They will not get out, Annie is clamped to Gwen, held so tight he's surprised she can breathe. He resents the breasts. Resents that he cannot comfort Annie that way. That the first she turns to is her mother. Stop thinking this.

'You all right?' Gwen says, opening the passenger door. 'You're shaking.'

For this, glad. The rose hip of the cheeks of his girl, the closed eye on the breast.

'She's okay,' Gwen says. 'No breaks I think.'

'We need to get moving,' he says. 'Dangerous here. Anything could come off the road.'

'No,' Gwen says. 'We stay here.'

'No,' he says. 'No.'

Show no fear. Four hours, no more than that. No fear as he turns the key; no fear as he hears nothing but whine. No fear when trying again; no fear as the whine gives way to nothing. The Ford logo looking back, blue and white, clean and shining. The engine not turning over. The windscreen unblemished, not even a scratch, not even spritzed with mud, but nothing from the engine. The rain is sheeting. Again and again, and nothing and nothing. Four hours from safety and nothing. What did you call them, Curtis? Was it dreams?

8

On the back seat, he removes his soaked trousers and his now see-through underpants and dries himself with a towel. There is oil on the trousers where he has wiped his hands, oil on his drenched jumper, but she does not tell him to watch the uphol-stery. Both she and Annie watch his quiet ballet, his awkward movements, pulling on pants and jeans, covering up the whiteness of his legs. The speed of it. Off now the shirt and jumper, drying his chest and torso like a boxer after a round in the ring. No idea why he packed towels – surely Carter would have more than enough – but happy at his foresight. Happy the engine is running, the heater blowing warmth onto Annie's legs and her lap. Happy at least that they will soon be making a move.

He climbs around the driver's seat, not wishing to get wet again. Two hours out there. Testing, checking, looking for the culprit, her wishing they'd joined the RAC, but saying nothing. There is oil on his cheek. Just a single fleck, like a beauty spot. He puts the car in gear and pulls onto the road, the car hesitant, snarling through its exhaust. Annie looks like she is about to say something, but Gwen puts her finger to her lip. Annie says nothing. No one says anything until Drum wipes the condensation from the inside of the windscreen.

'We were lucky,' he says. 'It could have done serious damage. There's not even a chip in the windscreen.'

'It's a good job you were driving slowly. Any quicker and I don't know what would have happened.'

'And you're fine, aren't you, Annie?'

'Yes, she's fine.'

There is silence, then the conversation again; how lucky; what might have happened; how well he did. Loops and spools, winding and rewinding. His hands shake as he drives. They have drunk all the tea; all the food is now for Annie. They sing songs to keep her entertained. She plays with a rattle, Gwen tells her several favourite stories. Drum starts the same conversation again and again – how lucky, what might have happened – so much so Gwen thinks Annie might soon join in.

'Yes, we were lucky,' he says.

'Yes, lucky,' she says.

She leans over and kisses Drum on his stubble-brushed cheek, leans her head on his shoulder the way she used to when they took the Underground. He smiles, but she can feel his discomfort. An irritation. She keeps her head there, leaves it on the bone of his clavicle, closes her eyes.

'Did I tell you about the supermarket this morning?' Gwen says.

'No,' he says.

'It was bedlam,' Gwen says. 'I went in to get some bits and it was full of old biddies fighting over tins of peas and tins of peaches. You wouldn't have wanted to get in their way. Some of them looked like they were going to lamp each other for a can of oxtail soup.'

He doesn't laugh, doesn't look towards her, eyes forward almost not blinking.

'Apparently it'd been like that all morning. The woman at the checkout said she was hiding some beans for her tea in case anyone got to them. They think it's the end of the world, she said to me, the mad old ducks.'

'Maybe they've got the right idea. Maybe they know more than we do?'

'Ah yes, the rumours of impending international nuclear conflict coming from the Women's Institute?'

'It would explain it.'

He laughs then. Annie laughs too.

'I think Annie agrees.'

He turns left, the road deeply dark and then light as they drive through a town. Orange sulphur light and bungalows, streetlamps and closed-up shops.

'You're not worried?' he says as they take a roundabout.

'About Cuba?'

'Yes.'

'I haven't really thought about it.'

Annie laughs again. They laugh at her and she smiles and she keeps her eyes on the dark outside the windows.

Old Nick once wrote a long, blank-verse play about the aftermath of an atomic war. *The Stars Shine Down from Heaven*. There was murder and incest; a vague suggestion of magical powers, of the divine amongst the rubble and madness. A curio, he claimed: a play born out of nightmares. It had been staged at the local theatre. He had extended Gwen an invitation and she had attended. It was melodramatic, verbose, poorly acted and badly staged. He took it all in good humour.

'At least,' he said, once the run was over, 'when the apocalypse does come, we'll have something to compare it to.'

Nick said he thought about the end of the world every day. Not one day without it crossing his mind. On good days it was a fresh wind blowing through the earth, a Godly broom sweeping away the trash; on bad, a man-made inferno, venal and pointless.

Gwen lets Annie hold her finger, let it go, grip it again, the way she did when she was younger.

'Are you worried?' Gwen says.

'No point in worrying,' Drum says.

'That's not what I asked,' she says.

She looks down at Annie.

'A friend of mine died,' Gwen says. 'From back home. Da said in his letter.'

'Oh, I'm sorry,' he says. 'How awful.'

'She was old, but it was sudden. Wasn't expecting it. The funeral was last week. John had the wake at the pub. She was a bit crazy, but I liked her. Used to come in every day with her brother. Pint and half of mild, a packet of scratchings.'

She laughs. Nick's demented side-whiskers, pint of black and tan, now a woman with half a mild. A final transformation. From death to resurrection. Ecclesiastical almost, that.

'You should call Carter,' she says at last. 'Let him know we'll be late.'

'Yes,' he says. 'If I see a phone box, I will.'

9

Either Carter is at home or he is not at home.

If the house lights are on, Carter is at home. If the house lights are on, you tell Gwen to stay in the car and you go to the door. If Carter answers, he will understand. Carter will play the game. Carter will make nice with Daphne. If Daphne answers, you explain things. Carter will be not far behind. They will understand and wave you in.

If the house lights are on, Carter is at home. If the house lights are on, but there are cars parked outside the house, you tell Gwen to stay in the car and you go to the door. Either Carter or Daphne will answer the door. If Carter opens the door, he will know what to do. Carter will make nice with Daphne. He will introduce you as late-arriving weekend guests. Gwen will put the baby to bed and you will have a drink. If Daphne answers, you explain things. Carter will be not far behind. They will understand and wave you in.

If the house lights are off, Carter is not at home. If the house lights are off, you tell Gwen to stay in the car, and ring the doorbell, shrug, then look down and pick up the note you've written. You know the spare key to the back door is in the plant pot under the window. What things you remember.

If the spare key is not there, you will force the door. If you cannot force the door, you will smash a French door or small window. You will make sure Gwen does not go into that room. Sometimes these things are simpler than you think.

Plans. Contingencies.

He takes a right at the end of a road. Not much further now.

Either Carter is in or he is out. A binary. Just the two options. Are you in or out?

Annie cries. In her mother's arms, she screams. Annie cries and either Carter is home or not at home.

'She's awake,' Gwen says, flatly, as Annie howls. 'How far now?'

'Not far. A couple of miles.'

Annie screams. Annie has filled her nappy and Drum can smell the settling.

Shhh, Annie. Shhh, Annie-moo. Home or not home. Shhh, Annie-moo.

'She stinks,' Gwen says. 'We should stop and change her.'

Annie screams. Hot tears on pink face. Annie wriggles out of her mother's arms.

Shhh, Annie. Shhh, Annie-moo.

'We're almost there,' he says.

Home or not home. Shhh, Annie. Home or not home.

10

The track up to the house is waterlogged, full of crags and puddles. It is almost eleven and the car makes bogged progress, the headlights revealing a rabbit, turning over mud and clod, and the house on the hill looks regal, each room lit as though with fire.

'It's beautiful,' Gwen says. 'Look, Annie, look at the house.'

Drum smiles and it does not look like his smile, not like his smile at all, the muscle movements and display of teeth nothing like she has seen before. He looks more like Montgomery Clift than he ever has. She has not thought of Montgomery Clift in a long time. Stars they come and go.

They pull up just outside the house, alongside Carter's cars.

'You change Annie,' Drum says, 'and I'll go ring the bell.'

Drum smiles that strange smile again and is gone, his bootprints in the dirt, trouser cuffs already muddied, hair wild from the wind.

II

Carter's cars are parked out front. The lights are on inside. He is home. Drum rings the doorbell, the sound echoing behind the door, deep and rich. The door is glossy, black as the Jaguar's paintwork.

The door begins to open. Either it is Carter or it is Daphne. It is Carter. Carter is wearing a white linen shirt and blue linen trousers. There is the shrug of a smile beneath a new and tweedy moustache; not quite welcoming, not quite not. Carter looks at his watch. All in the timing.

'So you made it,' Carter says. 'I didn't think you would in this filthy weather.'

Drum tries not to look surprised. Carter is holding a glass of red wine, it swings in his fingertips.

'I was worried you hadn't got my messages,' Drum says. 'I've been calling the telephone.'

'We tend to unplug it,' Carter says. 'I don't like its tone.'

Drum laughs, but Carter does not. There is no welcome embrace. Carter swirls the wine in the glass.

'I would have called you,' Carter says, 'but as you don't have a bloody phone it was impossible.'

He stands in the doorway, the door not completely open, like dealing with a tinker or door-to-door salesman. His eyes are whisky and wine; his teeth tannin and tar.

'But I keep my promises, Drum. No matter what. It's a point of principle. Now, bring your stuff in and I'll get you settled. Daph's in bed with Tommy, so keep it quiet, okay?'

He turns away, down the hall, leaving the door wide open.

Drum looks to the car, sees the crest of his wife's hair. The air is clear and clean and tastes new in his mouth. There are stars and all of them are looking down on him. They shine down and say to him that he is safe. That he has arrived and they all will be safe.

THE MOOD FROM THE PICKETS

As the world holds its breath over Cuba, the massed strikers of Ford's of Dagenham are focused solely on negotiations closer to home. For those I spoke to in the packed canteens, on the pickets, in the pubs, the threat of nuclear war seems to be little more than a sideshow to the events going on in the factory. 'We're not distracted,' said Richard Allanson, a forty-six-year-old veteran of several strike actions. 'We're determined to see this through, to get the right result for all the workers at Ford's.'

It is a sentiment heard time and time again, the roar of militancy drowning out the fear of atomic destruction. In the Eastcote pub, however, I was told by a group of younger men that one of their number had been seen leaving town, a car fully packed, sensing an opportunity to escape. It is a rumour that provokes both laughter and ire; one that ultimately has the quality of a Chinese whisper – they all admit it could just be someone visiting family. Stories and rumours are rife during an out. They keep the men enlivened during the cold business of striking.

Whatever happens in the wider world, I get the impression, one derived from observation and a childhood spent in orbit of the Ford plant, that the launch of nuclear weapons would be met with shrugs and a few moments' reflection before holding a meeting to ratify another series of demands. To the men and

women who toil here, Ford's is the world, the centre of
the earth, and no amount of geopolitical turmoil will
stop them in their quest for social and industrial justice.

Raymond Porter, 'The Mood from the Pickets',
Herald, 19 October 1962

13

Entering the house is to retire from the century; to step into an era removed and out of time; curated, piece by piece, from what has gone before. That's how it feels to Gwen. The hall is its gangway and portal; a precarious balance of the inherited and the acquired, the modern and classical: a grandfather clock beside the telephone table; riding boots racked next to kitten heels; a bag of golf clubs leaning against a shyly enclosed radiator.

And how lit. How lightened by the chandelier's crystal drop; the soft, slow burn of an oil lamp; the glow of a green-visored desk lamp; the solemn flames from red tapers burning in a silver candelabra. And how scented. Pollen and leather; log-smoke and wax; dusk notes of tobacco and rum, dark as the parquet stretching beyond the mahogany sweep of staircase, its newels unhung with jackets or scarves. And how staged. The doors off the hallway, tantalizingly ajar: a swatch of wallpaper, flocked and scarlet, its silver motif dappling from an unseen fire; a light switch in gold, a dial instead of a rocker; the dark spines of leather-bound books behind smoked glass; the ankles of a Queen Anne chair tipping a wink. And how empty, but full. Unpeopled, but sentries and hosts mounted to the walls. Oil portraits of military men, women in mourning clothes, young boys dressed in sailor suits. The three of them standing there, laden and heavy-breathed, unable, or unwilling, to leave the large dun-coloured doormat.

How they must look. Like emigrants or evacuees. Their belongings on the doormat, a child in her arms, the hum of just-changed baby, mud and muck on their shoes. How they must look.

Carter emerges from a doorway, hair flopping into his eyes, arm aloft in greeting, smile constricted by a moustache.

'Thank God you're here, Gwen,' he whispers. 'I had the awful feeling old Drum had come here solo.'

Carter is aftershave and alcohol, a damp kiss on her cheek. He makes a face at Annie who neither cries nor simpers, but looks curiously at Carter. She touches his moustache, brushes it with the tips of her fingers, recoils at the sensation.

'She's a little bobby-dazzler, isn't she?' he says. 'Cute as a button. Anyway, let me show you to your room. But quiet, see? Old Tommy's liable to wake if we make too much noise. Would you like a hand, Drum?'

Drum looks down at the suitcase, the boot still laden with bags and boxes.

'No, I'll be fine,' he says.

Carter nods and sets off at a clip, the three of them in his antic wake. Soft stairs, then the softer landing. It feels like walking on the beach at low tide, as though she could leave footprints in the twill. The landing is long, so many doors off, one of which Carter opens and allows them to enter before him.

There is a four-poster bed and a dresser with a pitcher of water already poured, two glasses beside; peach sherbet carpeting; the bedspread patterned with roses and briar. Towels are laid on the eiderdown and two doors lead off from the room, both open and lit: one a bathroom with a claw-footed tub; the other with a cot in its middle, alongside it an armchair.

'I'm afraid I'm absolutely done in. Was just off to bed when you arrived. Sorry to be such a baby, but we'll catch up in the morning,' Carter says. 'No rush. Get up when you like.'

A smile and then gone. Poof. As though never there. The three of them say nothing, just look at each other, until Annie breaks free from her arms and begins to explore her new territory. Gwen does not stop her, does not blame her.

'Did we die?' Drum says. 'Maybe we died on the road.'

'You think this is heaven?' she says.

'Not heaven. But maybe a rooming house on the way.'

'So purgatory is needlepoint samplers and duck-down pillows?' she says.

'Purgatory sounds less . . . luxurious,' he says. He runs and swallow-dives onto the eiderdown.

'Me,' Annie says to her mother and pointing at Drum. 'Throw me!'

Gwen picks Annie up and throws her onto the mattress, the girl landing wide-eyed next to Drum, too excited even to say *again*. Gwen flops onto the bed and lies beside Annie and Drum. The three of them lie there looking up at the floral canopy, stilled like they have been dropped there from a passing aeroplane, quiet and open-eyed.

14

He has become accustomed to waking alone, to reaching out for Gwen and touching only eiderdown or pillow. Six nights from seven these days; the fold-down bed permanently set up in the spare room, Gwen too tired to make it back to their room once Annie's finally back down. They have tried having Annie in with them, but the possibility of smothering her with his bulk is unnerving. So before sleep, he kisses Gwen goodnight and in the dark she disappears, like a magician's trick, and he is left to face the morning alone.

In Carter's spare room, it is the light that wakes him, not the scream of a child or the buzzer of an alarm. He has forgotten how that feels; how natural to be woken by subtle ambient shifts. He feels the warmth of the winter sun, its bright eyes through the thin curtains. Silence in the room. No sign of anyone around. He is again the last man alive. The slow terror of that. To have somehow survived while all others have perished. To stand and open the window onto the blistered earth, the bodies in the fields, the burned bones where once there stood cattle. He can smell it. The cook of it. What he can smell is bacon. What he can hear now is the chatter of voices, the whoop of a child, the cry of a child. He turns over in the bed, feels stupid for letting the idea get too far; is ashamed he is the last to make it downstairs.

Drum checks Annie's room and sees evidence of morning routine, the fine dust of talcum on the dresser, the unpacked bag of nappies and creams. All this without him; all this without his even realizing. How deep the sleep to not stir; how deep the sleep to just snore through it all. The peace of it.

He can hear voices as he descends the staircase. There is a radio playing, the sound of cooking, a family getting on with their usual Saturday breakfast. He does not quite dare go into the kitchen. He watches from the doorjamb as his wife feeds porridge to his daughter, as Daphne feeds porridge to her son, as Carter fiddles with a coffee percolator. As though this everyday, normal. But no place for Drum. Drum just watching. Not serving food to the infants, not making the coffee, but waiting by a door, useless and mute.

'Oh, it wakes,' Carter says, spotting Drum, waving a finger. 'I was beginning to wonder if you'd ever surface.'

'You've only been up a half-hour yourself,' Daphne says. 'And Drum at least has an excuse. He drove most of England yesterday.'

Thank you, Daphne.

'Hello, love,' Gwen says. 'I thought I'd let you sleep, after all that driving yesterday.'

He kisses her on the top of her head, Annie looks up at him but says nothing, just accepts another spoonful of porridge.

'Thanks,' he says. 'I must have needed it. Hello, Annie-moo.'

Annie smiles and he would love to know what the smile means, if it means anything at all, whether there is so much packed within it he could never hope to parse the individual notes. Gwen pours him tea and the light bounces from marble surfaces and copper pans to the tea pouring from the pot.

'Help yourself to bacon and eggs,' Daphne says, pointing to the two lidded silver trays on the table. 'I'll make us some toast once Tommy's finished his porridge.'

His grandmother, when she was alive, would tell Drum stories of her years in service. What it was like to work a big house, how being neat, effective and silent was the key. Something she said coming back as he forked bacon and eggs onto the plate: gentlemen and ladies always serve themselves at breakfast. You're never on duty then.

'Gwen was telling us all about your journey,' Carter says. 'Sounds like quite an ordeal.'

'We were lucky,' Drum says. 'It could have been much worse.'

'So I hear.'

Drum tells Carter of the crash and the repair work in the torrential rain, and how lucky they were, but at some point during the retelling Drum understands that Carter is not listening. He shows all the signs of attention – his body leaned in towards Drum, nodding his head at each narrative point, shaking his head in sympathy – but it's clear Carter is away from the conversation, working deeply on something else.

'That sounds awful,' Carter says, just at the right time, just at the correct juncture, but there is contempt to the commiseration, also a sense of finality. What else to say but yes, yes it *was* awful?

'Yes,' Drum says. 'It was awful. But we're here now.'

Carter takes a cigarette and lights it, lets the smoke pipe from his nose.

'Yes,' Carter says. 'You're here now all right.'

15

Annie watches Tommy eat; Tommy watches Annie eat. They are both *good eaters*, a fact Daphne and Gwen established early this morning, long before Carter put in an appearance. Does Annie eat porridge? Yes, she loves porridge. So does Tommy. I'm so glad he's not a fussy eater. Annie won't eat eggs, mind you. How strange. Yes, it is.

So many such conversations of late, it's hard to remember what Gwen talked about before Annie came along. People see baby and baby is all they see: a plump-cheeked conversation starter. The same for all women, the same conversations in every language, in every corner of the globe; the same conversations stretching back through history. Does he sleep? Does she do that too? Do you think that's normal? Does your little one eat her vegetables?

Dismal, these conversations, yet so easily reached for, and neither party truly knowing if the other isn't just simply going through the motions. Daphne is particularly difficult to read in this regard. She appears interested in such topics as good recipes for children, how long naptime should last, and breastfeeding; her face one of utter concentration when listening to Gwen, a sense of almost note-taking. Yet, for all that, there's a sense that this behaviour has been learned through observation, rather than through natural aptitude. There are moments when Daphne seems to drift, just slightly, like a radio station detuning, then returning stronger than ever.

'Last one, Tommy,' Daphne says.

Daphne's hair is light pine against the dark wood of the kitchen; her sheath dress powder-blue, the club-collared jacket likewise, the ensemble covered by an elegant, translucent housecoat embroidered with lilacs. The kind of fashion Gwen slicks through in magazines when at the hairdressers: perfect for the button-nosed and waifly-hipped, for those with book-balanced deportment and bank accounts.

It is hard to be in such company; hard it seems for both of them. Gwen gets the impression they both see rather less of people than their husbands realize. At first, meeting mothers at the park is solidarity; but later it is routine. Like when the factory is on strike: all the men just waiting for something to finally happen.

'I thought,' Daphne says as she wipes Tommy's face and takes off her housecoat, 'that after breakfast we could have a little tour of the house, then take a stroll down to the brook. The weather's supposed to be fine this morning.'

'Then after that,' Carter says. 'Back here for a spot of lunch, then I thought we'd drive into the town and have a wander around the shops. There's a terrific market.'

'Sounds wonderful,' Gwen says. And aside from the house tour and the shopping expedition, it does sound something like wonderful. The night-time walk from the car to the door had given her a perverse thrill. Her feet in the suck of mud, she'd suddenly realized how much she missed the muck and mulch, the scent of manure. Here was the promise of stagnant water, perhaps even a rope swing. To show Annie this. To show her the dirt roots of her life in northern England, in its disordered fields and wilding copses.

'What say you, Drum?' Carter says.

'Sorry?' Drum says. 'What was that? I was just . . .'

'Away with the fairies, is what you were,' Carter says. 'Well, be careful; they say there's all kinds of woodland folk around these parts. They might come for you.'

Gwen smiles at Drum and he gives an apologetic smile back. He's seemed dazed since coming downstairs, as though he's left crucial pieces of himself in the bedroom. So still when asleep, so peaceful-looking. Could not have woken him. Would have been too cruel. Looking now like he needs more sleep. Another few hours to recharge.

It's something on the radio that's got to him, she realizes. She can see it in the jokingly concerned looks between Carter and Drum, the stuff about woodland folk some kind of cover. Cuba again, most likely. If it had been the strike, he'd have shushed the room, asked to turn up the bulletin. Gwen watches her husband, the pallid smile he forces out.

'I'll keep on my guard,' Drum says and puts his hand on hers.

After stacking the breakfast things in the sink, they are given the tour. Gwen makes all the right noises, and Drum tries to do the same, but he sounds like a busted echo. And this is the library. Oh, lovely. And this is the drawing room. Ah, lovely. And this the dining room. Oh, how lovely. On and on. So many rooms and no more words for the rooms, just beamed smiles and appreciative nods.

Carter keeps himself to the outside of the four, someone always between him and Drum, no matter how Drum positions himself. He carries Tommy, too; a little boy amulet warding Drum off. It is strange; as though they should not be seen together for fear a scandal will be exposed.

They are shown another bedroom, the blue room. Carter fusses with a blue ashtray on a blue-stained dresser. Drum slips the other side of Gwen and pretends to inspect a seascape in a gilt frame. Seamlessly, Carter sets down the ashtray and put his arms around his wife's blue-clad waist.

'With that dress on I thought you'd disappeared,' Carter says. 'I just wanted to check you were still here.'

She takes his hands from her waist.

'For now, yes,' she says, ushering them all out to the landing.

'Now,' she says, opening the next door. 'This is Thomas's room.'

Carter has miscalculated his position and Drum is now beside him. Drum taps him on the shoulder and Carter turns sharply, anxious-eyed, with a long finger to his lips. He nods down and Tommy is in his arms, asleep. Curse the child, the morning nap, the protector. He thinks of Patty for a moment; a strange face from the recent past. The way she must have felt; to be cast off, to be an embarrassment perhaps. A reminder of more primal times.

'He mostly sleeps through the night now,' Carter says to Gwen in a whisper, his back to Drum. 'But for a few months it was hell.'

'It was, yes,' Daphne says. 'It's slightly better now.'

They take the staircase down to the hallway. It looks like the kitchen has been tidied in their absence, but Drum does not recall anyone doing this. Perhaps there are staff they have not been told about, secret servants tidying in the shadows.

'You have such a beautiful house,' Gwen says. 'I've never seen anything like it.'

'I'm so glad you like it,' Daphne says. 'And I'm so glad you're the first to see it all finished.'

Carter looks at the clock on the wall. He looks at the watch on his wrist.

'Well,' he says, 'let's get this one in the pram and we can walk down to the brook. Did you bring wellingtons?'

'We brought everything,' Drum replies.

'Of course, you did,' Carter says. 'Always prepared, isn't that right, Moore?'

Over tea and cake, their daughters playing on the sitting-room rug, Gwen's friend Bridget often tells stories of back home; half-remembered gossip about the Lagos of her childhood. Gwen likes to reciprocate, telling Bridget all the tales she knows from Millom. When they talk of back home, they talk of different streets but the same cast of blowhards, tricksters, devil women, low-lives and love rats. It always makes her feel blessed her family is closer than Bridget's, though she has seen them no more often that Bridget has seen hers. My people, Bridget often says.

Standing beside the brook, in the shade of a birdwatcher's hide, Gwen is shamed by Drum helping Annie throw sticks towards the brook; shamed by Carter's encouragement; shamed by the small talk she is making to a rigidly cold Daphne.

Where are her people? They are not so far north of here: her father, her brother, her nephew. Her people, the ones she does not think about enough. Her people, the ones who are yet to meet Annie. Her people who do not even know how close she is to them.

To come all this way and not stop by, to not make the effort. Shaming that. And yet, would they come to see her, all things being equal? Unlikely. John and Barbara have their hands full with the pub, with Jack and with Da. Families move on, move away; it happens and there is no remorse or recrimination. When people leave the town, they stay left until they return. Everyone knows that. It's like they've never been there in the first place.

'We don't come here enough.' Daphne says and smiles, frigid with cold, a scarf coiled just up to her lips. Tommy has woken and is sitting up in the pram, sleepy eyed and running nose. 'I don't make enough of an effort.'

It is the closest to a confession either of them has made; the closest it seems to hearing a true voice on Daphne's lips. It is chastising, it is bitter. As though a lack of effort worse than any other sin. Daphne smiles, but it is an attempt to catch back those words, to rebuild the facade.

'I'm the same,' Gwen says. 'We have a park five minutes up the road and I don't go nearly enough.'

Untrue this, but met with a thankful nod of the head. To the park most days, in most weathers, there to meet with Bridget and her Susan. But to have this? This on the doorstep? Gwen imagines it for a second, running through the fields, scampering through the brook. Throwing sticks, cracking ice in the winter.

'Oh, look,' Daphne says, pointing to Carter and Drum. 'It's got competitive. What a surprise.'

Drum and Carter have left Annie with a stick while they skim stones on the brook. On the third attempt, Drum manages five bounces on the dimpled water; on the fourth, Carter manages six. Daphne slow claps, as does Gwen, until she looks down to Annie, the stick by her side.

'Hey, Annie, don't do that, my love,' she says.

Annie has a handful of silt and pebbles and is smearing it around her mouth. Gwen takes a handkerchief and wipes Annie's mouth, Annie smiling, gritted lips and cheeks. A rush of love at that moment. A rush of it, endorphins surging like they have been charged and let go. Her people.

Dried-out and warmed by the fire, Daphne and Gwen head upstairs to put down the children for their long naps; the two mothers delighted that Tommy and Annie have the same sleeping patterns.

'I'm going to lie down with him,' Daphne says.

'You should do the same,' Drum says to Gwen. 'You were up with the larks.'

Gwen gives him the ice eyes, the wide eyes, but Annie is crying and he knows Gwen usually naps in the day, though she says she doesn't. Can tell from the way the bed is remade, the corners not so neat.

'We'll be fine on our own,' Carter says. 'Don't you worry about us.'

'I don't doubt it,' Daphne says. 'But if you insist on going to the pub, no more than three, okay? I don't want you crashing into any trees again.'

'On my honour,' Carter says and salutes to her already-turning shoulders. Drum kisses Annie goodnight, Gwen goodnight.

'You be careful,' Gwen says.

He watches the four of them vacate the room, Tommy now howling, Daphne shushing. Clever Carter. The evasions of the morning, the stilted conversations over breakfast, during the house tour, down by the brook, the quickly shutting down of talk over Cuba – not now, Drum, not now! – he should have seen there was reason to it. All about timing. The kids having a nap. The mothers too. The perfect time for a further tour. No, not a tour, but an inspection. An inspection of the bunker and a briefing as to the latest intelligence from Cuba. A glass of whisky in the sanctuary, Carter opening doors onto toilets and billets, showing him the space, the specifics of it.

'Okay,' Carter says and claps Drum on the back. 'Let's get going.'

Drum has been trying to work out where the entrance to the bunker is situated. He assumes it is in the cellar, probably somewhere below the pantry. They walk through the kitchen, quickly over the flags, past the pantry, then through the side entrance and out to where the cars are parked. Carter opens the door of the Jaguar, gets inside and opens the passenger-side door.

'Come on,' he shouts. 'We've got an hour before the Wolf stops serving.'

Carter reverses the car with the passenger door still wide open.

'Come on,' he says. 'Look lively. This'll be the only chance we get to go to the pub.'

Drum gets into the car. The leather of the seats is the same colour as Carter's hair. He does not want to think that the car purrs, but it does purr, it's the only noise he can compare it to, and like a purring cat it is distraction enough. The burr walnut of the dash is distraction, the smoothness of the gear change distraction too. But not enough. Not nearly enough.

'The latest is good,' Carter says, pulling away. 'From Cuba, I mean.'

'On the news it sounded worse,' Drum says. 'Reports of a plane being shot down?'

'Mrs Eyre informs me that there are rays of light amongst the dark. She says they're beginning to realize how high the stakes really are. That plane being shot down is nothing to worry about.'

'And Mrs Eyre is . . .?'

'My mole,' he says with a smile. 'My father's old secretary, but disgustingly well informed.'

'And she says there's nothing to worry about?' Drum says.

'You don't believe me?'

'It's not that.'

'It rather sounds like it is to me.'

Carter swings onto the road and puts down his foot, flooring the accelerator and hurtling the asphalt. Drum tries not to look concerned, though the road is still slick from the previous day's rain and Carter does not slow when the next bend comes, but leans himself into the turn like a rally driver. The needle hits eighty, then ninety. Drum closes his eyes. Another ironic death. St Peter now saying, 'Welcome back, Drummond. Now, where's the family?'

*

The Wolf is a large stone cottage with a harried appearance, as though the effort of keeping its bricks in its foundations is almost insurmountable. Carter has talked often of the Wolf, its landlord Bobby with the small hands; but Drum could have gone a lifetime without seeing it. Now seeing it, he is disappointed. He expected a thatched roof, for some reason; something more country village than farmhand boozer.

Carter cuts the engine but does not get out of the car. He turns to Drum but Drum is looking at the flinty exterior of the pub, the huff of smoke from its chimney.

'You're angry with me?' Carter says. 'Is that what this is? You come to my house and I take you in without batting an eyelid and you're angry with *me*?'

Yes. Angry, exactly that. Livid with it, in fact.

'I never said I'm angry with you,' Drum says. 'When did I say that?'

'You don't need to say it, Drum, I can smell it on you like camphor and shit.'

'I just thought—'

'What did you *just* think?'

'I just thought,' Drum says, 'you'd show me the bunker, not take me to the bloody pub.'

Carter's face lightens, his brow uncreases. He laughs that laugh and takes out cigarettes, lights one and does not crack the window.

'You're a proper comedian, Drum,' he says. 'Honestly, you should get yourself on the stage.'

He laughs and smoke gutters from his mouth.

'Only you would want to spend the last hours before an atomic war touring a nuclear bunker.'

And Drum laughs at that, laughs at the absurdity of it, at the anger that's stilling but has not yet been quelled. They laugh and there is smoke, and there is someone coming out of the Wolf, blowing on his hands. Drum can briefly see inside the pub. It looks cosy in there, warm and comforting.

'Come on,' Carter says. 'Let's get a pint in.'

★

Carter is right: Bobby does have very small hands. They are dainty, made odder still by the addition of a large sovereign ring. Bobby serves them pints and chasers with a gap-toothed smile, gives off a waft of beef dripping. The bar is bigger than expected, almost too warm inside, dogs sleeping under the feet of their masters, the room smoked by cigarettes and pipes and the fire in the grate. They walk to a table at the far end of the bar, past a man who nods at Carter but without any kind of warmth, more as in warning.

'I'm loved by all,' Carter says. 'You can tell, can't you?'

The long, low smile and they clink glasses, same as they have done in so many pubs. A last supper of beer and whisky. A last go around. Better to be here than underground. Carter always right on these kinds of things.

At the bar, Bobby bursts into a snatch of song, doesn't seem to notice he is doing it.

'I've been coming here a lot,' Carter says. 'After work, on the way home, I've been stopping in. It's calming, you know? Just look at these old skates. There's not a care in the world between them. I asked that one there –' Carter points to a man with a pint of stout and a pipe – 'what he thought of Cuba and he starts talking about cigars. Clueless, the lot of them. And I envy that. I envy that so bloody much.'

Carter shuffles the Scotch in front of him.

'You come in here and it doesn't seem possible, does it? Take this pint glass. The history within it. The invention of glass. The invention of beer. Yes, but what else? The invention of measurements, the invention of social conventions and codes. All human history in a pint glass. You think about that and you can't conceive of it coming to an end. Thousands of years of human endeavour over as quick as throwing a pint to the floor. You just can't imagine it.'

'I don't have to imagine it,' Drum says. 'Neither do you. We've seen it.'

'And that's just it,' Carter says. 'That's exactly why I don't want to show you the bunker. It's just like Doom Town. Once you've seen it, you can't not see it again. I took Daphne down to the bunker just after it was all finished and she was dead to the world for a week. It changed her. I can't even mention it around her, it terrifies her so much. It's the air, Drum. It's the air and the sheer, I don't know, *architecture* of it. It changes you. It's changed even me.'

Carter does not look in any way changed, there is no difference to the way he knocks back his whisky and motions to Bobby for two more. Back into an old routine, just the two of them again.

'And you're sure it's going to blow over?' Drum says.

'No,' Carter says. 'I have as much clue as Bobby here. But we'll be okay. Trust me.'

'Yes,' Drum says. 'I trust you.

18

'I do much prefer to eat in the kitchen,' Daphne says, ladling *cassoulet* onto plates. 'The dining room is so formal, and I love the low light in here. It makes me think of the lovely French farmhouse Jim and I stayed in last year with the McKenzies. A big round table laden with lovely food and lovely wine and all served without any kind of pretension at all. Just conversation and food and comfort. If it were down to me, I'd eat every meal in the kitchen. Every last one.'

'Yes,' Gwen says, accepting a plate from Daphne. 'It's so homely.'

Gwen looks at Drum, but Drum will not look at her, only at the incoming plate, superlatives spinning though he's not so much as dipped a fork in the sauce. It *is* homely: pans hanging copper above the range, candlelight kissing their wide bases, slate flooring and dark-wood cabinets, the round table laid with a red-and-white gingham cloth.

'Yes,' Daphne says. 'Homely is exactly the right word for it.'

Daphne looks pleased with Gwen for using the right word. Folk are simple. Even those with money, simple. Easily pleased. You take a moment to listen, a moment to observe, and the compliment becomes obvious. Hair or weight, house or car, intellect or beauty. Pub skills, the dark art of the nocturne.

'*Salud*,' Carter says. 'Or should I say *iechyd da*?'

He laughs and Gwen takes a tight-lipped taste of wine. She realizes she is smiling, despite the predictability, the obviousness of it all. What Nick would have made of this. How he would skewer them; Nick's accent thick as mince, words sharp as tines. Gwen smiles as she eats the simple stew with the ten-bob name; smiles and sees Nick join them, pint of black and tan in hand.

'The recipe,' Daphne says, 'was given to me years ago by a friend of my mother's, Madame Ganz. It's the one time I've ever been thankful I'm fluent in French.'

Carter laughs and Gwen wonders how many times Daphne has said these exact words; how many times she's thanked her French for the food before her guests.

I never much got on with French myself. French letters especially. Always found them a bit of a fiddle.

Hush, mischievous Nick. Quiet, you old skate. Back in your box.

This is the only box I've never wanted to get inside.

Be quiet, you old filth-monger, you'll make me laugh.

'Delicious,' Drum says. 'Utterly delicious. Gwen, you should get the recipe.'

At last he looks at her. This a look she recognizes; one they share and assume others cannot decode.

'Yes,' she says. 'Yes I should.'

She does not laugh, but she can hear Nick's cackling as he wanders away, suddenly out through the French windows, trudging towards the fields, black and tan in hand. She sees him wave and disappear into the night. Oh to join him. To walk the tracks and pathways and find a pub lit in the night, to sit by its burning fire.

The light is perfect for eating, for the avoidance of eating: Carter has barely touched his food, but is pouring himself more wine. He has been drinking all afternoon, even after returning from the pub, Gwen is sure; there are different drunks for different periods of time: this the long drunk, the long, slow drunk that ends with silence and maudlin stares, that gets a manic burst not long before its end.

Drum is talking to Carter about cars; Daphne is talking to her about France. Pub talent, to be able to follow two conversations at once and wish to be part of neither. She nods and agrees with Daphne about the wonderful books of Elizabeth David.

'Another strike then, Drum,' Carter says, changing the subject. 'What is it this time? Not enough biscuits during tea breaks?'

Heaven help us.

'I don't want to talk about it,' Drum says, suddenly serious in the gloom, shaking his head. 'Feels like I've talked of nothing else for months.'

There is piano music playing, something she hasn't noticed before, a record player in another room. Cutlery scrapes on plates. No one quite knowing where to look, least of all Drum, who seems to be inspecting the large pepper grinder in the centre of the table.

'But at least you get to come and see us,' Carter says. 'So it's not the end of the world.'

The piano music. The scrape of cutlery on plate. And then laughter. The two men laugh, madcap laugh, banging the table and making the plates jump, just the two of them laughing, heads lolling over the table, shoulders chugging, putting cotton napkins to their eyes.

19

As Daphne serves a baked-dark tarte Tatin, the telephone rings. Not the one in the hallway, but one off in Carter's study. Two lines, two numbers. One to which Drum does not have access.

'I'll be right back,' Carter says, taking with him wine and cigarettes, a grim face smiling.

'I'm sorry it's a bit on the toasted side,' Daphne says. 'But I prefer it a bit chewy, don't you?'

'Oh yes,' Gwen says, though as far as he knows, she's never eaten tarte Tatin. Daphne passes him the cream and Drum pours some over the pastry and apples, the cool swim of white over the steaming dessert. Mrs Eyre on the phone. Could only be her.

'So, Drum,' Daphne says, 'how did you like the Wolf?'

Drum takes a forkful of tart, and feels the bunker lurch up from below, swallowing him, sucking him down. Mrs Eyre is telling Carter the latest and the latest is bad. The latest is the worst. It is happening, it has happened. And he has pastry on a dessert fork. It is drenched in cream.

'It's very homely,' he says. 'The beer's good too.'

'When I was young we tried to get in there for a drink,' Daphne says to Gwen. 'Three of us girls. They looked at us like wolves as we walked in and we ran straight out. Aptly named, is the Wolf.'

Gwen smiles and Mrs Eyre is still talking, still on the phone. Drum eats the pastry. It is claggy in the mouth. It's like a bad apple pie, too heavy with something cloying and fussy.

'At school I overheard some of the boys talking about trying to get into our pub. I didn't know what to do. Whether to tell Da or not,' Gwen says. 'In the end I did tell him and he just nodded. He let them all have one drink but not another. If I hadn't said anything he'd have clipped them round the ear and no mistake.'

Daphne laughs and he can't muster even the vaguest of smiles. Gwen looks at him and her eyes look muddled, expression confused presumably by his blankness. How does Mrs Eyre sound? How old is her voice? Does she speak the Queen's English?

He takes another piece of tart.

'This is delicious,' he says. 'It's so tasty. I've never had anything like it before.'

Daphne beams at the compliment, but both women are looking at him with something approaching concern. Something in his face. Something he can neither see nor hide.

'Sorry about that,' Carter says, coming back into the kitchen. 'Just work. Panic over.'

'On a Saturday night?' Drum says.

'As I've told you before,' Carter says. 'I'm a very important man these days.'

'And everything's fine, is it?' Drum says.

Carter swills his wine, drinks the remainder of the glass and pours himself more.

'Yes,' Carter says. 'Everything will be fine.'

20

Drum's hands creep inside her nightgown, his fingers massaging just below her breasts and down to the tops of her legs. The allure of a strange bed, of doing something they perhaps should not. It is a pitiful seduction, one that smacks of prepared desire, perhaps a deflection. He kisses the crook of her neck and she moves her hips towards the curtained window. He is hard against her back and behind.

'Are you all right?' she says. 'You've been all at sea tonight.'

'All at sea?' he says.

She sits up, hair bed-tamed and snaking over the pillow; he lies on his back, the sheets pulled down over his chest.

'My mother was a maid in a house like this,' he says. 'What would she make of this? Lying in one of their beds, but still treated like staff.'

'I thought they were very welcoming,' she says. Though Carter off, Carter strange. Just drunk, perhaps, but something bothering.

'Welcoming?' he says. 'Did you hear him? Hear her? We're like . . . a test case. Some people to show around the house before the important people are invited. We used to sit up all night, me and him. And now he's yawning at eleven . . .'

'Shhh,' she says. 'You're imagining things.'

She puts her hand to his face. She kisses him on the mouth. 'Would it help if I did it for you?'

She takes him in her hand. 'Do you think this might make things better?'

Fleetingly, it seems, yes. For the briefest of moments. Yes. At least then sleep. At least that.

21

In the bathroom he wipes himself down. He sits on the toilet and imagines the bomb babies being conceived; the magic unlocking, the anti-fission, across the US and Russia, in the cigar dens of Havana. How many last ditches, how many let-us-revels will lead to births amongst the bunkers and shelters, to pregnancies terminated from the skies? A long time with that. The different faces; different men and women. Bodies danced with glass as the bombs come, the babies dust as soon as they are conceived.

A long time imagining that. A long time.

22

On the armchair in the nursery, Annie on her breast, she can still smell cum, the high notes of it, some having sprayed her nightgown. She doesn't mind: she almost likes its disreputable stink. Would it have been better to have lain back and let him get on with it? Always promised she wouldn't do that. She used to suck him, back when she didn't want sex. Quick that. Always so quick. Quicker than the hand. But she doesn't do that with her mouth any more. Hasn't for a long time. Jaw ache and the taste, more pronounced after the birth.

Annie sleeps, loose lips on her nipple and Gwen hunkers down in the chair, pillow behind her head. Outside she can hear feet on the carpet, someone shushing, the noise going past the door several times. The start of a wail then, quick feet on carpet then on wooden stairs. Gingerly, Gwen plucks Annie from her breast, puts her back inside the cot. The gentle laying down, the holding of breath, the child not waking. Sleeping as though she never wakes; sleeping as though she drifts off and morning comes sooner than expected.

The landing is half lit from below stairs. Gwen stands barefoot looking down through the balustrades, a baby's tears and squall tucked somewhere below. Go back to bed. Sleep now while Annie sleeps. Go back to bed, ball up the duck-down pillow, and sleep. Sleep.

The wood is cool on her feet, the kitchen light burning at the end of the hallway. Stealing, she thinks. This an act of burglary. Indecent to do so, but she walks through into the kitchen anyway, Daphne there pushing a pram back and forth over the slate floor, back and forth, shushing the quietening child.

'Couldn't sleep?' Daphne says to her.

'Annie woke and then I heard Tommy and—'

'It's the only way he sleeps some nights,' she says. 'I can stand here for hours rocking him back and to.'

She picks up a glass of brandy, drinks from it, sets it down on the counter top.

'Medicinal,' she says, laughing. 'That's what my mum always said. And she said it an awful lot. Help yourself if you'd like. I must keep pushing on.'

Gwen poured herself brandy from the decanter, sat down at the same kitchen chair she'd been seated in at dinner. Daphne's house-coat was translucent roses, beneath it silk pyjamas. To feel those on your skin. For those to be your clothes. Your buttons to fasten.

'Annie's still on mother's milk. At night mostly.'

'But you get to lie down. Barely even awake, I'd imagine, while you're doing it. Not that I'd want to start all that again. As soon as he got his teeth . . .' At this she shudders.

'He sounds settled now.'

Daphne stops pushing the pram. Thomas screams as soon as he is stilled. Daphne pushes the pram back and forth and the screaming stops.

'That's just what he wants you to think. Sly little man he is. Sly and vindictive.'

Gwen has not drunk brandy for many years; it reminds her of shock, of old movies, hip flasks and Mr Elphrin from the bank who came in for a glass after closing on a Friday. The brandy tastes different to what she's had before. The good stuff, no doubt. The best.

'So you like the house?' Daphne says.

'Yes,' she replies. 'Very much.'

'I hate it,' Daphne says. 'Honestly, Gwen, I've come to loathe it. Each day I hate it more. Two years of work, two years of getting rid of his parents' terrible taste, and I already want to rip it all down and start over again. The rugs are foul. The parquet is the wrong colour. And as for the wallpaper . . .'

She finishes her drink and shakes it side to side.

'Would you, dear?' she says. Gwen pours her a large measure and passes it back.

'It's to be expected though, isn't it?' Daphne says, 'The emptiness at the end of a great project. Nothing left to do, just time to sit back and marvel at your own mistakes.'

'Annie's room isn't painted,' Gwen says. 'There are three stripes on the wall. One pink, one yellow, one blue. We couldn't decide.'

'It must be nice to have a girl,' Daphne says. 'The one we lost was a girl. I was going to call her Clarissa.'

What to say to that. Where to even look. Daphne pushes the pram and Gwen drinks the brandy and a clock ticks and the wheels of the pram make a sound like rubber soles on a dancefloor. Go to bed. Go to bed now. Leave her pushing the pram, alone and spooling. Leave her with the decanter and the ticking clock.

'I should go to bed,' Gwen says.

'Stay and drink some more,' Daphne says. 'Keep me company.'

Her voice is soft, sisterly almost, but not one to disobey.

'Tell me, do you miss home?' Daphne says. 'I can't imagine moving all that way.'

'I miss my friends,' Gwen says. 'My family too, but friends most of all.'

Patty no longer sees Gill. Gill is now friends with Glenda. Patty has made friends in Aberdeen, but says she sometimes struggles with the accent. Gill has had another baby, but Frank works long hours and she is mainly alone. Gwen has Bridget. Gwen likes Bridget but not as much as she likes her friends from home.

'I loathe my friends more than I loathe this house,' Daphne says. 'Goodness knows what they'll say when they finally see it. Something vile, I shouldn't wonder. Spiced and sweetened, but underneath utterly vile.'

'I can't think why,' she says. 'It's beautiful. We're both so grateful for inviting us to see it.'

Daphne laughs, a small and throaty chuckle, the sound of which echoes off the copper pans.

'Inviting you?'

Gwen feels something unsettle, come unstuck somewhere in her stomach, beneath her rib cage. Just the faintest sense of a complex problem suddenly revealing its simple, logical answer. Back and forth the pram wheels go. Back and forth. The large stone in the wedding ring going back and forth with it.

'Yes,' Gwen says. 'We needed the break.'

'I don't doubt it, dear. I don't doubt it for one moment.'

Daphne looks back at the pram, bends down to see inside, to see her sleeping boy. She chances a stop of the pram and the boy instantly screams. She pushes and he quietens.

'He looks so beautiful when he sleeps,' Daphne says. 'In the daytime he looks like he's made of light and rainbows. It just radiates from him. And I watch him crawl and shuffle and I wonder when he'll learn to lie. When he'll learn to cheat and deceive and when I'll notice it for the first time. When I'll see his father's face look back at me and tell me he's not lying.'

Daphne pushes the pram harder.

'Our men are liars, Gwendoline. They're not dishonest, but they're born liars. Dishonesty – and I've thought about this a lot – is an active thing. You must choose to be dishonest. But lying just comes naturally to some people. They can't help it. They'd lie about anything and have no idea why. It's just who they are. They're liars. Yours and mine. Both born liars.'

'Well I wouldn't—'

Daphne just laughs. Laughs so much she forgets to push the pram and the screaming starts again. She pushes the pram one-handed, grabs the brandy glass with the other.

'You wouldn't, would you?' Daphne says. 'Okay, so what would you say if I told you that I didn't invite you here? And that my lying husband didn't either? What would you say to that? We didn't invite you here. Your husband *asked* to come. He begged, in fact. And my husband, the man who lies straight to my face, couldn't bring himself to make the most politic of untruths. Couldn't even do that! Won't break a promise. Won't break his word. You have to laugh, don't you? Won't break his word! The lying hound.'

Gwen looks down at her glass, away from the hot face of Daphne, away from the frantic movement of the pram.

'Yours is as bad as mine. Peas in a bloody pod the both of them. Did you honestly think I'd invite you up here at a moment's notice? On a whim?'

The pram stops. They both instinctively look to it. Hold their breath. No scream. Peace.

'I should go to bed,' Gwen says.

'No,' Daphne says. 'No, stay here. Let's have a drink. One last drink, yes? I'm sorry. I didn't mean to be so inhospitable.'

She pours the drinks, giddy in the light. She looks like she means the apology.

'He invited himself?' Gwen says to the newly full glass.

'It's not really his fault,' Daphne says. 'He was doing what he thought was right. Don't they always? Years ago, Jim's father said he was going to build a bunker under the house. He had plans and everything, the Ritz of bomb shelters, it was going to be. But he never quite got around to finishing it. And Jim has never got around to telling Drum there isn't a bunker. That there never has been. Instead, he keeps on promising Drum a safety he can't even offer us.'

Her laughter. Even closer to Gwen now. The ire. She could strike her. So close.

'So when this whole Cuba thing starts up, James starts to panic. Because he knew what would happen. Drum would be up here like a rat up a drainpipe. Expecting to see the bunker. Protecting you and Annie. The telegram came, but there was no way to get hold of you. No way to stop you coming. The horns of a dilemma right up his jacksy. Genuinely, I don't know what he fears most: the bomb or having to tell Drum there isn't a bunker.'

Gwen could think of Doom Town. What Drum has told of her it. Think of his waking in the night, his constant ear for the wireless. She could think of the drive, his determination, his leaned-forward body as he steered, the white of his skin after the collision. But what the point in that.

'Oh well,' Daphne says. 'It's not the end of the world, now, is it?'

A slight pause and then a madcap laugh, the brandy in the glass jumping, a hand on an arm, eyes closed and laughing, the boy not waking, the boy not waking at all.

23

Drum's wellingtons pinch his feet as he shields his eyes from the morning glare, the sky looking scrubbed as a mortuary slab. Annie stands beside him, holding his hand, more confident now on her feet, waiting on Carter to join them, to hold the other hand and swing her down to the brook. It was fifty-fifty, Carter said before heading to his early bed, according to Mrs Eyre. A fine clairvoyant, Mrs Eyre. Either it will happen or it won't.

'Mama?' Annie says.

'She's just having a lie-down,' Drum says. 'She'll be back soon.'

Gwen looked white and wiped out when she woke, first day of period, most likely, another month to wait on. Often angry then, often distant, often blaming, though mainly of herself. He went to kiss her and she gave him her cheek. Best to leave alone. 'Take Annie,' was the only thing she said to him as he got up from the bed.

'Mama?'

'Yes, she's inside. Now, who can see a cow?' Drum says and points at the Friesians in the next field, cold-looking and sleek. One pisses and steam rises from its yellow arc; the others mooch, butt their snouts against the hard earth. Annie follows his hand and points towards the cows.

'Clever girl,' Drum says.

The countryside baffled Drum when at first he saw it on walks with Gwen. It had confused him with the openness of space, the highness of the skies, the broadness of the fields. He knew nothing of the names of fauna or flora, had no clue as to what kind of tree was which, the only one he could name for certain was the yew, for its appearance in graveyards. It was not quite beauty he saw, not quite the divine in blades of grass and hillocks. He did not see himself smaller or larger, as part of a grander plan or insignificant mite. What he saw, he saw filtered through Gwen's eyes, twisted by her giddy pleasure in the greens and browns and blues. That was divine enough. To appreciate the beauty because of her appreciation, her sense of belonging. The keenness of that. It always seemed implausible a bomb could destroy that, that a work of mankind could rent it so utterly. Looking out now, with Annie, it seems impossible.

'Cow,' Annie says.

'Very good, Annie,' he says. 'Very good indeed.'

One day she will talk in proper sentences. One day they will have a proper conversation. One day they will argue. One day she will tell him a lie. One day she will tell him she loves him. One day she will tell him she hates him. One day she will be a woman and he will be an old man and he does not know who that man will be. He picks her up and hoists her high so she can better see the cows.

'Dad-dee,' she squeals.

He pretends to drop her, catching her at the last moment. They laugh and laugh until he puts her down and sees Carter standing in front of him, something bundled underneath his jacket, a look of gravity on his face, despite the broad smile. Annie takes steps towards Carter, trips on a divot and falls flat on her face. Annie does not cry. Annie is scooped up into her father's arms and her small boots make dirt footprints on Drum's coat.

'It's over,' Carter says. 'All bar the shouting. But it's over.'

There's a heat rising across Drum's shoulders, shooting down into his sternum.

'You're certain?' he says.

'The Yanks gave in. Or the Reds. Something to do with Turkey. Either way . . .'

Drum puts Annie down and Annie totters off. They watch her make a beeline for a stick, pick it up and hit the ground with it, then find another stick and hit the sticks together, a marshal beat.

Carter unzips his jacket and takes out a bottle. He opens the whisky, drinks and passes it to Drum. They pass the bottle between them as Annie hits her sticks. Drum thinks of the ground beneath his feet, the bunker below the turf and sod. The safety he feels in that moment. The spectacle of it, the sensation of it. Something evaporating, melting like the morning frost, slowly, but thawing nonetheless.

Drum looks at Annie, playing with the sticks. He watches her and wants to pick her up, kiss her, smell her cold cheeks, the scent of her hair. She ambles towards him with the sticks, like she knows. He picks her up and kisses her. Oh, Annie. Oh, my love. I am back, Annie. I am home, Annie. I will never disappear again, Annie. I promise you, Annie, I will always be here, Annie.

My Sweet Lord

1971
February

I

In dark and drear, Coca-Cola red and white; Cinzano blue and red. Flashing the statue of Eros, flashing those in hats and coats, the neon red and white and blue. No rain, but chill wind on dirty pools from the afternoon pour, dead black the sky. A playbill light in red, *Vivat! Vivat Regina*. Coca-Cola in red and white; Cinzano in blue and red; Skol in red and gold. Bright the lights. Don't look on them for too long, look too long and the logos imprint on streets, on unclad buildings, on the puddles. Know that of old.

Once took Nathan to show him the lights, he liked the lights, looking up in gurgle wonder at the Coca-Cola and the Cinzano. The Skol there? No. A new one, the Skol. Never liked the stuff, lager-beer too fizzy, tastes of nothing. An ugly word Skol. Like skull, Skol. All the commuters, all the youth, all got skulls. The men in the bowler hats, thought they'd all been culled, but no, there they are, walking alongside, all have skulls. The men in the bowler hats, the woman in the pink minidress and long red hair, all have skulls. A cunt too, the woman. Every woman. Since when you use that word, even in thought? So horrible a word. Like Skol. All the words to use and Skol and cunt. Disgust yourself with your thoughts.

On Shaftesbury Ave a pigeon pecks at a rubbish sack, pigeons everywhere, on the concrete and the breeze; gas and diesel, sulphur and fume, thick as steak, smoked as coals. Forgot the smell: rot of tramp, piss of alleyways, burn of flicked cigarettes. Unnerving and beautiful with Gwen, all those years before; now the city flashing darkly, voices in the dark.

Killing time, a half-hour early, the pubs inviting, the St James, the

Groom, but just coins and a note, still odd in the pocket, in the hand. A few weeks since the changeover, and still unsure about new money. Knew where you were with shillings; knew where you were with tanners. Knew how much you didn't have. No idea what a pint now costs. What's that in old money?

Money the reason to be here. Carter always offering whenever they saw each other, Drum refusing, then quietly accepting. The dance done and folding cash in pocket, an offer to repay, unmeant and ignored. The only reason for coming. Say it enough times and must be true; the only reason to be walking Shaftesbury Ave.

A longhair playing guitar on the street, 'My Sweet Lord'. Everywhere that song, 'My Sweet Lord', Hari Krishna. Seen the Hari Krishna once, their orange robes and the little cymbals, their faces melted in reverie amongst streets still scarred from bombs. The young man singing, and his guitar just out of tune and new and old coins in his guitar case, a fifty-pence piece, rigged and placed, no one doling out fifty-pence pieces for this.

Down the Charing Cross Road, past the bookshops, the coffee bars, the trolleys of mildewed paperbacks, stop there to browse, soak up the time. It's free to browse, always free. Stacks of books, something for Gwen in there, a present perhaps. Guilt present. But no money for books, no money for anything tonight but beer. Money to beget money.

Hand in pocket: this is a ten pence, this is a five pence, this is a pound note. Twenty pence a pint, a rough guess. A quid fifteen in pocket. Almost six pints, not quite six, five pence short, so save the fifteen or get a half somewhere. Just a half. How can that hurt?

In to the Roundhouse pub, a half-pint, ten and a half pence. Sip the drink, open the book. The latest from the library, Gwen bringing back the new releases, perk of the job; still disbelieving she works in a library of all places. *A Clubbable Woman*, a murder at a rugby club. Drink slowly, kill time, turn the page, sip the drink, check the clock.

A man at the table beside the bar, hair growing out, losing on top, is with a tart, an actual prostitute. The tart laughs and she has a skull, and the skulls of prostitutes . . . what was that? A memory of another book, the thing the killer did to women. The tart she has a skull and a life and a skill, most likely, and we're all killing time to a greater or lesser extent, aren't we? Killing time on the strike. Another strike, the longest yet, or so it seems. Strikes harder as you get older, days without work a tense in the shoulder, an imaginary rivet gun in the hand, have that till the day you die, the old ghost of the machine.

The tart laughing. How much in old money for that? How much in new? Does she take old money or is she strictly new pounds and pence? Perhaps they're in love. From john to sweetheart, sure it happens. In novels all the time, it happens. Don't say what it feels like to come home stinking of men though.

Kissing now, the tart and the john, and good luck to you, tart and john. Good luck john, hope you don't get a dose. Good luck, tart, hope he's not kind who wants to see your skull. How long in the city and these the kinds of thoughts. Counting down to meet Carter, to having to make the right kind of conversation: to talk of the kids, of Gwen, of the strike, the fucking strike, and then to listen to Carter talk of his kids, and of Daphne and the job he will only allude to.

Drink finished and onto Garrick Street, Maiden Lane. Rules' awning a deep bold red and the doorman outside, whistling. The doorman pivots slightly to allow entry and through the hallway, beyond the stash of umbrellas, Carter is sitting at the bar, martini and cigarette in hand, wearing spectacles now. He waves from the bar and stands but does not put down his martini.

'It's like coming out of hell and into paradise, isn't it?' Carter says.

2

The bath is meagre, topped up with kettle-boiled water, just enough to cover his scraped knees. Nate is talking about something that happened at school, an altercation over a football, the reason for the red welts and scratches on his kneecaps. Happens all the time, the falls and damages.

'Did you say sorry?' she says, and it is a rote response, easily applied to any situation, but clearly not this one, the look on his face.

'She hit me, Mam,' Nate says. 'Why do I have to say sorry?'

'I said, "Did he say sorry?" not "Did you say sorry."'

'It was Lucy, Mam. The one who hit me.'

Caught red-handed. Guilty, your honour, distraction in the third degree. Concentrate now: smile and sorry and shush. Nate smiling, Nate saying silly Mam. Six years old and proper little man now, proper little boy. Boy that took her tits, gave her the sag in stomach, bundle of joy, quick as an eel, brushing his own teeth these days. Looks like his father, like his uncle, like her father, all of them, all at the same time. Everything to all people. And her ignoring him, not listening, though whatever happened is the most important thing in his life right now.

'Time to get out now, Nate,' she says. 'Story-time.'

'But I haven't done my lengths, yet,' he says. 'How will I swim like Daddy and Annie if I don't do my lengths?'

'Okay,' she says. 'Ten lengths and no more.'

His eyes widen, and he pretends to swim, back and forth, in the small bath. Knowing her vulnerable to appeals as his father's not there. Better him not there. Bath-time her preserve while Drum's at work; only taken from her when he's out on strike. Trying to *help*. To *lighten the load* while she's the only one working. But she misses the routine; the bath with Nate, the calling to Annie so she can bathe in peace while Gwen wrangles Nate into bed, forces him through at least one book.

Nate lacks concentration, asks questions irrelevant and annoying, something Annie never did. Not that Gwen read to her often; that falling to Drum most nights as Gwen attended to Nate. She'd hear them reading in her and Drum's bedroom before she went in to say the coast was clear and carry Annie to the top bunk. Annie long since reading her own books, recently in her own room. There are still kisses at the end of night, still the warmth from her breath, but there are secrets now, secret landscapes Annie will not share.

'Annie, my love,' she says, 'bath's free now.'

It will take at least three more calls before she acknowledges receipt. Lost in Narnia again, rejecting the books Gwen has brought for her from the library. Sometimes picking them up, but never sticking, these books; the ones Annie loved she found herself on a Saturday morning before swimming.

'Coming,' Annie says and she is there in the bathroom, will not undress until they are both safely in the other room. This modesty is new, there are no signs so far of change, but her best friend Susan has started her monthlies and is wearing a training bra, and Annie is looking at her own body for hints of swelling, growing, hairing. Gwen has talked to her about it all, said all the right things: it's natural, normal; it happens at its own pace; it happens to some girls *much* earlier than others, and Annie seems happy for the information, though somewhat surprised it will happen to her. There are no periods in Narnia; there is no puberty under Aslan. At least as Gwen recalls.

'Is everything okay, Mam?' Annie says.

'What?' she says.

'Are you okay? You look like you're a hundred miles away.'

'Yes, *cariad*,' she says. 'Just a bit tired, that's all.'

Annie closes the door. Always closing doors, it seems, these days. She sees her only for a moment before there's wood between them both.

'Don't be too long in there,' Gwen says. 'Lights out at eight.'

She settles Nate down on the bed, picks up the two books she is to read to him. Annie able to read at his age; him not yet able. Should not say anything. Should not think anything, but unable not to. Men should read, always thought that. Men who do not, a paucity in their soul. Old Nick's words, what he'd make of her son, his slovenly southern accent, his estuarine twang, his lack of interest in anything that isn't a ball.

Nate lies heavy on her, already lolling, exhausted from running and falling. He will hold out though, resist sleep as much as he can.

'You missed a page,' he says.

She apologizes and reads several pages without realizing she has done. He does not complain, so the words must be right. How this happens. Mysteries of parenting.

'Too fast,' he says. 'You're reading too fast.'

And she is reading too fast, and she is getting words wrong, and she is not okay, Mam. She is not okay. She is remiss in her reading; she wishes only for him to sleep. She wants to go downstairs and drink a gin by the fire, with a book and her own thoughts. She wants to toast herself for her fortitude, and commiserate with her cowardice. She wants silence and calm, and she is still somehow reading her son a book though she is thinking of a man who is not her husband, and what it means to be a mother, and what it means to be a woman, and thinking of what her daughter would think of her. What her husband would think of her. And what it is like to get away with something. Is it ever really getting away with something if you know you have transgressed? And the shame of that, and the life within that, and having no one she can tell. No one to share the weight of it.

3

Drummond orders the steak-and-kidney pudding, the cheapest option on the menu; Carter the squab pigeon. He looks upholstered now, Carter, plumped up like a scatter cushion. The moustache has been recently shaved, but his upper lip remains shadowed by its memory. His hair modishly brushes the collar of his shirt, a few lines on his face, here and there, awkward scribbles writing of his coming middle age.

'Is Gwen still working at the library?' Carter says. 'Such a hotbed, the library, isn't it? All that quiet. All that unspoken tension. The silent thrill of it!'

Carter wrinkles his nose. To be one of those nights. Carter in a high pitch of excitement, all filters relieved for the evening.

'It's Dagenham Library, Carter,' Drum says. 'Old women reading romances. Old men reading the newspapers. The only hotbed is the seat after some tramp's pissed himself.'

'I think you'd be surprised.' Carter takes a sip from his martini. Nothing better to say than this. Nothing better to share than innuendo.

'Get your mind from the gutter,' Drum says, almost snapping, but not quite. A softening smile. A whoops-oh-shucks look heavenward. *Ooh, you are awful.*

'Shame,' Carter says. 'It's where I do my best thinking.'

The waiter brings oysters on a chipped ice platter, six of them, shells foreboding. Carter takes one, slurps down the clotted innards. Around them, other men, older and redder of complexion, fatter and balder of pate, do the same. Silence and one room-wide gulp and the hitting of the shell on china, a sigh from the room, the waiters filling glasses of champagne and Riesling. Drummond lets Carter finish them all. After last time, best to avoid.

'Actually, talking of books . . .' Carter says, wiping his glistened chin. 'I've been asked to write one.'

He picks up his martini and takes a sip, preserving the moment.

'Well, part of a book at least,' he says. 'A friend of mine was having dinner with this writer chap. Terribly clever by all accounts, terribly clever and wondrously fat. Anyway, he's getting people to write little memoirs of their time on National Service. My friend suggested me to this Bryan and he wrote inviting me to contribute.'

Drummond looks at the oyster husks on the chipped ice, the platter swiftly removed from the table as he's watching it, as though he's drawn eyes to the waiters' inattention.

'What'll you say?' Drum says.

Carter stretches out his arms and leans back in his chair, as though this kind of literary talk is commonplace.

'I don't know,' he says. 'I'm tempted, obviously. There's a lot to write about. The first thing that came to mind was Doom Town, of course. I hunted out my old journal and had a look through. There's so much I'd forgotten. You remember Jerrick?'

'Yes,' Drum says.

'Completely forgotten about him. Total blank. You remember when he scared us to death in that library?'

The hush of the library, a different kind of still to the one in which Gwen worked. The books in there quietly seething, quietly warning.

'I've not thought about Doom Town in years,' Drum says. Carter will not call him out on that. Will agree, otherwise the night gone.

'Nor me,' Carter says. 'But I set to remembering all that I could, and when I did, I realized no one would quite believe it. There's more chance of them believing our little stories of Cyprus and the Sudan.'

Carter laughs and the waiter arrives with the wine, uncorks it, lets Carter taste it. The waiter does not look at Drum once. Carter nods, not even looking at the waiter.

'But then,' Carter says, the waiter pouring the wine, 'I started to think of those months right at the beginning, when we were in the kitchens. How lucky that all was. So I thought I'd begin with our meeting—'

'You leave me out of it,' Drum says. Carter looks mock hurt, surprised.

'Well I can't very well tell the story without you in it, can I?' he says.

'I don't want you writing about me like that,' Drummond says. 'Like I was your batman or something.'

'I'd never do such a thing.'

'You wouldn't know you were doing it.'

Carter laughs. Already almost drunk. Already on the way.

'Well, if you insist,' he says. 'I'll give you an alias then. Like Alan. Alan Spencer. Yes. You look like you could be an Alan. I might start calling you Alan from now on. What do you say to that, Alan?'

Drummond thinks of the name Alan Spencer. Who Alan Spencer might be. To be made someone else, just like that, with the change of a name.

'Well, *James*,' Drum says, 'I'd say you've had your ego stroked and you'll promise fat Bryan something and at the last minute you'll make your apologies and say you're too busy.'

Carter smiles, picks up his wine glass and raises it to Drum.

'Oh, Alan, you know me too well.'

Over their main courses, Carter talks of Daphne's new hobby, yoga (drill exercises for hippies), the work about which he cannot freely speak (one day soon, I'll tell you all), the new Jaguar he's just bought (goes like shit off a shovel). He asks Drum about the strike and they spend a needless, mutually unsatisfying half-hour arguing about the union movement, equal pay legislation and other political matters which sound hollow and ill-informed even to Drum, let alone to outside ears.

Their plates are taken away; Carter has eaten little, drunk a lot, smoked more than he drank. The last ten minutes he has been quieter than usual. He lights a cigarette and leans over the table.

'Are your children scared of you, Drum?' Carter says. The baldness of the question is surprising, as though this has been the one thing on Carter's mind throughout dinner.

'I was scared of my father,' Carter says. 'Petrified of him. But my children, they don't seem to be scared of me at all. Rather the contrary. I think they find me somehow slightly amusing. When I ask them to do something, it's always conducted with a thin veneer of insolence. Like they know something I don't.'

Carter pulls on his cigarette, the smoke plumes and he waves it away.

'I lose my temper with them, I shout and bellow, and they don't cry or cower. Neither of them.'

'You want your children to be scared of you?' Drummond says.

'Of course,' he says. 'Don't you?'

'Why would you want them to be afraid of you?'

Drum shouts at his children rarely; when he does they listen. Not through fear, but because they understand when he raises his voice it's for their own good, their own protection. Is that fear? When Annie cries, is that fear? When Nate cowers, is that fear? No, not fear. Understanding.

'Because fear is the only way we learn, isn't it?' Carter says. 'No one learns from hugs and kisses. I blame the schools. The bloody teachers. Children aren't shown any discipline, any kind of rigour these days. Nothing like when I was at school. Nothing like it.'

'You always said you wanted to burn your school down with everyone trapped inside.'

Carter leans in close to Drummond. Two heads in a booth, dipping down low as though avoiding a train inspector.

'Fear gives you structure, Drum,' he says. 'It gives you a code and a set of principles to live to. Fear is the only thing that keeps us in line. Fear of hell. Fear of shame. Fear of exile. Without fear, there is only chaos.'

He looks around, the other patrons clouded with cigar smoke, deep into brandy and brag.

'I've lived in fear,' he says. 'These last years, I've become the man I promised I wouldn't. I've become emasculated. But a while back I came to town for a financier's function. It was ghastly, but the wine was top drawer, so I stayed. I talked to likely people, tried to make myself sound interested in business rates and whatnot, and then at the bar, a woman said to me, "Drinking like a fish out of water?" A good line, I thought. We talked and afterwards we shared a cab. When we got to her place, she asked if I'd like to go up for a nightcap. I said no. I could have said yes, but I said no. And do you know why I said no?'

Drum shrugs, never knowing him say no to anything.

'Fear,' he said. 'That was all it was. Not love, not devotion, but *fear*. Fear of the consequences, of the repercussions. Fear, that was all. I thought of you at that moment, actually. About how I said I was going to live in the shadows. But I haven't, Drum. Not at all. And so I wrote to this woman and we started up a regular correspondence. I wrote until I had no more fear left. Until I left fear at the door, chained up like a dog outside a pub.'

Carter has sweat on his brow, the heat and the food and the wine. Little drops of it, perfect pearls.

'Fear is what keeps us down,' Carter says. 'All of us. Your strike action? That's all about fear. Fear of getting less than others. Fear of the unions losing power. Fear of being trampled down. We all run on an engine of fear. But I don't fear any more. There's no more growl in the gut.'

Beside them, an old man begins to laugh. A laugh that even over the chatter and the service, dominates the room. Conversations pause as it goes on, the haw-hawing coming down then starting up again.

'How long do you think we can go on like this?' Carter says.

'The IRA, the Angry Brigade, the Black Panthers, the Trots and the Fascists? It's just going to get worse. No one fears the bomb any more, no one's looking at Russia. They're looking inwards. Making it all personal, waging war on the system. The queers are kissing in Trafalgar Square. The blacks are citing the fucking *Magna Carta* in their defence hearings. We're heading for collapse, Drum. The kids, they don't fear their daddies any more, they don't feel it in the same way. And that's what's dangerous. The kids will need to be reined in soon. They'll need to have a *new* fear. Not of being on the end of an IRA bomb or being beaten by racist coppers, but a real fear, a true fear that will keep them down.'

Animated, a fresh theory, the first time said, the first run-through. Would get better at it. Would have honed it the next time.

'Once people think there's nothing abroad to fear, they're dangerous. The Soviets know it, the West knows it too. They need people to look again at the skies and not at their lives. They need a real enemy, a real threat. East and West will be a disaster area if not. People will have to start being afraid again. Properly afraid, *existentially* afraid. It's the only way. And only the bomb can do that. Only the bomb has that power. It's coming, Drum. The cold will thaw and then it will be hot. White hot. You mark my words, it's coming.'

Carter leans back against the booth; Drummond looks down at the just-delivered cheeseboard, the oozing camembert and mould-jewelled stilton.

'So you're having an affair,' Drum says, 'because the bomb's coming?'

Carter laughs, full-throttle laugh, head back, almost as loud as the old general on the other table.

'You always cut to the quick, Drum. Always so very sharp.'

The spread of cheese, the cigarette burning in the ashtray, the cigar clouds gathering. Carter crushes out his cigarette and leaves it with the others, the small pile of them.

'Let's go,' he says. 'Get a drink in somewhere.'

Still the money to go. The few quid he's promised Gwen. Two quid wouldn't kill him. Maybe a fiver. Speculate to accumulate. Get the money. Take the money. Food on the table. See us through a while, that. Gwen will be pleased.

'I should get back,' Drum says.

'Oh, come now, Drum, the night's yet ours. It'll be worth your while.'

'Just one then,' he says. 'Just a quick one.'

Stand now. Stand now and walk as though not drunk. Drunk though. Wanting home. Wanting home and bedclothes and pounds in the pocket.

4

Nate asleep, Annie with the light off, but presumably under the covers with the torch she thinks Gwen knows nothing about. Gwen goes downstairs, pulls on another jumper, pours herself a gin, lights a cigarette. The gas fire stays unlit, the way it has all week. To put it on now, to turn the dial and hear the gas catch on the flame, just for her and her alone. To do that just once.

Before Nate was born, they redecorated, excised the last of Grandpa in the house, while he was quietly excising himself a few doors along the street. Picture of him and his wife on the mantel, now; pictures of Gwen's family, her father dead now too, the pictures only lightened by the beaming faces of her children, her niece and nephew she so rarely sees. A picture of Drum and Gwen's wedding day, black and white, though she remembers it in all its colour. Though not as she drinks gin. Will not look at the pictures, only at the glass on the coffee table, the library books beside them. His books, or at least were. Hers now. For a time, at least.

A year of working in the library; a year under crackling strip lights, static shocks from the shelves, the trundle of trolleys. She wrote to her brother of the new chapter of her life (ha!). Children in school, a salary of her own, an environment of learning and betterment. 'I can't ask for anything more,' she wrote, 'than a good husband, beautiful children, fine friends and a job where I could spend the rest of my days.' Meant it too. But should have known. Should have realized such a prideful sentiment would be quickly tested.

In amongst the stack of large-print titles the man checked out, there was always something surprising: *The Conquest of the Incas*, a V. S. Naipaul novel she was too intimidated to read; a crime novel set at a rugby club; *The Female Eunuch*. She'd stamp them out, pass them over, offer a smile and a goodbye. The same as for everyone; but for him quieter, her farewells almost inaudible. As though she respected the piety of the library so much she could not bring herself even to whisper.

A rare bird, a man of her own age in the library. On opening, old men settled down with the papers; late morning, the mothers and their broods; the afternoon a mixed bunch, but never men in fine clothes with close-cropped beards who smelled of sandalwood and patchouli, who bent calisthenically to read the spines of low-shelved books. Hen-tooth rare, men like him.

After he returned his books, she'd check them out herself, read them sitting next to Drum on the sofa, thrilling at her fingers touching the same pages he'd so recently held.

She did not tell anyone of the rare bird (what she called him, though she knew his name was Ray, and that the large-print books were for a mother or aunt, as he had no wedding band). Not recently divorced Patty, nor her friend Bridget. He was for her alone. She would have told Nick, though. He would have enjoyed the suspense. Was still enjoying it, no doubt.

Mid-morning, mid-March of the previous year, in amongst the stack of large-print titles, nothing for the rare bird. She looked up and he was holding out a chit.

'I have an inter-library loan,' he said.

In the loans cupboard his surname was written on a slip of paper around the spine of a thin hardback. She looked at the faded jacket image, the dustcover chipped and foxed. Heart and stomach in tandem, off downhill. She handed him the book and he inspected the inside cover blurb.

'This is the one,' he said. 'Thanks.'

There was always God. One of her invention, one to whom she never prayed, but knew existed. A Welsh God, part beard, part gorse and heather; a hydra of Yehova and the tales of the Mabinogion: terrifying, placating, elemental. She now saw a different side to him: a trickster, huckster God. And alongside him, pointing down from his oraculum, an accomplice, a bawdy ally: Nicholas Oldman, bouncing with delight as she read his name on the book's cover. His name in the rare bird's hand. The audacity of the plan, the mendacity of it, the sheer nerve of it.

'Do forgive me,' Gwen said. 'But can I ask why you ordered this book?'

The rare bird wore a black roll-neck, the wide-lapelled tweed jacket. His beard needed a trim.

'Research,' he said. 'My editor recommended it. It's a classic of its kind, so she says.'

Designed for further questioning, that. Are you writing a book? Have you written a book? Are you a writer? To be wary of such men. Those who suck you into interest, though you have no interest in them. Superb control of the social contract: ask a question, receive an answer, ask a further question.

'Why? Have you read it?' he said. 'I must confess I'd never heard of it.'

Say no. Say no, just say you liked the cover.

'I knew the author a little,' she said. 'The book's very much like him. Full of himself.'

The rare bird laughed, a low, library-minded laugh.

'I'll make sure to tell you how I get on with it, then,' he said.

The rare bird flew the library, his black trousers tight at the seat, Cuban heels clacking on the polished concrete floor. You won't get away with this, mischievous Nick. Why shake trees like this? Why from on high, reach down? She finishes half her gin before heading upstairs to check in on Annie, her blankets illuminated from within, her room still a state, the shame of that room.

'That's enough now,' she says. 'Sleep time, now.'

The light goes out and Annie emerges from the blankets, face just visible from the streetlamp outside.

'I can't sleep,' she says. 'I'm worried about the nightmare.'

Gwen sits down on the edge of the bed, strokes her thin, light-slatted hair.

'I'll stay for a little while,' she says. 'If you think that'll help.'

Gwen lies beside her daughter, shushes her and calms her, the nightmares she complains of all about her father. Father leaving. Father dead. Never her, always Drum. When Gwen was the same age, she'd had a dream about the local dentist playing a penny whistle only she could hear. Still sends a shiver. Happy to lie there, comfort her, send her off to unmet sleep. Dozing herself, thinking it all through. Hoping her thoughts do not bleed from pillow into her daughter's ear. A dream where her mother leaves, not her father.

He skipped a week, the rare bird. She did not look for him, did not check the door when it opened, did not wander the stacks when returning from tea-break, did not check the loan cupboard to see if *The Regional Forecast* had been returned. None of that. Thinking of what they would eat for tea, which books to take home for Annie, what to read to Nate last thing. Thinking of those things.

She read *The Regional Forecast* again, the copy Nick had sent her. She wondered what the rare bird was making of it, the passing of the seasons in a small town, the gossipy, self-indulgent tone. She imagined the rare bird looking for her in the text, seeking her out, finding her as the barmaid. He'd know it was her. He'd see that. Though it was not her. Not her at all.

The next week the rare bird returned his mother's books, and she did not say anything to him. So many patrons of the library, so many questions, how could she be expected to remember—

'I'd love to discuss Nicholas Oldman's book with you,' he said. 'He seemed like a character.'

She nodded. Said nothing. Say nothing.

'Perhaps we could have lunch or something,' he said. 'On me, of course.'

Say nothing.

'I'm Ray, by the way,' he said.

She wanted to say, 'Hello Ray By The Way,' but didn't. She didn't eat her sandwich in the staffroom as usual either.

'You mustn't take too much notice,' Gwen said, holding her coffee, sitting at the back table of Rita's cafe. 'He wasn't one for truth. The truth is as slippery as a pebble from the sea, he'd say. The *essence* was the thing for Nick. All the people in that book, none of them are real. Not *really* real at least. They're added to, blended with others, wholly invented sometimes. That bit when the policeman arrests the chimney sweep? That's an old tale. My da told me that as a nipper.'

'It reads like it's real,' Ray said.

'I'm sure he'd be delighted to hear that,' she said. 'He always loved putting one over on Southerners.'

Ray was wearing a dark-blue cheesecloth shirt, had trimmed his beard, was smoking a cigarette.

'Can I ask,' Gwen said, 'what it is you're researching?'

Ray waved a hand.

'Just an idea I had. An idea for a book about living here. You know, life in the orbit of Ford's . . .'

'And Nick's book . . .?'

'A different approach. Something my editor said. "You need to find an authentic voice."'

'So you read someone else's?'

Ray laughed. How smart her mouth; how subtly cutting. Where from, this voice? Where from, Nick?

'Something like that,' Ray said. 'The structure I like, the passing of the seasons. It's given me some good ideas.'

'Nick would be appalled,' she said. 'But probably flattered.'

Gwen left the cafe, returned to the library, pleased with her performance. Better than she'd expected; unpractised as she was in conversation with newly met men who talked to her as equal. The power of standing behind the library desk.

That night, Wednesday, their night for it, she took Drum in her mouth. Forgotten the last time she did so; her jaw working, lips and tongue. Swallowed. Drum on the bed, leg stammering. No connection. Do not make a connection. None to be found.

Now in her daughter's bed, thinking of Drum in that way. Indecent. Annie asleep now, so still when sleeping, almost dead looking, only the slight rise and fall of chest. We have children to protect ourselves from our own stupidity.

And how much stupidity! How much fantasy! To wake in a different bed; to wake with nothing to do but laze, occupy her own hours. No routines to adhere to, no traditions to uphold. To have a curry instead of fish and chips on a Friday, a Chinese meal, or no meal at all. An Underground trip into the city, drinking cocktails in loud and smoky bars. Dressed in what? Her slippers?

She tiptoes out of the room. My house. My brood. My family. Unsure whether they could smell her thoughts, their acrid funk. She loves them all so much it burns like braziers.

5

Carter stands the first drink at the Lamb and Flag. Two pints of best, Drum given a note and knowing he can keep the change. Sixty pence.

'This reminds me of that little souk we found just outside Addis Ababa,' Carter says. 'You remember?'

'Such charming hospitality, I thought. So very attentive.'

'Until that Tuareg chap came in.'

'Was he Tuareg?'

'I should say so, I recognized him straight away. After our Saharan exploits, how could one ever forget?'

'He was all smiles at first.'

'And then out of nowhere, he was out with the knife and going to slit that poor man's throat.'

'I still don't know what he'd done,' Drum says.

'I think he'd been coveting another man's ox. But the way you handled him! I'll never forget it.'

'It was nothing.'

'Nothing? I've still got the scars.'

Carter reaches down to shirt and began to unbutton it.

'Oh put it away, man,' Drum says. 'The world is weary of seeing your war wounds.'

Somewhere outside there is music, but no music in the pub.

'I miss this,' Carter says. 'I sit with all these people. All of them, and they're just dull. Full of shit or dull. Not you. Not old Drummer boy. Go get another round in. And two chasers.'

Carter gives him two notes. Enough that. Enough to go home with. No shame in it. No shame at all.

'Two pints of best and two whiskies,' Drum says to the barman.

The barman rolls up his shirtsleeves. His right arm is burned, the flesh pink, purple and rose.

'That's a war wound, son. That's a fucking war wound. You two come in here, talking of war wounds? A fucking disgrace, the pair of you. You drink these and then you can fuck off.'

Drum wonders if Carter will start something, be maddened by the slight, the calling out of his lie. But he just smiles. That smile. The barman goes back to his newspaper, offers them his tonsured scalp.

Carter looks around the bar, then shunts his stool closer to Drum.

'It's coming, Drum,' he says. 'And you need to be ready. You know I'm right. You need to have a plan. For you, for Annie, for Nathan, for Gwen. You need a plan.'

'We'll be fine,' Drum says. 'Don't you worry about us.'

The four of them, fine, yes. The strike will work itself out. Always be jobs in Dagenham. Experience counts for something. All fine. Money will come.

'You can see what's coming,' Carter says. 'So what's your Plan B?'

Outside, Coca-Cola and Cinzano. Skol and Skull. 'My Sweet Lord'. Hari Krishna. Tramp and piss smell. Outside, home and back and no work in the morning, the morning to sleep it off.

'Drum, you had a plan,' Carter says, even closer now, smell the whisky, smell the sweat. 'You knew just what to do about Cuba. Come to old Jim's place. We'll be safe there. Isn't that what you were thinking? So what are you thinking now? You know it's coming. So what's the plan?'

'I don't have a plan,' Drum says finally. 'No plan.'

And there he is. In the pub at Doom Town. The pumps at half mast, still at pour; the cash register ringing a permanent sale, charred notes and coins blackly inside; the smashed glass scattering the bar, the jug handles still hanging above. Sack-men in the window, a sack-man with burn marks behind the bar.

Carter knocks on the table. Big fists on the table.

'Well let's make one,' Carter says. He drinks the rest of his drink. 'Let's make a plan tonight.'

6

She takes a second gin, picks up the first book from the pile, tries to imagine which order he read them in. Today's returns, all seeming pointed. A book on the patriarchy, a travel memoir, a novel about adultery in an area of London she's never been. Books taken out after their sandwich lunch, the usual spot; the usual conversation.

'How's your mother?' Gwen said.

'The same,' Ray said. 'Sitting in the living room, waiting to die.'

'They say people go quick after they've lost someone,' she said. 'They die of a broken heart.'

'By "they",' he said, 'I take it you don't mean any member of the medical profession.'

Hate him for that. For the arrogance, the sly kink of the head, the smirking eyes and suggestive mouth.

'It *is* medical,' she said. 'If you live the same routine, day and night, for sixty years, you become dependent on it. When it's over, body and mind just don't know how to cope. Look at how many men drop dead a year after retirement. All those years doing the same thing, and then suddenly they have nothing to do. Their brains and bodies just collapse.'

Her father above-stairs. Her father speaking Welsh, clutching the picture of her mother.

'Okay,' Ray said. 'I'll buy that. But don't call it a broken heart. Call it collapsed routine.'

'But where's the romance in that?' she said.

She picked up her coffee and he lit a cigarette. She took one from his pack and lit it from his match.

'And Jenny?' she said. Hated to say her name. The wife name. No wedding band as neither wore one; a modern relationship. No less married, though.

'Just about,' he said. 'She misses London, her friends and so on. Spends a couple of nights a week in town, sleeping on people's sofas. I think she secretly likes it. Makes her feel young again.'

He scratched his beard, did this when uncomfortable, or when lying perhaps.

'At first she had these plans,' he said. 'We'd live rent-free at my mother's, save money for a house. We went for a few viewings, ate dinner in all these different parts of town, tried to decide where we might live. I think she subscribes to the same thesis as you. Probably thought Mum'd be dead within a few months.'

A glum, gallows smile and a pull on the cigarette.

'I'm sure she understands,' Gwen said.

'I don't think she does,' he said.

'Are you saying your wife doesn't understand you?' she said, smiling.

'She never has,' he said. 'She's Turkish, can't speak a word of English.'

They laughed. In the cafe, on a Wednesday, they laughed, this already a private joke between them. They laughed, then talked about the books he'd read, the books she'd read after he'd returned them, then a book they had both long ago read, and then the book he claimed he was writing, but she knew he was not.

And then to it.

'Is there any chance?' he said. 'Of what we discussed?'

There was a conference. In the Midlands somewhere. They were putting him up in a nice hotel. A double room, a shame to waste the bed with him alone. Every week now for three weeks, this begging coda.

'You know I can't,' she said.

When she thought of affairs, she thought of *Room at the Top*, Joe Lampton and Alice, their stolen time in the countryside, when their love was enough they had no need even to smoke cigarettes. Ended badly, that. They always do. Mangled in a car. That's the true end of an affair. Mangled. Broken-boned. Unsullied by the smell of stale cigarette smoke.

'Why not? You said yourself your friend wanted to see you. It's just the one night.'

'Just the one night and then what?'

'Well . . .'

'You have nothing to lose—'

'Well that's not—'

'A relationship you say is already dead, Ray. No kids. No one but your mother who really matters. It's a whim for you—'

'It's not a whim,' he said.

'What men will do for their own satisfaction!' she said. 'What lengths they will go to for just a few moments of pleasure. All that effort and it's over so quickly. How can it ever be worth it?'

'Women, too,' he said. 'Not just men.'

Gwen laughed and picked up her sandwich.

'It's different though,' she said. 'You know that.'

'It doesn't have to be,' he said. And she would have liked to believe him; would have liked to cave in and say, yes, you're right. Let's go now. Would have liked to, but not so stupid as to do so.

'Ray, my life is bound by three other people. I can't just run off to Nuneaton and expect there not to be reprisals.'

Perhaps there would be; perhaps not. It could happen and she could return home, revivified, new womanned, the act just for herself and not for him. Something to bring some spice back, some danger. No danger here save for lack of money. Yes. No. One thing or the other.

'I wish Nuneaton sounded more romantic,' he said. As if that were the issue. As if that were the only stumbling block.

'But I understand,' he said.

'You have no idea,' she said. 'Not the first clue.'

She thinks of Ray, she thinks of Drum. In the cold of the living room, lights a cigarette and sips her gin. Drum drunk by now, wobbling around the city, him and Carter out for the night, on the tiles, painting red. Drum better come home with the money. Drum better come back with something. Drum better make it all worthwhile.

7

Her tenth birthday brought Anneka a room of her own. It had been a campaign of sixth months' standing, its composition varied and relentless, designed and executed to wear down resistance. With her father, mournful sighs about the injustice of a spare room that had no need to be spare; with her mother, carefully judged stories of two girls, one real, one invented, who'd recently started their periods. To both parents, she presented plans of how her room might be arranged; blueprints labelled with their constituent parts – lamp, dressing table, wardrobe.

Her birthday morning she unwrapped the gifts waiting for her on the kitchen table: three doll-size cans of paint and a fine-bristled paintbrush.

'You might want to look upstairs, *cariad*,' her mother said.

Anneka ran upstairs; mother, father, brother following her barefoot stomp. The door to the spare room was open, the room cleared of junk and tat; in their stead an expanse of carpet, vacuum marks on its nap, a single bed pushed against the wall, a bedside table to its left, a lamp, one she had not seen before, set upon it.

Anneka surveyed the room, dragged fingertips over the peeling wallpaper, examined the broken roller-blind, switched on the lamp, turned it on, then off again. She sat down on the bed, the mattress softer than the bunk from which she'd been freed. The walls, the window, the bed, the table, the lamp. All hers.

'Can I take down the wallpaper?' she said.

'We'll do it together,' her father said. She jumped from the bed and threw herself into his arms, reached out for her mother, the three of them caught in a tight embrace, her brother pawing at her back. 'Happy birthday, Annie,' him saying. 'Happy birthday to you.'

A few weeks later and half the wallpaper has been removed, ugly snatches of it still clinging to the plasterwork, the wall by her bed attacked at night, a spreading tear as though the paper is eating itself. On the opposite wall, three swatches of paint, three possibilities. The roller-blind is still broken, stiff and aslant; her clothes still reside in her brother's wardrobe. She no longer makes plans for decorating.

The room dislikes her presence. The window rattles in the night, the floorboards do not creak but crack. The space, so coveted, now seems meagre, the ceiling lower, the damp more aggressive in its corners. Cats or foxes ravage bins, scream and mewl all hours of night; dogs tethered outside for bad behaviour howl at the moon. She misses her brother's snuffles and grunts; more so the smell of him and her.

'I know you're disappointed,' her father said, the morning after the strike started, as he made her packed lunch. 'I understand that, but it won't be for long.'

He put his nose to her nose.

'You've just got to be patient,' he said. 'Strikes never last that long. But while they do, we need to tighten our belts a bit. You know what that means, don't you?'

She tries not to be alone with him now; the apologies, the promises and slayed optimism too much to bear. He is hard to avoid. Haunting the house of a morning; an apron on and making tea when she gets back from school. Nate loves his father being home. They cuddle and scrap, throw paper aeroplanes at each other while she retires up to her unkind room and reads books, waiting for her mother to come home and re-establish some kind of routine.

Anneka has begun to spend more time at Susan's house after school. Anneka and Susan were born the same week, on the same maternity ward, and have formed a unit; their personalities tumbling into one another. They are quiet in company, shy girls in the schoolyard; caught and kissed not often, nor never. They play recorder passably, jump rope with enthusiasm and skill, chew hair while concentrating. Debra Bentley calls Anneka 'White Susan' and Susan 'Black Annie'. Debra thinks it's funny, and sometimes it is.

Their houses are identical in layout, so different in smell. Anneka likes the way there's always something simmering on Susan's mother's stove, some pot of stew, or pan of rice. Anneka loves Susan's mother: Auntie Bridget's stately calm and starched nurse's uniform, the tiny clock at her breast; but reserves her deepest affection for Susan's eldest sister, Della: the only child she knows with her own room.

Della is seventeen, her room door permanently closed, its insides only glimpsed when she floats out in a cloud of perfume, her afro perfectly round, past Anneka and her sister. Her room is magical. A record player on a small desk, beside a jam jar of flowers, an overflowing ashtray.

'That's how I want my room to be,' Annie said once to Susan.

'A mess?' Susan said.

'No,' Anneka said. 'Private.'

Susan shares her room with her other sister, Angela, fifteen and an athlete at county level. She trains after school each day, so Susan and Anneka mostly have the room to themselves, Susan on one bed, Anneka on the other, drawing pictures, playing games, or just talking. Conversations that spiral and eddy, run from the fantastic to the mundane.

On 9 November 1969, Susan and Anneka had this conversation:

SUSAN: When I die, I want to be buried with my hands folded on my chest like this.
ANNEKA: Why?

SUSAN: I think it'd look nice. You promise that if I die, you'll make sure I'm buried with my hands folded on my chest like this.

ANNEKA: I promise.

SUSAN: You'll want to be buried at sea, I suppose.

ANNEKA: Yes. At sea. Dropped from a helicopter. Boom, splash!

On 14 August 1970, this:

SUSAN: I wish every day could be like this.

ANNEKA: When I'm grown up I'm going to have my own swimming pool and swim in it every day.

SUSAN: I'm going to have a pool too so you can come over to my house to swim.

ANNEKA: We could live together. A big house in the countryside with a swimming pool.

SUSAN: Two pools. One indoors and one out.

ANNEKA: And you could have a pony.

SUSAN: No. Horses. Two horses. And a stable.

ANNEKA: I'd like a bright red swimming costume and a white swimming cap.

SUSAN: I'd like a red riding jacket and white jodhpurs.

ANNEKA: And no boys.

SUSAN: No boys *at all*.

13 February 1971, this:

ANNEKA: There was ice inside the window this morning.

SUSAN: Dad's like a ghost haunting the house. He just sits in his chair. He's drinking now.

ANNEKA: It's strange having him home when I get back from school.

SUSAN: Yeah. I don't like it. I wish the strike was over.

ANNEKA: When they say strike, I always think of matches.

SUSAN: I always think matches smell like birthdays.

ANNEKA: Don't talk to me about birthdays.

Anneka remembers that last conversation, fleetingly and without much consideration, as she turns over on the too-soft bed. She woke at just before midnight and cannot get back to sleep. She's tamped down by thick layers of blankets, but the outside chill permeates past and present, blasting icy through memories of sun. I'll never again wake in daylight, she thinks. I'll always come round with feet half-numb and fingers dug deep into pyjama bottoms.

In her and Susan's house the heating would always be on; every morning would be summer, even in the lash of autumn. She'd walk in her gingham pyjamas to the pool house, change into her red costume and swim lengths, the lights low and the dawn breaking around her. Afterwards, she'd wrap herself in a towel with a hood, its hem brushing her ankles as Susan clacked poolside, smelling of bridle and brushwork. Outside, the horses in the fields would skitter and neigh, a sheepdog called Meg would snuffle the hedge-rows. The radio would be on and there would be no news bulletins, just music and chatter and laughter. After breakfast, they'd drive to the beach in a drop-top sports car. Fine sand and no wind, the sea as meek as a lake, the whole expanse to themselves.

Yes. A perfect day. But others, too.

Susan was kicked to death by horses as she took her morning ride. There was a car crash on a coastal road; Susan in a coma, Anneka in a wheelchair. Meg got into difficulties and drowned. Men abducted them and their bodies were never found. Men killed Susan. Men came and Susan left of her own free will, laughing as she closed the front door. There was a bomb and everyone died. The pool was empty and she was telling Susan they would need to eat the horses. In her torn and filthy riding gear, Susan was crying. These the days she sees, these the ones she imagines.

There is a sound from downstairs, the front door being slowly opened. In the books she reads, there are burglars, smugglers, robbers, kidnappers. Anneka closes her eyes and holds her breath. The click of the door and the sound of keys falling to the ground, a metal splash on lino. She looks at the clock. She assumed her father was home, but it has to be him. No one else with keys.

Anneka steals out onto the landing and puts her hands on the balustrades, cold like school railings, and watches her father stumble into the sitting room. He is wearing his suit, his tie slouched around his unbuttoned collar. He hums a tune. Something he likes to listen to on the record player, a woozy clarinet instrumental. He goes to the kitchen and comes back holding a glass in both hands, sipping Scotch like it's cocoa. Even from upstairs, she can smell his booze, his sweat.

She's seen drunk at a wedding; she's seen drunk on the television; she's not seen it in her father. Never much seen him drink at all, aside from when they went to see the Carters. She watches him take off his trousers, sit there in just his underpants. Money for drink. Money for that, but not her bedroom. How much a rollerblind. How much for booze.

Her anger is close, close to her skin, how it broils and hisses. She knows some dirty words, some filthy words. Dickhead. Fucker. Bastard. Silent curses, hurled in silent rage. Money for this, but not to help her sleep, money for this but not a thought for her.

Her father stands and catches his foot on the hem of the rug, trips and lands close to the hearth. Anneka vaults down the stairs, puts her hands on him. He looks dead. For a moment dead, then alive and stinking.

'I'm okay,' he says. 'I'm okay. Just fell over.'

He remains in a mound on the rug, head so close to the tiles and brickwork.

'I'm fine,' he says again. 'Go back to bed.'

She goes to the kitchen and fills a glass with water.

'Drink this,' she says. 'Get up and drink this.'

She taps him with her foot, his stomach soft, rolling back into place.

'Drink this or I'm going to get Mam,' she says.

He gets up, takes the water and drinks it down. She helps him collapse into his chair.

'You can take me swimming on Saturday,' she says. 'And afterwards, we can go and buy a wardrobe.'

'We can't,' he says. 'I'd love to but I have to go away on the weekend.'

'Away?'

'Yes.'

'Where?'

He looks confused. He begins to put on his trousers.

'Up to Uncle Jim's.'

'Without us?'

'Yes,' he says. 'Just me this time.'

'I want to go with you.'

'Well you can't,' he says. 'Now go to bed.'

He returns then, him straggling out of the confusion. That look on his face, that familiar look. Do not disobey. She is already walking to the stairs, Annie; she is already retreating.

'You stink,' she says on reaching the safety of landing. 'Dad, you absolutely bloody stink.'

8

Gwen does not leave him tea, does not set a pair of aspirin and a glass of water on his bedside table. She does, though, fold his trousers, lay them neatly on the chest of drawers, remove his wallet and take three of the five notes she finds inside, the two remaining reserved for food. A dirty way to get money; but needs musting. She looks down on Drum, the damp on the pillow from his open mouth. A murder scene and her the pathologist assessing the body. Dirt under the fingernails, small red-wine fangs at the corners of his mouth, his smell acrid, spilled booze and beef in sauce. She opens the window. Let him wake frozen, knowing the window's a pointed comment.

Since the strike, Drum has taken the weekday breakfast shifts, letting her sleep while he fixes porridge and mediates the fights and disagreements. She suspects there are fewer when it's just him; that the children's behaviour is better, more loving, without her. For him, sitting at table, not arguing for more sugar, not complaining one had more or less than the other, neither claiming a stomach ache that prevents them from attending school.

She makes porridge as Nate and Annie bicker. Soon they will leave for school and the house will sigh, revel in the short silence, and there will be ten minutes before her bus to the library to fix make-up and style hair.

'*Gwell i chi fod yn dawel*, you two,' she shouts.

She is serving the porridge, but looks up to see her daughter screw her face into a witch's gurn and slap her brother across the face. The moment of shock and then his scream, the cries and the hot salt tears, him quickly into Gwen's arms.

'You nasty girl,' Gwen says. 'You apologize this instant.'

Annie looks directly at her mother, eyes locked and burning ice. Still in her pyjamas, child dressed but adult raged, her face now resting witch. Taunting, saying nothing.

'Don't make me wake your father,' Gwen says.

'Wake him up,' Annie says. 'See if I care.'

The defiance of the girl-witch face.

There was a day, years before, almost perfect. They'd driven to the beach, impromptu, the morning surprising bright and already hot. On Westcliffe Beach, the tide out and a rug thrown down, Drum took Annie and Nate into the water. She watched Annie swim parallel to the beach, Drum just behind, ready to catch her should she fall. She did not fall, her swimming stronger than Gwen had reckoned on. It was the first time Drum called her Fish.

Gwen had watched her dappled, dripping family splash each other, sink under waves and breakers, re-emerge, shaking like dogs. She lit a cigarette none of them saw, dug her toes in the cool shingle. When they eventually tired of the water, she stood and welcomed them with sun-warm towels. Drum bought ice creams, strawberry sauce on soft white mounds, wafers so crisp they threatened teeth. When she kissed him, his lips were cold from the ice cream, then warm.

The children had joined a game of stick cricket, a big group, their shoulders red, their teeth bared in victory or defeat. And she lay her head on Drum's naked chest, and they dozed under the sun as the kids played and the tide turned.

'You know,' Drum said. 'At some point Annie's going to be too big for me to pick her up.'

'I suppose,' she said.

'I won't remember it, will I? There'll be a last time and I won't even know it's happening.'

She saw something on his abdomen, flicked it onto the beach.

'I can't imagine them hating us,' she said. 'But they will. Kids always do.'

At this he laughed, took her and rolled her onto the blanket, lay on top of her.

'No one could ever hate you,' he said. 'It's not possible.'

They kissed. On that perfect day they kissed and she could remember it all: Nate's sunburned shoulders; the waves claiming the sandcastles; the look on her daughter's face as Drum carried her to the car, limp and exhausted. It could have been then, the last time he carried her. It could easily have been. She was reminded of that angel face as Annie looked at her, the hate in those eyes, pure-eyed that hate; combustible with it.

'What did you say?' Gwen says. 'What did you just say?'

'I said, "Go and wake him up, see if I care." Didn't you hear me? Are you deaf?'

Gwen crouches, covered in howling boy, looks up to her daughter; her daughter looking down on her. She looks freed and ragged. Gwen strokes her son's hair as he whimpers, shushes him as she eyes her daughter. She wants to slap Annie. Hard. Across the face. Watch her shocked little face with a red hand on her cheek. Annie just runs off, thudding upstairs, not waking her father, though she seems determined to do so.

'There, there,' Gwen says to Nate. 'It's all okay. You're fine. You're all okay.'

Annie leaves without saying goodbye, without her brother, a slammed door meeting Gwen's shouting voice. Sheepish Drum comes downstairs, unshaven and rough, but dressed at least.

'You should have woken me,' he says. 'I would have done breakfast.'

'She hit Nate,' she says. 'Did you not hear the screams?'

'No,' he says.

'Well you can take Nate to school, I need to get ready.'

Shouldn't be so harsh, shouldn't be terse, when all things considered. Went to get money, the same as going to the factory. The same thing, but with fewer ethics.

'You'll be back from picket before school's out?'

'Yes,' he says.

'Good,' she says. 'I've left a list.'

★

A sludge of a morning, the rain settling in, comfortable against the library roof, a smatter of it, the old men smelling of wet dog. Remember days like this in the pub, Nick steaming on entering, never one for umbrellas. Would like to see him walk through the door now, take a pew, offer his tasteless ear.

The morning is slow, toddlers and the mothers reading books and playing games, hiding out from the rain. In an atlas she looks up Nuneaton. Looks at the word on the page, sounds it out – *nun eaten* – and laughs at that. The virgin consumed. Gwen tidies the desk, does not think of eaten nuns, just tidies the desk, making nice, making neat.

She hears a tap on the desk and looks up. A woman in a red and stylish raincoat. Her hair is long and black, centre-parted, dead centre, defined as a line of chalk. From a large bag she takes a stack of large-print books and places them on the counter. There are six books. Gwen looks at the date stamped inside each one, but knows they are not even close to being overdue.

'Thank you,' Gwen says.

The woman looks at her, the look hard, pitying, angry, victorious. A week they have been out, some only a day. Ray's mother dead. Dead certainly. Or a message. Or both. Both dead and a message.

'Thank you,' Jenny says. She swings her bag gently as she leaves the library, opens up an umbrella at the door, and looks back at Gwen, smiling with a wide and violent mouth.

JAMES CARTER

When I think of Service, I think not of the food – no one would wish to remember that filth, especially, if like me, you were responsible for its preparation – or the training, or the routine boredom, or the uniforms, or the COs, or the privations of life on a base, but of friendship and camaraderie. That is the overwhelming memory, as I write this, some twelve years after demob; the sense of men from all quarters getting along, finding common ground, a common language.

Over the years I have met many other former servicemen, and few seem to have kept in contact with their comrades. All have fond memories, however; many of them talk with great affection for men they have not seen since. I feel that I am most fortunate, however, to have met one of my very closest friends while on the parade ground, and to still count him as such today. I have long since forgotten the best way to cook bully beef, how to polish boots to a mirror shine, how to fire a rifle or use a bayonet, but thankfully my friendship with Alan – not his real name; he asked me to 'keep him out of it', which is instructive of his char-acter and temperament – remains a part of my life.

Alan was the first member of what I suppose we would call the working classes I'd ever met, unless of course you count those people in my family's employ. He was also the first socialist with whom I had consorted, and the first person of my own age who had been at work since the age of sixteen. On our first meeting, he saved me from ruin in a game of cards run by a pair of youthful conmen, and from then on, we became if not thick as thieves, then close as charlatans.

We were both given lucky stations; both given the greatest of chances of survival, as members of the Catering Corps. No postings abroad for us, no gunfights and bombs. We stayed at the same base for the almost all of our two years, found the ways out into town, drank beer with locals, made chit-chat with local women. Long before the universities were opened up for working-class folk, Service allowed the classes to mingle, to be educated – at least after a fashion – and to show us all a different side of life.

Had I not been sent down from Oxford, I feel I would have moved entirely in the set direction one is ascribed at birth, from dreaming spires to gainful employment, from marriage to children and all that comes with such joy. But meeting Alan changed my trajectory, not by much, but still by the finest of degrees. Many of the friends and acquaintances I have made over the ensuing years have been from backgrounds that do not mirror my own. And for that, I will always be glad to Service and to Alan. Over the years, he has saved my life several times – once literally – and so Service will always hold an uncommon affection. Without it, I would not have my Panza.

James Carter (author), retrieved from B. S. Johnson Archive, British Library, File 414 (Submissions for *All Bull: The National Servicemen*). Marked with annotation in pen by BSJ – 'We have enough of these upper-class nostalgia riots! Reject with glad heart.'

A long walk around the estate to outrun the hangover, the old sensation of it, so long out of practice, so long since waking dry-mouthed and gut-punched. A long walk in the rain, ending up on the high street, shopping to fetch.

Greengrocer's as usual packed, but no one there he knows. A relief, that. The worst is bumping into other striking men accompanying their wives; the sense of being taken to the shops by mother. Avoid eye contact. Better for all to do so, better to say nothing.

The butcher is cleaning down after the morning rush, silver platters of heart and liver, kidney and tripe; pigs hanging from hooks, rabbits still furred, chickens unplucked. He looks at the kidneys, would like the kidneys but Gwen can't bear the smell in the pan. The soft face of Mr Dutton, the sort of man who dreams of anything but being a butcher, but once sure of his fate, embraces it with zeal.

'Hello there, sir,' Dutton says as Drum walks through the rainbow streamers. 'Weather for ducks, isn't it?'

At home, still sick from drink, he unpacks the shopping, begins the hoovering and the dusting, the wiping down of surfaces. He changes the bedding upstairs, resists the temptation to tidy Annie's room, then tidies it anyway. He does the same to Nate's room, then attacks the bathroom.

This what men do. Think of plans, execute them. Even when cleaning a lavatory pan. Better to be doing that than at the picket. Better to be doing something for the family. Carter's is a simple plan. One he's sure has been offered to others first, but by elimination has arrived at his door.

'Who else could I rely on?' Carter said. 'Who else can I trust with my family's life?'

A good question, one meant to ruffle peacock feathers. Appeal to their special affection, the bond between them, and their families. How good it would be for Gwen to be closer to her family; how good it would be for Annie to be closer to Tommy; how good it would be for Nate to live in the good, clean air of the countryside. How Drum was the only one Carter could trust to protect them if he were away when things went down. How he could trust him to run the bunker in his absence.

Carter looked like he believed all of this; believed it too, when he said that Drum would take to the work, would become a true farmer in a matter of months. Believed it when he said Drum was doing something the Carter family would never forget; believed it when he said that Gwen would understand.

'All you have to say,' Carter said. 'Is that I'm fronting the money for you to buy the farm next door. That you can live there for as long as you like, all on me.'

'She'll ask why.'

'So tell her,' he said. 'Tell her about the warring neighbours, just as I told you. The housing development, all of that. She'll soon see.'

Yes, soon see. See through it, tell him that it's a fool's move. A plan about which he does not have the full information. And be right about that. Right about it and Drum not caring.

He begins dusting the lounge. He should feel guilty for the meetings he's missed, the pickets he's abandoned. Should do, but does not. What good the struggle anyway, the constant battle? No good. No good at all. Too old for it now, to be keeping on with it. The endless in and out of it. The constant hope and its dash, the ache in the shoulders. The same faces through the same doors, the same talk and the same resolution. And all for what? To send Nate and Annie to the comprehensive? To breathe the same filthy air? To fear the estate at night? To worry on every penny? No matter how sketchy the plan, no matter how ill-considered, better than waking at fifty, facing another fifteen years without even the kids at home to make it worthwhile.

Just before three, the telephone rings. No matter how long, the ring still surprising.

'Hello, Drum,' Carter says. 'Just checking in. Are we set for Saturday?'

'Gwen'll be back later,' he says. 'I'll call as soon as we've spoken.'

'I'm counting on you,' Carter said. 'Counting on you to save the day, as always.'

Gwen opens the door on a silent house, no bone creaks or radio, no food on the stove, no feet on the stairs. Perhaps she wasn't the only stop on Jenny's rounds. For a moment, it feels like they've all gone; the children taken, driven away by Drum. But then she sees him in the kitchen, serious faced, set for a scolding.

'Where are the kids?' she says.

'At Vi's,' he says. 'We need to talk and I didn't want them getting in the way.'

There are new apples in the fruit bowl, new bananas. Not going anywhere. No one buys fresh fruit and then leaves. No packed suitcase, no stuffed holdall. Just the tea, which he pours, *A Clubbable Woman* open, just a chapter from its conclusion.

'You look terrible,' she says. 'Still, serves you right. What time did you get back last night?'

'Late,' he says. 'Carter put me in a cab.'

'Earned your money then,' she says. 'The hungover hooker, right?'

He looks up and if he knows, this is the time to say. She's given him the perfect in. *Well, you'd know all about being a whore*, something like that. Easy to follow that conversational line.

'I've been this close to throwing up all day,' he says. 'I'm out of practice.'

She nods and takes her tea. No sympathy.

'So what's so urgent we have to banish the kids?'

He puts his hands on hers. If they were not already married, she would expect a proposal. Something like the way Ray held her hand and told her his plan for Nuneaton.

'I want you to know,' he says, 'that none of this has been agreed. This is our decision, yours and mine, and I need you to be one hundred per cent sure it's what you want.'

'Okay,' she says. Into strange territories here; Drum never one for abdication of responsibility. Always decisive, stubborn once a decision made. 'You're beginning to worry me, but okay.'

He looks her straight in the eye, does not move his gaze.

'You know the farm next to Carter's place?'

She nods. Should have realized. Carter. Who else.

'Well, the man who owns it is selling up. Thing is, a property developer wants to buy it and build a housing estate. Carter's furious about it, but there isn't much he can do. There's bad blood between the families. Goes back generations, apparently. A mutual hatred. Carter did tell me the reasons, but that part's all a bit hazy. Anyway, Carter wants to buy the land, but the farmer won't sell to him. Won't even let him inside the door.'

'Poor Carter,' she says. 'Someone he can't buy.'

'Exactly,' Drum says. 'But he knows the farmer doesn't want to sell up to the developers. Not really. The farm's been in the family for forever, so what he really wants is to sell to someone who'll keep it on as a going concern. So Carter wants to buy the farm, but have someone else front the bid.'

He looks at her, asking her to join the dots. She shakes her head. It sounds like a lie. Maybe the telling wrong, maybe details mangled by drunkenness and hangover, but a yarn this, a story.

'You?' she says.

'Carter says if I can convince the farmer to sell, he'll let us have the farm for as long as we like. The money we make will be ours.'

She looks at his eager face, thinks of all the times she's thought of moving home, moving away from Dagenham. It's never seemed possible, plausible even. She's never risked mentioning it for fear of the argument that would ensue. It does not make the whole thing any less insane.

'What are we going to do with a farm, Drummond?' she says. 'What do you know about farming?'

The right question, one for which he has clearly prepared. Tumbling out now, all the justifications. How it's mainly a question of process, how there's a farmhand to help, how he knows enough about machinery to master the milkers. The wide eyes. The excitement, the slight sweat of his clothes, the booze still working out from pores. He has decided. Already in his head, there he is, tending his cattle, pulling on boots, hauling oats and dung.

'We'll be closer to your family. The kids will grow up away from all of this filth and pollution. Fresh air and good food. A fresh start. A new beginning. A better life. A safer life.'

And that the kicker, that what this all about. The bunker, the one Carter had at last installed.

'Drum,' she says. 'If you think you want this you're leathered.'

'I've never been more certain of anything,' he says. 'You think I want to stay here? I don't want to die in that factory and this is the only chance for me to get out. It's all right for you in the library, but what about me?'

She lights a cigarette, goes to the cupboard and takes out an ashtray. A choice once of Nuneaton or home. An easier conundrum that.

'So I'm expected to be a farmer's wife, am I?' she says, laughing. 'All apple cheeks and delivering foals?'

'Daphne says she can get you a job at one of the local libraries. She knows all the right people.'

Oh that face. Certain that he will prevail, confused at lack of enthusiasm. And what to stay for. Really what. A sight of Ray. The dour cold, the brown houses, the promise of the city they never now visit. What difference does it make? Here or there. Farm or council house. Near or far.

'I'll need to see it first,' she says.

Oh *that* face. Already organized. Already in train.

'I said I'd go up on Saturday.'

'Okay, so Saturday,' she says. 'We'll all go up Saturday.'

'All of us?'

'Yes,' she says. 'All of us. All of us or not at all.'

He looks down at the table. You never think your lies are as bad as others. They are explicable. She doesn't know why she wants the children there with her. Just that she does.

'I'll have to check with Carter. He's booked me a room at the Wolf, so—'

'We can stay there. Annie and Nate can spend the night with the Carters. It'll be fun for them.'

'I'll have to check with Carter.'

'It's that or nothing,' she says. 'Those are my terms.'

He leans across the table and kisses her. She kisses him back.

'I'm promising nothing,' she says. 'Remember that. Not a thing, you understand?'

Another kiss, and then somehow then up to bed. Part of the plan this? Up to bed and him doing the thing she likes and her not caring she's day dirty and hasn't washed since breakfast. Don't look for a connection. There is no connection. None at all.

12

Nate does not want to go to the Carters' house without Mam and Daddy. He wants to stay with them at the inn, but Daddy tells him it's a game and he has to hide out at the Carters' house and pretend he doesn't know Mam and Daddy if he sees them. A funny kind of game. Kind of game Tommy and Annie make up. The rules not always clear. The rules sometimes changing.

The inn is nice. He likes the inn. He wants to stay with Mam and Daddy, but Annie says it will be fun. And don't forget Tess the spaniel. She'll be missing you, will Tess. And Annie and Tommy will play with Nate and Natasha the whole time. Nate knows this is a fib, but Annie is being kind, and she is happy and he wants her to be happy, so he dries his eyes and stands up as tall as he can and Mam gives him a big squeeze of a hug, and Daddy gives him a big squeeze of a hug.

It is the first time he's been in a car without Mam or Daddy and the car is a big car with seats that make a squeak when he sits. Annie says he needs a secret name, but Nate can't think of another name except Tess, which is a girl's name, and a dog's name, so Annie says she'll call him Norbert and in the back seat of the big car driving to the big house she finds this hilarious.

When they arrive, Tommy and Natasha are at the front door, and Annie tells them to call Nate Norbert, and they all laugh and Tommy says, no, Nobby is better, call him Nobby, and they all laugh, and after a while it is funny and so Nate laughs too, laughs as they run up the stairs to the playroom and Tess is in the playroom, not that she is allowed to be there, and Nate fusses her, rubs her tummy the ways she likes and then gets out all the Meccano.

Tommy and Annie are looking at him like he's a baby, which is what they always call him, but it doesn't matter; the house is warm, toasty warm, and there are dolls and teddies and a rocking horse and all the fun of the fair, and soon Auntie Daph is up with a jug of lemonade and a plate of biscuits.

Tommy and Annie are plotting something, he can tell, but it doesn't matter because Tess smells like hair and outside and is licking biscuit crumbs from Nate's hands and trousers, and Natasha has opened the dressing-up box. The four of them laugh and drink the lemonade and later they will play out in the garden, hide and seek for real, play war, throw balls. When the rain stops. Yes. When the rain stops, they'll all play outside, and they will all forget to call him Nobby.

13

It is the first car he's driven that's not a Ford, a Morris of all things, its steering column too high, the clutch heavy, the acceleration sluggish. Insisted on by Carter; just in case Garner recognizes Drum's car, Garner more likely to remember a car than a person. Puffs and huffs as Drum drives the short distance from the Wolf, but he doesn't say anything to Gwen; he is wary of negative mood, of creating an atmosphere before they even get to the farm.

The rain has cleared, there are fretted clouds and the puddles dazzle. He has drunk too much tea, has driven for so long he feels he could sleep at the Morris's wheel. Gwen is smoking a cigarette and he wants to tell her not to, to at least finish it before they arrive, which she does anyway. There are no mints in the driver-side door. He would like one himself.

'You're sure about this,' she says, 'aren't you?'

'Only if you are,' he says. 'Anyway, still got to convince him to sell. No guarantee there.'

'I spoke to Daphne,' she says. 'She says we must be crazy.'

'That's what she said?'

'Not in so many words.'

'Carter said she was excited about it. Looking forward to having you closer by.'

'That man'll tell you anything,' she says.

He taps the steering wheel, once, twice. A magpie on the road flies off as he approaches, both of them instinctively wave at it. A warding off of bad omens.

'You know what to say?'

'Yes,' she says. 'But I'm not *rehearsing* this.'

'We need to be believable.'

'There is nothing believable about any of this, Drum.'

He pulls up at the traffic lights, he grips the wheel, shuts off the tepid heater with a quick turn of the dial. She puts her hand on his knee.

'Whatever happens,' she says. 'I love you. You have to remember that. If I hate it. If I don't want to go. This is about this decision, not you.'

He looks to her, she has her open face, the one that implores trust, same as on her wedding day, same as when they found out she was having Nate; but pulled slightly, as though an impersonation of something once glimpsed.

'I know,' he says. 'I know it's not been easy for, but . . . '

The lights change and he drives the junction, unable now to finish what he was going to say. That he fears dying on the line, dying on a strike. More than the bomb, more than the Carter-predicted uprisings, just the common, everyday fear of death, an individual one, just his time coming up. He fears the lack he feels at the start of each day, either at the plant or protesting it. Fears slowly grinding into obsolescence, unable to provide properly, dependent on Gwen's meagre wage.

A plot of land. A place to call his own. To work at his own speed. The books on modern dairy farming, borrowed from Carter, pored over like pornography. A quick scholar, enough to muddle through an interview – enough, surely – and how it would feel to open the door on turf and mud, feel the warmth of cow hide, the softness of the udders, the teats. The agrarian life, the seasonal life. Safe and not minded by others. No longer told what to think, what ideology to follow, but just to follow the natural order, jobs culti-vated over millennia, not created by Ford. No more line. No more shoulder ache. No more the fool.

14

They take the unfamiliar turn on the track, left not right, and Gwen looks to the big house, looks for her children, somewhere inside, somewhere in the gardens, down in the dell, out of sight. Rare this, for them to be so far away; only ever as far as Vi's, close enough she could get them in seconds if needed. Daphne said it would be good for Tommy to have Annie around; he was a shy child, one who forms close kinships that easily burn out. Good for Annie too, Daphne said, though this said unsurely, as though testing whether it sounded right. Good for Annie, to move from all her friends, move from the school at which she's doing well? Perhaps, yes, good, Gwen thinks. Better here, away from the smog and brick, the volume of the traffic and the volume of the people.

'We're here,' he says.

'So we are,' she says.

In front of her is the old stone cottage, one seen on so many occasions, but never minded. It is neither forbidding nor enticing, the most pragmatic of buildings: as strong as it needs to be, as big as is necessary. Not much bigger than where they live now, she guesses, a little bigger perhaps. Cold-looking though, no lights from inside. The cows are being herded back to the sheds in the late afternoon dusk, a man with a stick and a boy behind and she imagines Drum doing that one day, Nate doing that one day. The farmers she knew from the pub, the ones in fine cheer and those who drank as quick as they could, as long as they could. Always tell a farmer, her father said, the happiest or saddest in the bar.

In the wellingtons she long ago borrowed from Daphne and

never returned, she walks the mud track to the house. The door opens and there is Garner, a farmer if ever she saw one, instantly recognizable in dress and face: like a cragged bluff draped in waxed cotton. He holds up his hand in greeting, as though they might miss him, and Drum waves back. See his nerves in the wave, the deepness of the breaths. He is to be Carter, and presumably that makes her Drum. Gwen the convincer, Drum the roper. Read about that in a book about con artists; all the tricks of the trade.

'Mr Moore,' Garner says. 'Mrs Moore.'

'Nice to meet you, Mr Garner,' says Drum. 'But please call me Drummond. This is Gwen.'

Garner sniffs, takes a handkerchief from his pocket, hands like lobster claws, blackly veined, fingers swollen. He wipes his red nose, puts the handkerchief away with some effort, then beckons them inside.

They enter directly into the kitchen, one bigger than she expected, a huge table in its centre, a range cooker, a stained Belfast sink. It is the biggest kitchen she's seen aside from Daphne's, the warmest too. A working kitchen, she thinks: a kitchen at the heart of the home, a place for tea and for Sunday lunches, a touch of the Larkins to it; imagine a plump chicken in the oven, a ham ready to carve on the counter. A Christmas room, the slight scent of clove in the air, of orange peel.

'Tea?' Garner says, not waiting for an answer, with his claw hands filling the kettle, struggling with it to the stove, lighting the hob with an unsteady series of match strikes. Gwen wants to help him, but doesn't, not appreciated, do not bring attention to the hands. Carter said that. Values his independence.

'You're from London, I hear,' Garner says. 'That's a long way from home.'

'I'm from Cumbria, actually,' Gwen says.

'A Lakes girl?' he says. 'Used to go there with Elsie when she were alive. Never stopped raining, but we loved it up there. You from the Lakes too?' he says, pointing at Drum.

'No,' he says. 'Essex.'

'And you want to buy my farm?'

'We're certainly interested,' Drum says.

'You know I've had an offer?'

'Yes, but I was led to believe that—'

'Man came here the other week, saying he was led to believe something, turned out he was buying for someone else.'

Garner turns to face them, smiling below a rosaria-pricked nose.

'Buying for him, over the way. Carter. That skate. I could tell it straight off. All smelled wrong, it did. Came here from Oxford or some way. You're not buying for him, are you? If you are, I'll tell you the same as I told him. I'd rather sell the hole in my own arse than sell to that bastard. I ran that skate off the farm, you know, with me gun. You want me to get me gun?'

'Mr Garner,' Drum says, soothing, lowering his voice. 'There's no need for such language. We don't know anyone called Carter, and this is very much for us. Gwen's mother died, left us a little bit of money, not much but enough. And we've dreamed of this for years, haven't we, Gwen? Our own farm, a place for us to raise a family, live a bit closer to nature. But if you're not interested in selling—'

'Yes, we have other farms to visit.' Gwen says off script. 'Pickford's, isn't that the one, love?'

'I'd have to have a look, Gwen,' Drum says. 'But that sounds about right.'

Garner goes to the whistling kettle, takes it from the hob, laughs to himself.

'Pickford's isn't a farm, it's more like a petting zoo. Buy his place and you'll starve before the end of the year.'

'Let me do that,' Gwen says as he struggles with the teacups. She gives her best library smile. 'You sit down.'

He nods in obligation, sits opposite Drum, places his mitten hands on the scarred wood. He follows Drum's eyes, looks down at his own hands.

'Elsie died and then the hands went. A visit from Arthur Itus. It's agony, can't do a thing.'

'Same as my Uncle Nudge,' Drum says. 'He got it bad, had to sell his place too. Had a dairy farm down in Braintree, I used to go and help him on holidays, and then his hands went and he had to sell up. It's houses now, you know. Turn in his grave if he knew.'

Gwen looks at Garner. An overplayed hand, surely. Too much a coincidence, too smooth a leap. Only chance Uncle Nudge ever worked on a farm is if they'd had a henhouse at Broadmoor.

'How many cows?' he says. 'On your uncle's farm.'

'Three hundred,' Drum says, 'so I know about scale. Can we see the sheds? I'd like to see the set-up.'

'Have us tea first?' Garner says.

'Of course,' Drum says.

15

They steal away from Natasha and Nate, leaving them playing dress-up, and run into the garden. They hold hands as they sprint, the wind snapping at Anneka's face, pressing her clothes to her like a shadow. They hurtle, and he makes a long roaring sound, one that comes from deep inside, and they take the incline hard, but do not break hands. They are heading to the dell, their secret place amongst the trees, a shack covered in moss, the old hide. They are going too fast, much too fast, but she doesn't worry for her footing, doesn't think of anything but the speed and the descent and the feel of his hand in hers.

He slows as he reaches the edge of the dell, slowing her too, expertly, bringing them to a canter and then to a slow trot. Heart in her ears, in her throat, the mulch scent of the dell, the sour stink of the stagnant brook. All the journey here thinking of that, the slippery banks, the still water, the hide with its damp blankets, gas lamp, the ripped deckchairs.

She loosens her hand from his as he pushes past the brambles, the nettle copses, the unpruned tree leaves. Inside, pushing through into imagined territory, the colours and textures different, as though from tape to film. Taking the narrow pathway single file, him in front, turned to one side, the two of them like swordsmen or fencers. Through into the frith, a wide expanse of treelessness, in the middle the hide, beyond it the brook. The astonishment of the greens, the dirtiness of the browns, the long nose of its fragrance.

'I got us supplies,' he says, opening the door to the hide. She follows him, the smell changing again, the damp blankets and the sweetness of mouldering apples. He turns on the gas lamp and on a small camp table there are two cans of Coca-Cola, a selection of chocolate bars, the kind of swag she dreams of at the corner shop. He sits on his deckchair and she quickly takes the one beside him.

He raises his can and she raises his, they take off the ring pulls and put them on their fingers, the way they always do.

'I do hope you come and live here,' he says. 'It would be so much fun.'

She feels the Coke foam in her mouth, gagging at her throat and it comes out of her nose and her mouth, one big rush of bubbles and sugar. It sprays her T-shirt, the swept floorboards below.

'You what?' she says.

'You don't know?' he says. 'Have they not said?'

She looks at him, and in the mouth there's something amused, and something terrified, something young and something old. A different face than she's seen before.

'We're moving here?'

'Well, I think that's the plan. It's a possibility at least. I shouldn't have said anything.'

Knew not to say something, but too excited not to, see that in his fizz, in his red cheeks and sweated temples. Blonder than any boy she knows, the hair long now, ringlets, a page-boy cut. Almost feminine, such long eyelashes.

'I knew something was up,' she says. 'I bloody knew it.'

'Nothing's decided,' he says. 'It might not happen.'

'It'll happen,' she says. 'If my dad wants it, it'll happen. Always does. No wonder he never did my room. What's the point if we're going to move?'

'You got your room?'

'Yes,' she says. 'I hate it though. It hates me too.'

'Oh,' he says. 'So this might be a blessing in disguise.'

He smiles, disarming, and pushes her gently on the shoulder, his sincerest form of affection.

'I'm not moving,' she says. 'Not for nothing.'

He picks up his can of Coke, he drinks some and picks up a Twix. He opens the wrapper and hands her one of the fingers. She takes it and bites off the caramel, leaves the biscuit intact.

'Not even for me?' he says.

'It's not about you,' she says, pushing his arm, smiling. And would it be so bad, to be here, to visit the hide, to paddle in the brook. No. Not enough.

'Anyway, I have something to show you,' he says. 'A secret. Might change your mind.'

Always with the secrets, the codes, the games they play needing to be hush-hush, ones sometimes where they touched each other, but not for some years now. Secret touching game, that one called. She looks him up and down, expectant eyes, knowing she can't resist. Can never resist a secret, has never seen a locked door she doesn't want to peer behind.

'Okay,' she says. 'What is it?'

'Later,' he says, biting into the Twix, eating half in one go. 'I'll show you later.'

16

He has never been so close to livestock before, the feral hum of cattle, the steam rising from their backs, the shit from below their tails, the arcs of piss, the huff of breath. He nods wisely at what Garner says, the technical information of which he understands around three-quarters. He asks about the milkers, their power supply, how old they are, how often the gaskets blast, and Garner does not seem impressed, but neither does he see through him, raise a cotton-flax eyebrow and push for confirmation of knowledge. Drum watches the milk pumping, filling the containers and it feels like being on the line, each cow contributing to the finished product. He pats the flank of a Friesian, fondles the tag in one of their ears, listens to Garner talk of supply lines and the man who collects the containers at the end of day.

Gwen stands close by, thankfully says nothing, does not distract from the transaction at hand, from the confidence he is building. Deference important, but also knowledge, and passion. He tells Garner stories of his time with Uncle Nudge, all his own invention, all his own guile. No Carter for this. Carter's intelligence worth nothing when standing with Garner, his provided information just slightly off, what his grandpa called duff gen. All Drum, now. Gwen too, but him. Him closing this one down, making all the inroads.

'I think we've seen enough,' Gwen says. 'Can we go back to the house? I'd like to have a look there too, if we may.'

Drum does not look at her, does not dare, does not want to show his face, the anger at her talking over what he was about to say. But this good, though. The impatience, good, because she wants to see more. Good this, to smile and agree – ah, yes that would be great to see the house – but seething that she cut him off, the anecdote now forgotten, impossible now to recall, but a good one about Uncle Nudge and what was it now? Never mind, all over, interview conducted, examination passed.

Garner leads the way, takes them down the gulley back to the house.

'My great-grandfather built this place from the ground up,' Garner says as they walk. 'The old house was burned down, but that'd been standing since the seventeen hundreds or something. Last man standing, me. Last man.'

He takes them into the house, through the kitchen, into the sitting room, a fire in the grate, stone flags, rugs cast over them, a dog sleeping by the television set. Good-proportioned room, bigger than home, a sofa and two chairs, only one looking like it was ever used.

Up the narrow stairs, runner threadbare, on to small landing.

'Bedroom,' he says, opening the door into a small room full of junk.

'Bedroom,' he says opening a door onto a bigger room full of junk.

'Bedroom,' he says opening a door into a sparse room, just a double bed and a chest of drawers. A big room, one with potential, the light sure to stream through in mornings.

'Toilet,' he says, opening a door into a small piss-stinking room with a lime-silted bathtub.

'It's been a good home,' he says. 'Too big these last years, but a good place. Good memories. Some sad, but mainly happy. My boy were born here, in that room there, in fact. I tell people he was midwifed by a visiting vet, but that's not true.'

He laughs and takes them down to the kitchen, sits at the table, invites them to join him. His eyes are distant, he is seeing the past in the present, his kid, clearly gone, clearly dead, eating soup or baking cakes, and Drum is seeing the future, his kids, clearly here, clearly alive, talking to him as they eat their evening meal, the sound of their voices and the sound of his.

'How many children did you say you had?' Garner says.

'Two,' says Gwen. 'Nathan and Anneka.'

'And what do they think of all this?' he says. 'Moving to a farm and all that?'

'They can't wait to see the place,' Drum says.

Garner smiles, sadly looks inside his empty teacup.

'You're wondering about my boy? Why he isn't here?'

Dead, the boy. Can see his coffin.

'Setting up the summer fair, over at Timbersbrook. Carrying a piece of metal to set up a stage or something, touched an overhead powerline. Dead immediately.'

He put his claws to his face, shielded his eyes with them, though they could see the eyes through the fingers.

'Him and Carter were friends, at first. Carter, the man over the way. Used to get up to all sorts. They got caught one time doing something over at the reservoirs, think they were firing air rifles or something. Carter's father, may he rest in agony, made Billy take the fall for it. Our families, there's always been bad blood, but you don't know why until you see it. They sent flowers to the funeral and Elsie and I we burned them. You ever burned flowers? They smell terrible.'

Drum sees the tears, does not know where to position himself. Wants to ask more about the young Carter, someone he has never even thought about, the boy Carter, the young master of the house. The untouchable little man and the grieving father.

Garner looks up, takes out his handkerchief.

'But you don't want to hear all that, I know. Young couple like you, you don't want to hear it. You want a fresh start and all of that. I understand that. But sometimes, I have to tell people about Billy. Remind them he was here.'

He blows his nose.

'Anyway, if you want it,' he says. 'It's yours. Match the offer, and I'll sell.'

The relief is like Cuba all over again. To go back to Carter. To say he did it, that he convinced Garner, that he played his part to a T. Did it without Carter, without relying on him. To be able to say that. To be able to say that was me. Not you, me. And to work here. To work here.

'Well,' Gwen says, 'we'll need to discuss it, obviously.'

Garner does not look at Gwen, ignores her and looks straight at Drum, down, if it were possible, into what counts for a soul, down into his guts at least, into his marrow.

'But let me tell you this,' Garner says. 'That man over there. That Carter. He'll offer you money for the land. First day you're here, he'll offer you money. Good money. But you will never sell to him. You will never, never sell to him or his family. If I find out in this life or the next that they own this land, I will put you in the ground or haunt you for eternity. Do I make myself absolutely clear?'

Drum cannot avoid his eyes. They are red-lined, distended, searing.

'I promise,' Drum says. 'We just want the farm, nothing more.'

'Well good,' Garner says. 'We should have a drop before you go. Celebrate.'

Gwen begins to say something but the crash and the bang from the drinks cupboard drowns it out.

17

'You can turn back now, if you like,' Tommy says. 'I'd understand.'

'Not a chance,' Anneka says.

They are in the cool of the wine cellar. She knows where he is taking her; her father has told her of a safe place they go if there's ever a war, a safe place where they'd be warm and cosy, a place like the bear's winter house, the one from the book they'd read to Nate.

Thomas swishes aside a tarp and there is a battle-grey door with a wheel at its centre. He attempts to turn it; she watches him, smiling, as he struggles, the wheel refusing to open sesame. She takes the wheel, grips the bevel and heaves it herself. The wheel gives with a clank, so loud in the wine cellar, the clank. They freeze, as though they could take back the sound, their stillness sucking it back. No one comes, though; no one is alerted. They look past the door and see small pricks of light on the roof; another battle-grey door.

'Be quick,' he says. 'We don't have long.'

They race the corridor barefooted; spin the wheel and leave it ajar, blink in the light. Green brick walls, a set of double doors ahead, nozzles on the wall.

'This is the decontamination chamber,' Tom says. 'You put all your clothes in here –' he opens a hatch, and they both look into the smooth metal chute – 'and you walk nude through these doors.'

He looks flustered at the word *nude*, cannot look at her as he strides through the showers. She follows, the nozzles watching her, gas seeping from them, not water, doors bolted and them left to die. She touches one and a drop of water blooms in her hand. Another hits the rubberized flooring, evidence of their transgression.

'This is where we'll live,' Tom says as they enter the living quarters. 'All of us, all of us in here.'

He seems proud of the space, the white walls, the long table, the easy chairs. He shows her around as though no one has ever seen a living room before, a galley kitchen before, small rooms with small beds before. She feels Alice-like, underground and shrunken; in the small bathroom impossibly tall. It is a perfect winter house. She can imagine being there for a time, curling up on the small bed, eating at the refectory table, having midnight conversations with Tom, sharing scared stories of what the world will look like when they emerge.

'Do you think it will happen?' she says. 'Really?'

'Yes,' he says. 'It can't not happen.'

'That what your dad says?'

'It just stands to reason,' he says.

Thomas comes up behind her, she feels his arms on her back, his head too, resting himself against her as a pillow.

'We should go back before we're missed,' she says.

'Missed?'

'They'll be wondering where we are.'

Thomas turns, as if to say something, something important, perhaps the reason for breaking his promise to his father never to go down to the bunker alone, something that has gestated for time but now is impacted, impossible to chip from its mass.

'Yes, we should go.'

He doesn't move. The last opportunity, but he doesn't take it. Instead, from the pocket of his trousers he takes a pencil. He moves the piano from the wall and writes his name behind it. He offers her the pencil. She takes it and writes her name beneath his, beneath that the date.

'Proof we were here,' he says.

'Proof, yes,' she said.

'Like a promise to ourselves,' he says.

'Yes,' she says to his downward eyes. 'A promise.'

'That we'll always be there for each other, no matter what.'

'No matter what,' she says.

And she thinks he is about to kiss her. It is there, the possibility of a kiss, but then it goes. It drifts away as they look around the silent bunker, their present and future, their names written behind the old piano.

Can't You Hear the Drums?

1977

Saturday 17 – Sunday 18 September

I

On Saturdays he leaves the milking to Joseph and Pete; only checking in at end of day when Rick comes to collect the day's containers. Drum does not let anyone sign for them but himself; a rule Garner instilled in him before Drum took full ownership of the farm. Ownership, Garner said, is the most important thing on a farm. Ownership of every heifer and bullock; every pump and gasket. Know everything; all that comes in, all that goes out.

It is his day off, but he still wakes at four, same as always. It is a heavy-headed waking. He folds the pillow underneath himself, tries to get back to sleep. His dreams are always more vivid when he does so. Sometimes he dreams of clocking in at the factory, sprinting towards his station and finding a line of cars waiting for him, doorless cars reaching back an impossible distance, all the cars he should have made. Beside them, workers gather, laughing at him; their laughter loud as the cattle's lows.

Ford's is out on strike again; he read about it in the paper, heard it on the radio. Everyone striking these days, everyone wanting more. Negotiating, filibustering, grandstanding, their hands thrust out. Drum has come to despair of them all. When he and Carter discuss industrial relations, Drum still raises the odd red flag, but does so without conviction.

'You're too much a farmer these days, Drum,' Carter says, smiling an accusation. 'You're a traitor to your own kind.'

What kind are they, he'd like to know. Those he has forgotten, those who sent him off, surprised at his leaving? They'd do the same, given the same opportunity. Every last one of them.

Gwen wriggles in her sleep and he loves her; in other rooms, his children sleep and he loves them too. Happy all of them. Safe all of them. What else can a man ask than that? Don't say it though. Not out loud. Never say such a thing out loud. At moments like this, the still of the house, the cows not long awake, the day not yet to begin, he does dare to think it at least.

There is a problem with one of the pulsators; he should have mentioned it to Joseph. No chance now of sleep with that on his mind. Should not be checking on Joseph and Pete, but unable to just switch off. He dresses by the window, looks out over the fields, the darkness of them, the first brush of sun hours away. He likes it better in the dark; the hum of the electric lights, the covert feel of it.

In the kitchen he makes tea; the whistle of the kettle bringing Nate downstairs, the growing lad in the tracksuit he always wears.

'Up early,' Drum says.

'Heard the kettle,' Nate says. 'Couldn't sleep much anyway. A scout's coming to watch us later.'

'Scout?'

'From City.'

'Right,' he says. 'You want a lift? I could watch if you'd like.'

These are the things he can do now. The things he can give. The look on the boy's face. Drum can give him that look. It is his to give. A few words and that face.

'You'll come watch?' Nate says.

'Come up the fields with me now, and yes, I'll come watch.'

They welly-up by the back door, pull on matching wax jackets, walk out into the blast of morning wind. The ground is scrub dry, no rain for a few weeks, a good thing/bad thing. When dry, Drum sees the centuries in the fields; the history in the sod and turf. It is communion and pagan; it is shit and sweat and other excreta. There are four hundred cows now, there are more on their way; the bull in his field waiting to stud. Sex and death. Bullocks sent off for veal; calves suckling unaware of their inevitable fate. The feeding and the milking and the birthing and the nurturing. A production line of his own staging, of his own pacing. They'd kill for that in the factory; they'd riot for that at Ford's. Ownership, just as Garner said.

'Chris Birch says they're sending someone from Crewe Alex as well.' Nate says.

Nate thinks of little else but football; cares only for the *togger* and his dog, Harris the German shepherd. Harris hares between them as Nate talks about the scout, words Drum does not really hear. Best not to hear, so he doesn't say what he thinks: that football fields are a waste of good grazing; that there's no future in football. Just lets him chatter and chunter; talk of footballers Drum has never heard of. What is an *Asa Hartford* exactly? Why do City *need* a new centre half? What even are *schoolboy papers*?

In the first months on the farm, when entering the cowsheds, Drum would breathe through his mouth, the smell appalling, but now no recollection of the exact stink. He remembers thinking that smells are particles in the air, breathed in and processed, so he was inhaling spilled milk, flecks of shit, droplets of piss and not caring. Better than oil and filings, fume from the pneumatics. Natural at least.

He watches Nate lay a distracted hand on a cow's flank. Always something that, watching his son's way with the animals; nothing learned, but assumed: same way the road led from school to Ford's.

'Ay up. Pete,' Drum says.

Joseph and Pete are standing by haybales, steam draws from the cows' pelts above the moody noise of milking. Joseph in his sixties now, canted and broken; his nephew sixteen and covering for his slowing powers.

'Fine morning, Joseph?' Drum says.

'Aye, fine,' Joseph says.

'Scout coming today, is it, kidder?' Pete says to Nate.

'Supposed be,' Nate says.

'If I were you, I'd wait 'til United come knocking, play for a decent team.'

'They already did,' Nate says, 'but I said I didn't want to show 'em up.'

Pete laughs, big-muscled Pete; like Popeye, Pete, even a tattoo of an anchor on his taut bicep. Good lad, Pete. Instinctive with the herd; handy with the pumps. Him and Nate, one day. Generations and generations. Watch them now spar and joust with one another; the tick-tock banter, the good-natured laughter. Funny, how Drum's children carry him inside them, moments when they say things stolen from his mouth, strike poses he knows he adopts; funny the way they are different, Nate a total stranger to shyness. Will stand him in good stead that, on the farm. Dealing with the men from the dairy. All about confidence in negotiation. Ownership and confidence.

'Something's gone on twelve,' Pete says. 'You want to come help fix it, kidder?'

Nate runs to Pete, and they set about the pulsator. Drum wanted to show Nate the small trick for faulty pressure that Garner showed him. Good that Nate's learned, but it's his to show, not Pete's.

'Hey, not so hard, lad,' Drum says to Pete. 'And watch for the gasket, it'll blast if you stand so heavy. Out the way.'

Pete stands off, and Drum demonstrates the correct fix, the little jumps to kickstart the pulsator.

'Watch,' he says. 'I see either of you lumping on it like that, I'll take the gasket out of your wages.'

The pulsator kicks into life; Drum smiles and nods.

'You see,' he says. 'Good as new and no gaskets blown.'

A smile from the boys. Generations. History under foot. Everything working just as it should. A good life.

2

It is her father who rings the bell; her father who holds her overnight bag. Lissa's house is a small terrace, much like the house in which Anneka grew up. Anneka has told Lissa to dress down. If her father sees ripped jeans and punk make-up, he'll make some kind of excuse, place a phone call later to bring her home.

Anneka worries the elastic band around her wrist; a strum that brings Lissa to the door, dressed as though wearing a disguise: pastel T-shirt and flared slacks, hair back in an Alice band, all traces of make-up removed. She looks twelve again; same as when they first met.

'Hi, Anneka,' Lissa says. Anneka not Neka, just as instructed. Neka would rouse suspicion, an eyebrow at least.

'Nice to finally meet you, Melissa,' her father says.

'Please, come in,' Lissa says.

Anneka has told her to say this too; to prove there are no tricks and a responsible adult abroad. A risky strategy, but essential to ensure a night without interruption. A month of solid negotiation, of pleas to her mother and simpering good grace to her father, all for nothing if Lissa's mother is already slumped in her chair, fuck-eyed and a Valium down.

Lissa walks them to the kitchen, her mother standing awkward at the sink, hands in yellow rubber gloves, washing something up. She nods down at the water.

'Hi, Mr Moore,' Lissa's mother says, 'Sorry, I'm up to my elbows in suds.'

A pot of tea on the table, the sound of dishes in water, plates stacked on a drip-dry rack. It is perfect. Domestic, everyday, utterly normal. Perfect, though Janice is washing the same plate over and over, wiping it from centre to rim, then round the circumference, dipping it in and out of the water.

'Please,' he says, 'call me Drummond.'

'Janice,' she says offering him a slightly panicked smile. Lissa has done her mother's hair, combed it out and coiled it into a bun. She has been dressed too, out of the dressing gown and into a roll-neck and dungarees. Still cleaning the same plate, still smiling panicked, finally putting the plate on the drainer.

Anneka looks at her father. He leans his weight on his heels as he does when unsure or nervous, but there's nothing not to trust here; the gas rings unlit, no knives visible, not even an ashtray. The smell of Fairy liquid, of Flash floor cleaner, of PG Tips. So safe it could be a commercial.

Janice takes another plate and begins to clean it, the same concerted effort. Don't drop the plate, Janice. Keep it together, Janice.

'Thanks for having her, Janice,' her father says. 'You have my number, don't you?'

'Yes,' Janice says. 'We've got the number.'

Her father looks around the room, trying perhaps to drag out the goodbye, though he must sense that everyone is wishing him out of the door.

'I'll pick Annie up at nine,' he says to Janice, to the room at large, then turns to Anneka. He kisses her on the top of the head, brings her in close to him. He smells of farm, of his own sweat.

'Now be good,' he whispers. 'Do whatever Janice says and be polite. No drinking, no going out and please don't stay up too late.'

He smiles at her, down at her, pleadingly.

'Promise,' she says, the word just coming out, its seriousness amongst all the smiles.

'Good,' he says. And louder, again for the benefit of the room. 'See you tomorrow. Have fun!'

Anneka and Lissa walk him to the door. From the living-room window they watch him get into the car, watch him and Nate discuss something; hold their breath until they are certainly, finally gone.

Janice shuffles into the living room, exhausted from standing, worn out from company.

'Can I have the telly on now?' Janice says. 'And it's time for my pills, isn't it?'

'Yes, Mama,' Lissa says and turns on the television. Janice sits in her armchair, her skin queasy porcelain, glasses now on, stylish frames back from when she cared.

'I did well, didn't I, Mel?' she says.

'Yes, Mama, you did well.'

'I didn't drop anything, did I, Mel?'

'No you didn't, Mama.'

'I can have my pill now, can't I?'

'Yes, of course you can, Mama.'

Lissa goes to get the pill; Janice looks up at Anneka, struggling to focus, eyes at swim, then fixes her by the window.

'So, Neka, your dad, he's a strict one, is he?'

Anneka wants to say she thinks he's a tyrant; that she feels as hemmed in as the cows, as cooped as the chickens. That there's always an excuse for her not to leave the farm: too far from home, not enough notice, exams to prepare for. That she knows he searches her room while she's at school, though there's nothing there for him to find. A betrayal though to say that. Unfair to say that.

'It's the first time I've stayed over at a friend's house,' Neka says. 'He just worries, that's all.'

'For you, or for himself?' Janice says.

'A bit of both, probably,' Anneka says.

Lissa comes through with a tray, a pill on a plate, a glass of water, a pot of tea, places it on her mother's lap.

'I used to worry,' Janice says. 'But I trust my Melissa. Don't I, love?'

Lissa puts a hand on her shoulder.

'You don't have much choice, Mama,' she says.

3

In her bag the book is contraband: she is drug mule, jewel smuggler, diamond thief. It burns in her bag, hot coal inside, firelighters threatening to smoulder. She walks the high street to the car, passing people she knows, hiding the bag lest they ask why her bag is burning so, why smoke hunts from its clasp.

She could have ordered his book from the library, in keeping with their almost courtship, but she felt a violent need to possess it, as though by owning it the book would no longer exist. Would no longer exert a charge. But it fumes in the bag: it is afire, the book. The small receipt like kindling.

Inside the car, she takes the book from her bag. Brazen. In full daylight too. Anyone could see. Anyone could catch her holding it, looking at his picture on the inside back flap, his face in front of palm fronds and ash-tipped waves. Same face, same lines on the forehead, same creases at the eyes. Years in a foreign country and no change to the face. To think she's imagined him, after all those years, still waiting for her in Nuneaton, growing sallow and thin in his hotel room as he gave her another day, another week to arrive.

Put it away. Let it burn inside the bag. Do not read a word of it. Do not look for yourself in it. It is a travel book and you have not travelled. You cannot be inside the pages. You are not present there.

Gwen has travelled with him though. Over the years, she has enjoyed several imagined lives with Ray. When unable to sleep, she has plotted an alternative past, one beginning in Nuneaton and taking in more fragrant destinations. Another life, a dark-lit life, of travel and books and money, the scent of jasmine, frangipani, lotus blossom, coconut oil; the feel of fine sand between toes, the warmth of sea water. Notebooks with elasticated straps, cocktails heavy with rum, sex in humid rooms, naked sunbathing beside swimming pools, walking around the Colosseum, the Pyramids, the streets of New York City.

She looks at the book and it is sickening. To have her private dreams dashed that way, the book an account of all the places she has never seen, all the places they have not been together.

★

The house is afternoon quiet, cool in the kitchen, cool in the living room. Anneka is in her room studying; Drum and Nate are at the football. Quiet as Wednesday half-closing, when she comes home alone before heading to Daphne's for Secret Wine Wednesdays: Daphne's price for arranging Gwen's job at the library. But it is Saturday and there are no social calls to make, just the book to read. It eyes her from the kitchen table, dares her.

Kitchen or living room. Bedroom even. An hour or two before Drum comes back; a hundred pages, more if she skips. She makes tea and decides on the kitchen table, the formality of the hard-backed chairs better than the lounge of the sitting-room couch.

She opens the book, she flicks past a page of quotations, the title, *Frum*, the subtitle, *A Year With the Cargo Cultists*, then the dedication. To A. B. Could be anyone, A. B. Anyone but her though. Not her. Hoping for some oblique connection, a coded message. But no. To A. B. only. The whole book just for them. Relief and upset in four letters.

The opening chapter is titled 'Leaving'. She reads descriptions of the preparations to stay in a culture little more evolved than medieval peasantry. She reads of the labyrinthine process of booking his passage, the long negotiations with a man who will be his guide. There is nothing of Ray in these passages. It is just Raymond Porter. She has no idea who that man is. She doesn't recognize him in the pedantic and fusty prose.

Raymond Porter is at last boarding an aeroplane when the

phone rings. Only two people call, her brother or Daphne, and it is the middle of the day, so not her brother. She tents the book on the table; the crack in its spine.

'Hello, Daphne,' she says.

'I've tried,' Daphne says, 'But this bottle of wine simply won't drink itself.'

'I'm just in the middle of cooking,' Gwen says.

'Well stop all that, I need you to come help me drink this infernal Chablis.'

The book like a bird on the table. The flight about to be taken.

'Okay,' Gwen says. 'Twenty minutes?'

'Now, my dear,' she says. 'Otherwise it might just drink itself and then where will we be?'

Onto another bottle, most likely. Onto the gin, even worse.

'Fine,' she says. 'I'm on the way now. Just taking off my pinny.'

'I've told you before,' she says. 'It's an apron, not a pinny. Don't ever say pinny. It sounds like you're talking about your vagina.'

★

The bottle has already drunk half itself, and in the kitchen Daphne is talking about another murder in Yorkshire, another woman killed. The usual saving up of things. She likes to talk of murders, of atrocities, scandals and conspiracies. But there are never enough. Not enough for more than a half-hour, before talk of Carter, or Tommy or Natasha.

'Those poor girls,' Daphne says.

'Horrible,' Gwen says.

Daphne's blue trouser suit has a drop of wine at the cuff, her green scarf is skewed; she has been crying, or been at the wine earlier than usual. Her heart-shaped face, the thin application of make-up, the effortlessly styled hair, all unaffected.

'That's why you're drinking?' Gwen says. 'Because of the murders?'

'It could be Natasha dead in a ditch.'

'It's not though, is it? She's at horse riding, isn't she?'

'You know what I mean,' she says.

Daphne drinks and refreshes the glasses, drinks some more of her wine.

'Have you ever had an affair?' Daphne says. 'And be honest with me. You're a terrible liar. Don't think I don't know you hate my chocolate roulade.'

Gwen laughs. What to say to this. To admit anything with Ray would be to admit weakness, to admit her turned head, to admit she is sitting in Daphne's kitchen but her mind is in Vanuatu with a man not her husband.

'No,' Gwen says. 'No, I've always been faithful to Drum.'

'Are you sure, dear?' she says. 'Look me in the eye and tell me you've not. Tell me you're not having an affair right now.'

Gwen looks her in the eyes.

'I'm not having an affair,' she says.

Gwen looks down at the wine and something in the way the light hits the glass and the cock of Daphne's head, the alignment of them, speaks of accusation. Daphne is weighing Gwen's response for veracity; it's clear she's found Gwen guilty of something. And then it aligns, the glass and her face and the look, and it becomes as clear as the summer skies.

'Oh God,' Gwen says. 'You can't possibly think—'

'He's always liked you. Always said what a *sport* you are.'

'He's your husband, Daph –' and a cheat, a liar, a vain, self-satisfied bastard – 'I would never, never, do anything like that.'

Daphne's face collapses, shudders as she cries. Quick, quick, into Gwen's arms, the thinness of her, her bones through the polyester, the hoik and roll of her ribs and chest.

'I'm so stupid,' Daphne says. 'If he could see me now, like this, accusing you, the prick would laugh right in my face. I'm so sorry. So very sorry.'

The force of the word in the muggy kitchen, the wine sweat on the glasses. Two women close enough to smell their respective deodorants. The tears and the hidden face, the hair remaining still, lacquered perfectly, bouncing but not moving. Then Daphne up, as though suddenly inflated, back straight against the chair. Daphne takes a tissue from the metal box on the table, dabs at her eyes.

'I can always tell when he's at it,' she says. 'He thinks he's discreet, but he might as well have it written on his face in lipstick.'

She blows her nose, quietly.

'I hoped it was you,' she says. 'I did hope it was. I could rail at you. I could shout at you. I could forgive you. It would be okay if it were you. But I knew it wasn't you. I knew that really.'

At table, she is still, her back dead straight, taking small and consistent sips of wine.

'If I were betting, I'd say she was younger this time. Slip of a thing, most likely. A bit reticent in the bedroom, if you know what I mean. He always gets more amorous when there's some little slut around.'

The venom and then again the tears; again the head against Gwen's breast.

'The last time, he gave me the crabs,' she says. 'Once he gave me the crabs and he said it wasn't him, that I must have got it doing yoga or something. Accused me of having an affair.'

Gwen has heard this before, Daphne having told her several times of the crabs, the white lice itching her day and night. The doctor who looked at her like she was a whore or a bad wife, or both of those things at once.

Her tears are not slowing. A *there, there*, a shushing, same as she offers Nate, offers Annie. But nothing pure like that, no wish to take away the pain. Thinking of Ray, thinking she is as bad as Carter: supposing she could get away with it, believing herself undetectable. But having not done anything. Better to have done nothing, or the same as having done something?

'What are you going to do?' Gwen says.

Daphne looks up, somehow make-up still perfect, still no panda eyes, how expensive the eye make-up to leave no trace of tears. She smooths down her ruckled jacket.

'I'm going to have another drink,' she says. 'You?'

'I meant, what are you going to do about James?'

'Oh what is there to do, dear?' she says.

'You could take a lover,' Gwen says.

'I'm not *French*, dear,' she says. 'Besides, who am I going to snare looking like this?'

She finally removes the cork, pours herself a large glass and tops up Gwen's.

'Have you ever done that?' Daphne says. 'Taken a lover? Truthfully?'

'No,' Gwen says.

'You don't look sure about that.'

'I'm sure,' Gwen says.

'There's something,' she says. 'I can feel it. Something delectable you're just dying to tell me.'

They both laugh, so much laughter and so much booze and so much unsaid, evaded, quietly shared. Gwen imagines telling Daphne about the book, of Ray. How she would listen to it like a news item on the radio, ready to repeat the facts to someone later. Not for her that story, but something having to be given. Something offered up.

'I was almost unfaithful,' she says, 'just the once, before we were married.'

A door. A door and the sound of feet on stairs and the door opening. Not thought about in many years. Not thought about ever. Hello, Old Nick. Long time no see.

'Almost?' Daphne says. 'Please don't get my hopes up just to dash them.'

'He was an older man,' she says. 'A lot older.'

'How old?'

'In his sixties,' she says. 'Late sixties.'

Daphne splutters wine all over the counter, a grand spray of Chablis.

'And how old were you?'

'Twenty-one, twenty-two, something like that.'

'You slept with a man forty years older than you?'

Inside the small flat, the place immaculately clean, as though he knew she was coming. A sitting room with the gas fire glowing umber, books on the shelves, some she'd handled. Wordsworth on the armchair, a pencil keeping his place. Him fetching tea, her sitting on the sofa, him asking her something and her nodding, and then standing, both of them, and him taking her to his study, the small room a chaos of proofs and papers and scribbles and scraps. Into his bedroom, an electric heater already on, pyjamas on a chair, folded, tartan.

'I didn't sleep with him,' Gwen says. 'I thought I was going to. I thought that was what I wanted. He put his hands on me, on my waist, and the touch was . . . light. His hands were gentle and they were shaking, in excitement or age, I don't know. But he touched me and he moved to kiss me and we kissed and it was gentle and it was . . . light. And I kissed him back. And then I knew what I wanted. I wanted to say no. Not to run away, not to run away screaming, but just to say no. Calmly, gently. To say, this was nice, but I'm saying no. I wanted to prove I could do it. To be able to say no and mean it. So I said no.'

'And what did he do?' Daphne says, not looking at Gwen, looking well away, a story there, another memory not cared for, not recalled but dredged. A shallow-grave memory, just the brush from a boot, a dog's snout, from discovery.

'He kissed me on the cheek and said, "These things go better in books."'

How cruel that seeming now, and yet no sense of wrongdoing. To play on Nick's emotions, on Nick's sense of his own worth, the elation of challenging the physical world. And then to crush that. Snuff it out. A change of heart. Like a dare. Like a child's game.

Daphne looks up at her from the rim of her wine glass.

'Am I supposed to feel sorry for him?' Daphne says.

'I don't know,' Gwen says. Yes. No. Who knows.

'Because I don't,' Daphne says. 'Not one fucking bit.'

4

On the ball and off the ball, Chris Birch. Shirt untucked, stockings down, Chris Birch. His thighs – man thighs, Tommy Smith thighs, Asa Hartford thighs – Chris Birch.

The ball bounces against his thigh, Chris Birch. He controls the ball, long legs striding out from the centre of midfield, Chris Birch. The speed of turn, head alert, looking up, Chris Birch. A shimmy, a step-over, and accelerating past the defender, skin flawless, genuinely flawless, Chris Birch.

Planting foot and striking the ball, Chris Birch. The ball spinning past the prone keeper and into the sighing net, Chris Birch. He does not celebrate, does not acknowledge his teammates, Chris Birch. He jogs back to the centre circle and in his deep voice tells his teammates to keep going, to pretend it's still nil–nil, Chris Birch.

But it's not nil–nil, Chris Birch, it's six–nil and he has scored four of the goals, Chris Birch. The opposition know it, his teammates know it, he knows it: he is a player from another planet, Chris Birch.

He stands on the semi-circle, chalk marks on his boots, the best money can buy, the boots, the three white stripes, the same boots Asa Hartford wears, Chris Birch. He steals the ball from a midfielder and sprints off, looks up, weighs his decision, passes the ball wide right, Chris Birch. Wide right, Chris Birch. To you.

You run at the left-back, beat him, and look up, looking only for him, Chris Birch. You should shoot, but you square it to him, and he scores a goal, Chris Birch.

He does not celebrate, Chris Birch. He just stands still and points at you, his finger outstretched, Chris Birch. You, he is saying, you, no one else, but you, that's what he's saying, Chris Birch.

He jogs back to the centre circle and you do the same, having learned how to jog back to the centre circle from him, Chris Birch.

Later, he passes to you again, Chris Birch. At the death knell of the game, he passes the ball to you and you score and you do not wheel away in celebration, the way you would once have done, but you stand your ground and point at him, and he nods and the two of you jog back to the centre circle almost in step, Chris Birch.

The whistle blows and the opponents are all heading towards him, to shake his hand, Chris Birch. They're all thinking they'll be able to say they played against him before he was famous, before he played for England, Chris Birch. You shake the hands of the opposition and they do not look at you the way they look at Chris Birch. The way you look at Chris Birch. And then he is gone, into the changing room, Chris Birch.

In a book of football stories you read most nights, there's a story about two footballers, Archie and Glenn: brilliant when they play together; terrible if the other's not on the field. They have a kind of telepathic connection, and sometimes you think it's the same with you and Chris Birch: that he's the player he is because you're on the field with him. In the story, Archie gets injured and is forced to retire and on the same day Glenn retires too.

'People always ask Glenn why he retired,' the story ends, 'and he just tells them it wasn't the same without Archie. People wonder what might have been. The heights they could both have reached. But Glenn knows. They both do.'

*

It is a returning, the moments after a game: a settling of the blood. All outcomes now achieved, the facts established. A league position set in stone, a points tally unarguable. Nate is different off the pitch, the world is different off the pitch. It is more languid; there is less at stake. There is Chris Birch in the shower; there is hair on Chris Birch in all the adult places.

'No scout today?' Nate says, pushing the button for the shower, the cold needlepoint spray on his body.

'Not as I could see,' Chris Birch says. 'Maybe next week, Bobby.'

They call him Bobby, after Bobby Moore. Sometimes Dazzler, sometimes Daz. Only an accident him playing with the under-fourteens, playing with Chris Birch: a player dropping out late last season and Nate at the playing fields having a kick-around and only him tall enough, strong enough, good enough to play with the team, and no one afterwards caring he was a year or two junior.

Chris Birch finishes his shower, wraps a towel around himself. The game a waste now, a waste if no one sees Nate and Chris Birch play together. A scout might come for Chris Birch, but they'd also see something in Nate – not as obvious, somewhat raw, but something – and enquire afterwards about him. They would come for Chris Birch but they'd take Nate along too.

On the way out of the Portakabin, Nate sees his team's manager talking to Chris Birch's father and a man Nate doesn't recognize. Chris Birch is just ahead of Nate, and the manager calls Chris over, and the man Nate doesn't know puts his hand on Chris's shoulder. They look excited, all save Chris Birch who looks at the laces in his trainers. Nate walks past them. He hears the word City. He hears the word scout. He hears the word trial. Chris Birch nods as if this is to be expected. Chris Birch meets Nate's eye, but he does not beckon Nate over, does not introduce him to the scout. Nate slows, but no one calls his name.

In the car park, his father is looking at his watch.

'Come on,' his father says. 'Time's ticking.'

Nate says nothing, just gets into the car.

'You scored a goal,' his father says as he starts the car. 'I saw it.'

'I could have scored a hat-trick, it wouldn't have mattered,' Nate says. 'The scout didn't show again.'

To say it might make it true. Make it true.

His father looks at him, no sympathy, a placating face, condescendingly his father's.

'I expect they want to see that Chris Birch against better opposition than them lot,' his father says.

5

Rumour is that his parents committed suicide; rumour is that they were found in a Volvo by the lake at Rudyard. Rumour is that they didn't leave a note, just their house and only son behind. Rumours are that their son was once a talented artist, a talented musician, a talented scientist, a talented fly-half; rumour is that now he's alarmingly obese, practically welded to a long leather couch. Rumour is there was a party the day after his parents' funeral; rumour is that the party's never stopped. Rumour is that he listens to Abba's 'Fernando' all day long; rumour is that Fernando's front door is always open: all you need is the address.

It has taken Lissa a month to get the address; a mission undertaken solo and without Anneka's knowledge. Lissa will not say who gave it to her; will not say what she did to get hold of it: three times Anneka has asked, and three times she has been denied.

'I got the address,' Lissa said the last time. 'What does it matter *how* I got it?'

Anneka agreed. What *does* it matter? But Anneka thinks it does matter. Secrets matter. A refusal to share matters. Not knowing matters. Not knowing of what Lissa is capable matters. The things she's imagined her doing – blow jobs, tit wanks, shitting on a glass table with a man beneath it – matter. The acts Lissa has performed just to find the location of a party.

What does it matter how, now they are in a minicab, the windows wound down on the dark fields and shedding trees, the driver's eye in the rear-view trying to look beyond the slashes in Lissa's shirt to the skin where straps and cups should be.

'You're such a stiff,' Lissa said as they were getting ready in her bedroom. 'You're so straight.'

'Just because I want to wear a bra?' Anneka said. 'Just because I don't want everyone looking at my tits?'

'It's just a fucking bra, Neka,' Lissa said. 'Don't be so uptight.'

New words these: Stiff and Straight and Uptight replacing Boring and Immature and Stupid as the most irredeemable of sins. On their first day of sixth-form college the head of year told the assembled students they were not yet sixth-formers, just fifth-years who'd had a holiday; but it wasn't true of Lissa. Her summer had been taken in study of what to wear, what to say, the best way to blend in and stand out. It was like having two friends at once; one just met; the other close as blood and bone. Melissa the girl she has confided in these last four years; Lissa now, in her slashed white shirt, ripped jeans, leather jacket and boots, lighting another cigarette.

'You two off to a fancy dress party?' the taximan says. They both ignore him, Lissa studiously; Anneka as though she can't hear him over the sound of the wind and engine.

In the taxi, Anneka considers all the possible deaths, all the possible indignities, the night could yet bring. Murdered by the taximan. Dumped in Rudyard Lake. Sold into the white slave trade. Enforced prostitution; a drug overdose in a Manchester squat. Abducted, battered and left for dead, no one ever to know. Where were they going? When will girls learn? When will you learn, Annie? When will you understand I only have your safety at heart?

The trouble she is courting, the sanction if she is caught, and for what? For Lissa? Yes, perhaps for her. To keep pace with her, not to lose her. But for herself too, for the new iteration of her. Neka at college. Introduced as Neka, even the tutors calling her Neka. Neka looking forward to the party as Anneka hopes they never find the address. Neka wanting to know if the rumours are true as Anneka prays for quiet retreat back to Lissa's house, uncaught and yet still with the thrill of transgression.

The taxi pulls up outside a wall and a gate, nothing either side but field. No sound of music, no sense of habitation, no obvious structure even.

'Here you are,' the driver says. 'You're sure you've got the right address?'

'Yes,' Lissa says.

Lissa hands over the fare and the driver juggles with the money, touching her hand, her wrist, eyes on her shirt, coins spilling in his lap. A ten-pence piece lands in the footwell, dull against the shine of Lissa's boots.

'It won't pick up itself,' the driver says. A routine of some years' standing, a tip at the end of the ride. Nipples seen; cleavage viewed.

'That it won't,' Lissa says and gets out of the car.

Anneka wants to pick up the coin, make nice, make excuses; they might need him to pick them up, might need to rely on him for an alibi or some such. It is the first taxi she has taken; he is the first taximan she has met. He looks like all the things her father has said about taximen. The way they take advantage, the way they are not to be trusted, driving around all day, stuck in their own thoughts. An unhealthy profession, a lonely trade. Does bad things to people.

It is a coin, just a coin, nothing more. She picks it up and hands it to him. He does not offer any kind of thanks, just flicks it into the ashtray with the other change.

She gets out of the car, heads towards Lissa. She walks but wants to turn, to check the taximan has not got out of the car, is not approaching them with bat or brick or spanner. There is a murderer at loose. Somewhere up north. Perhaps he has come south to kill again.

The taximan sounds his horn, even Lissa jumps.

'Oi,' the taximan shouts through his wound-down window. 'Try not to get raped, you jailbait slags.'

And then gone, fan-belt whine into the dark, and the two of them there, alone in the silence, not even a house to walk towards.

Lissa takes a long drag on her cigarette, a true smoker already, another thing studied over the holidays. In the late light, she looks wintry; as though dressed for sleet. Anneka is wearing Lissa's clothes, but on her they feel ill-considered, underinformed. Lissa knows what her clothes actually say; Anneka just mimes the same words.

'You're sure about this?' Anneka says.

'It's the right house,' Lissa says.

'That's not what I meant.'

'Go home if you want,' Lissa says. 'But I'm not going anywhere.'

'I can't even see a house.'

'It's just over there,' she says, looking up the hill, past bushes and hedges.

'Just stay close to me, okay?' Anneka says. 'Don't go running off and leaving me.'

'I won't, Neka,' she says. 'Promise.'

They walk the scrub path up the incline, too riven with thought and counter-thought to talk. Will they both laugh when they arrive at nothing? Will Lissa be furious at the busted transaction? They walk and Anneka wants to hold Lissa's hand, Hansel-and-Gretel-like, but Lissa is already striding up the hill, hair wildly backcombed and ill-tempered.

Anneka feels dragged in her wake, the sensible one brought along for support and ballast, the one to put the pieces together on the way home; but there is nothing sensible about any of this. Sensible would have been to stay home; sensible not to risk it; sensible to say, no Lissa, if my dad finds out . . .

'See?' Lissa says. 'Look, told you!'

Just over the brow of the hill, a house, but not the kind expected; Anneka having imagined something forbidding, old-fashioned, a manse or twisted farm building. Instead a building that looks gusted from one of the luxury estates over the other side of town. It is an awkward wedge shape, its roof peaked at a reflex angle, large windows, a vast extension that does not quite match the rest of the property. It looks placid, sleepy almost, but as she nears, Anneka sees its scratches and nicks, the welts it has accumulated.

Windows are splintered, curtained or boarded; the panelling is peeling, verdigrised, filth-lashed. There are cars and bicycles abandoned outside, people smoking on a roof terrace whose wooden surround has been broken and breached in several places. There are roof tiles missing, the guttering has become unmoored and rusty stains stripe the stucco extension like mascara tears. The kind of house you see on the television: the scene of a murder; a cult's residence after the poisoned punch has been served.

By a clutch of motorcycles, they stop, watching the halfway-open front door. They can hear music, they can see disco lights bounce against the sacking draped over the picture window, they can see ripped wallpaper etched with graffiti in the hallway; a picture of a seascape askew, a knife slash running diagonally across it.

Lissa lights another cigarette, passes Anneka the box of Embassy. Anneka takes one and lights it, blows out the match, and then it comes, a warm flood of sensation, down from the shoulders, fairy-lighting her back, settling in the sacrum. Something Lissa described: a feeling she had the first time she'd ridden the bus to Manchester alone. Unencumbered freedom, a sense that the outside world was connected, was cheering her on, that all the traffic lights were saying go, go, go, that all the lampposts were exclamation marks.

Feeling it now, having felt it before, once before, that weightlessness of liberation; the time Anneka swam away from her father at the seaside, refusing to be shadowed by him, kicking away from his grasping, protectorate hands.

A bus. The sea. The howl of that, the thunder of that. What did it matter *how*.

'Shall we, Lissa?' Neka says.

6

On the far side of the cowsheds, unsighted from the farmhouse, a two-berth caravan occupies the former paddock. A relic, the caravan, late-fifties design: once white with aquamarine trim; now dirt-drifted, its windows the colour of dust. For years forbidden territory; the children told not to approach, to leave well alone.

On weekends and in the holidays, Nate sneaks to the caravan and imagines himself a woodsman, whittling things from tree bark and bits of lumber, listening to a transistor radio. His space. His dominion. He can defend it if he wants. He has three knives. Were a burglar to come, a prospective squatter, he'd gut them like a fish, a skill he's developed down on the brook, his quarry taken home, his father impressed at his deft work.

Sometimes Anneka comes into his bedroom and babies him, cuddles him like he's a toddler; sometimes she ignores him for days. At school he has his pals, he has his football; at home he has the caravan. No one asks him where he goes. No one asks what he's up to. His parents are in the living room and he should be in his room, but instead he is at the caravan, looking for possible assailants.

He thinks about cutting the Achilles tendon on Chris Birch's right ankle. He thinks about Chris Birch in pain. He thinks about Chris Birch telling him to stop. He thinks about Chris Birch in an England shirt. He thinks about Chris Birch and has to leave the caravan.

With three knives in his backpack, he walks down to the main road. It is dead dark and it takes time for his eyes to adjust. He stops at the bottom of the track and takes the knives from the bag.

Across the road is a huge oak tree, heavily girthed. He throws the first knife and it falls to the ground yards from the tree trunk. He throws the next knife harder, but it flies past the tree.

An hour later, he is still throwing the knives across the carriageway, trying to get one to stick in the trunk. He thinks of Chris Birch when one finally goes in. The satisfaction of that, the knifepoint deep in the bark.

7

Though her accent hasn't changed since the move north, she uses the same slang as her adopted home: butty, slat, ay up, blart. A small step to integration. Girls and boys impersonate her sometimes, good-natured mainly, good-natured because Lissa is her friend and won't take that kind of shit. A science teacher used to speak to her in cockney rhyming slang, the whole class laughing; Anneka laughing along to prove she could see the funny side. When 'Come up and See Me' made Number One, the PE teacher called Anneka *Cockney Rebel* for a whole year.

When she told Tommy some of this, about the gentle ribbing, he shifted on his chair in the hide where they sometimes still met.

'People always look for something to pick upon,' he said. 'You're lucky it's just an accent.'

No one had told her that Tommy boarded, that he was only home one weekend in three, that the promise of 'all the fun they would have together' from her father would be condensed into brief meetings in the hide, lunches at the Carters', the odd day during the holidays. They walked the pathways, they fished hopelessly in the brook, they made up games their siblings could not understand. They were always in the throes of farewell or welcome, bridged by a solemn exchange of I miss you and I'll write, though neither ever did. Each meeting was like collecting a picture postcard: the excitement of the image and such a small space for messages.

He changed, inevitably. His accent had been modified, his deportment corrected, his moods altered. He could be priggish; patronizing in all new ways. Once she was telling him about the technicalities of the Viking 1 launch and he'd stopped her mid-train.

'Where did you learn all of this? I mean, do you even understand it?' he'd said.

'Of course I do, you arsehole,' she'd replied.

But these disagreements were rare; mostly he wanted to regress, fall back into old routines. She did not introduce him to Lissa. She did not talk of friends, and neither did he until he turned fourteen or so, a distraction, she thought, from looking at her breasts.

Nothing of that sort, not since the Secret Touching Game as children. Not quite brotherly, but not quite not. Lissa told her she should fuck him; get it out of the way with someone she trusted, and the thought appalled. Could not imagine him undressing; could not imagine her undressed before him. She wishes now, perhaps, she'd done exactly that: she'd be less shaky, less apprehensive, of the man she's sitting with, if she'd done this all before.

The man has a hand on her thigh, an accent the same as hers, a name she can't quite remember. He is a student from London and is staying with a friend who has sloped off with Lissa to neck. Neka looks around the room to locate her, finds her in the darkest corner of the room. Relief at that, and then to the right of them, she sees a man who looks just like Tommy.

'Everything all right?' the man with the hand on her thigh says.

'Yes,' she says.

She watches the man who looks like Tommy and she is sure it's not Tommy. She hasn't seen him for a few months, but it's not Tommy. Too tall, and he would never be seen in T-shirt and ripped jeans. The not-Tommy is smoking a large joint, laughing. Not the way Tommy laughs. Too loud. She has never seen Tommy amongst men. But even so, not him.

'Thought I saw someone I know, that's all,' she says.

There are cigarette burns in the sofa's arms, her fingers in them like she's holding a bowling ball, the airy itch of the foam, the wire struts cold on her fingertips. A drink in the other hand, the man's hand on her thigh.

'Do you miss it?' he says. 'Home, I mean.'

It takes her a beat to follow the conversation: accents, accent, the South and home.

'Sometimes,' she says. 'Less and less these days.'

He takes a sip of his drink. Name forgotten. Remembered. Sam. Friend of the red-headed man kissing Lissa in the darkest corner of the dining room.

'I couldn't live anywhere else,' Sam says.

'You think that,' she says, 'and then you move and you wonder what all the fuss was about. Dirty streets. Bomb threats. Strikes. I don't miss any of that.'

Word for word her father. Words like sick in her mouth, washed down with vodka, the vodka not making her appreciably more drunk, keeping her just the right side of reckless.

'But it's *life*,' Sam says. 'It's a cauldron, a melting pot, a fiesta and a wake. It's everything, the city. It *is* life.'

'There's more than enough life here,' she says.

And she kisses him, and it is wild, it is the taking of the bus alone; it is the swimming in the sea. His tongue is in her mouth, her tongue is in his, the curiousness of two open mouths pressed together. A hand straight on her breast, no lead up, a straight grab and instinct saying move the hand, but not moving the hand. Knowing Sam will say let's see the garden lights, let's go find a room.

He stops the kiss, keeps his hand on the breast.

'Shall we go upstairs?' he says.

The bus-sea thunder. The disco lights saying go, go, go. His hand in her hand, dragging her up from the sofa and her laughing. Walking through the rubble of the dining room, the upended table and the ripped carpets. Walking through, the man who is not Tommy looking at her. The man who is not Tommy staring at her as she crosses the room. The man who is not Tommy putting a foot towards her, then stopping, then turning away.

'You know him?' he says.

'No,' she says. 'I don't think so.'

'His name's Tommy. Posh lad comes here every Friday to buy dope from Tolly. Sells it on to his boarding-school mates. Arrogant prick.'

'Never met him before,' she says. 'I think he might be a friend of Lissa's though.'

Tommy looks at her and she looks to the floor. She takes Sam's hand and leaves the room, Tommy's eyes following her, two hot coals on her back.

8

From outside the side entrance he can hear the argument, the volume of their voices, the television getting louder, Natasha presumably trying to hear her programme over her parents' fighting. It has the desired effect, the row stopping, replaced by the distorted sound of a television turned up to its maximum. Natasha turns the volume down as Drum knocks on the door. He waits, Daphne or Carter. Natasha, possibly. He knocks again, louder now. He could let himself in; he has been invited after all. But he waits until Carter opens the door, his eyes bloodshot and looking unsure as to why Drum is there, then remembering.

'Welcome to the madhouse,' he says. 'Inmates always gladly received.'

The evening is warm enough to sit out, but Carter shows Drum into his study rather than out onto the veranda. End of summer, another hot one, and into autumnal retreat already, whisky to drink now rather than beer or wine.

'We haven't done this in a while, have we?' Carter says.

'Not for a couple of weeks, no,' Drum says.

'Feels like longer than that.'

Carter hands him a tumbler of Scotch, Drum sits on the Chesterfield, but Carter remains standing.

'*Salud*,' he says. 'Good health and happiness!'

Carter takes out his cigarettes and lights one. Soon they will be forty. Soon their children will leave home. Soon they will be old. Carter does not look old. He is cast in amber; he is stalled at his early thirties. There is no grey in his hair, no hair in his nose.

'How are you?' Drum says.

'I'm well,' he says. 'As well as can be expected in this house. If it's not Daphne it's Natasha. And if it's not Natasha it's Tom back from school, acting the fucking idiot.'

He downs his Scotch and pours another few fingers.

'How about you?'

'Annie's staying over at a friend's house tonight.'

'You let her?'

'She's sixteen, that's what Gwen says.'

'What I was doing at sixteen,' Carter says. 'It doesn't bear thinking about.'

He smiles that smile, he sits down on the Chesterfield opposite Drum, shakes his head.

'I'm just joking with you, Drum,' he says.

Carter is silent for a time, stubs out his cigarette in the ashtray. He leans in to Drum, uses the lowest of his voices.

'You're okay?'

'Yes,' Drum says. Though the twist in his gut says otherwise, the sense that his body is being overworked, dealing with too many things at the same time.

'Good,' Carter says. 'Because I'm not. Or at least that's what Daphne says. Says I'm not right in the head. That I'm acting strange.'

Carter laughs.

'Daphne saying *I'm* acting strange. Would you credit that?'

He has been acting strange, he has been taking something, can tell when he's been taking it. Something prescribed or perhaps not. Making him manic. Making him hectic.

'Does she know?'

'About Eileen? No, of course not.'

'You're sure?'

Carter drains his drink, Carter pours another. How many drinks, how many had already.

'It's not that,' he says. 'She's not that perceptive.'

Carter looks at Drum, his blue eyes bloodshot. He crushes out his cigarette.

'I punched Tom last night,' Carter says. 'Not a slap, a proper punch. The little bastard was giving me lip about something, can't even remember what. And I just thought, that's enough. I've had it with you. And wallop. Landed him one on the chin.'

Drum must look startled. Drum must look appalled. Drum must say nothing. Drum looks at his friend and does not quite recognise this man, the look upon his face: anger, spite and vengeance.

'It felt good, Drum. The way he looked up at me. A new kind of respect. Fear, yes, but respect too. I apologized of course, blamed work, blamed stress. Tommy said he understood. And I think he did. One day he's going to come for me, you know? I know that. It's healthy. You always want a shot at the king, right?'

Sometimes Drum wanted to punch Carter. To knock some sense into him. No chance of that. No hope of that ever occurring.

'I shouldn't have done it,' Carter says. 'But I'm glad I did. I'm so *glad* I did.'

9

Even through the weight of boot, Neka can feel the deep pile of the carpet; its giving luxury after the hard stomp of the landing's floorboards. It is a different kind of room than the ones she's frantically scanned in search of Lissa, one of both utility and comfort: a fridge and small electric oven set against a flock-wallpapered wall; a series of unvandalized paintings above them; a large flickering television, either side of it tall speakers playing Abba's 'Fernando'. On the couch, someone is lying, difficult to tell who, in the television dark.

'Lissa,' she says. 'Is that you?'

Like she's playing hide and seek. A childhood game in a stranger's house. Lissa there one moment, gone the next. Last seen wearing. Last seen with a red-headed man. Coming ready or not.

'Tolly's downstairs,' a man's voice says. 'Second on the left.'

It's a voice as warm as the room, a depth to the voice, a richness, plump as pillow.

'I'm looking for my friend,' she says.

The man sits up, face lit in flickering blue and grey. He wears a kind of smock that makes it hard to see where he ends and the sofa begins. Creases of fat pucker at his neck, jowls flap, cheeks shine bloated and smooth. It is an attractive face; attractive because of the heaviness. It feels to Neka like it is his correct face, his natural face. Not like Sam, kinder than Sam. Sam with the hands and the yesses to her nos.

'It's just me here,' he says. 'Maybe I'm your friend?'

'No,' she says. 'We've not met before.'

'We've not met?' he says.

'No,' she says. 'I'm sorry—'

'You're sorry we haven't met?' he says.

His laugh is surprising light, childlike. The turntable clacks back its arm and restarts 'Fernando'. Deep inside the rumours now. At their heart. And relaxing in the warm room, feeling everything suddenly clearing, vacating. An urgent need to urinate, something unpleasant in her guts to expunge, Sam to wash away.

'No,' she says, 'I'm sorry, I just really need the toilet.'

The light laugh and something thrown at her feet: a single key on a Ferrari key fob.

'Use mine,' he says. 'That door there.'

He points to the right of the television and there is an unnoticed door, one summoned perhaps just for her benefit.

'Thank you,' she says.

She unlocks the door and walks into a large bathroom. A fragranced candle burns on the cistern, casting purple shade over a jacuzzi-style bath the shape of an oyster shell; his-and-hers wash-hand basins; a wall of framed family photographs beside a spotless rectangular mirror. She looks at herself in the glass and feels herself pleat inside, the back of her mouth watering like it's raining there. She vomits into the sink, the female one with the carefully arranged creams and products surrounding it.

Her sick is pink from vodka and black; it looks acid, like it could burn through the porcelain. She runs the tap, the pink scattering as though panicked, and vomits again. It feels like she could expel everything; her pelvis, her liver, her kidneys. Turn herself inside out. Vomit until she's dead on the floor; her father later to identify her exsanguinated body, weep over her disobedience, grab her lifeless shoulders and shake her, ask her how she could be so stupid.

As the heaves subside, she catches a glimpse of herself in the mirror. She looks like the stucco of the extension, black lines down her white cheeks. There is a bottle of baby lotion and cotton-wool pads in a half-open porcelain jar. She hesitates to use them; a desecration to help herself to a dead woman's toiletries. Her father's voice is so loud he might as well be sitting on the toilet. I raised you better than this. Don't even think of it. Don't you dare.

The cotton pad is cool on the skin; the smell of baby lotion reminding her of when her brother was little. Flooding back. The house down south, the room that so hated her.

Clean up now, Neka. Find Lissa, Neka. Go home, Neka. Back to Lissa's. Avoid the hangman's noose.

She puts the blackened cotton pads in her back pocket, tries to remember the exact placement of the porcelain jar; approximates it, hopes it atonement enough. Disappointed in you, Anneka. I thought you had more sense. She pats her face dry with a mono-gramed towel. She does not leave black marks on the fabric, a relief that. The taps are gold, she notices. Gleaming gold.

'Feeling better?' Fernando says as she opens the door, locking it behind her.

'Yes,' she says. 'Must have been something I ate.'

He laughs, his body in the smock shuddering. Fifes play through the speakers, another spin of 'Fernando'. On the television a man talks to a panel of guests. She approaches the sofa and offers him the keys.

'Thank you,' she says.

'You're going?' he says.

'I need to find my friend.'

'What if she's looking for you too?' he says. 'You might never find her if you keep moving.'

The kind of thing her father might say. Be on the safe side. Don't leave it to chance. Think things through. Don't go into a darkened room with a man. Don't put your hand there. Don't move your hand. Do not open your legs.

'Stay, have a drink,' he says. 'There's room on the sofa, or you can pull up a chair. There's bottles in the crate.'

There are drums, Fernando. Something to the air, Fernando.

There has been badness, Fernando. Something has been surmounted, Fernando.

He looks up at her and there is no pleading, no interest in his face. She can say no and he will say goodbye and she will never see him again. She picks up a bottle of rum from the crate and drags over a highbacked chair.

'Here,' she says, passing him the bottle, sitting down on the chair.

He drinks from the bottle, long unguilty swigs, wipes his hairless mouth with the sleeve of his smock.

'I don't let just anyone into my bathroom,' he says. 'You should feel honoured.'

'It was kind of you,' she says.

'Did you get what you came for?' he says. 'Have you had fun?'

He does not look at her, but she feels that he sees her; another young girl come here and for what? For drugs. For sex. For release. For the trading and the allowance. Yes, you can put fingers there. No, not there. You can do this and no more. I will not do that. Yes I will do that.

'I don't know,' she says. 'I think so.'

'Well that's good,' he says. 'That's the most important thing.'

She listens to 'Fernando'; she watches the muted chat show. He passes her the rum and she shakes her head, and he goes back to drinking it.

'You can ask, if you like,' he says, still watching the television. 'I don't mind you asking.'

He has long lank hair, threads of premature grey amongst the chestnut straggle. Old and young at the same time.

'I know you have questions,' he says. 'You would've left if you didn't want to ask me something.'

He turns to her.

'What did you hear about me?' he says, 'Did you hear that my parents were murdered?'

Impossible to know if confession, or mystery, or bait. A seduction technique perhaps, the girl consumed not by lust but by curiosity. What would Neka do to find out the truth? What would Lissa do? Somewhere a penis beneath the fat; somewhere perhaps growing hard.

'No,' she says. 'That's not what I heard. Why, were they murdered?'

He laughs, deeper, more masculine, a dimmer switch turned down on a chandelier.

'No,' he says. 'Not at all. I just wondered if that's what you'd heard. Most people say they heard old ma and pa were murdered. The stories I've heard! That they were shot, poisoned, stabbed, cut up with axes, raped to death . . . my poor parents have been murdered more than anyone in history, I think.'

He shifts up in the sofa, cradling the bottle, wears an expression of deep, offended glee. He holds up the bottle in triumph.

'You heard suicide!' he says. 'I bet that's it. Yes, I can tell. Where were they found? Rudyard or Stapeley?'

He looks excited by the development, brow knitting, making further creases in his face.

'I heard Rudyard,' she says.

'Brilliant!' he says. 'That one's my absolute favourite. Hand in hand in a Volvo, right? Have to laugh at that. My dad wouldn't be seen dead in a Volvo.'

He takes a long pull on the bottle.

'And luckily for him he wasn't.'

Struggling, he gets himself up from the sofa, opens the fridge and takes out a bowl of roasted chicken, shuffles back to the sofa. He offers her a leg but Neka shakes her head. She should make her excuses and leave. But one question. Just one. No way to resist it.

'So, how did they die?' she says. 'Really?'

'Does it matter?' he says. 'Really does it matter in the end? They're dead, I'm not. That's really all that matters.'

He rips the flesh from the chicken, the whole bone stripped in a matter of seconds. 'Fernando' reaches it chorus again.

'I should go,' she says.

'You keep saying that,' he says. 'But I don't see you going.'

He tears the flesh from another chicken leg, continues with his mouthful of fowl.

'Because you *need* to know, don't you?' he says. 'You're the same as everyone else. Desperate to know *why*. Because there always needs to be a reason, doesn't there? But what if there isn't? What if the why isn't important, only the asking of the question? Better to be asked about than explained, don't you think? Better to be legend than case study.'

'So you're a legend now?' she says.

'I *am* a legend,' he says, putting down his chicken leg and wiping his hand on the sofa. 'The thing is, I won't remember this conversation tomorrow. By the time you walk out that door, I'll have forgotten all about you. For all I know this is the tenth time we've met, the hundredth. But *you* won't forget. You won't *ever* forget. In twenty, thirty years, you'll still remember me. Every time you hear "Fernando" you'll think of me. When you see chicken legs, you'll think of me. Everyone who comes here, not one of them will ever forget me.'

He looks so young as he says this, so childlike; the way she looks when she argues with her parents, the sense of standing too close to her infant self.

'And that's why?' she says. 'That's the reason for all this? A kind of immortality?'

She thinks of the sperm that landed on her stomach, the teem of life from Sam's circumcised penis. The hundreds of potential lives in those waxy puddles.

Fernando takes more rum, wipes his hand on the sofa again. He shrugs, adulthood returning, the veneer of it.

'Perhaps,' he says. 'It's just a theory. There are several. Hundreds most likely . . .'

She takes the bottle from his hand, drinks some and does not cough, the rum slides down and it is warming. She likes the way she does this; does it again, to impress, to create her own legend.

'I have a theory,' she says.

He takes back the bottle, puts the bowl of chicken on the floor. She does not know what her theory is, it is not yet formed, but she can feel it like the beginnings of a headache.

'Well, do share with the class, then, my little punk princess,' he says. 'Enlighten us all!'

She moves from the chair to the couch, folds herself into his bulk, puts an arm around his shoulder. It does not surprise him; he accommodates her but nothing more, there is no stirring from his crotch, his hands do not move towards her. She can smell chicken grease and over-proof rum and she is close to his ear, whispering.

'Your parents were strict, weren't they?' she says. 'They kept everything just so, including you. They had such plans for you, didn't they? And now they're gone, you're doing everything they disallowed. You trash their house, you sit here alone, and it's punishment for them, isn't it? It's retribution for all the things they expected of you.'

She feels his whole body shake, at first she thinks tears, but no, just the lighter laugh, the child laugh. He puts his fleshy fingers on her face, holds her there, kisses her on the forehead.

'Oh that's priceless,' he says. 'Such wisdom in one so young and in such bad make-up.'

He gets up from the couch, quicker this time, less lumbering. It's hard to say if he is spooked or genuinely amused.

'Do tell people that, please do. It's wonderful. So very astute. So very plausible. Tell the world! With my blessing tell the world! It's the best theory I've heard, the very best yet!'

He drains a third of the rum, wipes his face, still laughing, his smock like angry cats.

'It's such a perfectly neat theory,' he says. 'What ever made you think of it?'

The record player begins to spin 'Fernando' again. They both hear distant drummers.

'Because it's what I would do,' she says. 'It's exactly what I want to do.'

IO

In bed they have sex. They feel further apart from each other as they do, Gwen thinks, though she intended for it to do the opposite. When he did what she likes him to do, she itched her stomach, her arms. He was impatient and she had to slow him, tell him gently, gently. She didn't know what was on his mind, but she knew the book was distracting her. He is impatient inside of her now. He comes and quickly rolls off her body. At that moment, she misses cigarettes, the way smoking one shifts the atmosphere from mutual desire to selfish whim.

They lie in silence for some time. She goes to the bathroom, comes back, cuddles up to Drum.

'What did Carter want?' she says.

'I don't know,' he says. 'Absolution. Something like that.'

'Is he having an affair?' she says. 'Daph thinks he's having an affair.'

'I don't know,' he says. 'He doesn't talk to me about that stuff any more.'

'Was that good?' she says.

'What?' he says.

'You know,' she says.

'Yes,' he says. 'It's always good.'

'I thought you were a bit distracted.'

'No,' he says. 'Just a bit surprised, that's all.'

He smiles and he looks far enough away to join Raymond Porter on his island of curiosities.

'I hope she's okay,' he says.

'Who?'

'Annie.'

'She'll be fine.' Gwen says.

'Melissa's mother's a strange one. Kept washing the same dish. Over and over, washing the same dish.'

He rolls over towards her.

'I should have called her,' he says. 'I should have checked everything was all okay.'

'She's sixteen,' Gwen says. 'She'll be fine.'

'I know she will,' he says.

He kisses her on the cheek.

'You mind if I read?' Gwen says.

'No,' he says. 'Go ahead.'

She turns on the bedside lamp. She looks at the book. She's thought more about the book than her absent child. Thought more about Vanuatu than a place a few miles up the road. She's seduced her husband and thought of the book and not her child. She says a small prayer to the huckster God and ghost of Old Nick, prays for her mortal soul.

'Don't stay up too long,' Drum says.

II

What does it matter how. What does it matter how we get home, so long as we get home. What does it matter if Sam is drunk. What does it matter if Sam is stoned. What does it matter he forgets to turn on the headlamps. What does it matter he doesn't know where to go. What does it matter Lissa has her head out of the car window. What does it matter if this is Sam's car. What does it matter if they are still drinking vodka. What does it matter that Lissa took an hour to find. What does it matter if she is on the pill or not. What does it matter how fast they are going. What does it matter that the sun will soon be rising. What does it matter that the car finds Lissa's house. What does it matter that Sam hoots the horn as they leave. What does it matter how they get inside. What does it matter Lissa's mother is where they left her. What does it matter they are laughing and shushing as they go upstairs. What does it matter if they stay up all night. What does it matter if they sleep. What does it matter now. What does it matter now it's all done and cannot be taken back.

Just Pete and Drum in the cowsheds, quiet when just the two of
them; the most harmonious of working situations: Drum in sole
charge. Sundays and Pete is always slightly hungover, green-gilled
and permanently attached to a flask of tea.

'You go feed the calves,' Drum says. 'I'll finish up here.'

Drum herds out the cows, smoothly done, a tide of black and
white into the fields, the cows' slow mooch. Another warm
morning, the sun coming up and the shadows small, and he walks
back towards the house, all jobs done quickly and early, hours
before picking up Annie from Melissa's.

He wonders what it is they have talked about; what secrets they
have shared. How it must be to be so young and have the whole
world to dissect. He hopes she has had fun. He hopes she has a
true friend.

At the gate, Tommy is waiting for him, sweating in a tracksuit,
hair matted, sticky underneath a Bjorn Borg headband.

'Been running?' Drum says.

Tommy doesn't say anything, almost as if he hasn't even noticed
Drum standing there. The vacancy of these kids. The fact you have
to ask them three times to do the simplest thing.

'Yes,' Tommy says. 'Running, yes. Clears my mind.'

A pretty clear mind in general, Drum always thought. An absent
sort of kid, a nothingness about him, a sponge. Destined for great-
ness then, destined for some sort of power. The kind who worked
the offices at Ford's, sports jacketed, suspicious of the shop floor.

'Uncle Drummond,' he says, though he has not called him that
for years. It is a softening, a reaching out of hands. Drum cannot

remember the last time they spent any time alone together. Perhaps they have never been alone together. He doesn't much like the experience: the pause, the heavy breath before he doesn't quite speak.

'Go on, lad,' Drum says, 'Spit it out.'

'It's Anneka,' he says. 'I'm worried about her.'

Tommy looks coy, ashamed of himself, almost like he could take the words back, gobble them up like chocolate air.

'Why's that, lad?'

'I think I saw her,' he says. 'I think I saw her in a car about four this morning. I was out running, training for cross-country, and I saw her in a car with her friend. Lisa is it? Melanie? I saw them in a car with two men.'

You wait for moments to happen, the plummet stomach and the realization you've been right, your instinct has been right, and it is never as clear as the preparation. The strange iciness of knowledge you already knew.

'Where?' Drum says.

'Heading towards town.'

'You're sure it was them?'

'Positive,' Tommy says. 'I think they were coming back from a party. There was a big party one of my friends was going to up near Leek. I think she must have gone there.'

Tommy looks down at the ground. Tommy looks up at Drum.

'Thank you,' Drum says. 'You did the right thing.'

SCHOOLBOY PAPERS

We'd heard rumours that scouts from City and Crewe Alex were coming to watch our games. They were started by our coach, I think. He knew that was what we all talked about, being scouted and being signed, and so every match we played out of our skin, thinking there might be someone from a big club watching. He was canny, our coach. He really kept us on our toes.

I'll never forget the day it happened. We'd just destroyed Northwich Albion and I was coming out of the changing rooms and my dad was talking to this stranger. My dad looked serious and I thought maybe I was in trouble, though for what I didn't know. Then the scout introduced himself and told me he thought I had what it took. That he was recommending a trial at City. It was literally a dream come true. It was unbelievable. It was like walking on air going back to the car. You want a moment like that to live forever.

When people used to ask about those years at City, what it was like to be an apprentice there, I'd tell them about shining boots, the freezing changing rooms, the long commute from home to school to training and then back home. People liked all that. But now they ask different questions. They want to know if I noticed anything back then. They want to know if I heard the rumours. They want to know if I suspected something was going on. It shames me to say that I didn't notice a thing.

All the stuff that came out in the investigations and the court cases, I had no idea. No clue at all. I was so committed to my football, I just never saw it. What my teammates and the other schoolboys were going through, I just didn't have an clue. No one said anything. We wouldn't have believed them anyway, I think. We'd have probably just told them not to be so fucking soft.

I used to look back at that time with great fondness, but it's been tainted now. You start to see things in a different way once you know the truth. I've always been a big believer in making your own luck. Mostly, I still think that. At least in your professional life. But some things are just out of your control. There's nothing you can do about them.

When I pulled on the England jersey for the first time, as an under-sixteens, I came out and there were City fans singing my name. They shouted Birchy, Birchy, give us a wave. And I did. And I felt like the luckiest boy alive. I didn't know how lucky I was.

Chris Birch, *Near Miss – My Autobiography*
(Halfway Line Books, 2004)

14

Janice pushes open the door and rouses Neka from the bed on the floor, turns on the light.

'It's your father,' she says. 'He wants to speak to you.'

She's in her nightdress, the sun has only just risen. Neka runs downstairs, picks up the telephone.

'I'm coming to pick you up,' her father says. 'I'm coming now.'

'But, Dad, you said—'

'Never mind what I said. Get your things,' he says. 'Be ready in ten minutes.'

Anneka hands the receiver back to Janice. Anneka can feel herself turn white, so white she is translucent. Janice looks at her, looks at her daughter.

'What did you do?' Janice says. 'What on earth did you two do?'

15

Even upstairs Gwen can hear the sound of his voice; its rage and howl. There are words – stupid, irresponsible, unbelievable – but also noises, animal grunts, cattle lows, that score his raging. Then it stops. She hears something crash and splinter and she runs downstairs. In the kitchen the telephone is cracked in several places; Drum kicking at its Bakelite shards.

'What on earth's going on?' Gwen says, running to him, not finding him there; finding instead a man she can only dimly make out behind the wild eyes. He pushes her away, a dismissive, hardly forceful push, but one that sends her skittering on the stone flags.

'What's going on?' she says. 'You're scaring me.'

A murderer on the loose. Up north somewhere. Gwen's idea this. To let her from the gilded cage, out into the dangerous world. Her idea and her baby dead. Murdered and for what?

'Is it Annie?' she says. 'Is she okay?'

There are welts on his fists; he has punched something; there is blood.

'When she gets home, she won't be,' he says. 'When I get my hands on her.'

'She's okay though?'

He stands by the fridge and it is for a moment normal; the usual kitchen conversation, talking about what to eat for dinner, what the plans are for the week. Just the bloodied hands and the glass eyes and the heaving breath saying different.

'Yes,' he says. 'Yes, she's okay.'

'So what happened?'

'I said, didn't I? I warned you, didn't I? Trust her, you said.'

'Can you just tell me what's going on,' she says. 'Please?'

He sits down and she sits down with him.

'She went to a party,' he said. 'Got in a car with two strange men. God only knows what happened.'

Her baby girl not murdered; her baby girl just a lying, deceitful teenager. Relief in that. Alive and in trouble, but alive nonetheless. The relief of that. The stupidity to be so scared about something so minor.

Gwen offers her arms, wraps him in them, but he refuses the embrace.

'I said, didn't I?'

'Yes,' she says, 'I know. But she's okay, isn't she? All in one piece.'

He fills a glass of water, empties it, fills it, three times this, then downs the water and looks out the window.

'She's okay, yes,' he says. 'I spoke to her. She's fine.'

'How do you know she went to a party?' she says.

'Tommy saw them in a car when he was out running.'

'And you're sure?'

'Positive. Knew it from the get-go. She's planned this, I bet you.'

'Shouldn't you wait to hear her side?' she says.

Upstairs is the book. Upstairs is Raymond Porter's book. Upstairs, in another life Drum is reading it and suddenly piecing it all together, the way people sometimes can, a spiritual under-standing of disloyalty. Instead it is Annie to answer. Annie to apologize and promise it won't happen again.

'You stay here,' he says. 'I'm going to get her now.'

'Maybe I should—'

'You stay here,' he says. 'You've done enough already.'

16

Nate hears the door go for the second time, and goes down to investigate the silence. No radio on, no sound but shoes being removed, coats being hung. From the stairs he watches his mother embrace his sister, the whiteness of her skin against her mother's shoulder. His father is behind them and Nate has never seen his father look so grim-faced, so tensed in jaw and shoulder, like his body is constricting his movements to the absolute minimum. Nate inches down the stairs and waits behind the doorjamb. He watches them sit, her mother pour tea.

'You're not going to lie to me, are you?' his father says to Anneka. 'You wouldn't do that, on top of everything else, would you?'

Anneka says nothing.

'Who's was the party?' his mother says. 'Someone from college?'

Anneka says nothing.

'What scares me,' his father says, 'is the danger you put yourself in. Getting a lift with total strangers? What were you thinking?'

'Who said I was in a car with total strangers?'

Her father gets up from his seat and the chair makes a loud scraping sound; it teeters on its legs as his father looks out of the window. Nate can see him breathing, the pushed-out breath.

'It doesn't matter who saw you,' her mother says. 'We know it was you.'

'How could you be so fucking stupid?' his father says to the window.

Nate has never heard his father swear before, never seen him so close to explosion, to actual violence. And yet it feels rigged;

artificial. As though he's been preparing this for years, taking rehearsed positions, only the players around him unsure of where to stand.

'Was it Tommy?' she says. 'Was it him?'

'I told you it doesn't matter,' he says. Admits it then. Admits it was Tommy. To do that to his sister. The grassing bastard.

'He was at the party too,' she says. 'I saw him.'

'It don't care if Lord Lucan was there,' her father says. 'Only that you were.'

Nate's seen this look before; the look that only his father can give. The precursor to a sanction that cuts to the heart of punishment. Like he's seen into your soul and knows the one thing you want, the one thing not be taken away. A year before, the confiscation of football boots for fighting at school. The same face as then, almost delight in it.

'That's it, as far as I'm concerned. You can't be trusted. You've taken my trust and you've burned it right in front of my eyes. And so you're going to have to earn my trust again. This is what's going to happen. You're going to leave college and you're going to work on the farm here with me. You're going to earn my trust every day, right here.'

'Dad, you can't—' Anneka says.

'Drum,' his mother says. 'We should talk—'

'Look at what happened the last time we talked,' Drum says. 'Just look at the *state* of her. She has to learn. I won't be disrespected. I won't be deceived like this. Not in my own house.'

The silence of the three of them. The panting breath, the odd look of victory on his father's face. The sense of nowhere now to go, the script run out and now pure improvisation.

'Now go to your room,' he says.

Anneka looks at her mother and between them a mute conversation, an apology, a promise to fix this, a further apology.

'I'm—' Anneka says.

'I don't care what you are,' her father says. 'Get out of my sight.'

17

Late in the Sunday afternoon, Drum herds the cattle, his dutiful girls coming in for the night, all of them seeming quiet, subdued just for him; the cows taking his temperature, holding off on truculence. His daughter is not speaking to him; his wife is not speaking to him. It is him, somehow, who is being judged; he who is somehow in the wrong. The whole affair has been handled badly. He will relent about college; he knows this, it is obvious. But he will set new sanctions. He will drive her to college and he will pick her up. She will not be allowed driving lessons for her birthday. She will learn to be trustworthy. It will seem like a fair compromise.

From down near the brook, he sees a thin column of smoke; more than a campfire, bigger of build. He walks down the incline towards it, sees flame in between the newly shedding trees. The hide is on fire; its roof just catching now, flames languid, almost calming. He heads back to the house, runs the incline and gets together buckets. He fills them from the brook, throws them over the hide, five or six of them to control the blaze, another ten or so to put it out.

Inside, it is blackly burned, the camp seats broken, remnants of paper on the singed carpeting. The smell of char and damp; of steaming wood. Plastic has melted into the flooring, pens and old toys. Not placed or arranged, just caught in the fire.

He walks the incline back home, stinking of smoke. He goes straight upstairs for a bath and does not tell anyone of the fire. They'll find out soon enough.

The Winter House

1980

Friday 4 January

Three drawers removed from their chest; the drawers on the carpet, the clothes on the bed. A rummage of them: socks inside pants; bras inside T-shirts. Anneka kneels at the bedside, hands out, fingers extended, casting a spell. No movement in the fabric; no cotton twitches nor dancing singlets. One day. One day they will tango.

She begins with the socks, rolling them tightly, setting them flush against the left of the drawer. Knickers next, a fold across the waistband then laid on the right. Count them. Ten pairs. Ten pairs knickers; ten pairs socks. Bras next. Five. Draped between socks and knickers. Two black; three white. This taking half an hour. A further thirty minutes on T-shirts, arranging them in the lower drawer; changing the order, deciding eventually, as always, on three rows of three.

The clothes that remain on the bed are ragtag; garments that do not fold flat or keep their shape. A gym skirt; a thick-knit cardigan with buttons; two swimming costumes, both too small.

She'd once loved to swim. Loved it so much her father had called her Fish. For a time, he'd called her Fish more than love, or darling, or sweetheart: more even than the hated Annie. As she packed her swimsuit and towel, her father would say: 'My Fish, time to swim!' at the municipal pool he took her to, 'My Fish, let's swim!' on swimming her first length a month after her sixth birthday. 'My Fish, I'm so proud of you!' Those once gilded words.

A reminder of that. Of that time. The piss-and-bleach smell, fogged eyes from chlorine, floating plasters and verruca socks. Not every time. Not every time a memory, but right now, yes.

On a summer holiday, she swam in the sea rather than paddling in its shallows. Her father followed her as she waded out, the grey cold up to her waist. She took small explorative steps, testing for shell and rock, until the seafloor suddenly gave and she was unmoored, adrift. Her father was on her quick and fleet, his hands on her torso, her arm. She was already at swim, though, already righted. She looked at him with disdain.

'Even fish can drown,' he said.

'No they can't,' she said and turned away, swimming parallel to the beach, her eyes ahead, her father a vigilant distance behind. That shiver of freedom. He could have called her Water Baby, Sea Otter, Dolphin or Shark; instead he called her Fish.

She puts away the swimming costumes, clears the bed, job for the night done. She's been quick. Under two hours, not even one o'clock yet. No chance of sleep before three. Never before three.

The wardrobe has been already sorted, but she considers starting on it again. No. She says this out loud. No. The wardrobe is only to be sorted before the drawers; any time afterwards is cheating. Cheat the ritual and there's no chance of sleep at all.

Once there was sleep. When first they'd moved to the farm, she'd slept soundly, her room liking her in a way her old room never had. There were no nightmares, no city sounds to wake her. She adapted quickly to the quiet, the night-time animal noises; she was up with the larks, yes; but that normal in a farming house, the morning always loud: the cock crow and low of cattle, the suck of hoof in mud. Years of that. Then, around the turn of her eighteenth birthday, the last months before her A-levels, sleep abandoned her, disappearing like candle smoke.

She moves to the small desk by the window, the insomniac sky a jeweller's cloth. There are three piles of papers on the desk: three subjects, three failures, three exams to re-sit. She turns on the lamp, a letter from Lissa on top of the history revision. A short letter, the shortest yet. Soon it will be postcards: picture postcards of the Roman Catholic cathedral, the Cavern, the Liver Birds. Wish you were here. Come visit. Must rush.

Had she been able to sleep, she would be in Liverpool now, with Lissa, in the flat they said they'd share. Had sleep not deserted her, Anneka would have passed exams as predicted, made good on her promise. Maybe if she'd had the night-time ritual then it would have been enough. Maybe if she'd never gone to Fernando's party, she would now be gone, able to strut the streets rather than rot in the farmhouse.

She picks up her copy of *Wuthering Heights*, tries to read around the pencil annotations, the underscorings. Time was she could not read the set-text. Time was she hid it under her bed. Time was she saw, in the window above the desk at which she now sits, the ghost of Cathy Earnshaw clawing at the glass. Time was she heard scratching as the waif tried to gain entry. Time was she saw Heathcliff on her bed. Time was she saw, at the foot of the bed, Kate Bush dancing, all linens and silk, stark staring eyes and whooping shrill. Time was Heathcliff whispered and Cathy moaned and Kate Bush wailed. Time was that her father would come into her room, hold her shaking body.

'Shush now, shush now,' her father would say. 'A bad dream, that's all, a bad dream.'

And she'd want to say she could not sleep. That she could not sleep, let alone dream. But she'd say nothing, just flit her eyes around the room, watching for the ghost Cathy, the banshee Bush. Not telling her father. Keeping it back for herself.

On her desk, the letter from Lissa. Miss you, it says, by way of signing off. Lissa came home for Christmas, talked of people Anneka did not know, of hanging out at News From Nowhere, a bookshop not a club, and Eric's, a club not a bookshop, where she saw all the bands now, The Raincoats, her favourite. The third loss this.

The first after Fernando's party. She was allowed to continue at college, but good to his word, Anneka was never far from her father's orbit. College and home and no points between, him there in the morning, there in the afternoon. She remained friends with

Lissa, but it changed things: Lissa finding new extra-curricular friends; Lissa finding new music, new clothes; Lissa with stories from her weekend; Lissa with a boyfriend.

The second when Anneka stopped sleeping, started acting oddly. Lissa asking if she was on smack. Lissa telling her to see a doctor, to get some Valium. Anything. The way she pleaded, and the way Anneka said no. All was fine. Just tired, that's all. Nothing to worry about. The tutors were worried though; they saw the spiralling of her work.

Her English tutor, a young man with a ginger beard and a flat Mancunian accent, was the first to take her aside, to ask if all was well.

'Why do you ask?' Anneka said.

'This essay,' he said. 'It's incoherent. It's poorly written. It has no logic. It also has quotes from *Jane Eyre* in it.'

She did not believe him, but there they were: Rochester and Heathcliff transposed, Orson Welles not Laurence Olivier.

'Whatever it is you're up to, Anneka,' he said. 'Knock it on the head. You look like raw mince.'

The second time, her history tutor asked her to stop behind after a lesson. He took off his glasses, as though she would trust him more if she saw his eyes, and asked if everything was okay.

'After what you did to me, you think anything is okay?' Anneka said. 'After all the filthy things you did?'

She accused him of all kinds of interference. Saw him upon her. But also Heathcliff watching. Cathy laughing. Kate Bush strumming a zither. Then knew. Stopped there. The history tutor white-faced and almost cowering.

'I'm so sorry,' she said. 'I'm so, so sorry. I didn't mean any of that. I've been . . .'

But she didn't know what she'd been, and the tutor took her to the dean, and the dean sent her home, and her mother sent her to the doctor, and the doctor prescribed pills she pretended to take but did not.

Seven exams all told; seven failures. In the exam on *Wuthering Heights*, she saw Orson Welles, and he whispered in her ear, 'I am no bird; and no net ensnares me: I am a free human being with an independent will.' She transcribed it as he whispered, filling furious sides, enjoying every semi-colon. On leaving, she did not know she'd failed; she thought she'd written the essay of her life.

Anneka gets up from the desk, sits herself in the window alcove, the distant lights of town and the darkness below; no Heathcliff now, no Kate Bush, no Cathy laughing. She opens the window and lights a cigarette, the cold air parading the smoke. She looks down to the road, past the dell, and there are lights, headlamps on the road. Then on the track, a white skittering through the trees.

She does not recognize the car; it is large, old-fashioned. It bucks the tracks and a light comes on inside the Carter house; Daphne in the kitchen window, fully dressed, pouring gin. The car pulls up outside the house, a man gets out. A tall spindle of a man carrying a small case.

Anneka watches him disappear inside, reappear in the kitchen with Daphne, her glass empty and hidden in the large sink. She watches them talk, Daphne all nods, like she's taking orders. And then the telephone rings. Not in the Carter house, but downstairs. Anneka hears her parents' door open and her father hurriedly take the stairs, the muffle of his voice from downstairs. She hears the receiver click in its cradle. She hears the silence of the house.

Someone has died, she thinks. Someone has died suddenly. Perhaps it is her. Maybe she has become as wraith-like as Cathy, haunting the dark spaces, never to leave. She doesn't know how that makes her feel.

2

It is a woman who calls; something Drummond did not expect. In the imagining, in the preparation, it was always a man. A pause after his message and then a gravelled *good luck* before ending the call. Import. Seriousness. An understanding of the weight and implication of his words. Instead, a woman, the breeze and speed of a secretary, emotionless and dutiful, another task ticked from a list. No pause; no good-luck coda. All the things to think, and this the first. Distracted as a condemned man eyeing the dandruff of his executioner. Should have been a man.

Drum's hands shake, exaggerated the shake, welcoming-an-invisible-figure shake, both arms jolting up and down, in different rhythms, at different speeds. The things we say. *I thought I'd have a heart attack*. Thinking that now, thinking he'll soon clutch at his chest, fall to the farmhouse flags, his last sight clumps of food unswept from under kitchen cabinets.

It has been a good life. Yes. A family safe. Money, tight, but always food on the table, a car to drive. Good kids, mostly. Gwen happy, provided for, loved. His days free from bodywork and production; up at the crack with the cows; at the end of day, watching the cattle into their sheds, dung and flies, the sense of a day's work done. Nights watching the sun set over the fields, whisky in hand with Carter, reading books with Gwen in the sitting room. His back cracks and his joints ache, but it is a good life. Has been a good life, well lived.

It passes. The clutch at the heart releases, the hands and arms settle. Ashamed at the reaction. The adrenalin cooling. He washes his hands and face. Calm now. Trained and diligent now. To follow the drill by rote. Still, it should have been a man to call. A man to wish him good luck. He deserves that at least.

3

Over time, Gwen has got used to wearing earplugs; those she uses to deaden Drummond's snores. They give routine, the plugs. Once the radio is switched off, the last page read, she puts them in and offers a kiss goodnight. They are punctuation; a provider of grammar. They say no more conversation; they say quiet; they say no chance of sex. A kiss without earplugs has potential. Not uncommon those kisses, and always successful.

Each morning he forgets about the earplugs, talks for a time before stroking her arm to wake her. A dance that. A quick foxtrot of pretending to be asleep before putting on dressing gown and slippers.

The way he strokes her arm now is different; insistent, running to rough. She looks up and there is sweat on his brow, the grey at his temples darker. She takes out the earplugs, and he is shaking his head. Somewhere she can hear the run of water.

'We need to go,' he says.

'Where?' she says, though his face and the sweat tell her exactly where.

'Under,' he says. 'Just a drill, I expect.'

There have been many drills over the last year, but never at night. She sits up and touches his arm, the slight stammer to it. He smiles, the falsest smile she has seen on his face, one he does not believe himself.

'Are you running a bath?' she says.

He sits down next to her, eyes already cried, already wiped dry and glassily prepared.

'You never know how long we'll be down there. I'd like to go in clean.'

He takes her hand.

'Come,' he said. 'The bath's warm. Almost ready.'

In the dark he leads her to the bathroom. There are bubbles in the bath; the best towels folded on the toilet seat. Be calm. Just another drill. Never a bath on the drill though. Never like this. *Go in clean.*

She vomits into the lavatory pan, three quick expulsions. Nausea like the worst of the morning sickness, body fried with tremens, gooseflesh on her arms as she flushes the toilet.

Looking up from the pan, she sees the panic in him, the disappointment in himself. 'Get in,' he says.

The water is piping, her skin quickly red. He smooths a soaped-up sponge over her body. *We go in clean.* To have thought this for so long, the preparation and planning to think that. He pours water from a jug over her head. He massages shampoo into her crown. She closes her eyes and smells jojoba, tries to hold on to that smell, that smell and not scream.

'It's not a drill, is it?' she says.

'I don't know,' he says. 'But we'll be okay. We'll be safe.'

'You talked to Carter?' she says.

'No,' he says. 'All communications are disconnected. We can't call anyone. They can't call us. But we'll be fine.'

She thinks of Ray. Immediately, Ray. Not thought of for some time, and now urgently with her, combing his hair in the mirror.

Drum gets out of the bath, wipes steam from the mirror, picks up a can of shaving foam, fills the basin with water.

'How can you be so calm?' she says. 'How can you just stand there and . . . . *shave?*'

He looks straight into the mirror, not at her. He dips the razor in the water, scrapes away a strip of white.

'We need to be calm for the children,' he says. 'If we go crazy, so will they.'

She wishes he'd cut himself, for the blade to nick him, remind him he is blood and skin and bone. You think you're prepared. You think you've thought it all through, practised it enough. But you can't practise the real thing. There are baths in the real thing. There is shaving foam.

She gets out of the cooling water, presses herself against him. She shakes and he dries her, still foam-bearded, her shakes not stopping, the shakes shaking themselves.

'Hush,' he says. 'You need to calm. You need to be calm for Annie and Nate.'

He goes back to his shave, the white and the dark in the water, the sound of razor on stubble. Calming the sound, calming as she dries.

'Remember when they shared a bath?' she says. 'When they were young enough for that?'

He looks at her in the mirror, he smiles and his teeth look fang-yellow against the white.

'Go get them and tell them it's just a drill,' he says. 'Don't worry. They know what to do.'

In her bedroom, she opens the wardrobe. A dress would be defiant. A long black chiffon number. A floaty gown in soft pink. A floor-length purple dress. All Daphne's cast-offs. She shuts the door on them. Leaves them for the archivists, for the historians, for the archaeologists. Confuse them. Who could have lived in this simple cottage with such lavish garments? Let them wonder. Let them think. She puts on underwear, jeans, a jumper. She looks at herself in the mirror. The last time. This is who I am. About to disappear. Poof.

OPERATION MID-OFF

It begins with an accident, a computer malfunction. There have been several over the years, all of them intercepted at the last moment, the world none the wiser as to the proximity of Armageddon. On this occasion, the computer malfunction is not discovered until the Americans have already spotted the movement of missile sites. In the wake of the Russian invasion of Afghanistan in late 1979, increased tensions have made such movements a catalyst for action. The Russians claim a malfunction, but the security council in the US believes this is a smokescreen for a pre-emptive strike. Between Washington and Moscow, the conversations are terse. The Soviets begin to wonder whether this is a work of espionage; the malfunction designed to allow the US to launch their own pre-emptive strike. The UK's Regional Seats of Government are placed on the highest alert. Designated people of importance are contacted and told to make their way to the nearest safe facility, the first time this action has been implemented. The code name for the action is Operation Mid-Off. In the RSGs, we wait for further news and instructions.

Bryan Jerrick, *My Cold Wars*
(Underworld Press, 2001)

5

It doesn't feel like it is happening, more that it has already happened. The way they shoulder their Go bags, the quiet as they descend the stairs. The same as a regular drill, no different to any practice run, as everyday as school and work. Happening, having happened: both the same.

They put on boots and walk to the Carter house, Drum unlocking the padlock on the storm hatch, letting his family crouch, descend first. The drills are principally about the normalization of process. The repetition dulling the senses, without that shrieking bedlam, blind panic. He follows them as he always does, into the creosote-and-sacking smell, the damp cold air.

They wait at the end of the cellar for him. He opens the door using the wheel at its centre, releasing the catch, pulling the door towards him. A corridor beyond, stone and steel and lead, lit by small spots in the roof, pricks of light leading to another battle-grey door.

He holds the door open, extends an arm in invitation, an invitation none of them takes. They stand in the cool, their breath visible. Gently Gwen ushers them into the corridor, holding one hand back for Drum to hold, which he takes, though he doesn't want to. He knows if he doesn't, the first few hours will be worse than the second time they rushed underground. Then the children looked not to him, but gravitated to her. They hid amongst Gwen's petticoats as she asked them if they were hungry, if they'd like baked beans or spaghetti hoops. Neither of his children looked to him then.

Nate begins to turn the second door's wheel. Not waiting for

Drum, but turning it himself. The door opens before Drum can get there, behind it the decontamination chamber, strip lights reflecting off the chrome doors. The pipes and brickwork are painted the same shade of soothing green, nozzles are arranged in a regular pattern: one high, one at waist height, one for the ankles. Beyond the swing doors is a changing room, painted the same shade of soothing green, hooks on the walls, small wooden benches beneath. They take off their boots there, all of them, as they always do. Well drilled. Well trained. Then push through the doors into the living quarters.

In 1965, when Carter had eventually revealed it to him, the bunker project taking some three years to build and not an inconsiderable amount of his inheritance, the living area had appeared vast. If anything it now looks bigger. It still takes Drummond's breath away; he feels genuinely winded whenever he sees it. A space for them to share, when the moment came. Enough room for both families, Drummond to lead them while Carter was at the Regional Seat of Government bunker. That the plan. Always the plan.

The large room is divided into specific spaces: the back wall dominated by a long refectory-style table; the right-hand wall home to a series of sky-blue easy chairs circled around a glass coffee table; the left wall a piano, and shelves filled with books, records and a radio set. The floor is black linoleum, the walls white, uplighters bracketed on them, brightly illuminating the space. There is a touch of the institutional, but it retains a simplistic comfort he admires.

'Is anyone hungry?' Drum says. 'I could heat something up if anyone's hungry.'

'It's the middle of the night,' Anneka says. 'How can you think of eating?'

Anneka sits on one of the easy chairs, tucks her legs underneath her the way she does when she sits on the sofa to watch television. So simple a motion: engrained and surprising. Drum doesn't know where to put himself, where to stand or sit, but she has already decided, taken the space as her own. The fortitude of her. The strength of her. Does him proud.

'On the bright side,' Anneka says. 'If it is the end of the world, at least I can't fail my exams again.'

She laughs and it is flinty, her laughter directed squarely at her father. He smiles as the swing doors open: Daphne, Thomas, Natasha; behind them a thin tall man, suited in pinstripes, thick spectacles on a snub nose, chin weak as mild. Daphne walks towards them, drops her bag by the door, slackly embraces Gwen as though this a regular meeting. The two friends stay like that, holding each other, Daphne's three companions standing by the settling door, two teenagers and a man in his fifties, blinking, their bags still in hand, looking at the congregation around the coffee table. Drum hopes the doors will open a last time, and Carter stride in, but they remain shut.

'Come in, all of you,' Drum says. 'Come, sit. We were just about to make some tea.'

The two teenagers slope towards their contemporaries. Tom wearing a shirt open at the neck, slim-cut trousers, boat shoes, hair combed straight, the spit of his youthful father; Natasha wearing a similar outfit, a striped blouse and jeans, boat shoes. A holiday look. The way they dress when they pack the car to head to Spain.

The thin man strides towards Drum, takes his hand, it is a clammy handshake, confident in its pump.

'You must be Moore,' the thin man says to Drum. 'Gault. Pleased to meet you.'

'And you, Mr Gault.'

'Could you show me to my berth?' Gault says. 'I'd like to change, if I may.'

'But of course,' Drum says, 'it's just through here.'

He thinks of Carter's face, serious in the darkness, looking out over the fields. He wonders how Carter is coping. What he's seeing on the telex machine. Drum walks Gault to his berth and opens the door: a small double bed, a nightstand, a chest of drawers.

'Well,' Gault says. 'Seems I dropped lucky. You should see the shelter I was supposed to be billeted at. Double bunks. Four to a room. This is like the Savoy in comparison.'

Gault takes off his jacket; Drum thinks he's about to hand it to him to hang on the back of the door, but he folds it on the bed.

'What's the latest, Mr Gault?' Drum says.

'You know as much I do, I expect,' Gault says, unbuttoning his shirt. 'As I understand it, the Americans are being painted into a corner. All I know is that it's not looking hopeful.'

Drum looks at the thin man, the way he removes his vest, opens his case and takes out a fresh one, then a linen shirt. A man on a weekend away, unfazed and judging the accommodation.

'We'll be fine here,' Gault says. 'A few months at worst. Probably won't even get that far. But with people like you, your family and so on, it'll be the making of us. I believe that. I really do. A chance to start again. To begin again. A friend of mine always says that from the ashes came the phoenix, and from our ashes, we shall build a utopia. I believe him when he says that. Whatever the sacrifice, whatever the hardship, when we look back, we'll see this was needed. We'll see the privations were, in the end, worth the toil.'

It has the air of a speech oft-performed; the soft chin and watery eyes, the buttoning of the shirt, easing its passage. A man like that, saying those things, yes; succour there. Hope there. Belief there.

'But I'm sure it won't come to that,' Gault says. 'Though we must be prepared if it does.'

'I'll leave you to change, Mr Gault,' he says. 'How do you take your tea?'

'With lemon,' he said.

'I don't think we have any lemons,' Drum says. Gault clicks his teeth.

'If not I'll take a small amount of milk, and a half-spoon of sugar.'

Drum closes the door on Gault. He passes the room he and Gwen will share, the children's rooms with their single beds. He stands at the doorjamb, looking into the galley kitchen, Daphne and Gwen busying themselves with the tea, silent and looking through cupboards, checking stocks of tea and sugar.

'Do we have any lemons?' he says. 'Gault likes his tea with lemon.'

The two women turn, pause their movements at the same time.

'Well you tell Mr Gault,' Daphne says, 'that when we were preparing for the end of the world, we forgot to put fucking lemons on the list.'

6

Her mother and Daphne put down their tea; the radio now on, low hiss, an orange dial, the needle over to the very right of the band. All the stations to its left, playing Top Forty, playing opera, doling out the news, forecasting the weather, all oblivious. Already knowing this not a drill. Gault not a man for drills. This the real thing.

How many underground, Anneka wonders, how many like her, sitting with family, friends, colleagues, strangers. How many thinking suicide, planning pacts, unable to face the survival. She could blow her brains out. Overdose on pills. It's an option, holocaust or no. When the lack of sleep got out of hand, she thought about it often.

In the bath, her father's razor in the medicine cabinet, the easiest way out. Slash down not across. Where did she read that? The ease of it; of walking out into traffic; motorcycles, strangely, the most provoking, the meagreness of them compared to cars, but the impact just as total. Electric pylons from the school information films, throw something over them. Wasn't there something about shoelaces, a kid in flared trousers looping them over the pylon and catching flame? Always her father's voice though, always the soothing voice, sometimes the shouting voice, but mostly the soothing voice: my love, my girl, be safe, that's all.

Gault enters the living quarters. He looks strange in the linen shirt, the fawn slacks. He is trying too hard, he is too casual: she can already only imagine him in pinstripes, a suit like the father from *Mary Poppins*. The kind of man she's seen arriving at the Carter house, greeted by Uncle Jim, backslaps and bottles of wine in hand, ushered into the big house through the front door she and her family never use.

'Here you are, Mr Gault,' her father says, handing the man a cup and saucer. 'No lemon, I'm afraid.'

Gault sits down at twelve o'clock in the circle of chairs. He sets down his cup.

'Thank you,' Gault says. 'Thank you for accommodating me. I know this is a difficult time, but if we all pull together, I'm sure we'll all get through this.'

He picks up his cup, stirs his tea, looks blinking round at them all. Anneka wonders if anyone else is thinking they'd kill and eat him first.

'I think,' Gault goes on, 'It would be a good idea to introduce ourselves to each other, so everyone knows who we all are.'

'We know who we all are,' Nate says.

Anneka watches her father flinch, his stepping in, his phoney laugh, the one he uses when Carter says something she does not understand, but her father clearly does.

'This is my son, Nathan,' says her father.

'Nathan was it? Nice to meet you, Nathan. And you are?' he says to Thomas.

'Thomas Carter,' he says. 'We've met before. With my father.'

'So we have! Nice to see you again, Thomas.'

Gault displays no sense of recollection, a weary expression instead, his hand-rubbing joviality already waning. Stuck here with a bunch of resentful teenagers, an obsequious father, two women to make tea and comfort the kids. It is the first note of worry; the first sign of wavering. Bombast bombed out, scuttled by the scowling faces on the easy chairs.

'And you, missy?' Gault says.

'You've met me too. I'm Natasha.'

'My, my,' he says. 'You've grown since the last time I saw you.'

Gault's eyes perhaps linger on her longer than they should. Or perhaps she just thinks that.

'This is Gwen, my wife,' her father says. 'And my daughter, Anneka.'

Anneka says hello though she wants to remain mute, to stare at his weak chin and make some sharp remark, make the words scratch, leave a mark.

'And you know me,' Daphne says.

'Yes,' he said. 'I know you, Mrs Carter.'

Gault takes a sip of his tea. Anneka feels him look at her, long eyes on her. Lissa would say something. Take a photograph, it lasts longer.

Lissa in her flat on Granby Street, Lissa doing make-up, heading for lectures, Lissa asleep, still stinking of sex and cider. Lissa and the boyfriend Anneka's not met, her lecturers and fellow students, all soon to be shadows and burn and bodies under rubble. Rats and cockroaches surviving; no one else. Impossible to think it actually happening; happening, and with a man looking her up and down, calmly judging, perhaps thinking which one he'd fuck first, when it came to it. The plumper, more buxom girl; the taller, lither one. Reducing herself to this, a pick, as in netball at school. The world now, this room. This room reduced to basic, primal thinking. The world reduced and Thomas Carter sitting looking at his finger-nails, refusing to look at her.

Gault speaks to the parents, turns his legs from the four teen-agers; small talk and reassuring words, Cuba mentioned several times, a wash of words.

'Hello, Anneka,' Thomas says.

'Hello, Thomas,' Anneka says. 'Dressed for the party, I see.'

'As are you,' he says. 'I'm glad to see you've outgrown the punk look. It never suited.'

'Oh don't start, you two,' Natasha says. 'We don't know how long we're going to be down here, and I'll go mad if you're at each other's throats all the time.'

Since Fernando's party, there has been no contact, no exchanges. He rarely returns from school these days, and when he does, he makes sure not to leave the confines of his property, though she has spied on him from her window, watched him swan and preen around the house, drink with his father, not seem to care he made her a prisoner. She likes to think of him beaten in alleyways, battered with lengths of pipe, strapped by lashes. And now here, a fingertip away, all too real, all too hateful.

The Thomas who looks at her now is no longer the boy from the hide, if he were ever that boy. He is the boy who burned down the hide, who relished in her punishment. The boy from the hide would not have done what the arsonist did. That boy would not have given her up simply out of spite and jealousy. That boy would not smooth away his hair, laugh, look at his fingernails as if bored.

'So Nate,' Tom says. 'How's the football?'

'Good,' Nate says. 'Playing for the under-seventeens now.'

'Really?' Tom says. 'Gosh.'

'There's a scout coming from City next week.'

'Well, good luck,' he says.

Nate sits embarrassed. A conversation exploded by tenses. Next week. A scout coming. Playing for the under-seventeens. All lies now, all made lies. She wonders if he realizes. Maybe she is wrong. Not possible to believe it, not truly.

Fernando's party, still going on, coming now to an end, one out of his control. Death of a myth, a legend. She can imagine him watching the bombs from his window, smocked and drinking the over-proof rum, asking the party if they can hear the drums. Can't you hear the drums? The drums are coming!

'How are you, Anneka?' Natasha says.

'Tired,' she says.

'Me too,' she says.

'I can't believe they got us out of bed for a drill.'

'Me either.'

'If it gets to it, do you want to sleep in with me?' Natasha says, abruptly, as though the question surprises even herself. 'It'll be like camp. Or like a sleepover.'

305

'You don't want to share with me,' Anneka says. 'I don't sleep much. I toss and I turn.'

'I don't mind that,' Natasha says. 'I just don't want to share with Tommy. He snores and his feet smell.'

Natasha laughs at that, the first time Anneka can remember sharing any sort of joke with her. Natasha's eyes cast down, expecting rebuttal, an easy rejection. Anneka has known her since her birth and yet can't recall any specific bit of knowledge about her. Anneka has seen her in dresses, being driven off to dances, made-up and graceful in new gowns, but cannot imagine an interior life for her. She has no character, as far as she can see; quick to tears, she remembers, but what else? Some people, she thinks, are locked to us, unknowable as rock; they pass into our lives, and pass out just as quickly, glancing off us, never really meeting. And now Anneka is stuck with her, her only female contemporary, a fifteen-year-old, sitting baffled in rich-girl clothes.

'If you want,' Anneka says. 'If that's what you'd like.'

'Yes,' she says. 'It is.'

'Nate,' Anneka says. 'I'm going to sleep in with Natasha. You sleep in with Thomas.'

'Okay,' Nate says.

Thomas is talking to her father and Gault. She gets up and taps Thomas on the shoulder. He ignores her, continues to talk of his interview at Oxford, his witty and thoughtful answers. She taps him again.

'Thomas, you're sleeping in with Nate, okay?'

Thomas turns. He smiles, that smile.

'What was that, Annie? I was just talking to Mr Gault here.'

'You're sleeping in with Nate.'

The radio scuffles then, whining until a voice pierces the static. All eight of them are drawn to it, filings to a magnet. Gault turns up the volume; her father tunes the dial for better reception.

'In Vestry Park,' a clipped male voice says, 'the annual rainfall decreased by three-fold over the months of November and December.'

They all look at Gault. He sits as the voice continues with its incomprehensible bulletin. They know he knows what it all means, but dare not interrupt.

'January saw an abundance of snow, five inches falling in a single day on the twenty-second. Flood warnings could be in place in February, with fine weather for the time of year promised in the last week of the March.'

The report repeats, then concludes with static. They all look at Gault.

'My God,' he says. 'It's starting.'

7

The family hold each other. The four of them. They hold each other and remain embraced; arms around arms, their heads bowed, locked temple to temple. No matter the rehearsal, opening night always a leap. Metaphor redundant, comparisons blithe. No words for it. No way to pinion it, no linguistic trap a suitable snare. It is the totality that evades us. The exuberance of the whole. Every possible emotion, every single reaction, experienced at its most heightened, at its most intense. Terror, yes; but more than that; grief, yes, but more than that; anger, yes, but more than that; thrill, yes, but more than that; pity, yes but more than that. On and on. Every last emotion dialled up, jacked up, blended and pulsed, no drug invented or imagined as powerful. An implosion of emotion so savage, so various and so concentrated, the body is placed under the most extreme of pressures, every part of the human ecosystem straining under its weight. It is the hit that every addict craves; somewhere between the delivery of a healthy child and a stillbirth; between surviving a knife attack and stabbing someone dead; between whole body orgasm and the first signs of cardiac arrest. It is all of human history and human experience in one ten-second fury.

8

After the message on the radio, after she has hugged her family, Gwen turns to Daphne. They look at each other, the way they sometimes do, as though checking each other's make-up. Daphne gets up, heads to the kitchen and returns with a magnum of champagne. Unasked, Gwen goes to the kitchen and comes back with glasses. Daphne opens the bottle, the pock as the cork flies echoing around the room. She fills the glasses and hands them around, the early evening hostess, a painted smile on her lips.

'I promised my husband I'd do this,' she says. 'I promised him we'd toast everyone. Wish everyone bon voyage and safe sailing.'

Her hands are shaking, all their hands are shaking, they look like they are aboard a cruise ship experiencing heavy weather.

'Bon voyage,' Gault says.

'Bon voyage,' Gwen repeats.

Daphne downs her glass; everyone follows suit. And, as at Christmas, they all turn to listen to the voice of the Queen, addressing her subjects from the radio's orange glow.

OPERATION MID-OFF

At the RSGs, we played the recorded Queen's speech on the designated frequency. Some had heard the words before, most had, but they were still surprised. NATO was trying to calm the situation, but there was no way to calm something this far in train. British missiles were primed. The Russian missile silos were trained upon London, Manchester and Glasgow. The Queen was aboard her nuclear submarine off the Scottish coast. We sat waiting. Working, but waiting.

Bryan Jerrick, *My Cold Wars* (Underworld Press, 2001)

IO

In the small bathroom, Drum sits on the chemical toilet, lets loose his bowels, wonders who will come in next and vow never to follow him into the privy. If the attack is light – amusing, like being lightly pregnant – then six weeks should be enough. Two months at most. The radio will give the all-clear, the instructions. All that training, so long ago, and all so meaningless, if it had meaning even then. The idea of walking out, a few days after, looking for survivors, for those in the lintels of buildings, trapped under rafters, absurd now, laughable.

Drum wipes and hears a different voice, a different timbre to it, something on the radio. Piss splashes his underpants and he pulls them up, rushes from the toilet. The first news and not there to hear, the first word and him shitting. He runs into the living space and wants to ask what he's missed, but Gault has a preventative finger to his lips. He is standing closest to the radio, ear bent to the speaker, a BBC voice talking, dinner-jacketed, smooth and warm, treacle on crumpets.

Warheads in the industrial north and the capital. Casualties unknown. America and the USSR attacking with multiple warheads in multiple locations. Citizens to stay indoors, underground until further notice. More instructions will follow. This bulletin will be repeated every half an hour until more information is made available.

There are no embraces, they stand as mannequins around the wireless, waiting for more, but nothing more coming. Gault removes his spectacles and wipes them thoroughly with a handkerchief.

Drum thinks of the blast radiuses learned on Service, the heat maps, the orange sectors of total destruction. Burned into retina those maps, though useless now; the tonnage of the bombs so much bigger than before. Industrial north, Manchester or Sheffield, Newcastle, close enough. The fucking impotence of it.

'When it happens, and when you're panicking,' Carter said, a few weeks before, 'think of me. Holed up in a tiny berth, sleeping in a bunk bed below some farting, wanking counsellor or some red-faced copper. Think of me buried there, away from my family, wondering if you got there in time, wondering whether I'll ever see you all again. Think of that. Think of me and think of them. Remember, down below, you are me. You understand? When you go down, you are *me*, and you think like *me*. You understand?'

This just before the invasion of Afghanistan, the growing tensions; must have known then, but not able to say. And what would Carter do now? Tell stories? Tell jokes? He would be useless. He would not be dependable. He would jitter in the aftermath, waiver in the confines of the room, kick things over, lose his mind. When he said he wanted Drum to be him, what he really wanted was Drum to be the Carter he'd always assumed he was: in control, born to lead, a rock on whom to depend.

Drum can be that. Drum can do that. There are months ahead, but at the end of it, he will reunite Carter with his family. Drum will show him he was in control; show him that he'd led the Carters to safety in the new life. Safe, yes. All of them. Just as they'd planned. A glass of Scotch on his homecoming; a glass of Scotch and a promise upheld.

II

'I'm glad Jim's not here,' Daphne says, the two of them in the kitchen. 'I thought I'd mind. I thought I'd miss him, but I don't. Strange, isn't it, that when you need someone most, you no longer need them?'

Not to think of Ray. No. Not now and not here. Dead Ray. Shadow on a wall, Ray. Conversations in the afterlife with Nick: Ah, dear boy, I have been so wanting to talk to you, do you have time for a pint of black and tan?

'At least he's safe,' Gwen says.

'Do you think after it's all over that wedding certificates will still be valid?' she says. 'Surely the records will be destroyed, won't they? He could come back and I could say I don't recognize him, tell him to leave my property. We have guns. Maybe I could threaten to shoot him if he doesn't leave . . . '

Daphne refills their glasses; in the living quarters, Drum and the children are playing Monopoly like it's a wet afternoon on a summer holiday.

'I always said I'd go when the kids left home,' Daphne says.

'Yes you did, Daphne.'

'I think they've left home now, don't you think?'

'It's probably not the time to tell them you're seeking divorce,' Gwen says. 'That could be stressful for them.'

The two of them laugh.

'He's probably wondering who to fuck first,' Daphne says. 'Maybe I should fuck Gault.'

She finishes her champagne.

'I would if he didn't look like a skinny version of my father,' Daphne said. 'I honestly would.'

Gwen vomits in the small sink. Sudden it coming and then all out. Arms around her, Daphne's arms, and more fucking tears, tears they should be catching, reserving for bathing and drinking; salty, endless as oceans. Fish dead in oceans, risen to the surface, a teeming shine of gill. Fish dead on beaches, swept to shore, a bounteous catch without a net in sight. Birds on the ground, felled from trees and the skies, beaks blackened, feathers singed. Cattle cremated, the smell of hog roast, beef brisket, lamb chops. Ray and Jenny, dead together, entwined, melted into one another, fused as solder-work.

Daphne off her now; instead a different body. Drum's sour smell, his arms around her, so many times, so many times over the years.

'Got to be strong, love,' Drum says, 'for the kids. Come now, for the kids.'

That smile and that face. Right of course. The right words and the right sentiment. Dry eyes now. Swirl out the sink, make clean, make right.

12

As pieces round the board, money changes hands. Wooden hotels sit on Trafalgar Square and Regent Street and Nate embroils himself in a concerted effort to bankrupt both his father and Thomas. He goes for the corners first, those around Free Parking, Go and the Jail, and builds up his portfolio. He is tense every time his father rounds the Go square, hoping he'll fall foul of his East London trap. His father dodges it eight times in a row, which seems somehow impossible; Thomas the same.

He does catch them both at Fleet Street, collects from both with glee, counting out the paper bills into stacks of the same denomination. Thrilling that, the beating of the two men, the sighs as they hand over their tithes. When he lands on Regent Street, Nate expects Tom to exact revenge, to slide his finger down the card to reveal the huge amount to pay, then revel in the winnings. He doesn't. He just says the amount and Nate passes it over.

Nate moves his pewter motor car, but instead of concentrating on the game thinks of his friends. He can see Gary, Richie, Dave and Al dead. Can see them, peaceful almost, laid in their beds. He thinks then of Asa Hartford and Colin Bell, the two of them combining to score a goal just as the bombs drop. He cannot imagine Colin Bell or Asa Hartford, Kenny Dalglish or Trevor Francis dead. He cannot imagine they would not be safe. They would be down below like them, surely?

Under floodlights, hundreds of feet below ground, he sees them, the greatest footballers of their generation, playing endless games, labyrinthine tournaments. The greatest games ever played and no one there to see them, no crowd to go wild. Chris Birch is with them. The young midfielder showing the older men up. Chris Birch and his thighs, Chris Birch and his boots. He can't imagine Chris Birch dead.

Nate rolls a five and a four, moves his car around the nine spaces. He looks around the table, the blank, bored faces, and he wants to fucking destroy Thomas. Deep, deep the burn, the tightness in his arms, the clench of teeth. Headbutt first; a knee to the groin as he goes down. Sitting there, looking at fingernails, not caring, not playing, calm and casually dressed. Rolling the dice and moving his speedboat and missing his fucking properties again.

'Cheat,' Nate says.

Thomas looks up from the board, a little smile there, thin the smile.

'What's that, Natey?'

'You're cheating. No way you could have avoided my properties this many times.'

'How on earth can I be cheating?'

'I see it when you roll. I can see what you're doing.'

'Why would I cheat?' Tom says. 'I don't even want to play.'

'Why don't we take a break from Monopolizing?' Nate's father says. 'We can pick it up later.'

The players stand as one, stretch legs and arms, a warm-down.

'Let's play cards,' Nate says to Thomas. Thomas laughs and shakes his head.

'I've played enough games for one day,' he says.

'Scared you'll lose?'

'How old *are* you, Natey?' he says. Tommy sighs and puts a hand on Nate's shoulder.

'Look, we're all in shock,' he says. 'If it helps, take a swing at me. It looks like you'd like to, though God alone knows why. You want this to be *Lord of the Flies*? Fine, we can do that. Go on, son. Lay it on me. I won't fight back.'

He smiles. That smile. Smug the smile, knowing the smile.

'Thought not,' Thomas says. 'Let's not say anything more about it, okay? It's over and it's done. Pals again?'

Nate looks at the floor.

'Pals?' Tom says.

'Yes,' Nate says. 'I'm sorry. I just . . .'

'You don't need to explain,' he says. 'I understand. I really do. But don't take it out on me. Okay? Never, ever take it out on me.'

They join the men by the radio, waiting for the next broadcast. Thomas yawns first, then his father, then Drum.

'You should get some rest,' Gault says. 'All of you. We'll take it in shifts to listen out for news. Let me take the first one.'

'He's right,' his father says. 'Time for bed.'

Nate does not argue, says goodnight to his sister, to his parents. He has an erection, one that will not abate, no matter the images of destruction and death he can muster.

The report repeats the same information. Stay indoors, do not leave your place of residence: a come-on, these words. Natasha's bra is sometimes visible when she bends down and the sight of the strap is also enough. He watches Daphne, drunk and sloppy on the sofa, and wonders if she has ever been fucked in her arse. He has stuck his fingers in his own hole several times, experimentally, up to the knuckle. He likes the sensation, the smell of his fingers afterwards.

'Goodnight,' Nate says to Thomas.

'I'll be through in a little while,' Thomas says, eyes on him, a warning, as though he can see his purpose.

Nate closes the door and undresses, takes a sock, the whole thing messily over as soon as he touches it. He puts on pyjamas, hides the wet sock down the side of the small bed, gets under the blanket. He punches himself in the arm, then on the leg. Hard blows. You stupid twat, he says, punching his arm again, you dick, as he slaps his own face, beats at his head, you twat.

The door then. The door and he freezes as the corridor light shines through.

'I don't want to hear anything,' Thomas says. 'You understand?'

'I don't know what you mean,' he says.

'Then that's understood then,' Thomas says.

Thomas gets undressed in the half-light, a well-toned body, defined around the abdomen and torso, lithe, rather than athletic. Tom wears shorts rather than pants, his arse flat, a small patch of hair, a perfect rectangle at the base of his spine. He pulls on a T-shirt and a pair of long-johns, gets under the blankets.

'You okay?' Thomas says.

'It doesn't feel real,' Nate says.

'I know,' Thomas said. 'But it is real. It's real, but it won't be as bad as people make out. The Earth will keep spinning, and we'll live long lives. We'll start a new world. A better one.'

Tom shifts over in the cot, leans over the divide between them.

'Don't have nightmares about the bombs,' Thomas says. 'Just think about the day we get out. What that will feel like. Like the first day of the summer holidays. Just think of that. Think of that and sleep well.'

Nate looks at the walls. He closes his eyes. He thinks of the irradiated. He thinks of football. He thinks of Chris Birch, of the first day of the summer holidays and the bomb blasts. He thinks of all of these things, sees them all in dreams. Long, riotous dreams of pornographic intensity.

13

Natasha sleeps as if dead. Anneka cannot hear her: it is almost as if she has erased herself, teleported back to the aboveground world, the real world; whatever that now means. Anneka dozes, wakes, sleeps, wakes, mentally arranges her drawers and wardrobe. She opens her eyes and closes them, reminds herself where she is, what has happened. No breath in the room, no breath and then breath. Something panting, almost.

In the shadows, she is sure it is Heathcliff come again. Heathcliff in the shadows, the shape of him by the doorframe, cur-like and huffing, face and body obscured, but him, for certain. She can feel him there. She holds her breath, closes her eyes; no way he can see her, no way to know without her breath, her open eyes. Eyes closed, breath held, stiff as board under blankets. The burst in the lungs, the fire, the slow exhale, gently, softly through the nose. Eyes still closed. Blink open, quick, quick the blink, enough to see him still there, alone in the shadows. No Cathy. No Kate. No Natasha either, her bed a nest of blankets missing a hen.

Not Natasha, by the door. Can tell that. The breathing is male, large of lung, the breath over the tongue. Breath inching closer, foot by foot, slow, slow steps, the lips pursed and teeth behind, shush, shush, from his lips like a parent's comforting of a child; shush, shush, darling quiet now, darling, that's enough, my love.

Travelling the shush, coming near, and with it scent and heft, a body-smell of groin and sheet-cooled sweat. Closer, the shush, and the body and its smell lying down beside her, the mattress gulping, settling, the body not quite touching hers, but close, so close, almost touching. Shush, shush, through the lips, her hands by her sides, protecting nothing, ready to scratch perhaps, but the body on the top of the blanket and her trapped under it.

Shush, shush in the ear, shush, shush, as the hand roams over the blankets, palms on her breasts, layers between his palms and her chest, the hands resting there, as if searching for the beat of a heart, the hands not rough, not the Heathcliff hands she has fought and pawed away, his smell not the smell of ash and fire and damp hair. Not her Heathcliff. Something real, tangible. Weight to the hand, weight to the fingers, wandering down, settling around the crotch, resting there, fingers grabbing down, trying to find a hole through the blanket, any hole.

'These are the days we've waited for,' the body says. 'Are they not, Annie? It's just us now. The two of us. It's all down to us now, the two of us. No choice now, Annie. Just the two of us. Down here, it's you and me. It's going to be months, months down here. And we said we'd look after each other, didn't we, Annie? We said we'd take care of one another, didn't we, Annie? We said we'd do that. We made a promise, didn't we, Annie? Signed our name on that promise. We wrote our names together behind the piano, didn't we, Annie?'

A more forceful grab with the hand, pushing the fabric of her pyjamas almost inside her.

'I know you've always wanted me. I've always known. It was always going to be this way, war or not. Bombs or not. It's fate. I said what I said to protect you. You going with that man at Fernando's? That should have been me. You know it should have been me. You no longer need to be scared. You no longer need to mess with scum like that. It's us now, Annie. This is our world now, Annie. We will populate it in our image, Annie.'

Anneka spits in his face. Reaction as a grass snake, projectile towards the assailant, surprise the only weapon. He moves his hand from her groin, wipes away her spit. He drags his spitty fingers down her cheek, four wet track marks down to her chin.

'Or maybe you'd prefer to spend your time with Gault? He's the only other option, Annie. That's the reality of it all. You have a choice, Gault or me. Some desiccated old bastard, or me.'

He puts his arm across her chest, heavy like a log.

'Or maybe it's your father you want? Perhaps that's it. You'd like to fuck daddy, is that it, Annie? Is that your filthy little secret?'

He laughs and she tries to move her arms, nails ready to scratch, fists ready to punch, but the blankets are tight over her.

'Shush,' he says. 'I'm joking. Just joking around. I know it's hard. I know it's difficult for you, but why make it harder? Why not just accept it? We'll be together. The two of us will be together. Our children will repopulate the earth. We will be heroes. We will be gods.'

She wants to stab him. With blood, so much blood, she wants to make it stop. She can do it. She's sure she can do it. Just a weapon needed, improvised, a blade of some kind. Talking, him talking, but her hearing the gurgle of blood in his mouth, the lurch as the blood sprays free and clear.

He kisses her. Finds her mouth and she clamps down her lips, and he surrounds them with his; strong hands around her thin wrists, erection pressed against her. She manages to move her mouth away.

'Get off or I'll scream,' she says. 'I'll scream the fucking place down.'

'Scream,' he says. 'Go on, scream. You think anyone will care? We're all screaming. You say not tonight, but what of tomorrow? A week from now? A month? What then? Your fight will burn out. And then you'll start to enjoy it. You'll pretend not to, but you'll enjoy it. With every no, there is a coming yes.'

She pushes him from the bed and he falls to the ground, a thump and whack as he hits the flooring, the edge of the bedframe. Where you find strength, where you find ire, where you find courage. He doesn't move. She looks down and hopes for blood. His eyes are closed.

'You'll start to enjoy it,' he says, eyes still closed. 'You know that.

I know that. That's why you didn't scream. You could have screamed, but you didn't.'

And she screams then. All the screams, all those locked inside, flooding. She screams at him, but he is gone, out of the door and gone. She runs after him. The corridor is empty, all the doors closed, and she screams and screams.

Into the living quarters, him not there. She upends the crockery on the table. She throws a chair at the wall, starts taking books from the shelves, hurling them at walls.

'Come out,' Anneka shouts. 'Come out here. I'll fucking kill you. Come out!'

Gault watches her, but she does not notice him; does not notice her mother and her father, the two of them coming for her, all shushes and calming words. Arms around her, arms in comfort, arms in restraint.

'Get off me,' she says to her father. 'You should be after him, you should be getting him, not me!'

'It's okay, darling,' her father says. 'Just a bad dream, a nightmare.'

'No,' she screams. 'No. He was in my room. He was in my room and he touched me and he said things and—'

Behind Gault, her brother and Natasha, Daphne and Thomas appear. Thomas is wiping sleep from his eyes. Confused face. Strange face. Amused almost. Almost that.

'I'll fucking kill him,' she says. 'Keep him away from me.'

'Darling, sweetheart,' her mother says. 'Please. It's just a nightmare. A bad dream. No one was in your room. No one.'

'He was there,' Anneka says. 'He –' she points at Thomas – 'was in my room. He lay on my bed.'

'What's she talking about?' Thomas says.

'Go back to bed,' her mother says. 'You and Natasha get back to bed. We'll sort this out.'

'He's the one who needs sorting out. He was there. He was,' Anneka says.

Daphne ushers her children from the room. Gault stands watching, observing. Like he has a clipboard, a touch of the medico about him, an intrigued consultant.

'Can you give us some space, Mr Gault?' her father says. 'She suffers from terrible nightmares.'

The man nods, but does not move immediately. He keeps his eyes on Anneka. Close eyes on Anneka, shrewd eyes and reckoning.

'What happened?' her mother asks. 'Did Thomas come into your room?'

'Yes,' she says. 'I just said that, didn't you hear me?'

'And Natasha was there?'

'No,' Anneka says. 'No. She wasn't.'

'It was just a dream,' her father says. 'A terrible, awful dream.'

'No,' she says. 'You have to believe me, I know when things are . . .'

The weakness there, the weakness of the words, and the weakness of herself. The troubled look on her father's face. So many times that look, fear and shame that look, pity and anger that look. Heightened though, like the wind has changed and he is permanently stuck within it.

'I know what happened,' she says. 'I know he came into the room. And he—'

'Like Mr Hartson?' he says. 'Like you knew what he had done?'

And she sees the future then. The repetition. Overhearing her father tell Gault about the teacher she'd accused who had done nothing more than have the misfortune to appear in a dream. An apology to be made, the scraping and penitence. To Thomas.

'You don't believe me?' Anneka says. 'You think I just made all this up?'

Her father comes for her, with his arms and his eyes set on hers, the way he does when he means something serious.

'I believe you believe it,' he says. 'But it's hard, when you've said so—'

She busts out from his embrace, throws herself against the piano, screams there, kept screaming, the lung burst of the scream, so loud she feels her eyes might explode, her heart emerge from her throat.

'Don't come near me,' she says. 'Don't you come near me, either of you.'

Anneka weeps and she heaves and she screams and it is like she is no longer in the bunker, no longer anywhere but inside the noise and the heat and the fire and the rage. It does not feel it will end.

Gault returns to the living quarters and then it does end. Quickly, perfunctorily. They watch as he puts his hand behind the radio and produces a handset. A receiver. He pushes its button and talks into its grill.

'Site seven, a four seventeen. Concluded 4.16 a.m. Copy.'

'Copy that,' a static voice says. Gault puts down the receiver.

'Can I speak to you, Mr Moore?' Gault says. 'In my berth, please.'

The soft steps of his slippers. The ashen face of her mother. The sheer violence of her father's face. The rapt silence after the screams.

OPERATION MID-OFF

The plausibility was the test's main success. Even those who knew it was a test began to wonder if the fiction had become unwitting fact. Those involved were made to sign further Official Secrets Act paperwork. The threat of punishment was draconian, even for those dark days. I left the RSG the next day and thought of all the underground survivors, mole-like, emerging into a world they expected to have disappeared. The results were catastrophic, and no further tests were ever held, at least as far as I have been able to ascertain. I still think of them now, those survivors. How they see the world, how it changed them all. I like to think that they saw life in a new way and found it more precious than ever.

Bryan Jerrick, *My Cold Wars*
(Underworld Press, 2001)

15

Gault has the voice, the correct voice, the one of gravitas and import, sufficiently gravelled. His explanation is succinct and calm. You understand, he says, using Drum's forename often and deliberately, you understand, do you not, Drummond? The importance of this. The absolute necessity, Drummond. The need, in times of extreme pressure, to ensure the safety of the country.

Nodding head, Drummond. Nodding head and thank-you-sirs.

'When there are threats to safety, however,' Gault says. 'We have to stop. There is a clear directive. No one wants to see a death over this. So we have suspended the exercise and you are free to go, all of you. Once the paperwork is in order.'

He takes out papers, the penalties listed in bold type. Drum signs. He signs and Gault asks him to show in the rest of his family.

16

'You understand the consequences,' Gault says.

'Yes,' Anneka says. She signs below the bold type, below the regular type.

'I suggest you seek some help for your nightmares,' he says. 'You are clearly not well.'

She stands.

'Will that be all?' she says.

'Yes,' he says. 'Thank you for your attention.'

She shuts the door on Gault, collects her Go bag and walks to the living quarters. Her father, mother and brother are there. The bag is on her shoulder, like she's ready to go to school.

'Did you know?' she says to her father.

'No.'

'Did Carter know?'

'I don't know,' he says.

They look at each other and she knows Thomas must have known.

'You still don't believe me, do you?' she says.

Her father starts to say something, but she spits in his face. Second time the spit. She walks past him, past Nate, past her mother. Saying nothing, heading for the doors, heading for the exit.

'Where do you think you're going?' her father says. 'You come back here now.'

She keeps walking.

'If you leave now,' her father shouts. 'That's it.'

She keeps walking.

'I mean it,' he shouts. 'You come back here right now, Anneka Moore. You do as you're told. If you go now, that's it. I mean it.'

She keeps walking.

'You leave now, you never come back, you hear?'

She keeps walking.

'I mean it,' her father says. 'One more step and that's it.'

'Please, Anneka,' her mother says. 'Please, please come back.'

Anneka keeps walking. She keeps walking until the voices behind her are muffled by doors, by earth, by elevation. She keeps walking until she starts to run.

Woven in Fabric

1984

Sunday 23 September

I

There was summer in the late September morning; Sunday sunlight through an unhitched curtain hook, a square of pale just below his crossed feet. Neka placed her hand on his bicep, her skin pale as the square on the bed, his skin dark as the curtains. She'd promised not to do this; it made him uncomfortable, he said, the laying on of hands; it made him angry. He used words like fetishized. He used words like slave. He used words like dark meat. Later, he would apologize; say sometimes he said things he didn't mean, though she knew he meant exactly what he said. She promised not to touch him that way, but while he slept she'd put her hand on his skin and leave it there. He only caught her again the once. Caught her white-handed. A long jag that, some home truths coming.

'You only do this to scare daddy,' he'd said.

'I don't have a daddy to scare,' she'd replied.

'There's always a daddy,' he'd said. 'For women like you, there's always a daddy.'

She took her hand away now, imagining her leaving her fingerprints on him. It was the third night in three he'd shared her bed; a pattern emerging. It would not be long before it was broken. A few weeks and something would happen. She would upset him; he would upset her. They would fight, scream in the street, slam late-night doors, throw abuse through open windows. There would be weeks of silence, then one would make an apologetic approach, rhythmic as the tides, and they would both fall back into bed.

★

Cities are composed of conductors and soloists; soloists, if lucky, introduced to a conductor soon after arrival. Conductors exist to show the places that define their city; to reveal streets that become your streets, bars that become your bars, clubs that become your clubs. In this they revel, in this they dance. But they need a soloist; a soloist casts the city anew, shows it afresh through their eyes. Without conductors, the city is soulless, sprawling, sharp and empty, impossible to truly know. Those who do not love a city are those who never found their conductor.

Robin was there the night after Neka arrived at Lissa's, in the first-floor sitting room of Lissa's student house, holding a can of beer, dressed in a slimly cut suit, a black turtle neck, suede boots the colour of beach. An outfit of outrageous nostalgia. Neka was still dressed in her bedclothes. She sat in the cigarette-burned armchair, tried to cover herself, tried for invisibility, as Robin spoke to Gaynor and Kate, Lissa's housemates.

'Some of his followers call him John Frum,' Robin said. 'Some call him Tom Navy. Some say he's black, some say he's white. What they all agree on, though, is that during the war, an American GI came to their tiny island with all these modern miracles. Guns and walkie-talkies and I don't know what else. Their minds were blown, and so they decided he must be a god of some kind. A god! And now they want independence and their own nation state, free to worship this mythic American GI. They've built runways to encourage him to come back, too. They think he'll return, like Jesus or something. It's insane.'

Kate and Gaynor nodded. Lissa had said Neka would like Robin, even if he never did shut up. Listening to him talk to two uninterested women, she liked him well enough.

'I read about that,' Neka said.

'Insane, right?' Robin said.

'I think it's logical,' she said. 'If you've never seen a gun or a walkie-talkie before, never even conceived of such things, what are you going to think? You're going to think magic. You're going to think divinity. You're going to worship something with that kind of power.'

'Better to worship than to fear its wrath?' he said.

'Exactly,' she said. 'It works for every other religion, doesn't it?'

He nodded and pulled on his can.

'You're Nico?' he said.

'Neka,' she said.

'Coming to the Mayflower, Neka?' he said.

'Maybe,' she said.

She took a quick, spiteful shower; the water warm then cool, never getting to hot. The bathroom was filthy, hair-clogged and mildewed, the sink, bath and toilet cracked and unclean. The smell worse than farm, than her brother's bedclothes.

In her room, Lissa was blow-drying her hair: a new cut, a flicked bob.

'Try the black dress,' Lissa said over the sound of the hairdryer. 'It'll look good on you.'

Neka went to the wardrobe, took out a dress roughly the same age as her. Short, a collar at the neck, black buttons running down its front. She racked through the other dresses, similar vintage, similar styles. Gone now the rips and slashes in jeans and T-shirts; instead nostalgic elegance, a resurgent formality. Neka put on underwear and then the dress, zipped its back with a fumble, checked herself in the mirror.

She looked like she'd not only left home, but also her own time. There was something safe in that: to go back rather than forward; to slam on brakes, to stand and feel that a better, more artful era surrounded her. She pulled on a pair of Lissa's black tights, a pair of Lissa's shoes.

'Perfect,' Lissa said. 'Told you it'd look good on you. Now, let me do your make-up.'

A conductor and her soloist. One of many.

★

Robin snored lightly, rolled over onto his front. Neka got out of bed and went to the bathroom. It smelled of bleach and Jif, the small mirror wiped clean of toothpaste spits, the chrome taps' just-installed sparkle against white porcelain. Lissa's nerves expressed as household chores. A job interview, details sketchy, some time on Friday and then to her parents' for the weekend. The water in the toilet was still blue; the lino had been mopped. Grown-up, this cleaning; Lissa's ambition there to see.

Neka knew she should make plans, should think about getting qualifications, should think about a job that wasn't admin and service. Knew that she was behind her contemporaries, was idling as they sped. Lissa's voice, her father's voice. Urging her to think ahead, to think of the future, think of herself. Deaf to those voices now. Deaf and defiant.

'Shift starts in forty-five minutes,' Robin shouted from the other side of the door.

'I know,' she said.

'What time will you be back?'

'After shift.'

'I'll cook then.'

'There's no need. I might go out with Lissa. Depends when she gets back.'

'So you won't be back after shift?'

'I don't know,' she said. 'Depends on Lissa.'

'You going to be much longer in there?'

'Give us a sec,' she said. She ran the bath, let herself out and Robin closed the door behind him.

In the bedroom, she looked through the curtains, down onto Hartington Road, some kids messing around on bikes. She watched them for a time, their mute laughter and mock fights, the chrome dazzling in the sun. Liked the boys from this vantage; hated them on the street. The things they said were vile for lads barely in their teens.

Robin's arms around her then, big arms around her narrow shoulders.

'Bath's almost run,' he said. 'Give me a ring later, let me know what you're doing.'

'I will,' she said. Then stopped.

'No,' she said. 'Actually I'm not going to work. Fuck it. Day's too nice to be waiting tables.'

She turned and saw the delight; let him believe this change of heart was all down to him. Perhaps it was. She called in sick, put on her best weak and incapacitated voice, then took her bath.

Clean, pinked from the heat of the water, Neka slipped back under the blankets. She put her arms around Robin, the more of him now than when they'd met; lugs of flesh on his hips, a tum forming, too much drink. She put her hands on his biceps, she bit his earlobe. She pulled at the scrappy hairs on his chest, tight coils, springing back when released. She disappeared under the blankets, took him in her mouth, him unwashed and almost unwilling, the tang of it in her mouth, enjoying the surprise of him getting harder, enjoying the mischief of it. Not what she should be doing. Not the kind of girl she was; but certainly now the kind of woman she was.

His hands were on her head, not pushing, not pulling, but resting there. Little licks on the softness of the head, the way he liked it. She stopped and rolled over. At first he said he didn't like it that way. A political reason, he said. The same way he'd at first stopped her from sucking him, saying it made her subservient. She'd soon changed his mind on both.

She touched herself while he slowly moved inside and out of her. Furtive this: he did not like that she needed manual stimulation. But she touched herself whether he realized or no. She felt him climax inside her, the shoot and spray of it, and they lay there, both in a cycle of spasm and release, muscles like gears and cogs, his mouth at her ear, kissing her neck and shoulder.

'So what do you want to do now that you're playing hooky?' he said.

'That,' she said. 'Again and again.'

'You don't mean that,' he said. 'I wish you did, but you don't.'

'I sort of do,' she said. 'I think I'd like it.'

'It's still sunny out.'

They both looked up to the unhitched piece of curtain, the light stronger now, closer to midday.

'We could go for a picnic in the park,' she said. 'Make the most of it before it's all rain and cold.'

He stroked her hair.

'It'll be nice,' she said. 'Perfect in fact. I'll get a bottle of sangria.'

'Sangria?'

'Like in the song.'

'Yes,' he said. 'Perfect Day.'

★

Outside St Bede's they stopped to hear the gospel for a moment, the joyousness against the dirt streets and the smutty brick. They walked on, hand in hand, and an old man, skin white as parchment, came in the opposite direction. He wore Sunday best, a hat. He saw them, looked at them both, and tipped the brim of his trilby as he walked past. Rob nodded and the man nodded back.

'You know him?' Neka said.

'No,' Rob said. 'Never seen him before in my life.'

At the off-licence they bought crisps and nuts, a couple of Yorkie bars.

'Mate, you got any sangria?' Robin asked. 'We really fancy some sangria.'

'Fuck off to Spain then,' the man said: accent broad Scouse; face Indian subcontinent.

'Do you have any though?' Neka said. 'I know it's a long shot, but we woke up this morning thinking sangria was what we wanted.'

'You even know what sangria is?'

They looked at each other.

'Wine and orange juice,' the man said. 'And it's bloody disgusting if you ask me. Get a bottle of red, some orange juice, mix it up and there you go. Wine's there. Orange there. There's paper cups there too.'

The man watched them as they picked out the items; Neka now unsure why anyone's perfect day would include diluted wine. They paid and the man behind the counter opened the wine using a corkscrew attached to the cigarette display. He passed over the bottle and smiled.

'Make the most of the sunshine,' he said.

★

They entered the gates, rounded the obelisk and headed towards the large trees under which they would shade, the familiar clock-wise progression around the expanse of grass. She'd first walked Sefton Park in the aftermath of a snowstorm a few days after arriving at Lissa's flat. She walked it in a loop, lap after lap, seeing her boot-prints melt in the snow. It became ritual. She could get lost in bars, take the bus to the city, trash about in clubs, but the park became a place of deeper solace, of retreat. There she heard voices. Her father and mother, her brother, Thomas. A battle-ground of sorts. She'd murdered Thomas there often; she'd thrown accusations at her father; slapped her mother. In the park, she'd replayed the bunker so many times its memory had lost its power.

It was in the park that she'd kissed Robin for the first time; a few moments later told him she loved him. Almost three years of friendship hung in that moment. Three years she'd spent in icy celibacy; fending off men, fending off women. No interest, none at all, and then the low level pulse of interest, the returning feeling of desire. She allowed a man to kiss her. She allowed another man to share a bed with her, but not to see her naked. She did these things without Robin around. Testing herself, seeing how far she was willing to go. And then ready. Not looked back since.

They stopped at their usual spot, not far from the ruined glass of the Palm House. She spread down a picnic blanket and she opened the crisps and he poured the wine and orange juice. It looked musty, red and cloudy. The light was so bright she wished she'd brought sunglasses. They tipped their plastic cups together.

'Chin, chin,' he said.

She sipped the drink. It was summer and heaven and all things in between, simultaneously disgusting and delicious.

'It's . . .' he said.

'Yes, isn't it?' she said.

They read books in the shade of the tree, distracted, both of them, by the lives around them, the giggles and screams of children. Screams of children in delight, in tantrum, in pain when falling, all sounding the same. No clouds in the skies, no aeroplanes or vapour trails. She saw herself give a bottle to a baby; Rob kick a ball to their son; swing their daughter around by her arms. A safe space, the park. No chance of exposure. Just looking at the people playing. Not thinking. Not imagining. Not prognosticating.

'More sangria?' Robin said.

'Yes,' she said. 'More sangria.'

He poured the wine and added the juice.

'We should go see a movie too,' he said. 'In keeping with the sangria.'

'I think I'd fall asleep,' she said. 'Anyway, wouldn't we also have to go to the zoo?'

'I'm not feeding any animals,' he said.

He ran his fingers through her hair, the short cut she was growing out again.

'I used to come here to fight demons,' she said. 'Used to walk the whole place round. It was green but it was ugly. I'd look at people and think they were my mother, my father. I'd be fucking spitting with rage.'

She took a sip of the sangria.

'I miss my brother,' she said.

And it was true, at that moment. As Rob played with her hair, she missed Nate and his low honk laugh and his foot smell and his quiet smile.

'It feels good,' she said. 'To miss him. Like something's changed. Like . . . something altered.'

'You could write to him,' he said.

'I don't miss him *that* much,' she said. 'Just seeing the boys playing football. Makes me wonder if he's still playing. Another person now, I expect. A whole other person.'

'I don't know how you do it,' he said.

'Do what?'

'Not have him in your life.'

Robin had once said that all belief was hardwired. That no amount of evidence, empirical or otherwise, could shake that faith. For some it was religion, for some politics; for Rob it was the primacy of family. Robin's family was large, with branches and orders distributed around the globe like missionaries. They threw parties for returning cousins and aunts up and down the country, celebrated Christmas in Robin's mother's terrace in Kidderminster, the downstairs rooms packed as nightclubs. Neka told everyone her parents were dead. A car crash. A lie easier than the truth. Her brother she could not kill off, however. She couldn't seem to do that to Nate.

'Does it bother you?' she said.

'What?'

'Does it bother you that I don't talk to my brother?'

'You said you had your reasons,' he said. 'I respect that.'

'There's always reasons, Rob. Always justifications. It depends on what side you see it. Does it worry you?'

'What?' he said.

'That I might leave you like I left him.'

He adopted the considered pause of deep thought. Same as when the kids in his community group asked him difficult, adult questions.

'It crosses my mind, from time to time, yes.'

She watched the families pick up their belongings, fold picnic blankets, ruffle hair, buckle sandals, put on coats, load up buggies. She'd once had plans. London or something. Birmingham perhaps. Some terrible plans to Interrail Europe. Job though. Money though. Lissa though. Of late, Robin though. Plans, so many forgotten.

'Would it help if we moved in together?' she said. 'Would that make a difference?'

She felt the fingering of her hair stop, his pause.

'Move in with you and Lissa?'

'No,' she said. 'Just the two of us.'

His look of surprise and shock, the calculation of it: a test, perhaps, yes.

'Are you serious?'

'When am I not?'

So easy, words. So easy, out of the mouth, as though decided and binding, but unthought, ill-considered, no way to take them back. All the progress in the world and this never changing, the contract of unintended words. She felt giddy, unnerved by her actions: her father's voice telling her to take it slowly, to be careful.

No. No care. Careless. Care less. In the park, on a perfect day, why not be carefree and do something rash without due consideration?

Robin was giddy too. They talked of the kind of place they would live – a terraced house, a basement flat. Somewhere light and airy; somewhere dark and cosy – until the light dimmed and dusked. When the sangria ran out, they walked to the Albert on Lark Lane, a quick pint in the smoke of the boozer, the old men at the bar, then home, skittering drunk in the now-dark streets, detouring for fish and chips, eating them from the paper, the salt and vinegar on their fingers, the steam rising from the paper.

The house lights burned inside as they let themselves in, all of them lit. Not to tell Lissa tonight. To give her a night and then tell her in the morning. Neka called for her, but it was clear she was in the living room, the television up as loud as possible. They inched inside and in the living room Lissa was sitting hugging her knees to her chest, crying, a bottle of gin beside her.

'Lissa,' Neka said. 'Lissa, what's—'

They sat down on the corduroy sofa. The deafening television showing something that looked like a documentary. The world was black. There were dead in the street, men in radioactive suits wandering around.

'What's this?' Robin said.

'*Threads*,' Lissa said. 'When the bomb drops this is what it's going to be like. Just like this. I can't take it. I can't take it, but I can't look away.'

A nuclear winter. A shambling woman, blasted heaths and charred bones. Lissa could not take it, but neither could she look away. Neka watched the aftermath. Neka watched the survivors. Neka saw herself in their number. She saw her father and her mother, her brother and the Carters and she saw it all, the lived experience, the quality of the air, the sense of life amongst the death.

She put her arms around Lissa. She put her arms around her to soothe her. And she saw the men below ground and she saw herself and she saw the end of the world for a second time.

2

It was a dress of her own choosing, bought with her own money from Pedley's in the town: the uncompromising assistants swishing open the fitting-room curtains to suggest other styles. Should have gone with Daphne, but Daphne unavailable, and Gwen forgetting why she'd decided to buy a dress, remembering it was because no dress of hers now fitted.

In front of the mirror in the spare room, looking herself up and down now in the dress she'd bought, the most expensive thing she'd ever owned, scrawny and short-haired, highlights dimming, thinking of excuses. Any excuse not to go to the lunch.

Drum came into the spare room, smell of his cologne, a present from the Carters at Christmas, expensive and strong; smart trousers, his shirt well-pressed, shoes polished up, the brown brogues, a birthday present from the Carters.

'Almost ready?' he said.

'Just need to do my make-up,' she said. 'Ten minutes.'

'Well, whenever you're ready,' he said.

'We won't be late,' she said. 'We've got lots of time.'

He looked at her in the flesh, then in the mirror, then in the flesh.

'You look beautiful,' he said. 'Absolutely beautiful.'

She looked at him first in the mirror, then in the flesh, the way he stood there, rocking on his heels, the brogues' leather.

'You don't think it's too much for lunch?' she said.

'No,' he said. 'It's perfect. You look wonderful.'

He stood there and she knew what he was thinking. That they did not dress any more. Did not undress either, so much as shed outer layers and collapse into bed. He sometimes said she was beautiful but when he did, it felt nostalgic, as though he was looking into deep time rather than saying it of the woman in front of him. Appreciated though. Always appreciated. The patience too. Always the patience.

He kissed her on the cheek. His lips lingered, his arm around her waist. She gently pushed him away.

'Get off,' she said. 'Otherwise we *will* be late.'

She smiled into the mirror. He caught it and smiled back as she smoothed down the fabric of the dress.

★

She read a book that year, one that opened in glacial calm, a chair and a room by a lake, a woman alone and looking to find her 'serious and hard-working personality' somewhere in a secluded hotel. Gwen no longer looked for herself in books; it felt juvenile to do so, the way she had when Old Nick had schooled her, the thrill of finding herself buried in the language and manners of invented characters. She sought only escape in books now, but that escape had become limited. She avoided certain genres these days, the kind of authors who had once given her so much pleasure. P. D. James, Ruth Rendell, Colin Dexter, even Agatha Christie.

She read about a murder and she read about the murder of her daughter; she read of disappearance and she read of the disappearance of her daughter; she read of prostitution, drug addiction, domestic violence, rape, sexual molestation, and she read the fate of her daughter. Once a safe space, books became dangerous. They offered untold imaginative harm. So she chose her books carefully, scanning blurbs for warnings, for mentions of dark secrets, family traumas, and rejected so many that she mostly stuck to re-reading the books Old Nick had recommended.

The book she'd read had won the big prize; she always read the book that won the big prize. And from the opening, in the room overlooking the lake, she saw herself waiting to find her own serious and hard-working personality. Gwen's house resembled the same kind of out-of-season hotel, light with guests, without hope of a summer coming to banish the autumn hiatus.

She cooked breakfast in the morning, four eggs for her two men, before they set out to the fields and sheds; the house silent as they slammed shut the door, no one sleeping upstairs, no one breathing as she passed the bedrooms.

The silence of the house, the silence of the car, then the silence of the library, then home in the car, the dinner to prepare, her husband and her son, starving at 5 p.m., talking of cows, talking of gaskets, as she spooned out casserole, looked not at the vacant chair, not at the odd number of plates and bowls and glasses.

There were few arguments, the doors only banged on her on account of the wind, and if Anneka's name was mentioned there were stone faces and avoided glances, a curt reminder not to mention that. Not to mention her.

Gwen and Drum had discussed finding her, had gone as far as contacting Lissa's mother, who was unhelpful, even to Gwen. They'd gone to Liverpool to investigate, gone to Lissa, asked her if she'd seen Anneka. The look on her face. Pained and surprised, worried, almost shaking with it. Hard not to believe her. Lissa promising she'd be in touch if she heard anything, but said they'd had a falling out. Lissa said Anneka had stayed only a couple of nights. That Anneka had said something about London. Something about Birmingham.

They kept her room as it was, until enough was enough and Gwen ripped off the wallpaper and stacked Anneka's things in the attic. How slim the life. How unlived. Her few diaries Gwen read, no revelations within them, no codes to decipher, nothing she had not known or surmised before.

The absence was the thing that got to her, the lack of mention of her. Some pages were devoted to Drum – unsurprising bouts of anger towards him – but Gwen warranted barely a mention. So little of Gwen, it would be impossible for a detective or critic to reach any conclusions save that she was a minor character who cropped up from time to time but was not material to the author. How callous to be disappeared by the disappeared.

Gwen had painted the walls of Annie's old room a shade of lilac. Some nights she would make her way there, sleep on the bed, sleep deeply, as if to prove it were possible. She was always up before Drum though, always ready to kiss him awake and tell him breakfast was ready, before doing the same for her son.

For a time, Carter and Drum did not speak – a few months after the bunker, a crippling time for Drum, soon smoothed over – but Daphne and Gwen had continued their Wednesday afternoons. The first months, they'd talked about it. Talked of it, around it, through it, below it. Gwen would confess her worst doubts, her most terrifying of dreams, and Daphne would pour and cluck, hold her when the shaking started. For months they did not discuss anything else; Gwen saying all the things she could not say to Drum.

The days moved on and there were snags, always snags, little tears in the reality, a missed phone call, a letter from the bank, a voice like hers whispering in the library stacks. Snags in the books she read, snags in the records she heard on the radio. They faded, they sagged; but they did not go, they did not disappear. Those left behind have no agency. They cannot do anything until the disappeared decides to rematerialize. And she accepted this. Every day, she accepted this.

★

They walked the shingle path in strong sunlight, the fields refreshed by recent rain, the hedgerows smudged with the last of the brambles and blackberries. They held hands as they walked, fingers laced, arms swinging in time to their footsteps. There was a new car outside the Carters' house, a white Ford Sierra; Thomas standing beside it.

Gwen had not seen much of him since he left for university;

drinks to celebrate his engagement, drinks to celebrate his wedding, the odd other times he popped home. She tried not to spend too much time with him, if she was able; he just made her think of Annie. Made her wish she would just pop home, now and again. Looking at him, an adult now, straighter of back, assured in his yellow Oxford shirt, pink sweater sleeves knotted around his neck, and wondering how her daughter was, whether she was as adult as him.

'I've not seen the XR4i before,' Drum said. 'Not in the flesh at least. That's a hell of a spoiler.'

Drum pointed to the back of the car. A pair of fins stuck out from the top of the boot and below the back window. It looked like a pair of duck lips to her; like Mick Jagger's pout.

'Goes like shit off a shovel,' Thomas said, 'if you'll pardon my Français. No Nate?'

His fair hair fell into his eyes a little, the sides short but the fringe on the long side, like his father way back. Looked like his father, but softened by his mother's features: less harsh in the nose, his eyes less piercing. He was the kind of man her father would have shunned at the bar, affect deafness if his attention was sought, add ice to his Scotch if not asked for; forget it if ordered. A barman's sense of a bad egg: the kind of men who on seeing a bus wonder who they might throw under it.

'He's been in the fields all morning,' Drum said. 'He might join us after he's had his nap.'

'Sounds like our Josie to me – she's hell if she doesn't get her nap.'

'So I hear,' Gwen said. 'Shall we go in? If we stay here any longer, Drum'll be asking about torque and miles to the gallon.'

Thomas laughed and they laughed along with him. His daughter Josie. His darling daughter, his beautiful cherub. That fucking child.

★

A Wednesday, one of the bad days. Not so long after Natasha left for Durham University, the two of them in the kitchen. Of all the conversations they had, this the one that stuck.

'I promised I'd leave him after the kids left,' Daphne said. 'And believe me, I've packed those bags so many times, but I just can't do it. But one day . . .'

'But you'd be leaving me, too,' Gwen said.

'Oh, doll,' she said. 'I wouldn't ever leave you.'

Daphne did not leave, but in the space of a year was twice taken from Gwen. After his graduation, Thomas married some pony-like woman from Surrey. The wedding was, so Gwen was told by Victoria, to be a small show down in the countryside, close family only, though it was clear this was a lie. A lie, and with it relief.

Six months and all Daphne's conversation was of the wedding: the flowers, the arrangements, the absolute lunacy of the bride's parents. Wednesdays became truncated, the trill of things to do, things to do. Gwen saw Annie everywhere during those months. Could not read even a newspaper without seeing her.

Two months after the wedding, the pregnancy. The second loss. Worse this, so much worse. The updates on Victoria's terrible pains and privations, the potential names, the guessing game of the sex. Months of this. There were other topics of conversation, but they were only a few roads from the subject of baby. The baby who arrived three weeks prem; Daphne scuttling off to Surrey to watch the wet wriggle of a thing in its plastic box. She called Gwen in tears, but was hopeful that the poor little mite – said so often it sounded like the infant's full name – would pull through. Gwen never thought that. Not that. No. No she never once thought of its death. That would be too cruel.

Daphne came back armed with photographs and stories, but did not really ever come back. So much of her was down in Surrey, in the nine-pound sack of skin. Daphne missed several Wednesdays. Sometimes she was in Surrey; sometimes she was just too busy.

'Do you ever wonder,' Gwen said to Drum, in bed one of those bitter Wednesday nights, 'about what Annie's doing? Where she is?'

'I try not to,' he said.

'I think she might have had a baby.'

He looked up from his book. His new spectacles made him look donnish, slightly confused.

'What makes you say that?'

'I feel it,' she said. 'I can see her, big-bellied. Carrying a little boy around. Lying him down in a cot.'

'She'd tell us,' he said. 'I know she'd tell us.'

'It must be great to know everything,' she said. 'To be so bloody *sure* of everything. You said she'd be back in a week, remember?'

'Babies change people,' he said. 'Your perspective changes, you remember?'

She looked down at her belly, wondered if she could conceive a child now. Still possible, surely. The child once there, a child inside of her now, the Russian dolls of it all.

The next week, Gwen walked into the Carters' kitchen and Daphne was beaming, lighthouse-bright and radiating, though she did not look like she'd been drinking.

'A surprise for you,' Daphne said and led her into the living room. Connected to the television was a video camera. The television held a single image, white lines bouncing up and down over it, a woman holding a baby.

'Now, let me see here,' Daphne said, bending down and fiddling with buttons.

The stopped image unpaused: Victoria with Josie in her arms. Holding her up to the camera, waving her daughter's arm as though hailing a taxi. Thomas taking the baby, throwing her up in the air, catching her, the baby giggling and gurning. Then Thomas passing the child to Daphne, and Daphne kissing the baby on the nose, holding her in the crook of her arm, laying down the kisses, raining them down.

'Very nice,' Gwen said and stood up.

It went on. A half-hour. Almost an hour. So much video. Gwen got up again.

'I can forward it,' Daph said. 'They videoed me giving Josie a bath. She looks so—'

'I'm sorry, Daphne,' Gwen said, 'but I just don't fucking care.'

She thought the video had paused, the people on screen watching them, not each other. Silence on video, silence in the room.

'And don't I know it!' Daphne said. 'The whole time you've been sitting there, not even pretending to care. You've shared in none of this. You've just sat there looking bored, like you'd rather be anywhere else.'

'That's not true.'

'Isn't it? All the times I listened to you, comforted you, and you can't share in my happiness. You just sit there, jealously sucking all the joy from it.'

That face. The fire in the eyes. The righteousness of the anger. The same face shared between them.

'You think this is easy for me?' Gwen said. 'Watching you with your precious Josie? My daughter's gone, Daphne. She could be dead for all I know, and all I hear is that Surrey's so far away and how much you miss that child. It's all I ever hear! And you don't for one single moment think how that makes me feel. You think it just ends? You think I don't think about her all the time? And you have the fucking *nerve* to be angry with me. To be disappointed in me? Well fuck off, Daphne. Fuck off, with your fucking children and fucking Josie.'

Gwen slammed out of the back door, went home and straight to the attic. She read Anneka's diaries again, saw herself disappeared again, removed again, not there, not there at all.

*

'Well hello you two,' Carter said, coming out from the kitchen. 'Better late than never.'

349

'Tom's just been telling us about his car,' Drum said.

'Ah, that explains it then,' Carter said. 'Daph's in the kitchen wrestling a chicken the size of Stockholm.'

Gwen watched the three men leave her, Carter throwing a lazy arm over Drum's shoulder, a joke or something, the three of them laughing. How would Annie feel if she came back now to find her parents wetting the head of Thomas Carter's daughter, making nice with his new wife? Come back, let us find out.

The kitchen smelled of roasting meat, sage and onion, thyme and rosemary, the perfume Poison. Daphne looked up from stirring gravy. She picked up a glass of wine and poured it into the pan.

'I was wondering if you'd come,' Daphne said. 'I thought you might have a migraine or something.'

'I'm sorry,' Gwen said. 'I shouldn't have—'

'No,' she said. 'No you shouldn't. Shouldn't have had to. I'm sorry too. But no more on it. Forgotten, yes?'

She turned to Daphne, they embraced; the gravy began to simmer.

'Gwen,' she whispered in her ear. 'Don't let me drink any more. Please don't. I'm really, really drunk, Gwen. I'm really fucking drunk.'

*

Victoria handed Josie to Gwen. Little Josie. The body so small, the head so heavy. Forgot at first, so long since she'd held one, then back to the old routine, looking down into the eyes, the dark eyes miraculously open, and like holding Annie, back when she was small, the gentle weight of her, the promises made in the darkness, the small room in which she gurgled, screamed sometimes. Not so much, not a bad sleeper. You never forget, but never quite remember. Imagine Annie with her own child, holding him, nursing him. Imagine that. Her own daughter, her own daughter in her lap. Annie. Come home. Only once. Only once to think it.

Just allow me this once. A prayer of sorts. A prayer yes, to be answered, Lord please. Bring her back to me. Her and her child. The child I do not yet know. I will be there, Lord. I will be there, Annie. There is nothing we cannot overcome. So, home, Annie. Back here, Annie. Understand me, Annie. Reappear me, Annie. Bring me back, Annie.

THREADS, SISTERHOOD AND THE BOMB

We were gathered and told our positions: the lucky pointed to stations in the shade; the unfortunate to those in the full glare of the sun. Our group was a broad church: a family with two small children, a clutch of twenty-somethings, four or five who had been in the original film, a few fellow writers, pretending not to recognize each other. This was not surprising. Had more of us known of the reconstruction, the whole ensemble would have probably been made up of journalists. For writers of my generation, the film we were there to reshoot is a cultural totem unlike any other. Mention it – mention *Threads* – and our faces form the same horrified mask; mention it and silence meets shudder.

Threads was broadcast on Sunday 23 September 1984. Filmed in documentary style, cold, meticulous and terrifyingly objective, it dramatizes the effect of an atomic strike on Sheffield. The initial panic, the all-engulfing fireball, and most shockingly, the aftermath; the few survivors eking out lives in dark medieval fields, lit by the bitter light of a nuclear winter. It is the single most terrifying work of art ever made. Nothing else comes close.

My scene was over quickly. The director called action and I ran demented, trying to outrun the bomb. The director shouted cut, and we all stopped, all imagining the bloom of a mushroom cloud. It took just under a minute. The director watched the rushes back on his iPhone; called it a wrap.

Threads Redux was part of the Sheffield Documentary Festival, the largest of its kind in the world, and back at its hospitality hub, I drank a large gin and tonic as if it were Fanta. Jude Rogers, a fellow writer, came over to join me, set down her wine and asked me how I'd found the experience. I had no words, and was thankful Jude began to talk of the first time she'd watched the film, on a battered, oft-copied VHS, on a date at a boy's house. A compelling seduction technique: shattering a girl and then giving her a shoulder to cry upon. She was not born when the film was broadcast, I imagine.

As Jude told of cowering in a nameless boy's arms, I was taken back to another pair of arms, that of my childhood best friend. Her and *Threads* are bound together, woven and stitched into one another: I cannot think of one without the other.

We first met at school, a quiet yet resilient – perhaps even hostile – twelve-year-old. She was mordantly witty, scabrous at times, always capable of surprising with an out-of-character moment of personal revelation. We became inseparable; the two of us riding our teenage angst at the same pace.

In the last year of A-levels, she fell apart. I remember offering her some of my mother's Valium to help her sleep and her declining, though she must have heard the plea in my voice. She failed A-levels. Spectacularly failed them, even though her predicted grades would have been good enough for Oxbridge. I went to Liverpool and left her behind with the parents she'd long come to resent.

Then in the February of 1980, she appeared at my

door, a backpack on her shoulder, asking if she could stay. She didn't leave for several years.

Anyone who has had a ruinously close relationship in their early twenties knows what happened next. You become symbiotic; you meld into one another. We shared clothes, we drank ourselves stupid, did things that in retrospect were astonishingly dangerous. We did not so much finish each other's sentences, but fill in the next lines in an ever-stretching paragraph. And as anyone who has had a close relationship in their early twenties knows, it couldn't last.

The Friday before *Threads* was broadcast, I told her I was going to see my parents; this the only way to ensure she would not try to tag along. I took the train to London to interview for a job at a music magazine. The editor was from Liverpool, he liked the sound of my recently acquired Scouse lilt, my disdain for the Beatles, my love of The Raincoats. We got drunk in a pub afterwards and he made a pass. I declined. He still gave me the job though. There and then.

On the train home, I wrote down all I would say to my friend, though I never said a word of it. *Threads* meant I did not have to say it. *Threads* meant she understood when eventually I cleared out without saying goodbye.

After *Threads*, I thought about the bomb constantly; thought about it even more than my act of cowardice. For a small feminist press, I wrote an essay about patriarchy and the bomb – reprinted in this volume – about how ships and planes were all female, but bombs always male. It is no coincidence that the first bombs were named Fat Man and Little Boy. I thought about the bomb more than my friend I left behind.

I have not looked her up, have not typed her name

into search engines or social media platforms (I made this mistake before, only finding an electronic book of remembrance for my former lover, lost to multiple sclerosis). I do not look for her, but prefer to think of her holding me as we watched that film, holding me and saying it was all okay, that it was just a film. And for that moment forgetting what I was about to do, and what I had already done.

Lissa Capel, *Kingdom Cum: Selected Essays, 1984–2018*
(Influx Press, 2019)

4

They opened the French doors onto the veranda; Carter disallowed from smoking inside while Josie was in state. The two chairs, wicker, cushioned in red cotton, looked out over the fields, a rattan table between them, heavily ringed from Scotch and wine. Their lives together: two men in two chairs, a table between them, a fair approximation of their berth in Shropshire.

During the months they didn't speak, Drum had missed Carter with a visceral, physical hurt. He'd tried to talk to Gwen in the way he spoke to Carter, but their exchanges were laboured; she did not quite follow the internal logic, the bends and swerves, could not cut flesh and plaster wound within the same argument. She was game for it, she understood. Transparent old Drum. To lose a daughter, inexcusable; to lose a friend, unimaginable.

Détente was reached with a bottle brought round on a Friday night. Carter's invitation to the veranda to make some inroads into it. Seconds to decide. He could feel Gwen's smile warm his back. A phoney war over, the sun down and the outside fairy lights lit, red, blue, yellow, green. A drink of Scotch, the smell of Carter's cigarettes, the averted eyes of his apology.

'I know this isn't your fault,' Drum had said. 'I shouldn't have blamed you.'

'It's forgotten,' Carter said.

'I keep thinking she'll come back,' Drum said. 'At the start of the day I think this'll be the day she comes home, tail between and all that.'

Drum looked into the lights again, the muddle of them through the tears he would not shed.

'She'll be back,' Carter said. 'Mark my words.'

He thought of that night, that reconciliation, the absolute conviction of Carter's words. Four years now. Four, soon to be five. Her birthdays came and went; so too the lightening of the mornings and the pulling in of the nights. Long times in the fields, alone with imaginings and cows. Days in rain and sleet, the smatter of it on the milking shed's corrugated roof, the snap of the inflators on the cows' teats, the checking through of jobs and routine.

For all the hard work, for all the worries of money, of the safety of the livestock, of milk prices, of the creep of pipeline production and bigger, more economically viable farms, he would not swap the life. The closeness of his son, the days spent with him, precious now, unsaid but precious. Annie might have run away, but no doubt would have one day run away regardless. You change a life, but the material essence of it can't be altered. She was always going to leave him; she had always been leaving him. She would come back though. When it was time. She would return and he would forgive her.

'You'll be watching tonight?' Carter said, sitting down on the wicker chair, lighting his cigarette.

Drum nodded.

'I wanted to watch it with you,' Carter said. 'But with Tommy staying . . .'

'We can watch it together another time,' Drum said.

'You're recording it?' Carter said.

'Gwen and Nate have been on at me to get a video for ages. Got it yesterday.'

Carter nodded and blew out a swatch of smoke.

Drum took a sip of his Scotch. The wind was up and Carter's limp hair danced like children.

'Daph won't watch it,' Carter said. 'Tom neither.'

'Fatherhood suits him,' Drum said. 'You can tell.'

'He likes the control,' he said. 'That I can see. He's read all these books. Has all these ideas. Thinks he's raising the next Iron Lady.'

'He looks happy.'

'She's a good girl, that Victoria. But I told him, I said, there's more to life than just kids and wife. You need to live a little before all that, or you'll live too much when you shouldn't. He said to me, "Not everyone's like you, Dad." The little skate. Bastard thinks he knows it all. I told him, I was in Service, every one of his ancestors fought a war at some stage, but he thinks he knows it all? He just laughed. They have no fear, these kids. If they fall, we'll be here to help them. If we're not here, the state will be. We had it good, but this lot, they've got it made.'

Carter stubbed out his cigarette and opened his pack for another. He looked at Drum.

'Sorry,' he said. 'It gets me like this when he comes here. Worse now there's a kid. All Daph ever talks about, all she cares about.'

'Gwen's convinced Anneka's pregnant. Says she knows it.'

Carter beat his hand on the table. Something done when playing backgammon. Hard lines. Drum had dreamed of Anneka's baby; already talking, already dressed in school uniform. Drum talking to the child but the child not understanding, deaf perhaps, or not understanding his accent. He'd watched Gwen cry in the night when she thought he was sleeping, heard her move to the spare room that always smelled of Anneka no matter how many dishes of potpourri were left on the dresser.

'I thought Gwen was going to leave me,' Drum said. 'There was a time not long ago, I thought she was just going to jack it all in.'

Carter raised an eyebrow.

'You never said.'

'I'm saying now.'

'She's always seemed so strong. Even after everything.'

'You're not the only one who can put on a show,' Drum said.

Carter took in a long lungful of smoke, blew it out in two straight beams from his nose.

'We should go inside.'

'Yes.'

They stayed in the wicker chairs, looking out over the fields, the only sound Carter smoking and Drummond drinking.

★

Drum set the video to record before the programme started. When he came to watch it again, so many times later, the first ten minutes of tape were coverage of a darts match, Cliff Lazarenko forever beating Leighton Rees three sets to one. The darts hitting the board, Cliff victorious; Tony Gubba congratulating him on his progress to the next round. Dart after dart, on fast forward; the players waddling ducklike to the board, ripping them from it.

Gwen came into the living room as, on screen, a spider constructed a web. Over the sound of birdsong, a voiceover, stentorian and authoritative, the voice he had wanted to hear on the phone, the one wishing him luck, said:

In an urban society, everything connects. Each person's needs are fed by the skills of many others. Our lives are woven together in a fabric. But the connections that make society strong, also make it vulnerable.

The birdsong and spider disappeared, replaced by the smoke and engine noise of a city.

'I'm not sure I can watch this,' Gwen said.

But she stayed. She stayed and she held his hand as the bomb dropped and the people screamed. She stayed as everything burned: bones and bodies; buildings and fields; an ET soft toy: a pointed, nasty detail. The tea on the table grew cold. He watched, burned alive and bunkered both. He felt the cool air of down below, what he'd imagined was going on above while he was down there, happening now on the television, much as he'd seen it. The panic, the desperation, the white light and nothing. The collective trauma, the one experienced now up and down the country. The audience watching this, watching the horror unfold over time, a day, a week, a month, a year, the power of that.

359

Having lived through it once, here to live through it again; worse this way, worse with the concrete of the visuals. He could smell Gault. He could see Anneka screaming. He could see Nate and he could see Anneka and he could see his wife and he could see Gault at the radio, calling off the exercise. He could see the nuclear winter. The nuclear winter as he had not seen it. The years of the survivors. The cold and black, the tilling of unfertile land.

It was him on the moorland, the hills, the blasted black territories. It was him almost mute, surviving there, day by day. It was them all together under the slate-black skies. And at the end, it was not them. It was Anneka. Anneka alive and pregnant, pregnant and giving birth.

A symbol of hope that birth, in the squalid makeshift maternity ward, and it was Anneka, not the actress, who was handed her baby, wrapped in swaddling, the swaddling covered in blood. And it was Anneka, not the actress, looking down on her baby, her face curious at first, then disbelieving and then in terror. Absolute terror, the actress, the Anneka, absolute terror and her face contorted and just the sound of a scream, so loud the scream the wooden housing of the television shook, and then the end, the very end, Anneka, the actress, dissolving and the film ending. Credits rolling, but the scream still shuddering the living room.

He took the two mugs of cold tea through to the kitchen. Gwen followed him, poured two glasses of Scotch. They sipped their drinks in the kitchen, standing and not looking at each other.

'I know what you're thinking,' he said. 'And this isn't the time.'

'When will it ever be?' she said. She looked at him in ice and fire, in bomb and blast, in love and rockets.

'Whether you help me or not,' she said. 'I'm going to find her.'

He looked at his drink, he looked at his wife. He saw his daughter birth the terror child, saw her scream, the noise audible around the world.

'You can't stop me,' she said.

5

They were ambivalent to him, the cows. They seemed to love his father, but treated Nate as mere wrangler, and somehow they were worse on Sundays. Seemed to know he was probably hungover. The only time it was different was when he watched the births, the guts and matter of it, the blind, jellied calves emerging. His father was moved by it. Every time he was moved, and Nate could not help himself either. The cows looked at him differently then, but not now.

They used surge milkers still, though others had upgraded to pipeline systems, a development his father had steadfastly opposed. The speed meant more cows could be milked, the graft was less than with the surge milkers, but his father had seen pipeline in action and thought the cows looked unhappy. It was a fear of not being able to fix them, though; Nate thought. Of having to learn something new after so long herding the cows into the herring-bone enclosures, affixing the teats, setting the rate of suction just so, fixing pulsators, reattaching blown air hoses.

'You know where you are with surge,' his father would say. 'Know to the gallon what's coming. Keeps the mastitis at bay too. They're happy girls, why change that?'

Because I already have the back of a sixty-year-old. Because an hour less with the cows would be an hour free of them. Because I spend too long replacing gaskets, getting evils from the cows as the suction fails once again.

He put the inflators on the teats of a cow his father called Patch, set the pulsator. He'd tried to speed up the process once, but his father had shaken his head, told him impatience would be the death of him. His father right, of course: no way to short-cut the process. The pump started, the milk flowed, he set about the next one, the one his father called Jem.

It was an automated process, both he and the cows. An animal production line. There were other things he could have done. An ex-professional footballer gave them a talk at the college, a question-and-answer thing. The ex-pro regaled them with his meagre glories, then told them he was now a physiotherapist, something he'd become interested in after a long injury. Nate had looked into a course; he did not have the qualifications, did not ultimately have the interest. Easier to stay on the farm, easier to be with his father, take his money on a Friday, live without worry for bills and food.

The fifth milker would not work, nothing happening when he attached the inflators. He turned on the vacuum pump and leaned his bulk on top of it, the pressure on the gasket kicking the pulsator into life.

'Make a farmer of you yet, boy,' he said, aping his father.

Though he was already a farmer, at least in the daytime, at least when working. To look at him, yes, a farmer, a farmhand, close to the land, close to the cattle, his little whistles to them. Harris the dog, his German shepherd raised from a pup, alert and lively, as suspicious as his owner about the cows. Nate could talk as a farmer, could make like one, but it still felt like something temporary, something he would outgrow, like thinking he'd play for City.

In a fight, someone did his ankle. An accident, not intentional. He watched City lose the Cup Final replay on the television with his leg up. Football dying for him then. The posters came down from the walls. He no longer nutmegged Cruyff, no longer thought of Asa Hartford, other things having taken over. The farm mainly; the farm and Pete. The working week and then Friday-night fighting with Pete. Pete now living in the old caravan, his uncle Joseph disowning him. No word of why. Later, Nate understanding. In the caravan, understanding. Things always different in the caravan; a place of greater safety.

It was warm in the milking shed, and he watched the cows while smoking a joint, his right hand bruised, the knuckle flattened, more so than usual. Making a fist still smarted a couple of days on from the ruck. The knuckle had gone on the extreme of his right hand. A tattoo there would now read love and hat. A smile at that. Him and Pete on a Friday. Fights and then to the caravan, to inspect the wounds. Kiss the wounds and welts away. Pete now sleeping; Nate's turn to herd.

Nate had seen them arrive: Thomas with his hair gel and slip-on shoes; the wife, posh bird, the kind that liked him well enough sometimes, the kind who would touch his arms and giggle, the way they did with Pete. Like Pete, he had no trust in these women. 'Like horses, men like us,' Pete had said. 'Horses, but not for breeding.' They'd done men like Thomas. Beaten them in the town centre, outside pubs. Not much sport, but fun nonetheless.

Nate flexed his good fist. Would like to do Tommy. Didn't matter if he did it or no. Didn't matter, in the grand scheme. Without Tommy, he wouldn't be there still; Nate was sure of that. Would have done something. Got out. Not feeling the need to stay with his family. Without Tom, everything different. Anneka still there.

He finished his joint and went back to the farmhouse; Harris labouring behind. His parents were at the table, eating toast, the two of them in low conversation about something. His mother smiled at him, his father too.

'All right out there?' his father said.

'Nice morning,' he said. 'Like the last of summer.'

'I can take more summer,' he said.

'You coming over to the Carters' for lunch?' his mother said. 'Thomas has brought his little girl up.'

'I should have known she was here,' Nate said. 'I saw this big star in the sky and there were shepherds and these funny-looking blokes in flowing robes.'

'Very funny,' she said. 'Are you coming over?'

'No, I'm washing my hair,' he said, running his hand over his buzzcut.

He could have said about Anneka. He could easily go down that road, but his father was already a pot with the lid on, the steam escaping from the sides. Ready for it. Ready to shut it down. Learned this, his look that said, in quiet, sad tones, do not push me. Do not make me lose the grip I currently have.

'I'll try to come over after my nap.'

His father nodded, the pan cooling.

'What did you do to your hand?' his mother said.

'Trapped it in the shed door last night,' he said.

'You're the clumsiest lad I've ever met,' his father said.

★

He spent the late morning and early afternoon masturbating and sleeping. He showered at three, got dressed and looked at the house through the binoculars. He could see his mother and Daphne in the kitchen, the baby on his mother's knee, the two of them talking and drinking white wine. He watched them for a while, watched as Thomas and his wife came into the kitchen, arm in arm, and plucked the girl from his mother.

Four years older and Thomas out in the world, like Anneka; Nate stuck here. You say it's a choice, but it's not a choice. You say you love the fields, the sweat of work, but you do not love the work, you just know it's easy. You say you're glad you're not a brainbox like the Carters and your sister, but you're not glad. You wake in the dark and you know your day and you know how it will end and begin again.

He masturbated again. Images coming, all of them. Images of Daisy, a short woman, a year or so older than him, stout and forthright. The first time she'd wanked him off it felt like she was doing something agricultural. He imagined he'd probably marry her. Daisy didn't.

'You need to relax,' she'd said. 'You're all . . . tensed up. Like you're ready for your whole life right this second so you can get it over with.'

He wondered if it was because he'd taken so long to cum when they eventually fucked that she'd stopped and offered to finish him off with her mouth. He'd declined and kept at it, no image or sensation making any material difference. He never had that problem when alone. Nor when in the caravan.

He heard his parents come back a little after four. He put on his Walkman. His father came into the room, tapped him on the leg.

'You'll go deaf as a post listening to that thing.'

'What's that?' he said.

'It's no joke. Most of the men from the factory were deaf by sixty. You'll be the same, you carry on.'

'It wasn't that loud.'

'You should have come over. Thomas was asking after you.'

'Maybe I'll go see him later,' he said. 'Catch up with him myself.'

His father smiled.

'I think he'd appreciate it,' he said.

★

Nate rode the 50cc to the Wolf. Blew off some cobwebs, drove a loop around the pub, then parked up. Bobby behind the bar, old as hills and fields, still gleam in his eye and a sharp word if there was any disrespect. Smoke fumed the dark wood and dark bar. Nate was the youngest in the pub by some distance, always the way, unless Giggsy was around. Worked the Chivers' farm a half-mile back, good sort, handy in a fight. After one of the dances at the Young Farmers', Nate had got in a scrap and Giggsy had got his back. Handy to know, blokes like that.

Nate ordered a pint, sat at one of the small tables, lit an Embassy. The beer was good. Pete and he came here, just a couple of pints together some nights, Nate riding pillion, quiet drinks, and quiet cigarettes and then to the caravan. The best nights those. This after the year of college, the swell of the people there, the number of them. Hated the number, hated the vastness. Better just with Pete. Things always better with Pete.

They talked about it, though Nate did not want to talk about it. They talked of shame.

'You're ashamed of this?' Pete said, his hairless chest and ripped abs, the cock Nate had recently sucked. Like velvet the head. That what he thought the first time. Something plush about the skin.

'Don't give a fuck,' Nate said.

'You don't worry people'll find out?'

He had a round face, the only part of the body he didn't seem able to primp or pump into athleticism. It remained slightly doughy, his brow ridged and too low, a sag of skin just below his jaw. It was the closest he'd seen him to ever looking nervous.

'Who's going to find out?' Nate said. 'It's just us. It doesn't mean nothing.'

Pete kissed him then and they went at it in the slow way. No shame. Not then. But Nate knowing something was coming, an ending coming. That there would be a time they came back to the caravan and his hand would be pushed away. A time when he was told this was wrong. A time when Pete told him not to come back.

A couple walked in, older types, man ruddy-faced in a burgundy Gabicci jumper; the woman in a shimmering blouse, the shoulders puffed up. They sat on the table next to him, talked in low voices about their plans for the week. Squash and pop mobility. So calm, he thought. The two of them, so calm nothing could unbalance them. Just the fucking *ease* of it all. Everything in place, shipshape. What that would feel like. To have the edges smoothed, ironed flat. There was an advert on the television for a brand of electric iron, a landscape of hills and tors made of denim, the iron moving through it, the denim flattened, perfectly wrinkle-free. That's what he wanted. The neatness of it. The perfect press, without ruck or hillock.

'Hi Natey,' Thomas said. 'Fancy seeing you here.'

Thomas Carter was lighting a cigarette, holding a pint of best, standing in front of him.

'What you doing here?' Nate said.

'Always come here when I'm back in town,' he said. 'The beer's so well-kept, isn't it?'

He took a long swill from his pint and wiped the froth from his top lip, sat on the small stool opposite.

'I was just going,' Nate said.

'Oh, I think we both know that's a lie,' Thomas said, 'You've only just got here. I saw you on your bike not twenty minutes ago. Let me buy you another.'

'There's no need. I'm heading off.'

'I insist, young Nate. I insist, dear boy.'

No point in arguing, never any point. Be calm. Don't let him get to you.

'I'll have a half,' he said.

'You'll have a pint and like it,' Thomas said, slant smile and cold in his eyes.

He watched him at the bar, the wide stance of his legs, the cream colour of his trousers, the tassels on his loafers, the highlights in his bouffant hair. He walks in and authority with him strides; Thomas the kind of man who knew no one on entering a bar, but would leave with phone numbers, well-wishes and everyone remembering his name.

'There you are, Natey,' Thomas said setting down the drink. 'A nice pint, just for you.'

'What do you want?' Nate said.

'I just wanted to catch up with my old pal, Natey. Find out how he's doing these days.'

'I'm fine.'

'Yes, working the fields. Mucking out the cows. Such honest work, I'm almost envious.'

'It suits me,' he said.

'No girl as yet, I hear. Heard you pulled some pig at the Young Farmers' dance though.'

Nate looked across the table at Tom, tried to use the face that Pete used, the cocksure face that said he could never be hurt, especially by someone like *this*.

'Still,' Thomas said, 'you're probably over it now you've got your bum chum in the caravan. Pete, isn't it? With the muscles. I bet his arms make you go all girly, don't they?'

Nate set down the pint pot, worried he might crush it with his left fist. That face. That fucking face. He could glass him. He looked into that face. How it would feel on the end of his boot. And yet good that someone knew. Not his mother and father, but someone at least. Pete and him existing outside of the caravan. Nate smiled at Thomas, clearly not the reaction he had expected. Don't think you know me, Thomas Carter, you fucking prick.

'I don't know what you think you know—'

'I know everything, Natey,' Thomas said. 'There isn't anything I don't know. Try this one, for example. I know where your sister is. Have done for years. I've got an address, even a phone number. I went to see her once. Just hung around in the car outside. Wanted to be sure it was her. And it was. Would recognize her arse anywhere. Shame she's cuckoo.'

Fist clench and the burn of the fist and remember to breathe. Smile and breathe. Pete's face. His face.

'I'm not rising to this, Tommy,' Nate said. 'You can try. Give it your best shot. But I won't.'

'Oh, but you are, Natey,' he said. 'Go on. Do it. Give me that hiding you've been so wanting to dish out. I hear you're pretty handy with your fists. Go on, Natey, do it.'

Drink the drink. Pick up the cigarettes. Do not clench the fist that will not quite clench. Do not launch yourself. Do not beat him until he's begging for mercy.

'Go on,' Thomas said. 'Do it. You know you want to. It doesn't matter either way, really. You'll be off my land sooner or later. And

I'm going to take such joy in that moment. Seeing you all packed up and leaving. I'm going to have the best day ever then. The likes of your family finally off my birthright. What a day that will be. The scum washed away!'

Smile now.

'Go on, Nate. Give me a slap. You know you want to. Go on, make this easy on me.'

Finish drink.

'Fancy another?' Nate said, smiling. 'My round.'

Thomas shook his head. He stood and picked up his cigarettes, leaned in to Nate's face.

'One day I might pay your sister a proper visit. Finish what I started.'

He patted Nate on the top of the head.

'Mind how you go, pilgrim.'

Thomas turned and walked out of the pub. Playing an angle. Do not leave. Finish your pint. Smoke an Embassy and do not follow him through the door. Do not follow him. Listen to the man in the Gabicci jumper talk of a bistro that's just opened in town. Think of Pete. Think of parents. Do not go out into the darkening night. Order another drink. Another one after that. Think of Pete. Of Pete. Not of kicking off the head of Thomas Carter. Not to think of him. Not to think of Anneka.

★

Nate dragged his way through the hall, past the open door to the sitting room. His mother and father were watching the television, holding hands, like they were in a seance. He wanted to say hello, but didn't want to say where he'd been, who he'd been with, how late he was back. He looked at the television screen. It looked like they were watching a horror movie.

There was a woman in a greenlit cell, giving birth, the grunts that of a birthing cow. The baby presented to her, in bloodied rags. The look on the woman's face, the scream she let out, one that shocked Nate and his mother and father. He sneaked up to his room. He put on his headphones. He thought of Pete and he thought of Anneka and he thought of Thomas Carter, dead at his hand. Over the music, all he could hear was a scream. A long, long, terrified scream.

No Other Place

1991

July – October

July

In the window, a cross. In the morning bathroom, in the empty house, a cross in a window. With pissy fingers, she held the test, shook it, washed her hands under tepid water. Persistent, the cross: it did not trick the light. She could see how women took to religion, the divinity of that moment: a cross come from nothing; a cross slowly emerging, a cross for all our sins.

She'd seen the sign of the cross twice before; both hoped for, anticipated; this one a shock. She wouldn't have thought even to check had she not found a rogue test while hunting out antacids. For two days straight, she'd suffered morning vomitus, but Robin was away, and she'd been out two nights in a row, so hadn't really considered the possibility. But then she was also late, just by a couple of days. Couldn't harm to check. What harm. A cross or a line. Like a minus sign the line: taken away, taken from.

After the first sign of the cross, they'd walked Sefton Park and looked out for families like the one they would become. Dads who windmilled their children, played hide and seek, opened picnics, played football; mothers who tended scraped knees, read books, played hide and seek, played football. They wondered what it would be like to raise a child with a Scouse accent, how strange that would be. They called the foetus Sefton, after the park. Hard fought, Sefton. The routine had been gruelling: sex as chore, the tired, tight groan as Robin came, the rolling off and her keeping it in as much as she could, self-harvesting.

The second sign of the cross, they'd walked the park opposite where they now lived. They did the same thing, watched the parents, the children, thinking how strange that Lloyd – named for the park that was not hers – would have the same accent as Neka. It was important, Rob said, for them to be positive. To not let what happened with Sefton affect the joy of Lloyd. They made it out of the first trimester, the jelly on her stomach, the helicopter whumps of the heartbeat, began to argue over names. They eventually agreed on Benjamin for a boy and Sharmaine for a girl.

For Sharmaine there was a funeral. Just Rob and Neka in attendance, didn't tell anyone they were having it, worried people might find it macabre. The tiny coffin, the smallest thing she'd ever seen, the concise eulogy, Neka looking at her own body, her own mark of Cain.

A third now. The charm, yes. She took the test to the living room, stood by the telephone, above it a Post-it note with the number of the residential activity centre Robin had taken his kids' group to. Robin abseiling in a downpour, kayaking in the bitter cold, waiting for orienteers to return, oblivious, not knowing it all starting again.

If she called him, he'd wonder if the child was his, but not say that out loud. He'd say, did you miss a pill? She'd say no. He'd say something about fate, things happening for a reason, that nature, like magic, will always find a way. He would be panicked, excited, terrified and exhilarated. And he would be different from that moment on.

If she called him, it would start again. There would be arguments; there would be intrusion. He would scour ingredients lists for verboten items; give up alcohol and caffeine in solidarity. He would read new books on pregnancy, gather new medical research on mothers who had suffered miscarriages and stillbirths.

No. Give him this time. Give him this week of clear sleep. When he returned, she'd stage the test again. Leave him fretting in the bedroom as she pissed the stick and presented it crossed in blue. Third time's the charm. Hand me the rosaries. I shall work them for us; worry them smooth.

She walked to the Bell Corner, a black cab, its light lit, coming up Hoe Street. She hailed it and inside it smelled of valeting, menthol cough sweets, perspiration, veiled tobacco. Could have taken the bus, could have rode the rails. But something reminding her of Lissa. Waiting for Lissa, in a Liverpool bar, first week of moving there, still shaky, still unreal the world around her, looking up from her book and seeing a black cab pull up outside, Lissa getting out, alone, wearing sunglasses and a burgundy minidress, handing over money to the driver. The impossible glamour of that, the sheer indulgence of that, the excess of it. Some days, Lissa had said, you just can't take the bus.

Neka had been back to Dagenham once before; a trip for Robin's benefit. They'd taken the Underground, walked out from Dagenham East into a guided tour of Neka's early life. She told stories and Rob listened with solemn concentration, surprised then nonplussed by her candour. She told stories of shopkeepers, bus journeys, some light local history. Easy, this kind of past. No pangs, no nostalgia: the gates of her school; the library where her mother had worked; the playground where Neka had swung for hours; the swimming pool where she'd once been a fish; the door to the house in which she had lived. It was her and not her. Robin was welcome to it.

She got out of the taxi, the streets dirty, people scurrying quick on busy pavements; her standing there, a branch in the brook, a rock in the stream. Where now to go. What now to see. See herself walking with her mother, her brother in a pushchair eating an apple, her mother saying, be good Annie and you can have a gingerbread man from the pie shop. Her reading at bedtime. Enid Blyton. The Secret Seven. Something about a stolen horse. Smell of her when she'd been to the pub, sweet and fragrant her late-night kisses; Dad's just beery.

Neka walked down to the estate, the brick sprawl of it, the endless repeating houses. She did not remember walking these streets, though she'd walked them every day until she was ten. So little to show for it, a third of her life. Alone, she had expected deeper resonances, access to a further circle of memory; but it was the same thin fare, the same lacklustre memoirs.

The door to her old house was painted red. She was unsure what colour it had been when she lived there. In the window she saw herself waiting for her father's return from work, the throwing open of the door and him picking her up, all dirt and sweat and overalls, oil smudges on his cheek. The smile on his face as he stripped down, bounded up the stairs to the bath, her mother following with a cup of tea. Anneka wanted one day to be old enough to carry the tea, to present it to him as he got into the bath. How she'd wished to be older. So much older, to carry his tea.

At the same window now, an old man. He looked at her, rapped on the glass and mouthed 'Fuck off'. She laughed, and turned away. Where to now? Park and swings. Susan's house first though. Always stopped at Susan's house to knock for her. Susan's front door had been blue. She remembered the blue door. Knocking on the door, waiting for Susan to open up. Susan's mother Bridget in the kitchen, calling Neka through and offering her a wooden spoon, taste this, Annie, taste this, do you like? Flavours of sunshine, of desert. Too spicy? No, Auntie Bridget, not too spicy.

Susan's door was still blue. Neka got closer, just to see, just to check, then rapped the letterbox the way she always had. Done and no chance of taking it back. No chance of anyone being in, thankfully. No chance of that. But the attempt important.

The door opened. Auntie Bridget standing there in housecoat and apron, wiping hands on a tea towel. She let the tea towel fall. She didn't look a day older, not close to a day, as though she had been cast in aspic, awaiting Neka's return.

'Is that you, Annie?' she said. 'Annie Moore?'

'Auntie Bridget,' Neka said. 'You haven't changed a bit.'

'Oh behave, girl,' she said. 'I've lost three stone since I seen you last.'

A soft embrace, always soft, no care for the flour on her arms rubbing off on Neka's jacket.

'Come in, come in,' she said. 'I'm making dumplings, just in time.'

When she'd first visited Rob's mother and father in Kidderminster, the smell as they entered reminded her of Susan's house: the same spices, the same kind of frying oil. It was sweeter there, no tobacco to give an undertow of acrid, but it took her back, took her back to Susan and to Bridget and the wooden spoon and the taste of sun.

Standing there, the same smell as Rob's parents', but the house different than she remembered it. They'd knocked through a wall, the hallway gone and all one room. Once a dark house, lamps always lit, but brighter now, the walls painted honey blonde, the same ornamental women on the mantle though, the same map of Nigeria above the fireplace, the same smell of childhood.

'My goodness, girl,' Bridget said. 'You all grown-up now. And here's me thinking you'd be a girl your whole life.'

She put the kettle on, Neka sat down at the kitchen table. The only difference in the kitchen a microwave and a dishwasher. The same orange-fronted cabinets, the same scorch marks above the hob.

'You live round here now, Annie?' she said.

'Walthamstow,' she said. 'Been there a couple of years.'

'So what you doing here?'

'If I'm honest, Auntie Bridget, I'm not really sure.'

Bridget poured the water into the teapot, took a cake from the tin, same tin she'd always used. Quality Street.

'What you do with yourself when you're not wandering Dagenham?'

'Social worker. I work with disadvantaged kids.'

'You always was the clever one,' she said, and put her hand on her shoulders as she put down a slice of ginger cake.

'Susan's in Mile End these days. That's not far from you, right?'

Neka picked up the cake, took a bite and nodded her head.

'She did well at her studies, did Susan. Got herself a job as an estate agent. But we don't tell people that. Husband's an estate agent too. You married?'

Neka shook her head. 'I live with a man called Robin. His family's from Nigeria too.'

'Whereabouts?'

'Lagos.'

'Where in Lagos?'

'I have no idea, Auntie Bridget.'

'You have kids?'

Neka took another bite of cake, wishing she could be eating anywhere but here. A mistake this. So many questions. What else to expect, you turn up out of the thin grey nowhere and what else going to happen?

'Susan's got two boys, five and two.' Bridget motioned towards the fridge, pictures of the boys attached by magnets. First day at school photo, on a beach, in a toy car at a funfair. Be the same age as Sefton and Sharmaine these, give or take. A picture there of Susan. Thin now, athletic, business-suited, hair like Janet Jackson. Next to her a man in an expensive-looking suit, thick spectacles, smiling and pointing into the camera.

'Aren't they the spit of Susan? Oliver looks just like her, same hair, poor thing.'

A picture of them in traditional dress, the boys too, Bridget at the centre, beaming matriarch.

'I'll give you Susan's number,' she said. 'I know she'd love to hear from you. I promise she won't try and sell you a house.'

She wrote down address and phone number, gave it to Neka, pulled her into her arms.

'Whatever brought you here, darling, I'm glad it did. And it's all going to be okay, my love. God is watching down on you, and blessings be coming for you, I can promise.'

She let her down. Neka put the paper into her handbag.

'How's your mum and dad?' Bridget said. 'Still up north?'

'Yes,' she said. 'Still there.'

'Do remember me to them.'

'Will do,' she said. 'I should get on, though. It's been good to see you. Thanks for the cake.'

'God bless, Annie,' Bridget said. 'God bless you, child.'

Neka walked the streets up to the station, saw several cabs with their lights lit, but did not hail them. She took a westbound train and cried in the carriage, cried the hour it took to get to her stop.

She walked into Walthamstow Village, up past the large houses, on to the pub. She ordered a cider – just the one, my love, just the one – and sat looking at the payphone. No need to call Rob. No need to think of the child, to think of her parents, her brother. Just a pub. Just a glass of cider and a jukebox playing the Pogues. Nothing more than that.

When the baby comes. If the baby comes. Then tell them. Yes. That would be the time. Why now, this sudden change of heart? This sudden thawing? Why now? No reason. A series of photographs on a fridge. A sense of her mother being close-by sometimes, just hidden somewhere, a face in the crowd, an overwhelming sense of tiredness about the whole fucking thing.

August

The trousers were wide, so wide that with legs together they made a skirt. Carlie was in the bathroom, doing her make-up; he was modelling the jeans in the mirror, swaying as he zipped the fly and put his legs together, then spread them. Skirt and not skirt. Dancing in Carlie's bedroom, Carlie's voice next door singing over the beats from the stereo, the handclap sound of drum machine, the toytown plink of synth.

Hips moving, move your hips boy, and looking in the mirror, watching himself move, putting on Jazz, the aftershave she'd bought for him. The smell of Jazz, the smell of her perfume, the smell of her. Hips moving in the small box room, a space that contained all of her, child and adult. An archive of her, a working museum: the condoms they used in the bedside-table drawer alongside the hairgrips she no longer wore, the black nail polish long-since abandoned. It reminded him of Pete's caravan, the same sense of absolute habitation. Of a place that could only ever be hers.

Sometimes he felt there was cum running through his veins; that if he were cut he would bleed spunk. The build of the music and the build of the lust. The purity of that lust; the relief of it.

Hips moving and Carlie watching him, not laughing, not embarrassed. She pushed past him and he stopped dancing. She put her hands on his hips, move your hips boy, and looked at the two of them in the mirror. Dressed and ready. In the place.

'Jay'll be here any minute,' Carlie said.

'Still time then. Maybe we could –' he nodded to the bed.

'You're joking, right?' Carlie said. 'I've just done me hair.'

Carlie put her mouth to his ear, whispered, 'But you can lick my cunt if you like.'

Nate tried not to look shocked, tried not to look like he was still surprised by her use of that word. Tried not to look like he was worried about going out with her on his breath.

'Thought not,' she said. 'Worth a try though.'

'You like embarrassing me,' he said.

'Not as much as I like you licking my—'

He tackled her onto the bed.

'Get off,' she said. 'Downstairs, you. Ten minutes with my dad as punishment.'

'Five or I'll take your second pill myself.'

'Seven or I tell me dad what you wanted me to do the other night.'

'Five or I tell him you did it,' he said. 'Twice.'

'You're a right cock, you know that, Nathan Moore.'

Off the bed, mock hurt, then taking his hand, pulling him down the stairs, thudding into the living room; her brother, her parents, sitting on the sofa, watching television, some gameshow or other, a fat man making bad jokes, the familiar drear of a Saturday night.

'Off out?' Les said.

'Yeah,' Carlie said. 'Don't wait up.'

A knock at the door. Jay there, his car parked out front. Jay with the good hair. Tall Jay, tall man, six four, six five, complexion of Native American, unreliable and forever nice to Nate; like there was something he knew that Nate didn't. Jay who was legally allowed to drive, unbanned unlike Nate.

Nate watched Carlie kiss her mother, father, brother. Always this. Rumours people had died from pills. In Essex, somewhere down south. Just rumours, but Carlie making sure that a goodbye meant a goodbye, with kisses and a quick love-you-all as she closed the door.

Jay's Maestro was the colour of beer sick and guttered when it hit forty-five. Jay stood by its open driver's-side door, building a spliff.

'You're in front, mate,' Jay said. 'Navigator.'

'I can navigate from the back,' Nate said.

'Need you in front, mate, in case I need look at the map,'

Six months left on the ban. Well over the limit, caught and having to be driven everywhere. Shaming and emasculating. The people he could have killed; how many on the road that night. The ban longer the second time.

First time after Pete said no. After Pete said he was leaving. After Pete said it was a mistake. After Pete said it didn't mean nothing. He'd gone out and bought vodka and just driven, looking for trouble. Crashed into a railing in the centre of town. So drunk, still there when the police arrived.

Second time, driving back from Manchester, the morning after meeting Billy. Still over the limit at 10 a.m., the coppers delighting in the positive reading on the breathalyser.

Jay pulled on the spliff and started the engine; the car flooding with tune, the bass cones in the back rasping at the low end, tinny and shrill at the top, the wails of a siren, the electric stitch of beat. Jay drove and Carlie and Nate nodded their heads, shared the spliff with Jay, the roads and then the motorway a blur of bright lights in drab surrounds given a drumbeat and a bass line, given some insistence, some unconfected excitement.

The pubs would be heaving now. The pubs would be drunk by now. The pubs in their pomp now, before the crush for last orders, before the fights and nightclub. The end of the night already happening, the bells about to sound. Here, velocity, possibility, no knowing where to end up, who there, what to hear. Better that than a fight. Scotty now running around with Mawer and his crowd. He came to rave along with Nate once and said it gave him headache, the music. Said it was gay, the way the men were dancing, shirts off, all hands in the air, some of them wearing gloves. Didn't like the feeling of the pills.

Scotty, lad, missing out, mate.

On the M6, the pager bleeped with the address and vague directions. Nate plotted the route as Carlie rolled a spliff in back. He looked back at her, just a tangle of curly bleached hair, turret high. People thought she looked like Kylie. She hated that.

'I should be so lucky,' she'd reply with such withering contempt it felt like a punch. Different weapons; same effect.

'Next right,' Nate said, looking down at the map. 'Then on for about a mile or so.'

'How long before we're there?' Jay said.

'Half-hour,' Nate said. 'Give or take.'

Jay took a pill from his pocket and Carlie handed him a bottle of water. Nate gave Carlie a pill, took one himself. Not able to stop it in train, something he thought when taking a pill. No way to stop the train. Train's going to keep moving, all doors locked. Did not kiss his mother goodbye, did not kiss his father goodbye. Should have done that. Dad covering the Sunday shift and not a kiss goodbye. Milking the cows and starting work as Nate would be on his comedown.

They soon found the convoy: cars snailing up a B road, people leaning out of windows to see how far the jam extended. They crawled and arrived in a field already a car park, bodies pouring from the cars towards an old grain store. The surge, the shimmy and heat of it, starting on, the first inkling of it, as they got out of the car; Carlie giving Nate a kiss, all tongues and lips that kiss, like she hadn't seen him in months. They joined the multicoloured herd heading towards the grain store, huge and alone in the field, people disappearing into its maw, dry ice and strobe-blessed, entranced in, pied-piper rats, pulled in by beat and bleep.

The hot air of the summer night and the rush of the dancers, already the grain store humming with people, the taste of dry ice, the bright lights and bright clothes and the sweat already within. A good venue, better than the factories and warehouses; less likely to collapse. A happy place.

In amongst it then, moving inside, always to the right of the room, so they'd know where to find each other should they get split up. The smell of old grain and the euphoric rush, feet already moving, move those hips boy, and starting to sweat already, feeling it inside the hooded top, running down the inside of the leg. Hype man for the DJ asking if everyone's ready and everyone ready and the beat dropping and all going to mental, hands in the air, and Nate's hands in the air, his large arms and biceps up in the air, and two men with their arms in the air, and the shout of pure release, and then arms down and the beat coming back, onward rushing, no break, no dropped beat, Jay nowhere to be found, the music seamless, a block of music, a wall of it, the strobe and the pink light and the dry ice, the settling cloud of it, cool in the lungs, everything else white hot, and the searchlight inside the grain store, the patterns cast on its roof, the pinks and greens and reds swirling over Carlie's face, the stop-motion of her in the strobe and then back to life, arms in the air, hands in the air, his hands on Carlie, Carlie's hands on him.

Hours passing in this, hours passing until the next pill, swallowed with a kiss from Carlie, and Carlie covered in sweat, just in her bra, her pinched waist and little shorts, ripped the shorts and her ass to hold, sometimes her brushing against him and teasing him, and men dancing with them both, them rubbing against him and against her, and that being fine, we all connected, all of us together, yes, no problems, drop the beat, drop the needle, drop the break, everybody in the place, let me give you devotion.

He danced. He did not think. They danced. They kissed. They did not think. They danced. They danced. They did not think. No thinking. Not a thought. They danced. They danced and did not think. They kissed and did not think. They held their arms in the air and did not think until the music stopped dead, as though it had never played, not once or ever.

'Cops,' the hype man shouted into the microphone. 'All out.'

Flooding out the grain store, running for cars, the multicoloured dancers, the naked-torso dancers. He held Carlie's hand, ran with her, looked for the Maestro amongst the Escorts and Sierras and Astras, no clue where parked, no idea, and being overtaken by men, dodging cars reversing wildly, pulling away at speed, another high. They saw a Maestro, the same kind as Jay's but not his, kept searching the cars as sirens moaned in the distance, even through the tinnitus, sirens, definitely sirens coming, and Nate sure the car was where they stood, but spaces there, no Maestro amongst them.

The certain knowledge then, standing there where he was sure the car had been: Jay has gone. Jay has left them there. A moment of self-preservation, a moment of punishment. A punishment for Nate being a farmer; a punishment for hitching himself to Carlie, for escaping his puny life of shit pubs and shit lager and shit clubs playing shit music. Punishment for being a tourist.

'Jay's gone,' Nate said. 'He's fucking gone.'

Carlie shook her head. 'No way he'd leave us.'

'The car was here,' he said. 'I'm sure it was here.'

Carlie was shivering, still just in her bra, T-shirt disappeared somewhere in the exodus. His top was around his waist and he gave it to her, but it was dripping wet, unwearable. The siren and the gooseflesh on her wrists and arms. Two men came running towards them, heading for a small purple Mazda.

'Hey,' Carlie said, and they looked at her in her bra and shorts. 'Our ride's fucked off, could you give us a lift?'

They looked like ghouls the men, wide-eyed but faces so pallid they could be skulls. They looked at each other, the ghouls. A decision to make. A girl in a bra and shorts, shaking cold. A genetic, biological imperative. Even with Nate there, inevitable.

'We're going Sandbach Services,' the ghoul with the car keys said. 'We can drop you there.'

'You're a doll,' she said. 'Thanks.'

They had to fumble over the seats to get in the back, the car moving before they could even see if there were seatbelts in back;

needed the seatbelts, the crazy way the ghoul was driving. Music playing they couldn't hear through the tinnitus and the other ghoul turning it off, lighting a cigarette, passing the pack back to the both of them.

'I'm Lee,' he said. 'This is Jon.'

Nate took two cigarettes from Lee, passed one over to Carlie. The car juddered over the irregular grass, heading for the track out of the field, Jon following the hectic peloton of cars, the sirens getting louder, blue flashes in the distance.

Lee fumbled under his seat. Threw over two T-shirts, both dry, both white.

'Are you sure?' Carlie said.

Lee held out two more T-shirts under his seat, fresh in cellophane wrapping.

'Be prepared,' he said. 'That's my motto.'

★

Sandbach Services was a holding pen; ravers hanging around for news of a party like unemployed stevedores on docks. Kids sitting on bonnets drinking Coke, still wired, tricked-out cars booming beats from inset bass cones.

'You're lifesavers,' Carlie said. 'Thanks.'

'Keep safe,' Jon said and pulled away.

The two of them were together, said so as soon as they were out onto proper roads. He wondered if they knew Billy. Whether he had been in the same clubs as them at some point. Billy with the sad eyes and the thin wrists, the swank apartment and jutting chin, the racks of clothes and credit cards. Billy with whom he lived a shadow life, for a time, but knew there would be goodbyes sooner rather than later. Different to Pete's goodbyes. More formal. He knew that the first time Billy called off a Friday night because he had to go to a dinner party.

Carlie had guessed somehow, seen it perhaps in the way he danced with men. He'd confessed to her, after she'd asked. Yes, he'd been with a man. Just once. A lie, but plausible. He was high. It had made her excited. She'd been with a girl, she said, just the once. It was good to explore sexuality, to be open to new experiences. A few weeks later, she stuck her finger in his ass for the first time. It confused him. Was unsure whether this was something all couples did, or whether it was specific to him; a way to keep him happy, though he'd never been as happy, never once. Not with Pete, or with Billy. It unsettled, but it passed.

They went inside the service station and bought coffee, sat in the cafe to warm. She looked beautiful in the harsh light, her make-up wrecked and wearing a T-shirt advertising a Toyota car dealership.

'You know,' she said. 'There's no other place I'd rather be right now. I'm cold, we're miles from home, but still no other place than here.'

'Me too,' he said.

She sipped at her coffee, she opened up the packet of cigarettes they'd just bought. She passed one to him and lit it with a match.

'How are we going to get back?' she said.

'Someone'll give us a lift. There'll be someone you know hanging around.'

She nodded. 'Smoke these and then we can go hustle?'

'Smoke then hustle,' he said.

★

He blew the man and swallowed. He tasted old and musty. There was no velvet to his cock. At the bottom of the track to the house, right there. Risky business, with the sun rising and his father probably already out in the sheds, but Nate had to be sure he'd take him all the way home. The man groaned. Nate saw he'd left a little blood on the man's thigh. Nate touched the side of his head. A small cut that would bruise up bad. The man pulled up his trousers.

'You're sure you don't want to go to the hospital?' the man said.

'You ask me that now?' Nate said.

The man opened the door. Nate got out. Standing there with bloodied knuckles, his blood and Jay's blood. Both now on the man's thigh. The man did not say goodbye, just drove away, got what he came for. Lucky man.

Nate walked up the track, the short shadow of him. The look on Carlie's face. So happy inside the service station; so angry after, so angry it lit her up beautiful.

Out to hustle and they'd seen the Maestro, Jay sitting on its bonnet. They went over and Carlie started at him, and Jay was trying to explain, poor reappeared Jay, but whatever he said wasn't enough and so Nate hit him. Full force. Jay got a couple of punches off, Nate letting him have them for free, before he set to him. Fists and knees and Carlie somewhere a thousand miles behind trying to haul him off Jay, but it taking five blokes to stop him. Jay on the ground, battered and kicked and punched. The shock on Carlie's face. The horror. Her dragging Jay up with the help of some of the blokes, lying him down on the back seat, her getting in front, crunching the car into gear.

'Psycho,' she'd said through the open window. 'You're a fucking psycho.'

Then off. Onto the motorway. Nate abandoned twice in one evening.

In the service station bathrooms, cleaning himself up, the man had asked if he needed a ride. Why not. What else to do now? Knowing what he would need to do in return.

He sat down at the end of the track. Once he'd thrown knives at the oak tree opposite. Once he'd got the knife to stick in the bark. The thrill of that. The dead sound of the blade in the trunk. Chris Birch. There was a tear in the new trousers, a rip where Jay had tried to stop him from kicking. Nothing going to stop the kicking. Once he saw him, nothing stopping that. Not the ecstasy. Not Carlie. Nothing to stop that, once it started. A train on the move, all doors locked.

September

Wednesdays she opened the library alone. The same men each morning waiting for her to unlock the glass doors. Five came every day, there on the nose and out when then pubs opened. Of late, a young man called Silas too. At nine, his watch pinged the hour. Everyone looked at him, as they did every hour he was there.

Around half past, the first set of mothers arrived. A smile for them, the long-suffering mothers, and a smile for the kids; the women blear eyed from lack of sleep, the kids toddling off to throw books on the floor. Sometimes it reminded Gwen of mornings with Annie in the library: the books they read, the way they'd laughed at the strangeness of English language, its innumerable inconsistencies. When Gwen first skipped a period, she thought she was pregnant. She thought she was pregnant and thought of another Annie in her arms, another little Annie-moo, her reading *Mr Rabbit and the Lovely Present*; or Nathan inside of her, plump and untroubled.

'These are new in today,' she said to the woman taking off her jacket.

'Thank you,' the other woman said. 'Nothing like fresh books, is there, Hannah?'

The child looked up, ringlet hair and smudge brown eyes.

'Thank you,' she said.

How to melt a heart, young lady. How to melt a heart.

Gwen allowed herself to be pregnant for a month, drank no wine or coffee. In a medical textbook, she looked up vasectomy and it said there was a slim chance of being able to conceive after the operation. The next period she skipped, she allowed herself to be pregnant for another month. She wondered about names, she wondered about how she would cope, how they would both cope, with a new life to nurture. The third came along as though returning from a holiday. A *grande vacance* around Mitteleuropa. She cried in the bathroom, the water running in the tub, cried as blood lapped into an expanding wad of cotton. You're fifty-one years old, she'd told herself, what did you expect? What were you thinking?

She sat down and picked up *Mrs Dalloway*. A new edition she'd read twice straight through. Just to spite Old Nick, his bilious hatred of Woolf: her tin ear and outmoded aristocracy.

'Don't read her,' he'd once said. 'Woolf is the enemy of fiction. The enemy of everything that fiction stands for. It is bloodless, limp, dazzled by its own self-importance.'

She remembered Nick's rant against Woolf, the alarming biographical note – she drank her own urine, he'd said with a lemon-wince mouth – and the real reason for his ire: a spiky comment from Virginia about his appearance at a literary dinner. Had Gwen read *Mrs Dalloway* back in the late fifties, she would have agreed with him, she would have dismissed it as being shallow and without a shred of dirt under its fingernails. She would have been wrong.

A ping from Silas's wristwatch. A grandmother with her two young grandchildren, bundling one into a buggy, the other carrying the books they would take out.

'This is a good one,' Gwen said, holding out *The Tiger Who Came to Tea*.

'I can make a noise like a tiger,' the boy said.

'Not in a library,' the grandmother said. 'Now come on, time for home.'

You can roar in here, she thought. Just once, I'll let you roar.

She went back to Dalloway, she served the last customers, then closed the library. On the tick of twelve, proud of that. Errands to run, then home.

The Lion and Bell was the town's pub for underage drinkers; which left it dead in the day, lacking purpose. She ordered a glass of wine and took her drink to the back room. No nerves until seated, no nerves at all, not even thinking about it. Not happening. Easy to dismiss. What chance this happening. No chance this happening. No worries, because not happening.

Ray walked into the bar; the same face, same slender body, hair seasoned with the merest dash of grey. She stood. They embraced. An aftershave she did not recognize; something adulterous about that.

'It's been a long time,' Ray said.

'You haven't changed,' Gwen said.

'Neither have you.'

'I was glad when you wrote,' he said. 'Surprised but glad.'

She'd wanted to many times, wanted to when she read his profiles of the striking miners, the travel books he'd become known for, seeking out fanatics across the world, interviewing them, giving them voice. Hard to believe the same man she had abandoned. Or he her. Difficult to remember the exact manner of the parting. No matter either way. Two decades past, time having brushed their shoulders, not blown hard on their faces.

'You could have come to me sooner,' he said. 'I would have helped.'

'You know it's not as simple as that.'

He nodded. 'Still, I'm glad you came to me. There are things—'

'It was a whim,' she said. 'Desperation, really. I almost did years before, but Drum was dead against it. Said I'd break my own heart. He made me promise I wouldn't. But I need to know. I couldn't wait it out any longer. It had to be you. I couldn't pay anyone. Drum controls all the money, you see.'

'Same old, Drum,' he said.

'Don't say anything about him,' she said. 'That's my fault. I only ever told you the bad stuff. Wasn't likely to tell you all the good, was I?'

'I like to think I'm good at reading between the lines.'

'What you like to think and what's true are two different things, Ray.'

She sipped her wine. Some old anger there, sepia-toned, turned autumnal.

'If I hurt—'

'That's not why we're here,' she said. 'That's not why I'm here, at least.'

'I know,' he said. 'Of course, I know.'

From his leather briefcase he took a manila folder. It had been months; an investigation he said would take a matter of weeks. He'd insisted she meet him, only then would he show her his findings.

'She lives in London with her boyfriend. This is them.'

He handed her a photograph, the two of them walking through a park, hand in hand, her girl, certainly her, defiantly her, looking her age, as tall as her boyfriend; her boyfriend like an African prince, she thought. Like from that television show. Don Warrington. Her daughter dressed like the mothers in the library, those high-waisted jeans and fat-tongued trainers.

'His name is Robin Adebayo. He runs a youth group that has chapters over London. She's a social worker.'

She looked at the picture again, the lives led in the face, the lives behind smiles. How many photographs had he taken? How many developed and this one chosen? The happiest one, the one in which they are in love, unvarnished and unaware of eyes watching.

'Are there children?' she said.

'No,' he said. 'It looks like she had a stillbirth three years ago. There's a death certificate.'

Still holding the photograph. Three years. The stopped periods that came back. Building things now, building ideas.

'Thank you,' she said.

'Are you sure you don't want the address?'

'I'm sure,' she said. 'I just needed to know.'

'Will you tell him?' he said.

She laughed, and together they laughed, all the times they had laughed and no one to know, no one even suspecting that they laughed together.

'Did you ever tell him about me?' he said.

'No,' she said. 'Nothing to tell.'

'I came for you, you know?' he said. 'To the library. Wanted to whisk you away from it all.'

'How very romantic,' she said.

He looked around the tired bar, looked like he missed cigarettes for a moment, something to do, something other than flipping a beer mat.

'Don't you ever think what might have been?'

'Of course,' she said. 'Sometimes, once in a while.'

On good days, she contented herself that her life was the product of endless tests and extrapolations, that she had for centuries been changing small details of her life to see the ramifications before concluding this was the best outcome. On bad, she weighed the decisions she had made and could not see how they could be worse than what she had endured. There were few of these days. Fewer and fewer of them now.

'Jenny and I split up in seventy-two. She has two kids now, married some environmentalist or other.'

'Are you married now?' she said, feeling the clumsiness of the question. It's leading tone.

'Was for a time,' he said. 'It didn't work out. No kids either.'

'Just the world as your lover,' she said. 'All those far-flung places.'

'I never meant for that to happen,' he said. 'Just got the taste.'

'Always sounded like a death wish to me,' she said. 'All those war zones.'

He drank more of his beer.

'How do you feel?' he said. 'Now you know?'

'Nothing,' she said. 'It's like shock. Nothing has changed. She's still missing even though she's found.'

She laughed.

'Though I'm surprised. She always professed to hate London.'

'People change,' he said.

'Some stay the same,' she said. 'However much we change, we all still think we're bloody teenagers.'

She wondered what his behind would feel like in her hands, how heavy he would be upon her. There were rooms at the Swan, at the Bull's Head. No one would ever know. Does he not deserve favour? Does he not deserve reward?

'I'm staying in Manchester tonight,' he said. 'I'm often up around this way. Perhaps I could see you next time I'm around?'

'I'm not sure—'

'I'll check in on Annie before I come. Keep you updated.'

She paused. What would she give for that? Herself, perhaps. A gradual erosion. Every so often, him landing and them sitting at this table, talking of his expeditions and looking at pictures of her daughter.

She picked up the photograph of Anneka and Robin. She looked at it closely. Her daughter's eyes, the eyes of her boyfriend. Pregnant those eyes. Pregnant that belly. Tell by the look on their faces, a baby coming, a baby to come. A mother always knows.

The pub clock tolled the hour. She finished her drink.

'I think that would be okay,' she said. 'Yes, I think we can do that.'

THE SECOND SUMMER OF LOVE

We didn't realize we were doing anything especially groundbreaking back then. The raves were in the moment, they were very much present tense. You didn't think much about them, you just looked forward to the next one. The gay scene was different. It had history, it had nostalgia for the hedonistic past, it had a death toll, and it had importance. When they merged, when they came together, as they did, it changed things. Straights coming along because the homos had all the best parties. Before E, you wouldn't have got one of those boys coming into those clubs, now they were coming in droves, happy to kiss each other to get in.

Ecstasy changed people's lives, it changed everything. I think it was Boy George who said that the difference between gay and straight, in his experience, was a couple of pints and two tabs of ecstasy – we certainly saw that on the scene. Lads who had never thought of it, suddenly loved up and fucking anything that moved. I fell in love with one of them. Not a great idea.

Had it not been for rave and for E, I probably would never have met him, and he would never have broken my heart. It sounds dramatic, but I think that music showed the world the right direction. Those years, between eighty-eight and ninety-one, they were the best years of my life. The possibility, the end of history, the breaking down of everything, the collapse of all the rules. The old queens were dying, yes, I know that.

I should have cared but I didn't. I had this muscled boyfriend, beautiful and sweet, who was always there, when he was there. Until he wasn't.

He was a fighter. He liked to brawl. He liked to fuck and he liked to fight. He told me he'd fallen in love once, but it hadn't worked out. On account of his temper. Lucky for me, I said. Not lucky, as it turned out. He punched me once. It came out of the blue. I told him to get out and he did. The last time I ever saw him.

But the way it turned, the way he turned on me, that was like what was happening elsewhere. It had gone sour, it had been an act, this illusion of the future. The party was coming to an end. The police were raiding all the raves, the establishment was biting back. There was the Gulf War, there were gay bashings, there was still Section 28. With that punch, I cried not just for losing the man I loved, but for the world that was disintegrating around me.

Billy Lewis, *The Second Summer of Love: An Oral History*, ed. Lissa Capel (Influx Press, 2015)

October

In his hand a cassette, held as prize or reward; Carter standing by the open driver's-side door, shaking the case, the cassette inside rattling.

'A little stroll down memory lane,' Carter said.

Drum opened the passenger door into the perfume of relaxed luxury, the words 'touring car' on his lips. Memories of when he still read the motoring magazines, the photos of the large beast cars, the cream leather interiors, the width and breadth of them; sleek tanks, boots that could accommodate more possessions than Drum owned.

He unfolded the map, the route simple and direct, M6 and onto the new M40, opened earlier in the year, a treat that in itself, and then down the A34, lunch scheduled at a pub Carter knew in Oxford. Carter manoeuvred the Jaguar down the track, his glasses changing from translucent to tinted as they moved out of the shade.

'You'll get used to it,' Carter said.

'What's that?'

'Being a passenger.' He smiled, tapped the wheel.

'Put on the tape,' he said. 'It's real blast-from-the-past stuff.'

Drum put the cassette in the player. Tape hiss and spindle, a tremor through the speakers, the amplified hum of distant feedback, intergalactic transmissions, an ambient wash of electronic communion. He did not recognize it. And then the drums, marching in the drums, like hooves coming over the prairie, and behind the drums something coming, a buzz, like a saw or a swarm. Knew it then.

'I've not heard this in years.' Drum said. '"Telstar", right?'

He saw stars and planets, the infinite beyond, a rocket speeding through the dark, tourists waving down at Earth, looking down and humming along to the tune, subtle vocals over the electronics, the space-age cabaret of it.

'The bloke who wrote it, Joe Meek, he never saw a penny of profit,' Carter said. 'Some French composer said he'd nicked the melody from one of his film scores. Meek killed himself and his landlady before the thing was ever resolved. Poor bastard.'

'He murdered someone?' Drum said.

'His landlady. Shot her in the face.'

'And you feel sorry for him because he got shafted on his royalties?'

'The man wasn't well by all accounts. It's still a great song.'

'It's macabre is what it is,' Drum said.

'Meek wasn't a killer when he wrote it,' Carter said. 'And Caravaggio was a murderer. People still look at his paintings.'

Drum shuddered, the song different now, violent now. A noise from the tape player, a drift of static, not on the murderer's record, but just the hiss of no noise, then the louche, almost somnambulistic refrain of 'Stranger on the Shore'. The record he'd played more than any other, one he whistled when milking, when waiting for a kettle to boil. Thousands of songs he'd heard in his life, this the one he came back to, a constant soundtrack, always playing, deep down in the recesses.

'You're going to tell me now that Acker Bilk is a war criminal,' Drum said.

'No,' Carter said. 'Bilk was a gun runner for the mafia. There's plenty of blood on his hands though. You can hear it in the way he plays the clarinet.'

The two men laughed, the song played, its maritime drawl, something boat-like about being inside the Jaguar, an ocean-liner making swift passage through placid waters.

'Would you still like this song if you knew Bilk was a rapist or a pederast?' Carter said.

The beauty of the sound, the safety of that refrain.

'It'd sound different,' Drum said. 'It wouldn't be the same song.'

Carter took a mint from a bag in the side pocket of the car, offered them over to Drum. Glacier Mints. A cartoon polar bear and a cartoon fox on the packet.

'Did we always talk like this?' Carter said. 'Even back in Service?'

'Like what?'

'Like a confessional mixed with a comedy routine.'

'You think that's how we talk?'

'Maybe how I like to think we talk.'

Carter sucked on his mint, looked to the cigarette lighter, back to the road, then to Drum.

'I don't remember how we talked back then,' Carter said. 'We talked all the time, but I haven't got a clue what we actually talked about.'

'It's a long time ago,' Drum said. 'Probably for the best we don't remember.'

All those nights in the berth, all those days in the kitchens, the evening whiskies and the morning teas. Thirty years before, no time at all, and yet so little recall. So little that came to mind. Doom Town, yes. But little else.

'I read my Service diaries the other day,' Carter said. 'Names I'd so confidently written down, names I can't now place. Incidents I not only don't recall, but sound so fantastical they seem like lies. Why would I lie in my own journal?'

'Why not?' Drum said, smiling. 'You lie to everyone else.'

'Take the wheel,' Carter said and leaned over to the back seat, removed cigarettes from his bag, pressed in the cigarette lighter. He took back control of the car, put a cigarette in his mouth.

'I didn't write down the stories we used to tell,' Carter said. 'I just wrote things like "the Cyprus routine", or "the Sudan stories". As if I'd always remember them. As if they'd be imprinted on my mind for as long I as lived.'

'I remember the Cyprus routine,' Drum said. 'That was one of your favourites.'

'But the Suez routine? The Korea stories? Lost now. Utterly lost.'

Drum cycled through the lies, the routines they'd honed. Nothing for Suez. Nothing for Korea.

'We could try to remember them,' Drum said. 'We could work them up. We have time.'

Carter cracked the window and lit his cigarette.

'You go first,' Drum said. 'You were always the best at establishing.'

★

Halfway through an intense hostage scenario in Korea, they arrived at the Carter-selected pub. Drum felt somehow honey-trapped, as though the intention had always been to divert conversation from the present to the past; to play a parlour game in which they would both gladly engage.

On the day of Anneka's birth, her thirtieth, he'd ducked into a small church and lit a candle for her, a tenner dropped in the honesty box: Florence Nightingale to watch over her. Thirty. Already almost a decade older than his parents had managed; seven years older than the man who cooed over her, a cold day in 1961. To think of her skeins of lives; all her later unknown masks.

The pub was small, narrow, student-populated, sticky-floored, the air densely smoked. They quickly took a small table near the lavatories, the only one left, the stale air piss and beer and bleach.

'It doesn't look any different,' Carter said. 'Scruffier clientele, but the bar's not changed a bit.'

He got up from his seat, exhilarated for a moment, scanning the paintings hanging on the wall.

'Same pictures!' he said. 'The exact same. I remember this one. It's my college. I sat here once and looked up at it, and it was like my father was staring down at me. Go home, James. It's time to

400

study, James. Ha. I remember looking at it and saying, "Piss off, Dad, leave me be."'

Carter sat back down at the table, his brief high crashing. Nostalgia first as friend, then as assailant. The material things, the wood, the lino, the paintings, the pumps: a comfort, these. Those surrounding him, the patrons and the two barmaids, despoiled the stage; miscast and incongruous. No stout publican behind the bar, but a young American woman with a nosestud; no suited, gowned, short-back-and-sided young men, but youths with long hair down their backs, big baggy trousers, thick tongues poking through unlaced trainers.

'I'll get the drinks,' Carter said.

Drum watched Carter initiate conversation with the barmaid. She poured the pints, shaking her head. No I don't know him. No, I've never heard of him. Oh, he died years ago, I think.

Gwen once said the grand delusion of the pub regular is that they believe they're family. That if they don't come in one day, the staff and regulars will wonder after them. Old regulars who came back years later expected her and her father to remember their usual. It's the magic, she said, the bullet-trick of the pub: you think when you go back, you'll still belong.

'Bob might be dead,' Carter said coming back with the drinks. 'but the beer looks as well-kept as it always did.'

The beer was dark, pissy-headed, smelled of sulphur. Carter drank and lit a cigarette and continued his manic sweep of the barroom. Looking for what? Bobby-socked women who'd stayed miraculously young, waiting for Carter's return? Dons to tell him he was the most brilliant student they'd ever had? Something like that. This what friendship comes down to: knowing what the other is trying not to think about.

Drum wondered whether Carter was dying; whether this was the true meaning of the trip. This the kind of journey the dying take: to say goodbye, to wave a last animated hand at the past, at the ghosts who lately stalk; a passing-out parade of all lives led.

Drum looked at Carter, hale and leaner these days, a rose hue to his nose and cheeks, but not the face of a dying man. No suggestion of cancer, no intimation of vascular problems. Carter fiddling with his lighter, alive and living, still looking lithe despite his years, still looking invincible.

Someday Carter *would* die. The thought came as a sudden realization. Drum had imagined a life without Gwen, the harrow of that; the cold house, the unmade bed, waking and there being no eggs in the pan, coming home and finding no stacks of library books, her not sitting there, drinking tea. That, yes, but never Carter. The idea absurd that there could be a space unfilled by him. Not dying. No. Not that.

Drum looked around, saw some of Carter's Oxford stories play out, the few he remembered. In the corner, a don pissing into a bottle because he was too drunk to navigate to the lavatories; forgetting, then pouring the piss, thinking it whisky. In the back room, towards the garden, a French woman slowly stroking Carter's cock through the worsted of his trousers until he came with a gasp and she walked off as though nothing had happened. Both with the ring of inauthenticity; second-hand stories, effortlessly told. Carter's descriptions of the place were pitch-perfect, though; the place familiar through his eyes, through the precision of his words.

They decided on food and Drum went to the bar. As the barmaid took their order, Drum looked up to the optics, the photographs hanging behind the bar. Several were of a pair of actors pretending to pour pints from the pumps. The precision of Carter's words! The pitch-perfect descriptions! No such thing. The familiarity, the sense of proprietary knowledge of the place, coming not from Carter, but from barroom scenes filmed for a television detective show he liked.

'I used to come here alone,' Carter said when Drum got back from the bar. 'I read more in this pub than I did in any library, in any university room.'

'It's a nice place,' Drum said, wanting to mention *Inspector Morse*, feeling the conversation heavy in his mouth.

'I had friends,' he said. 'Don't think I didn't. There was Luke Ellison, Joseph Rowley, old Chips Henderson. Good fellows all. They'd come and join me here at seven. We'd have a few and then head out into the night for adventures.'

The expected stories didn't come. No high jinks, no saucy tales, no barroom catastrophes. Carter just sat and looked at the end of his cigarette, put it to his mouth, put his glass to his lips.

'You know?' Drum said, and Carter raised his eyes in something like anticipation, hope possibly.

'What?' he said.

'I'm just going to the lav. Be back in a tick.'

There was a latch on the toilet stall door, the door covered in graffiti, giant cocks and balls, numbers to ring for sex with men. He sat down and read the door from top to bottom, left to right. Should have realized, this the reason for coming here. Should have seen it. All the lives Carter could have lived, all the people he could have been, here was a crucible for them all. Should have realized. The excitement of remembrance, the sag of its quick passing. The possibilities ganging up, laughing like schoolboys in the nook and snug.

He wondered how it would feel to go back to Dagenham, to walk the factory again. He could be a floor manager now, deaf as a post; could be unemployed, off on the sick. The pub was possibilities; the factory their end. Both as blighting, both as immovable in the memory.

Their food was on the table when he returned, the service quick, or he had been gone longer than he'd realized. Carter was smoking, seemingly oblivious to both the food and Drum's absence. He'd drunk almost all his beer.

'Come in number two, your time's up,' Drum said, clicking his fingers.

'You know,' Carter said. 'They filmed some of *Inspector Morse* here. Right here in this bar.'

'Is that so?' Drum said.

'I must watch it one day,' Carter said, and took a bite from his steak sandwich. Blood dripped from the bread onto the plate, onto his chin. Smiled then. Alive. Would always be alive.

★

Drum had imagined Jerrick's home as a small cottage, a modest property, something slightly ramshackle, gone to seed. A place for a man to rewind old wars, compile his memoirs, decompose day by day. All he could see was hedge. A wall of hedge, twenty feet high, a hundred feet long, sheared perfectly, level as thatch. No breaks in the leaves, the livid green tightly woven, no sense of what was behind. The hedges protectorate, disallowing any glimpse of the house from the road, the gate only revealing a gravel driveway between two further hedges of a marginally smaller size.

Carter buzzed the intercom. A mumble of static and the gate swung inward, unsure at first, then reckless quick. Carter drove slowly over the gravel, took the car through the slalom, the car going dark, a canopy of some kind above them. They turned left and back into the light, and in the sudden brightness, in front of them, Jerrick's house, his pond and his gardens.

The house was squatly cruciform: a central tower tapering to a thin spire, four smaller spires beneath it; the brick a deep russet; the arched window frames, of which there were many, a deep black; the inset glass crisscrossed with lead. Gargoyles looked down from gables, wisteria spilled from under sloping, oxidized roofs. The house was too dark and gnarled for the brightness around it: the surrounding garden well-tended, a large pond at its centre, sprinklers shooting water at random onto billiard-table lawns. The house looked like it was scowling at them all, grousing at sharing the same space.

'Well, it puts your ancestral pile to shame,' Drum said.

'If you like neo-Gothic nightmares, yes,' Carter said.

He thought of Carter's death; he thought of Carter's funeral:

his white-piano-key coffin, the flowers and the raucous elegies, the chapel in Wildboarclough standing room only, mysterious women crying. A wake full of whisky, Drum in the corner, thinking maybe of this last trip, this last hurrah. And what then. What after. What to do. Silent crying in Gwen's arms. Unable to look beyond the field, the big house a brick-and-lintel reminder of his passing.

'Thanks for this,' Drum said. 'For organizing it.'

Carter nodded and they walked to the opening door, Jerrick standing there on the threshold, shrunken now, ruffles down an old shirt. As though every crease he'd ever ironed had come back to haunt him. He looked them both up and down, old inspection technique, unimpressed with what he saw.

'You're late,' he said. 'I said three o'clock, did I not?'

'Traffic was terrible, sir,' Carter said. 'And it's a long drive. '

'Depends on where you start,' he said. 'All depends on that.'

He smiled, crooked teeth, one side worn away with pipe; hairs on his top lip, missed by shaving, a stealth moustache.

'Yes, absolutely, sir,' Carter said. 'We're very sorry.'

'Well come, come, come. I don't have all day.'

Jerrick turned back into the hallway. They followed, walking the lozenge-shaped tiles on the floor, black and white, scuffed and in need of scrubbing. The walls black-blue, crowded with boxes of taxidermized seabirds and ravens. Jerrick disappeared through a door to his left, a sparse drawing room, walls peeling William Morris paper.

'You boys'll be ready for a drink by now, I expect,' he said and went to the dresser, took out a fresh bottle of whisky and three glasses filmed with dust. He poured without wiping the tumblers, handed them the drinks.

'To the end of history,' he said, holding up his glass.

They clinked their glasses. He stood by the bare fireplace, as though it were lit and roaring, warming himself though the day was humid and close.

'This is an incredible house, sir,' Carter said. 'Never seen anything quite like it.'

Jerrick laughed.

'It's a bloody monstrosity is what it is, soldier,' Jerrick said. 'My father's grand folly. Sunk everything into it. He was an occultist. Crowley held some of his rites here, Conan Doyle used to pop by. All before my time, of course. It was a house of scandal –' he laughed, motioning with his glass to the walls – 'and now it's just an old man's hermitage.'

Jerrick sat down in the armchair. Drum looked for somewhere they could sit.

'So, you boys are here to see the cave?' Jerrick said.

'If it's not too much trouble,' Carter said.

'No trouble at all,' he said, and then to Drum. 'You're not MI5 though, are you? MI6?'

'No, sir,' Drum said. 'We've met before. At Haverigg.'

'A Doom Town boy?'

'Yes, sir.'

'Same time as Carter? Yes. Vague bells ringing. Very vague bells . . .'

He finished his Scotch and poured more from the bottle on the coffee table.

'How does it feel to be part of history, soldiers? To be both of the present, and of the past?'

'Sir?' Drum said.

'The war is over and no shots have been fired. A million contingencies planned, and none ever arose. The only casualties mental health, the only fatalities caused by stress, cirrhosis and cancer. We are the most pointless soldiers in history. Fifty years of war-gaming and nothing to show for it. Just a lot of shadow lives, blinking now in the bright new dawn.'

He stood and beckoned them to follow.

'When those hardliners put Gorbachev under house arrest, how did you feel?' Jerrick said as they walked past the staircase, its newels grotesque parodies of devils.

'I jumped for joy,' he said, stopping by a closed door. 'Not literally. Not with these birdy bones. But I felt something like true joy. The world going back to its intended path, getting itself back on the rails. Yanayev! What a President he would have been! No concessions, no brokering of peace. The kind of man who would make a bomb a senator. For two days, I was beside myself. And then it was over. The whole thing finished. I was mortified.'

Drum had watched the news reports, the coverage of the attempted coup d'état, sick in the stomach. Jerrick looked at him and perhaps saw a fellow traveller, a flicker of recognition.

'It's not a popular reaction, I confess,' he said. 'But I'm old, and I no longer care.'

He smiled and opened the door. Inside, the room was almost total night, the large bay windows shrouded with thick layers of sackcloth. Jerrick flicked a switch and the light was blinding, strip lights, institutional and humming, suspended from the high ceiling where chandeliers had once shimmered. It was a former ballroom, a huge space dominated by three large desks covered in papers, maps and blueprints. The three unwindowed walls were shelved, crammed with books and box files, document wallets and boxes, thousands of volumes, flush to the walls, many more stacked on lines of library trolleys in front of them.

Jerrick shuffled to the nearest desk, picked up a piece of paper at random, put it back on the desk.

'You're surprised,' he said. 'People are always surprised.'

'I know you said it was comprehensive, but . . .' Carter said.

'It's mostly illegally gotten,' he said. 'Files I filched, memos I copied. It was dangerous for a time, I liked that, the danger of it. I had my little helpers. My little moles. But the service, they knew what I was doing. They knew what I was trying to amass. There isn't anything in here the Russians didn't know about anyway. When they closed Doom Town, they told me to take the library with me, they had no use for it. So I took it and added to it. This is the history of the ghost war. The last great conflict we shall know. A low, dishonest history. I used to come in here and feel the fire, feel the heat from the pages. And now everything is as cold as the grave. It's a museum, not an archive. There's nothing here but ghosts of ghosts, memories of a collective madness. People will look back on this archive, and they'll laugh. It will become a black comedy. All the things we did to protect ourselves will look like adults dressing up, creating their own ridiculous monsters. My bequest to the world is the world's largest collection of jokes.'

He went to the corner of the room and opened a box, took out a bottle of Scotch.

'I was a boy scout in my youth,' he said. 'Be prepared.'

Drum looked around the room, the insane amount of collated information. To his right was a wall devoted to novels about atomic war; below them hundreds of video tapes and reel-to-reel cassettes.

'It's overwhelming, sir,' Carter said. 'I had no idea you had all this stuff.'

'Stuff?' Jerrick said. 'This "stuff" is my life. Yours too. A grand devotional.'

Drum ran his hands along the metal of a bookshelf, jolted from a static shock.

'Yes,' Jerrick said. 'Do watch for that. Happens to me about a hundred times a day. Probably why I'm still alive. So is there something you're both interested in?'

'Mid-Off,' Drum said. 'An operation in '80.'

Jerrick walked back towards the door, climbed a few rungs of a ladder and took down a box. He placed it on the desk in front of Drum.

'That's all the materials for Mid-Off,' Jerrick said. 'All I have anyway.'

He smiled.

'Which is of course everything.'

Jerrick wandered off to refill his glass. Carter stood beside Drum and put a hand on the box.

'Are you sure?' Carter said. 'You can't unsee it, you know. Once you open the box . . . '

Carter was dying. Sure of it now. Should have thought. Should have known.

'Do you know what's in here?' Drum said.

'No,' Carter said. 'But please don't open it. Please don't.'

Drum looked for Jerrick. An arbiter. A referee. But he was gone. It was just the two of them in the vast room, the strip lights humming and a box with Carter's hand on its lid.

⋆

Alone, Carter unable to watch, Drum read the Mid-Off files. The speed of its introduction; the need to ensure full intelligence of what was likely to happen in the network of bunkers if the bomb dropped. There had been studies, but none so widespread or specific. What happens to the dynamics of a group when a stranger is introduced? How safe would the VIPs be? There were sixty registered private bunkers, and each would be tested. There were reports from generals and medical professionals arguing against the test. They were ignored. In the post-Afghanistan world, the defence experts argued, it was imperative to be as prepared as possible.

There were sixty reports of the Mid-Off tests, each in their own folder. They were dry: what had been discussed, the atmosphere of those in the bunker, the psychological temperature below ground. Drum read the first. The drill had lasted two days. The third a little over twelve hours. The third made it to three days.

'At 6.10 a.m.,' the third report concluded. 'The observer went through from his billet to the billet of the owners. There he found the four of them dead. There had been no warning of suicide. There was no indication it was planned.'

Names were not mentioned in the reports, just sex and ages. M, 46, F 39, M 4, M 7. The next report, another death. Suicide by gunshot, M 22. He stopped reading in any detail, skimmed them until he found himself in the twenty-third report.

'The father,' Gault wrote, 'was well-disposed, clear of intention, followed protocol, followed orders. Son on the edge, close to violence. Daughter lost her mind in the night. Was forced to abandon after an incident with the daughter. Conclusion that these be struck from the register of approved members of the public. Recommendation: unsafe.'

There was a final document, a debrief with future recommendations. All dignitaries to be armed on entering a civilian bunker, and to be accompanied at all times by trained handlers. All members of the programme to be rescreened; those who had already failed immediately expelled, all privileges revoked. Any dangerous elements to be removed from a bunker, in the event, by force if necessary.

All these years, he'd thought themselves safe, but not safe. No longer privileged with early warning; no guarantee they would be admitted to the bunker. All those years and no better off than the rest of the world. No safer than a factory worker, a librarian, or a farmer.

★

They drove to the hotel in silence, no cassette playing, no radio. Five deaths, one shotgun, four pills, a busted flush of a test. Annie running from the bunker, his last sight of her, running, screaming. Had she kept it back. Had she just been able to control herself, a matter of days and they'd have been safe. Safe for all time. Couldn't just keep it together, not just for a matter of hours. She put them all in danger. All these years.

'A drink,' Carter said, parking the car at the hotel. 'We could use one.'

'No,' Drum said.

'We need to talk,' Carter said. 'I brought you here so we could talk.'

'I thought you wanted to show me the archive. That's what you said.'

Carter turned off the engine, rubbed his eyes with thin fingers.
'A pretext. A sugar coating,' he said. 'Had to pique your interest.'

He laughed and it was the sad laugh of a man who knows something is coming to an end, to its conclusion.

'I don't want to hear it,' Drum said. 'Please, I don't want—'

Carter put his hand on Drum's shoulder.

'Please, Drummond,' he said. 'Please.'

The manners of the upper classes. Their perfect, perfect manners.

★

Carter had perhaps always drunk like a dying man; as though there were only a finite number of drinks one could consume before you die, and him ensuring he got his allotted. In the deserted bar, Carter lit a cigarette. Perhaps this was the place where death would finally come; a hotel in off season, the few guests trying to catch a glimpse of the cadaver as the receptionist explained the bar was temporarily closed.

'I'm in trouble, Drum,' Carter said. 'I'm in all kinds of trouble.'

Heard this before, heard it several times before, all with a wink, with the electric of drama behind it. Daphne leaving me, I'm in trouble Drum. Got the Hunter woman in the family way, I'm in trouble, Drum. I lost an important file, I'm in trouble, Drum. But nothing exhilarating here; enervating, rather, all fizz and vim fucked and bombed. Looking older than his age now, a mask slipping, revealing his true face, revealing his true features. Scared as the early days in Service, scared as those last days in Service. As though weeping in a small inaccessible part of his body. The pancreas perhaps, the lymph nodes.

It was possible Carter wanted his spleen. A transplant. Can you give a lung? A kidney? They would not be compatible, surely. Perhaps that was it. Perhaps that was always the plan. Found out years ago that they were both some obscure blood-type and Drum kept around for emergencies—

'Thomas has got himself into a spot of bother.'

The relief of that. Fucking Thomas. The relief and the quick taking of the Bell's, in celebration the bad whisky and Carter filling up his glass with the good stuff from his hip flask.

'I bailed him out, obviously. Drugs at first, then some trading matter. It was all fine, I smoothed it over. Pulled in some favours owed on my father. Thomas was contrite, said he'd pay me back one day.'

Carter laughed.

'I should have seen that coming, shouldn't I? When someone says they'll pay you back one day, you know it isn't going to be pretty, don't you?'

Drum said nothing.

'You can't trust sons,' he said. 'They want to fuck you. They might not mean to, but they can't help it. They're hardwired for it. Like Russians fleeing battle, they're a generational scorched-earth policy. I shouldn't blame him, the little skate. I shouldn't blame him, because I knew. I knew and I still went along with it. I listened to him, I listened to him and I wanted to trust him and so I trusted him.'

Carter, not dying, smoked his cigarette and looked around, but there was no one there save Drum.

'He had some hot tip. It was going to make him millions. Going to set him for life. Get his life back on track. But he needed money. No one else would front him. Said he would make everything back ten times over, just needed seed money. I gave him the lot, Drum. Everything.'

'Everything?'

'Everything, Drum. What part of everything are you missing? I gave him the lot and it went tits up. He lost the lot. I'd already taken a tanking on Black Monday, but this was like the bomb dropping, Drum. We have nothing. The house, yes, but I can't sell it; can't raise money on it without Daphne knowing.'

'I'm sorry,' Drum said. 'I don't know what to say.'

'Nothing to say,' Carter said. 'I just need money. Medium-term loan, just to set myself right.'

'So borrow it,' Drum said.

Carter shook his head.

'Nothing doing. No income for the foreseeable. They're closing the RSG. They let me go a while back. I just need some money for the next six months, a year tops.'

'You want the farm?' Drum said. 'Is that it? You want to take back the farm?'

'No,' Carter said, waving his hands. 'No, no. I made you a promise. And I always keep my word. I just need you to borrow money against it. Get me what I need and I'll pay it back when I can. All on me. Every last penny. You can save me again, Drum.'

Drum was not Drum at that moment. Sometimes, easy to forget oneself. To step out from skin, out from bone and brain, and become something wholly other. Seeing his son. Nate just there. Right in front of him. Save a son to save a son.

Drum will never understand that moment. That coming-out-from-self moment, when he looked at Carter and a fully formed response came, a quick deliberation, so quick it defied time. How complex the brain to come up with hard-and-fast plans in less than a lick of the lips; how complex the brain to conjure elaborate dreams in sleep.

'Okay,' Drum said. 'I'll do it.'

That look. The utter relief of that look. Bringing him back from death, that look.

'But the farm is mine,' Drum said. 'I do this and I own it one hundred per cent. You sign it over to me tomorrow.'

That face. How quick the calculations, how quick the brain working, how quick you see the sparks, the electrics crackle.

'I can't do that, Drum. You know how long that land has been out of the family. What it took to get it back. It's my legacy, that farm, you understand? On his deathbed, my father he looked at me and he said, "Do something I couldn't do." And I did it. I bloody did it, Drum. It was the best moment of my fucking life. You can't take that from me. You can't take that from me now.'

Drum sipped his Scotch.

'Then I can't help you,' Drum said. 'I need to look after Nate. It's his place now, or will be. You want to save your son, make everything right? I need to do the same.'

'You'd do this to me? You'd do this to me now?' Carter said.

'Without me, you'd never have had the farm.'

'You ungrateful shit,' Carter said. 'You ingrate. All the things I've done for you. You owe me your life, you know that?'

'And you owe me yours, remember that.'

Drum did not recognize the face. Not that face. Resignation, that face. Defeat. Carter stabbed out his cigarette.

'Okay. You win,' he said. 'But here's the deal. If you ever sell, you or Nate or any one, you sell only to me. To my family. No one ever gets that land but you or me. You have to swear on that.'

Just like that. As quick as that. The mind made up quicker than it takes to put out a Dunhill Light.

'I promise,' Drum said. 'But you don't make him an offer. You never make him an offer, nor anyone else. If Nate comes to you, fine. But you don't ever offer him anything for the farm.'

Carter held out his hand. They shook hands.

'Agreed,' he said.

Carter proposed a toast. They clinked glasses.

'I just hope I die before you,' Carter said. 'Otherwise Daph and Tom will kill me dead.'

Seven and Seven

2005

Thursday 7 July

I

She could not get hold of Ray. His phone rang through to an answer service, his clipped voice then a long tone. She left messages asking him to call her urgently; remembering the third time to say she hoped he was safe. In the kitchen, mid-morning, supposed to be at a Pilates class, good for her shattered back, ringing through to mobile, ringing through to an unanswered landline; the sound of the television loud from the sitting room.

Since switching from radio in kitchen to television in sitting room, Drum had not left the sofa. He leaned in close to the screen, mouth slightly open, as though he might miss something crucial. When the planes had crashed the towers, he'd done the same. Twelve hours and barely a toilet break. When aroused or threatened, the body shutting down such functions. He would be the day there now, the night: the commentators offering their insights, the constant repetition of the event, the estimates of casualties, the groups possibly responsible. After the towers, Ray had texted. *Don't worry. Anneka not in NYC.* Unnecessary, but appreciated.

She texted Ray. Belt and braces. She was in the kitchen because she needed privacy, but also to avoid the screen, the rolling ticker. She sensed thrill in the presenters, in the pundits and experts. Something almost sexual; the erections as they told of the destruction; the tightening of the groin as they said *deadliest peacetime attack on the capital.* The same for Drum, most likely; sitting there, tea cooling on the table, leaning forward, better to capture the images, hide the swell in his jeans.

Were Anneka dead, were Robin dead, Gwen would be able to claim Femi. She would be able to go to London and put her arms around her grandchild, and tell him he was safe, that he could come and live with them now. On a farm. Imagine that! Cows and chickens and birds in the trees, a brook in which to paddle. The smells and the sights and the warmth of the fire, the open air and the fields. And the love here, yes, the love. All for you, Femi, the love. The making right.

She called Ray. She heard his voice and the long tone. She left a short message.

She'd seen footage of the mangled bus; the punched-by-god Tube trains. A miracle not more dead; a miracle the whole city not aflame. Footage of the underground travellers above ground, blinking mole-like by the police cordons, looking over the lines of stretchers. To be blasted just a touch, just a little, enough for a story, enough to feel alive amongst the death. She knew that's how she'd feel. That she would want to be amongst it; to smell the sharp smoke and burned rubber; see the melt of flesh, the splash of spilled blood.

She'd watched the crowds for Anneka, watched them for Robin, for Femi. She did not see them, they could be on the stretchers, covered over and shrouded, perhaps. Laid out next to Ray, dying next to each other, a camera loaded in his pocket, the police puzzled as to why the only saved photographs were covert shots of a woman and a man and a child. How many secrets exposed by bombs; how many deceptions blown cover.

She called Ray. She heard his voice and the long tone. She left a short message.

The networks would be at breaking point. How many panicking up and down the country; thinking of partners and lovers, thinking of children and grandchildren? Ray would be safe. People like Ray do not die in these kinds of things. Never the known who die. Never the ones worthy of obituary.

The phone rang, Daphne's number. Immediate guilt at the number. She'd not thought of Thomas. His family. Natasha too, somewhere in the South now.

'They're all safe,' Daphne said. 'All of them. I just managed to get through to Tommy. He said it's carnage, but everyone's all okay. He spoke to Tasha, too.

'What a relief,' Gwen said. 'We've been watching it all morning.'

'We've had the World Service on. Sounds like no one knows what's happening.'

'That's what it sounds like,' she said.

'Well, I just wanted to make sure you knew, so you weren't worried.'

How many calls like this; how many placed from the deck of her Spanish swimming pool, a glass of wine for the nerves, though not even eleven o'clock, the white stucco walls and the terracotta cooler, Carter in the water no doubt, swimming to the moon and back. His new thing, swimming.

'Is it hot?' Gwen said.

'Sweltering,' she said. 'You?'

'It's warm,' she said. 'Balmy.'

Talk of the weather now, on the phone at least; long conversations about weather, about the heat and its lack. How had they got to this? Two old women, all conversation worn away, talking about the weather. No more Wednesday afternoons or Friday lunches; no more gentle back and forth, no more confessional. How it only hits sometimes how much you ache for someone's company.

The couple who rented the Carter house had a young family; they were scientists, uninterested in her and Drum. Hadn't even asked them to babysit; instead a slew of teenagers arrived in their daddies' cars. Their children seemed scared of Gwen, and of Drum. They sometimes crept towards the farm, but if she saw them, they ran away before she could offer them lemonade or cake.

'It'll be hotter when you come out,' Daphne said. 'You can forget all about warm and balmy.'

'I need to go,' she said. 'Something in the oven.'

'Molly coming over?'

'Yes. Carrot cake.'

'Well, I'll let you go. Call me on the weekend.'

Gwen put the phone in the pocket of her yoga pants and went into the sitting room, Drum's gaze not averted by her coming into the room, eyes only for the latest scenes from King's Cross, from Edgware Road.

'Looks like at least four,' he said. 'Minimum of four. No one's claimed responsibility, yet.'

'That was Daphne,' she said. 'Everyone's safe.'

He looked up at her, a moment's confusion, then thought catching up with expression.

'Good,' he said. 'That's a relief.'

'You'll turn this off when Molly comes over,' she said. 'I don't want her seeing this.'

'Of course,' he said. 'I wouldn't want her to see this either.'

He wouldn't though. It would still be on when Nate and Molly arrived. He'd inch towards the kitchen, only hitting the remote as he reached the sitting-room door.

'Good,' she said. 'I'm going to make that cake now.'

*

She made the carrot cake. Nate's favourite and Molly's too, Molly not allowed too much sugar, so carrot cake ideal, easy to make too, and fuck the cake, the cake, what, making cake when people are dead and dying? All that and you make cake? Grate the carrots as Anneka dies, as Robin dies, as Femi dies? No, not Femi.

She put the cake in the oven. The phone was silent; sirens from the sitting room, amateur footage of amateur bombs, the rotor blades of helicopters. She took wine from the fridge, put it back. Wouldn't do, not with Molly coming over. The look on Drum's face, on Nate's face; Molly understanding something not right.

From charity shops Gwen had bought Molly games and toys, kept them in a shopping bag she called Granny Gwen's Magic Bag. Cheap entertainment, cupboard love. Surprising the competition between the grandparents. Three sets to navigate, Molly knowing the choppy waters well, knowing who was best for what. Gwen for puzzles, for books; everyone else for fun. Why aren't you more fun? Molly said. Why don't you play? Why won't you dress up?

Count blessings. Could be a fourth set, five conceivably. Molly's father, biological father, disappearing before Molly born; Nate adopting her officially on her first birthday. Raised as his own, but not his own. Not really his; not really Gwen's. Not a real grand-child. A dark-haired thing, thick-limbed and bouncing with energy, hopped up on music and dance, beautiful but not really her own.

When Carlie finally left Nate, Gwen thought she might never see Molly again, thought she might become one of those women who rang up radio phone-ins to complain about grandparents' scandalous lack of rights. No rights with Femi, either. A true grandchild. Horrible to say that. A true grandchild. Molly, love, forgive me.

She took the cake from the oven, set it to cool. She called Ray again. Straight to voicemail.

Drummond wandered into the kitchen, stuck his finger into the frosting.

'They'll be here any minute,' she said. 'Have a shower.'

'I'm fine as I am,' he said.

'Have a shave then.'

'Molly likes to scratch at my whiskers. Like I'm a cat or some-thing.'

He came up behind her, put his arms around her, rested his hands where her apron was sashed around her middle.

'Don't worry,' he said. 'She hated London. No way she'd be there.'

'I know,' she said. 'But you get to wondering . . .'

'Shush,' he said. 'There's nothing to worry about. Nothing at all.'

2

In accordance with the new Thursday ritual, Nate met Carlie and Molly by the renovated play area at the park. The structures were futuristic: wheels, spokes and tyres hanging from wires; abstract ladders leading to floating platforms; the flooring beneath spongy from a seam of impact-absorbing rubber. He saw Carlie, and then Molly at the top of the spiral slide, watched her as she slid down, dress hitched, exposing knickers, face sombre. Already having the measure of the slide, already knowing its meagre thrills.

'Daddy!' Molly said at the slide's lip. She ran to him, bounced into his outstretched arms. For his benefit; for the benefit of upsetting her mother. Carlie sat on a pine bench, at her feet a carry bag and a small rucksack which Molly always packed though she knew she was not spending the night.

'Hey, Carlie,' he said.

'Hi,' she said.

'Push me on the swing, Daddy,' Molly said.

'Let me talk to Mummy first,' he said. 'You go swing yourself and I'll be right there.'

Molly smiled, scowled at her mother, so effortless the shift; effortless, also, Carlie's roll of eyes.

'She's been a perfect little shit for me,' Carlie said. 'So she'll probably be good as gold for you.'

She wore no make-up, there were grey stains on the sleeve of her black top, chips in her pedicure, dusty feet in flip-flops. Less effort each time they met, like when she stopped wearing thongs and switched to bigger knickers. Too old now to have something in my ass-crack all day, she'd said.

'Did you hear about the bombs?' Nate said.

Bombs a safe subject. Something even those at war could discuss without it leading down dark and personal pathways.

'Someone I know was on one of the trains,' she said. 'The King's Cross one. He's fine though. Vanessa called me to tell me all about it. I didn't know they were still in contact.'

'Who was that?' he said.

'No one you know,' she said. 'A friend from school. Haven't seen him in years.'

'Well, I'm glad he's safe,' he said.

Carlie knew so many people, had always known so many people. There wasn't one person he knew who would have been in London; not a one for him to worry about. When the IRA did Warrington in ninety-three and Manchester in ninety-six, there were conceivable casualties. Those he knew who worked there, shopped there. Billy was there, in Manchester. Nate had called him and Billy had answered, then Nate had put down the phone.

Bombs were always so far away, until they weren't. The Warrington one the worst; close, Warrington, but so insignificant; nationally probably only known for its Rugby League team. The bomb there was just to say no one was safe. To remind everyone, if we can do somewhere as pointless as Warrington, we can do anywhere. Look out. Be prepared.

'What you doing this afternoon?' he said. She laughed. He missed her laughter; the laughter that said he knew nothing, did not understand anything; not a malicious laugh, no bite to it, just something she did.

'Washing, tidying, cleaning and, if I'm lucky, after that I'll get twenty minutes for myself.'

'I could always take—'

'No,' she said. 'I mean thank you, but it's too soon.'

She handed him the small rucksack, the large bag.

'You understand, right?'

'Of course,' he said. 'Of course I do. And I'm trying. I really am.'

She huffed out. He had not wanted to say this, the same thing he said every Thursday, but he said it anyway.

'I look at you,' Carlie said, 'and it's impossible to tell how you're doing. You don't look any different. I can't see inside that head of yours.'

'One day at a time,' he said. 'That's all I can do. I have a meeting tomorrow.'

'Always tomorrow, the meeting,' she said. 'Always tomorrow.'

'Friday's a good day for meetings,' he said. 'Weekends are the most difficult for some.'

True this. The stories told in the group sessions so often started with *last Saturday*, or *it were Sunday* and the men would shake heads as they unburdened themselves. The things they said. Encouraged to be as truthful as they could, use the words they had used, the things they had struck, punched or kicked. It didn't matter how minor. A confessional without possible absolution. A strange push-me-pull-you in the room, the truth carefully stacked and weighted. Men he knew who'd had a punch up the weekend before would not mention it, but tell complicated allegories of the incident. Some he suspected were in some kind of Fight Club. There were old warehouses in the town; abandoned farm places nearby. Perfect for it. A chalk circle, money changing hands.

Years back, he might have made enquiries. Before Carlie came back with Molly; before he moved into her little place, the smell of nappies and nappy sacks and Johnson's baby lotion. A few years back, yes. Call it the nineties. Call it a decade of cows and fights and the odd excursion into the clubs. Last night at the Haç; the foray into Flesh. An AIDS test one morning, a blur that night, a damage to himself, he was. At Billy's house, the last time. Quiet, beautiful Billy. A rekindling, three months, a dinner or two, not just fucking. Scary, those months.

The last night, after a fight, after make-up sex, in his Manchester apartment, smoking an imported American cigarette, looking up and putting his hand on Nate's chest, Billy said, 'You're just waiting for the woman to come, aren't you, my dear? And when she comes, you'll come running, won't you?'

He'd wanted to say no to that. He'd wanted to say Billy was wrong. But Carlie had come running and he could not say no to her. No matter what had happened, could not say no.

Carlie picked up her bag.

'Okay,' she said. 'Well keep it up. I'll see you at seven. No later, right?'

'Seven at the latest,' he said.

'PUSH ME,' Molly shouted. And so he pushed her in the hard shine of sun, watched as Carlie walked away, waving without turning.

★

Nate drove them home. As always, Molly waved as they passed her house. Hard to look on the house now. A couple of years of walking up its stairs, taking a bath with Molly, washing the back of her neck, playing with a wind-up penguin. Not to think on that. Eight hours with her now. Up to see the cows, ice the cake with Granny Gwen, sit on Grandpa Dum's lap and read books the way he'd never done for him. The same as they had every Sunday before the crack-up; the same but minus Carlie; the same but something essential sucked from the day, like daylight-saving hours in the wrong season.

'Look, cows!' Molly said, pointing to the bored munch of them. Still excitement at that, the move from town to countryside. The strangeness of being on a farm, like a funhouse just for her. He saw the house bathed in light, saw the happy faces of those inside, the joy of her crossing the threshold, the transformative power of her little feet and girlish screams. Something his mother said – this house has never known a child – and this true, not a small child, not a toddler. A Boxing Day Christmas around the fire, Molly tearing wrapping paper from a seemingly endless tower of boxes. The look on his parents' faces, the smell of the roasting turkey, the gentle arm around Carlie. A picture-book idea of Christmas,

425

perfect, and frozen now in time, never to be repeated; perfection happening once and once alone.

'Yes,' he said. 'All the cows are out today.'

'Can we go and see Jemima?'

'After we say hello to Granny and Grandpa.'

Nate parked and unbuckled Molly, kissed her on the curl of her dark hair. Smelled of Carlie now, smelled of once home. He put on her long socks and pink wellies, pushed them over her delicate ankles.

'They okay?' he said.

'Yes,' she said and jumped down from the car, onto the still-muddy grass, the sun not having dried out the downpour of the previous week.

'It smells of poo,' she said, as always, and loped her way through the mud to the farmhouse. He locked the car, watched her negotiate the squelch, bang on the door.

'Granny Gwen! Open up, Granny Gwen!'

His mother opened the door, picked up Molly, held her as a trophy, took her inside, ignoring Nate, not even looking at Nate. He crossed the threshold and watched his parents fuss Molly, kiss her and take off her muddy boots, anointing her feet with the slipper socks they'd bought for her.

He poured tea from the pot on the kitchen table. There were sandwiches, a plate of pork pies, two bowls of raw vegetables that Carlie insisted Molly liked, but never ate when at the farm. Cake cooled on a rack, a bowl of frosting. A different house with a child in it. A different house entirely.

3

Molly was in his arms. His arms hurt these days, the ache in the joints, the pills he took for it doing nothing; cod liver oil at least better than when a kid, when it was a spoon of liquid, the stink of dissolved fish. In his arms, Molly heavy, so heavy these days. On his lap and him reading *The Lorax*, the rhymes she loved, Molly rubbing her hands along his stubble, sometimes upsetting his glasses. Had his surname, but not his genes. What genes to have anyway. Busted knees and twisted guts. She laughed, and her laugh giggled his belly, her riding it slightly, the weight gain from retirement, the odd shift now, no longer up all hours.

'What shall we read now?' Molly said and he shook his head.

'Dinner time now, Molly,' he said.

She jumped up, ran from him, a ride ended and off to a different attraction. He turned on the television, muted the volume, then turned it up slightly, just enough for him to hear. Leaned forward, the same text on the ticker. Still no one claiming responsibility. Remember the Angry Brigade. The bombs of theirs. Carter mentioned them in Rules that time. Another bunch of crazies. Sane now in comparison. None of them were ever Angry enough to blow themselves up for their cause.

New bombings these, new for that reason. How many people to cause so much death. Four. Five maybe. Not thinking big enough though. Why not the trains? Why not shopping centres? Why not football grounds? Only a matter of time. No matter the level of alert, the state can't suppress that. Enough will, enough ordinance, and they could bring the country to its knees. Find enough warriors, they'll bring enough war.

Times like this, he missed the bomb. Its certainty. The uneasy peace brokered on the assumption that both sides did not want to die. This a different proposition. The opposite of mutually assured destruction: a war fought for the afterlife and nothing else. Had there been a Red heaven, the bombs would probably have dropped thirty years before.

Turn it off. Watch your blood pressure. Reduce stress. Do not eat fatty foods. Take plenty of exercise. Rest yourself. Take these tablets three times a day. Do not rise your ire. Take it easy. They flew planes into a building. They bombed London. They are not scared to die and you want me to be calm?

'How many dead?' Nate said. Like a football score. Like asking who was winning.

'Still uncertain,' Drum said. 'Hundreds by the look.'

'One of Carlie's friends was on the King's Cross train. He's okay, apparently.'

'Well that's good,' he said. 'One of the lucky ones.'

There had been eyewitness interviews. The young mainly, astonished by their proximity to death. The audacity of it. The old seemed less willing to share; less staggered by it. He would like to know how they felt. Whether they were more worried about their hearts and their bowels than being blown ten feet in the air.

Nate sat down next to him on the sofa.

'What's up with Mam?' he said. 'She's acting strange again.'

'She seems okay to me,' Drum said.

'She's all sort of rushy, like she hasn't eaten or something.'

'We had breakfast same as always,' he said.

'I know, Dad, I was there.'

'So what are you talking about then?'

Drum looked at his son. The mess of that. Forty years old and staring down divorce, a child not even his own, back working the farm after Les sacked him. A wife, a child, a job, gone in an afternoon. No more company car, no more overseeing conservatories and loft conversions for his father-in-law. Forty and in his same old room, back in the same old routine. Drum had missed him in those short years of gainful employ. Missed their gentle routines, his hand on his back at end of day, like the two of them had a hundred years of farming in the genes.

After Carlie kicked him out, they'd talked, perhaps the only time they'd ever talked of *feelings*. All Drum could think to say was, you make it right. After what you did, you have to make it right. Nate had cried. In his arms, his son crying, the last time when Nate had scabbed up his knee, blood running down his leg, nine years old and his tears dampening the collar of his father's shirt.

'I'm taking Molly to see the cows after dinner,' Nate said. 'You coming?'

'With these knees?'

'You sound like a right old man,' he said. '*Oh, me knees.*'

'Oh go on, mock,' he said. 'I'll remind you of it when you're half crippled.'

He sounded old, felt old, looked old. Drum looked at himself in the mirror sometimes and remembered something Gwen had said about W. H. Auden. If that's his face, imagine his scrotum. He'd look at his scrotum then, the tucks and folds, no more wrinkled than he had ever seen it, though grey hairs grew there now, his cock at slumber for weeks on end. At first, on retiring, they'd made love more than in the previous ten years. Three or four times a week, morning sex mostly. Then that had worn off. Gwen or him, unsure who cooled first.

'When are you off to see Carter?' Nate said.

'End of the month,' Drum said.

'Looking forward to it?'

It was going to be hot; his knees would flare. There would be day trips and wine tastings at vineyards, dinner by the pool. There would be Carter, tanned and toned and strange without the cigarettes. Not his Carter, but another Carter, somehow spritzed and cleansed, somehow unencumbered, no longer with a tight rein, snapping Drummond back to him. Drum had the farm, but for the price of Carter's intimacy. Once the money was sorted, once everything had been settled and the capital built back up, off Carter went. Had always promised Daph a life in the sun, Carter had said, but it was something Carter had never expressed to Drummond. Not once and never.

'It's relaxing there,' Drum said. 'A beautiful spot. Lovely restaurants and stuff. Couldn't live there myself, mind.'

'Yeah, I'm sure Carter and Daphne are missing this plenty.'

Nate smiled, dumb smile he had, stupid as his laugh.

'How's Carlie?' Drum said.

'Fine,' Nate said. 'I think she wants to let Molly stay over, but she's worried what her parents will say.'

'Always blame the parents,' Drum said. 'Easiest thing in the world to do is that.'

'They were good to me,' Nate said. 'Always were.'

Drum had been jealous of the car. Jealous of the suits. The sudden ease of Nate's life. Left him in the lurch for a time, had to get a new farmhand and none as good as Nate. But he came back. At least he came back. No choice, but he came back at least.

'Just got to keep on, son,' he said. 'Just got to keep proving yourself.'

Hated himself for that. Winced at the words. Spent now, unable to help anyone, unable to make intelligent contribution. Perhaps never had. Perhaps always had said the wrong things. Once they looked to him, but not now. Just Dad. Just Drum.

Gwen called from the kitchen, dinner ready. Nate got up and Drum walked backwards, watching the ticker, hit the remote just as he reached the sitting-room door. Then stopped. He turned the television back on. Crowds outside the Edgware Road. He squinted, something spotted just before the screen turned black. Somewhere behind the reporter, he was sure he'd seen Annie. For a split second her. No doubt it was her. Her there, in the crowd, a purple top, a black shoulder bag. Walking past camera, surely her. And then not. No. Not her. Not Annie. Not his girl. Just a woman, a purple blouse, a black handbag, walking the road, not looking at the wreckage.

4

She was a good eater, Molly, a joyful eater, picking up sandwiches, deconstructing them, eating them discretely: cheese, then bread, then ham, then bread. Were she her child, Gwen would have told her not to, told her not to play around with her food. She'd had those arguments with Annie over the small kitchen table: don't pick up peas, don't eat just one thing at a time, hold your knife and fork correctly. It mattered so much then, but what difference did it make, ultimately? So many rules; so difficult to understand why so important. No singing at the table. No you can't wear a tutu to the shops. No, you can't read one more chapter. No, you can't go round to Lissa's house. No, you can't babysit, you can barely look after yourself.

'Did I tell you Granny Gwen and I are going on holiday, Molly?' Drum said. 'We're going to Spain.'

'Will there be a swimming pool?' she said.

'Yes,' he said.

'Am I coming too?' she said.

'No,' he said. 'It's just for grown-ups.'

Why mention this? Something to say, yes; but why this? Inevitable, what would happen. The crumple of Nate's shoulders, the excited eyes of the child, a holiday he cannot give her. No holiday, no home of his own, and his father goading. Still something of the grand game between them. Look at what I'd done by your age: two kids, a uniform once worn, a business of my own. And you, a driving ban the only thing the world knows you even exist. All said and unsaid.

Gwen excused herself and went to the bathroom, called Ray but

432

got a message that his mailbox was full. She called again and got the same message. They had not kissed. All the years and not a kiss, not once. Close sometimes, very close sometimes, but not. No Rubicon crossed, no line drawn.

When she'd been tempted, she'd reminded herself of fairy-tale kisses, how they bestow a contract. The frog becomes prince and claims the kisser; the prince kisses the sleeping woman and she belongs to him. Whatever the magic of the kiss, what ensues is practical, mundane, masculine. A marriage, a future, a goodbye to the fantastical. Once Ray had said, I will kiss you whether you like it or no. She'd been surprised, then replied. I will like it well enough, but whether *you* will is another matter. Suitably gnomic to give him pause, that.

How different could it be, she thought, with someone else, someone of the same vintage? Would he do things to her that Drummond could not? How much we will do for an orgasm, a few moments of pleasure. Take over kingdoms, sack cities, cut off oxygen, abduct queens. For a few seconds. A few seconds and then over. And again to need it, to do it once more. Again and again. So no kisses. No lingering hands.

She washed her hands and went back into the kitchen. No one seemed to notice she had gone.

Molly had made him name all the cows. Jemima, Jane, Joyce, Jennifer, Jody, Jessica, Joan, Joni . . . occasionally Molly shouting no, that's Jemima, look the black circle round her eye. And he would laugh and say how silly he was.

Twenty years, off and on, with the cows and not once feeling as a farmer, not once feeling that kinship with the beast, with the land. It just was. In Chris Birch's autobiography, which Nate read as soon as it was available at the library, Chris Birch wrote candidly about being a footballer; what it was like as a boy, what it was like as a former player. What it was like to not love football, but see it as a job.

After Chris Birch had retired from a career that never quite lived up to its promise, Chris Birch was in a bar and a City supporter started talking to him about his playing days. The fan knew more about his career than Chris Birch did. Eventually, Chris Birch lost his patience with the fan and told him he didn't give a shit. He hated football. Hated playing it, hated talking about it. It was just a fucking job. The fan threw a punch. Chris Birch wrote that, afterwards, more people were sympathetic to the fan than they were to him. When forced into situations with other farmers, Nate wanted to have the courage of Chris Birch. To just stand there and say, they're just fucking cows, mate, they're just fucking *cows*.

It was worse since coming back, tail between legs, after Les sacked him from his company; worse since his father retired. Dad still watching over him though, when he could, checking for error, for lateness, for a chink in the routine. They were being squeezed; money tighter than ever, madness to be in dairy still. He'd started planting vegetables over by the fields, applied for approved organic status. They'd survived foot and mouth, but some nights he was kept awake by the image of cows aflame, knowing it would have wiped him out it if it'd ever made its way to him. He wished it had sometimes.

'Daddy,' Molly said.

'Yes, darling.'

'When are you coming home?'

This the same every week.

'Soon, I hope. I need to stay here to look after the cows, you know that.'

She looked doubtful, but was distracted by a fine arc of piss from either Jocasta or Jolene. Saved by urine. When a dog dies, parents tell their kids the dog's gone to a farm. They said the same about Nate to Molly.

With her help, he herded the cows inside the sheds, showed her the milkers, showed her how to milk by hand, same as always. Each time like the first time, the wonder of the milk spurting from teat, the spatter as it hit the metal pail.

'Well, all done,' Nate said. 'Must be time for tea.'

She shook her head.

'I'm not hungry.'

'You will be,' he said. 'Race you back to the house.'

And they raced, and she won, as he always let her, though sometimes he wanted not to. Just to show her that you don't always win. That winning is something rare and special.

6

Drum went into the spare room, scrolled through the BBC News website. No real news, nothing really to report, but he read it all: the roundups and the what-we-knows and the timelines. He looked through photographs and could not see any footage of the woman in the purple T-shirt. Of course not there. Of course not.

'It'll make you go blind,' Nate said, standing at the open door.

'I was just—'

'I know,' he said. 'I know.'

'I thought I saw her,' Drum said. 'I thought I saw her in the crowd.'

Nate sat down on the bed, the spare bed only ever used by Gwen. Resented that bed. Drum had repurposed the room, made it his study; added further bookshelves, a new desk and a new computer, a broadband connection not much faster than dial-up.

'It's understandable, Dad,' Nate said. 'Something like this plays havoc with you.'

'Havoc?' he said.

'Yes,' Nate said. 'Havoc.'

'A strange word, havoc,' he said. 'A strange word, that one.'

That room had been havoc. Havoc and then its opposite, Annie's obsessive tidiness, the rigid order of her wardrobe and drawers. Once he had sat in there, looking through her things while she was out; opening drawers and fumbling under the bed, looking for something. Unsure what. A diary, something to explain the distance, the rowing out from the shore. He never found anything, just T-shirts folded tightly, knickers crossed at the waistband.

'When I worked at Ford's,' Drum said. 'We talked of revolution.

All the time, we talked of that. The red rising, the taking over. Like fairy stories, they were. Like Bible stories. It's the same with the stories these lads are told. The older you get, you see the truth, the boring, everyday, normal truth. They've tried, the communists, the fascists, but ultimately, people just want a quiet life. This'll pass too, this whole jihadi thing. And we'll be on to the next terror, the next panic. Because all we want is a quiet life, a home, a family. There's always something like this. There's never anything *not* like this. Bird flu, Al Qaeda, the end of oil, the millennium bug, climate change, there's always something. We're used to it. It doesn't change people. It doesn't change anything.'

'And yet you watch it all the same.'

Drum laughed. Yes, he watched it all the same. On the shelf, the books about the Taliban, the rise of the Right in Europe, voices of modern hatred.

His son stood from the bed.

'You really think that?' Nate said.

'Today,' he said. 'I think that today, yes.'

'And tomorrow?'

'Maybe you'll find me cowering in the bunker again.'

Nate put his hand on Drum's shoulder. Drum put his hand on his son's. Nate mussed the remaining hair on his crown.

'Don't stay here too long,' Nate said. 'Molly'll miss you.'

Drum refreshed the page, heard the door click. A good lad, despite it all; a good lad. Shared experience, shared conversation. Like on the factory line, the way you knew someone without even really speaking. Could see into their thoughts, their daydream fantasies. Knew them better than themselves.

This why Nate had found him on Millennium Eve; why Nate had found him though others were looking. They'd checked the gardens and the farmhouse, the bedrooms, assuming him drunk, having seen him set an alarming pace with his drinks. But Nate knew exactly where to look, knew also to give him some time alone there. Communion ahead of midnight.

437

Carter had thrown a large party, a local band playing the greatest hits of the last thousand years, hundreds of guests, cigars and champagne, the aching fug of perfume and aftershave. Drum watched Gwen and Daphne laughing with one another, giggling like schoolgirls. He felt erased, light in his body. Everyone laughing, no one thinking what would happen at midnight, the system errors, the catastrophic failures.

At half past eleven, he could take no more. He ducked down into the cellar, turned on the light and startled a young married woman and an older married man. They did not apologize, hurriedly pulled up or pulled down their garments, and silently filed past Drum. They'd spend the rest of the night worried they would be busted. To worry about such trivia.

The wheel was stiff, or he was not as strong as he once had been. It took several efforts before the door gave, opening up to the corridor, to the other door. He sweated as he did battle, and eventually won. The decontamination chamber smelled musty, like caves, and there was mould beneath the waterspouts, a lime-green pus.

He pushed through the double doors and into the living quarters, turned on the lights, all but one now dead, just the one holding on. How was this possible, if all bulbs installed on the same day, turned on for the same amount of time? He was thankful for it; for it not giving up.

The furniture was covered in sheets, clumps of dust on the linoleum, the same cave smell, but underpinned by something decaying. He breathed through his nose and took a bottle of whisky from the almost-empty box by the bookshelves. He removed a dustsheet from a chair and sat down, cracked the seal on the bottle. He put his wristwatch on the arm of the chair, the second hand counting down. He saw the bombs in their silos, the erecting launchers, the haywire codes and the looks of panic, of terror, as the military realized what was happening.

Not his wife, not Carter, but Nate. Nate finding him. Coming down, telling him they were looking for him, best look smart. Drum proper drunk then, Nate helping him above ground, half dragging him like one of Doom Town's sack-men. Nate deposited him back at the party, in the large dining room, as though he'd never left.

They counted down the seconds. Drum and Gwen and Daphne and Carter. The fireworks exploded in the garden. The sky erupted in violets, pinks, silvers and golds. There was no big blast to end the spectacle, not even a flicker of lights, not even a power surge. Just the fireworks and the cheers, and the kisses, and the hugs, and his son keeping quiet, his son saying nothing, saying nothing the best way he knew how.

7

Gwen hugged Molly close, that just-bathed smell, mint toothpaste and bubble bath, pyjamas washed in a pungent detergent. Taking off the slipper socks in the kitchen, putting them by the coats and shoes. For safekeeping, Molly. She would like to buy a pair for Femi, his slipper socks bright, red, gold and green, a touch of Christmas about them.

'I love you, Granny Gwen,' Molly said, kissing her on her cheek without prompt. Such sweet moments. Unexpected and still surprising. I love you, even though you're not my blood. Were you taken from me, I would miss you like I miss Femi. The same clawing ache, yes. But different. Where does one go for forgiveness for such thoughts? God, do not be listening. Be with the bombed and the blasted. Be not with me. Nor you, Old Nick.

'I love you too, Molly-moo,' Gwen said.

'I don't think I got my kiss,' Drum said and pushed his face into the girl, pretended to gobble her up, big-bad-wolf style. Molly loved it, as she always loved it. Jealous of that. Were Molly able to write a diary, Gwen would be missing from it too. Another excision from another life. When Carlie remarried, which she would, she would be excluded again. She would be a half-memory, a spectre on the farm, lost amongst the cows.

At night, unable to sleep, Gwen sometimes imagined there was a device that would alert you whenever someone thought of you. A terrifying invention. A kind of hellscape. The filtered rage of her daughter, the frustrations of her husband, the pity of her son. The sordid thoughts of men she had perhaps met only once. Ray only imagining her twenty years younger. Or worse, the machine registering no thoughts at all, eventually pointing to a true and inevitable death, one reached even before you've drawn your last.

'Bye-bye, Molly,' she said.

'I'll be back later,' Nate said. 'Going pop in the Wolf on the way back.'

'Drop the car here first,' Drum said.

'I always do,' he said.

He did not always do that. It was a miracle he'd not been killed on those roads. The future machine would tell Nate she thought about him all the time. This she hoped. This she was sure was true.

8

Nate knocked on the door he'd painted a cherry red, a good solid door, well hung, tight against draughts. Carlie opened up, bed-headed, tousled. Once he'd woken with her looking like that, like a French film actress, he thought, something natural, sexual about it.

'You want your men men, and your women women,' Billy had said. 'They need to be hypermasculine, hyperfeminine.'

Always thought a lot, did Billy. Too much thinking. Nate did not think on it almost at all now. When his parents were out, when alone, he didn't think, but used the computer. The images there. Everything he wanted. But no thinking.

'She's asleep,' he said. 'Nodded right off.'

'How much cake's she had?'

'Just the one slice.'

'No chocolate?'

'No.'

'Not even a little piece when Daddy wasn't looking?'

'No,' he said. 'Nothing like that. I'll bring her in.'

He checked the night nappy was correctly cinched, held Molly carefully and laid her down on her bed. He'd read her stories here, badly, but with effort; here he'd lain beside her when Carlie went out, Molly screaming for her, screaming in his face for Mummy, Mummy don't want Daddy, and that continuing for hours some nights. The screams like she was seeing the content of his mind, his thoughts of striking her, beating her, punching her in the throat to just stop her from screaming.

He was surprised that more children were not murdered; surprised that more parents did not lose their minds through lack of sleep, lack of control. Never touched her, never did, though once said he would, right up to her face, I'm going to fucking . . . and not getting further than that, but feeling the familiar urge to silence, to stop something in its steps. Carlie never knowing. Ever known, would not be here now, would not be laying down the child, tiptoeing away, hoping her to stay asleep.

The door closed, he walked down the stairs, Carlie at their foot, looking at her phone, not meeting his eyes.

'She's down,' he said.

Carlie looked up from the phone; the hated phone. Dreams of smashing the thing, its rinky-dink colour screen, its compact distraction, its constant beeps and glitches. So many messages, so many people; the type too small to read over her shoulder.

'She was good as gold,' he said.

The tap of her fingers, the speed of her typing, how quickly learned, how rapid the move up and down the keys. Couldn't have been more than a few years since he bought her first one; the delight at the small box, at the removing of the clear plastic from the facia; the joke she did not hear – now I'll know where you are at all times – and glad that she did not.

'Okay,' he said. 'See you next week.'

'Yeah,' she said. She looked up from the phone, held it in her hand as though weighing it, the candy-bar brick, the screen going grey, then black.

'Take care,' she said. 'Hope tomorrow goes okay.'

'Tomorrow?'

'Your meeting,' she said.

'Oh,' he said. 'Yes.'

He opened the door, was not pushed out of it, did not have blood on his knuckles and wrists; there was no hole in the living room wall, filled now, plastered over.

'See you, Carlie,' he said.

She took out her phone, and he closed the door as her fingers zipped the keypad.

9

She'd never heard a telephone ring in a bathroom before; she'd never felt the need to take one with her, and as it rang and danced on the copy of *The Line of Beauty*, it sounded like an alarm, a sonic panic, lighting up, flashing. She dried her hands and checked the phone; Ray's name and number there, Ray's name and number.

'Hello,' she said. 'Thank God, I've been—'

'Who is this, please?'

'Who is *this*?' Gwen said.

'It's Mary,' she said. 'And you?'

'Gwendoline,' she said. 'Gwendoline Moore. Why have you got Ray's phone? Has something happened?'

'We didn't recognize the number. It's not in his phone, you see. And you've called so many times.'

'I'm an old friend,' she said. 'What's happened?'

'We thought you might be a journalist.'

'A journalist? I've been calling all day, what's going on?'

'You're not from one of the papers?'

'Listen,' she said, realizing she was naked, feeling odd being naked, holding a phone, her body wet but hands dry. 'I've known Ray for thirty-five years, we're old friends and I want to know what's happened, *Mary*.'

There was a pause on the other end. Muttering in the background, a discussion had, several voices.

'There's been an accident,' Mary said. 'Nothing life-threatening, but an accident.'

'He wasn't on one of the trains?'

'What?' Mary said, perfectly neutral her accent, perfectly

mannered and cultured. Wife perhaps, long-suffering girlfriend, never mentioned, never even in passing.

'Oh, you mean the bombs?' she said, almost mocking. 'No, good God no, thankfully. He was knocked over. By a motorcycle of all things. He's in the hospital now. He's doing well.'

'What happened?' she said. 'Is he badly hurt?'

'A few broken bones, a cracked rib. Nothing serious, thankfully.'

And Gwen felt thankful, to the motorcycle and the collision and the hospital and the reassurance.

'Which hospital?' she said. 'I'd like to come and see him, see how he's doing.'

'Well,' Mary said. 'I'm afraid it's just close family at the moment.'

'I want to see him,' she said. 'It's important. Really important.'

'Let me speak to him, and if he wants to see you, I'll call you back.'

Clever, Gwen thought. Clever. No chance of calling back, no chance of a polite message with an address and the visiting hours. No chance of that. Well played, Mary. Sounding reasonable, sounding helpful.

'That would be most appreciated, Mary,' she said. 'I'd really like to see him.'

'Well, we'll let you know,' she said. 'But I really must go now.'

'Of course,' she said. 'I look forward to hearing from you. Give him my best.'

Mary ended the call. Gwen wrapped herself in a towel and left footprints on the linoleum, on the carpet to the bedroom. She started packing a case, an overnight bag, then went to the computer, the sound of the television loud beneath her. The AA website told her how to drive to London. She checked hotels near Walthamstow. One she could just about afford about a mile from there. She dressed and went downstairs to Drum, no idea what she would say, what excuse she would use, how she would manage to make it there without him in tow.

IO

Drum watched an interview he had seen before, an expert on suicide bombing, how many experts, how very niche their expertise.

'I love you, Drum,' Gwen said. He looked up from the television, her standing by the doorway in her dressing gown.

'I love you too, Gwen,' he said.

'Are you happy?' she said.

'Happy?' he said.

'Yes,' she said. 'Are you happy?'

Instinctively, the answer should be yes, because what else to say but yes. Not something to consider, not something over which to pore. Yes. Happy. Actively, no; but in general, as a broad concept, not unhappy. But not something to say, not the way to respond to the woman you love. Of course happy, with you, of course happy. Not to say, I've not thought about it. Not to say, it'll take me a while to reach a conclusion. Am I singing oh what a beautiful morning as I wake? No, but neither seething in anger, bitter in the chair, except when the politicians rankle, or another fool puts forward their foolish views. A simple binary: happy or not happy; no middle ground, no fair-to-middling.

'Yes,' he said. 'I'm happy. You make me happy.'

'Without me, you wouldn't be happy?'

'Of course not,' he said.

'You don't ask if I am happy?'

'I assume you'd tell me if you weren't.'

'Yes,' she said. 'I suppose I would.'

He watched her fiddle with the sash of her robe, the constellations in her mind, unknowable, unseen, yet sometimes illuminated.

Not then. No idea. The cool gust of strangers in the room, between them a gap, and a blank.

'Don't stay up too late watching this,' she said. 'It's not good for you.'

'I'll be up in a bit,' he said.

She nodded. She blew him a kiss. Could not recall the last time she did that. He went to the drinks cupboard and poured himself a whisky; looked at the clock and drank the Scotch until it was time to call Carter.

Carter had introduced Drum to a term he had recently read: retirony – a dirty little word, a gremlin portmanteau – the early death of those who had planned so long for the end of work. It seemed to them they were both ripe for it, the grip at the heart and the swan dive to the floor while looking over catalogues for cruises or brochures of the latest Ford motor cars. The article he'd read suggested new routines were important. Without routine, death. So he set routines, followed them to the letter. One of which their Thursday call. Not the same over the phone; not the same, but something nonetheless.

The phone rang for a long, continental tone, then Carter picked up. A background chorus of cicadas, water lapping at the pool, real or perhaps just in his head.

'Quite the day,' Carter said.

'Glad to hear everyone's safe,' Drum said. 'Daphne called this morning.'

'Tommy never takes public transport these days,' Carter said. 'I wasn't worried.'

'This fucking country,' Drum said.

'This fucking world,' Carter said.

Spain suited Carter, Spain and the restoration of his money. They popped back in late August to see the autumn come, but mostly they stayed there, getting deeply tanned, swimming lengths, learning the language. Carter read *El País* of a morning, conversed like a native, replete with shrugs and little details, avoided any nearby English settlers. The perfect diplomat: a career Carter said he now realized he should have pursued.

'A friend of Carlie's was on one of the trains,' Drum said. 'He's in hospital. Not serious though, I don't think.'

'Times like this I miss smoking.'

What Drum wanted to say was I miss you. But so trite, so childish to say that. Already implicit, surely, no need to overexplain, overshow. But yes, I miss you, I miss watching your eyebrows rise when I say something you do not believe.

'Fortunate, isn't it?' Carter said. 'Seven/Seven. Has that ring to it, doesn't it? Like Nine/Eleven? Do you think they chose it for that? And it works whether in American date form or British.'

'You've been mulling this one all day?'

'Numbers have always been important,' he said. 'Numbers at the heart of it all.'

'Lucky seven?'

'Something like that. In the States, a seven and seven is a whiskey drink, whiskey and 7-Up. It's no wonder the world hates them.'

'Hates us too, so it seems.'

'They've always hated us,' he said. 'Nothing's changed there.'

He heard the rattle of the whisky glass, the ice in the drink. Missed the sound of the lighter, the suck of the cigarette, the hiss as the cigarette was extinguished.

'How was Molly?' Carter said.

'She was fine. Must be confusing for her though.'

'They'll work it out.'

'Nate doesn't think so.'

'Give it a year and she'll be begging for him to come home.'

'Give it a year, and I'll be driving him round there myself.'

Carter laughed, different the laugh without the toasting of the cigarettes.

'Only you,' he said, 'could have one kid disappear and the other refuse to leave.'

'Why only me?'

'Because all you ever wanted was the simple life, and life just loves to shit in your kettle.'

They laughed, miles and kilometres apart; laughed and drank their Scotch, their wives asleep, upstairs and away, the sun now down and the lights burning, the drowsing lights of an outgoing day.

Nate left before the lock-in, a wise move; drunk and knowing it, hiccups and gas. Not calling Carlie, not texting Carlie, just holding the phone in his fist. Not calling her, done that before, sometimes done that, repercussions from that, three weeks of no Molly, her number now stored under DO NOT CALL, and he did not call, though he would have called had he not needed to piss so bad. He pissed onto the road, a Stinger of piss, shredding the tyres of any passing cars.

Bobby's son in the Wolf, some of the farming lot. Joined them for a bit, talking of the bombs. You live in Scotland, you get rain and snow; you live London, you get bombs. What else you expect? Then foot and mouth, as always; rumours of another suicide, farmer's son over Mow Cop way. Hanged heads at that. Always talk of a suicide, never anyone they knew. Nate had looked round the room and wondered who would come to his funeral. All of them, for the meat-paste sandwiches and the bar, and who else? No one knew of Billy. No one knew of Pete, wherever he was. There would be Carlie, distraught, forgiving him in death, him unable now to betray her. His parents. Molly wondering which farm he'd gone to this time. Anneka missing as usual.

He let himself in quietly. No want for lecture, no reminder of early starts and keeping the right hours. So long as job done, job done, no? In the silent kitchen, he took out leftover chicken, piled it into bread. He carried it up the stairs, the light on in the spare room. His mother was sitting on the bed, her phone in her hand. She looked properly old, frail even. The wrinkles around her chin, around her eyes, deeper set. Perhaps the first time he'd noticed it, the age creeping on her. How low her breasts; how round the shoulders.

'Can't sleep?' he said.

'No,' she said. 'A friend of mine, she's in hospital.'

'Oh,' he said. 'She okay?'

'She'll live,' she said. 'Nothing to worry about. I wanted to see her, but she said not to.'

'You'll see her when she's better,' he said. The words sounding fine, unslurred, unhurried, not too glassy.

'Yes,' she said. 'Anyway, get to bed, you.'

He kissed her on the top of head.

'Night, night.' He said.

'I love you, Nate,' she said.

'I love you too, Mam,' he said.

12

There were text messages on the phone. Ray's name, Ray's number.

Message #1:

> I knew you'd be worried, so I went to her house. She was there. Femi too. All safe. Couldn't see Robin but assume safe.

Message #2:

> I walked onto main Rd & motorbike hit me. Didn't see it coming. Cracked ribs. Broken shoulder.

Message #3

> Don't come. Please. Will explain when I see you. Don't call.

Message #4:

> The things I do for you x

She would have liked to hear his voice, would have liked to see him, yes; but Anneka more. To hold her. To say all the things she'd been thinking, all the horrors she'd seen. All calm in her arms, all of it slipping, the years and the horrors. To say, I thought I'd lost you, properly lost you this time, and the look on Annie's face, pure forgiveness, pure recognition.

Ray had taken that from her. A deceitful man. A lying liar. The things he did for her. The things he did not do for her. The things he kept. And the thing he had now taken. The reunion she'd felt sure she could muster, could follow through with. Unneeded now, unwarranted. Needlessly taken from her.

She curled up in the single bed, unable or unwilling to go to her own. She put the phone under the pillow, the messages now erased, gone from hers, gone from his, no doubt. Never having happened, never having been sent, or received, words never written, words never read.

FORTY YEARS OF *FRUM*

In the forty years since the publication of *Frum*, I have had little occasion to consider it in any great depth. It was well received at the time, the reviews respectable and encouraging, but it was hardly a bestseller, and, as with so many books, it fell out of print relatively quickly. Had it not been for a recent essay in the *London Review of Books*, which discussed the book at length, it would surely have stayed that way. Now, thanks to this reissue, it has a second life. Though, I must confess, this second life feels based upon a deception.

In the *LRB* piece entitled 'Frum Despair to Where', William Atkins writes, 'The true power of *Frum* comes from Porter's absence, his erasure from the text. To modern readers, it is almost shocking: a traveller travelling for their own interest, rather than spurred on some quest by personal tragedy, romantic palaver or mental breakdown. If this book were published today, Porter would be implored, begged and pleaded with to add a more personal dimension, to give some biography, to let us know our guide the more. We would not be presented with a narrative that is sympathetic, anthropologically astute, or spiritually aware; we would be left with the tepid musings of a white man pushed to discover the Cargo Cultists of Vanuatu, rather than one drawn to them.'

Mr Atkins is a sharp writer of the old school,

resistant to the overbearing vogues of current travel writing, for which I admire him; but it is with heavy heart that I must confess that he is wrong about *Frum*. At least the *Frum* of the first draft – which is, in fact, the latter kind of book he describes. What finally appeared, and what is the basis of this volume, is both a truthful and utterly fabricated tale. What Atkins admires is little more than cowardice.

Just before I began the long journey to Vanuatu, three major things occurred: my marriage dissolved, my mother died, and I fell in love with a married woman. In the first draft of *Frum*, these events are covered in obsessive detail; the nature of love, romantic, maternal, adulterous, are explored in more depth than the Cultists' rituals and spiritual mores. It is full of digressive asides, about libraries, about death, about the souring of relationships, which, though provoked by the islanders, are wholly a distraction from the point of the journey.

I remember the day I decided to delete myself from the book. It was a warm spring morning, my wife had long since left, my mother had been dead for two years and I had no idea where the woman I loved now lived. I felt that between the three losses, I no longer existed, and so decided to no longer exist on the page. I rewrote the book in a week, and the pages and pages on the affair – unconsummated, I must add – I eventually burned in a brazier while covering a strike action in Coventry. I wish I had it to hand; I wish I could see again how much I felt, how much I seethed with love for her.

We all have our masks and guises, the public personas versus the private selves, and the two versions of *Frum* feel like two sides of myself: one that is available for others' consumption, and one that is secret, dangerous and needs to be burned. I had not thought of this book for forty years, but it seems it was always waiting for me, reminding me, across the two versions, of the person I truly am.

Raymond Porter, Introduction to *Frum: A Year with the Cargo Cultists* (reissue, GD Editions, 2014)

13

Drum woke from a dream. Under the shattered spire, beyond the broken pub, he called for Gwen, but there was no answer. He called for Carter, but there was no answer. He called for Nate, but there was no answer. He wandered the obliterated streets, his hand bandaged and his uniform torn. By the post office, he called for Annie and there were noises on the wind, shrieks and hollers on the wind. They were saying Horse. The wind calling Horse, the draught from the water, Horse. Here, Horsey, Horsey. Here, Horse. We're coming for you Horse.

14

On birthdays, her father would tell her how lucky she was. How lucky she was to have such nice things; how lucky she was when so many had nothing. He'd told her she should think of those people as she opened her presents; guilting her even before she could unwrap the book or small toy she'd asked for. Though he'd watch her undo strings and bows with evident pleasure, that was what she heard. Remember how lucky you are; remember that this is my gift.

Thank you, Daddy. It's just what I wanted.

She wanted to tell Femi how lucky he was. How lucky he was that they let him sleep between them most nights; how lucky to have Robin; how lucky to have brains and imagination; how lucky to be there, breathing. To have made it out unscathed, cut from her, bloodied and bawling, all toes and fingers intact. She told Robin if she ever said to Femi that he was lucky, Robin could punish her in any way he saw fit.

Femi had made it between them in the night; neither Neka nor Robin now even noticing when he did so. He lay beside her, so still, the little sniffs of breath, the curls over his delicate ears, his mouth slightly agape. Her perfect little man. In private, she'd taken to calling him Beauty. Come here, Beauty. Would you like an apple, Beauty. Her name for him. Just between the two of them. Beauty.

He *was* beautiful, in an objective, modern kind of way. He was the kind of child who appeared in commercials for washing powder or toilet roll or brightly coloured clothing lines. His skin, other mothers told her, was a lovely shade of this or that; usually something sweet, something they would not pack in their children's lunch boxes. His eyes were always described in relation to nuts. Strangers would say he was good enough to eat. They'd say that to Neka's face, then look down again at her consumable, delicious boy.

(There were other strangers. Men who looked down at the baby and then approached her. Asked if the baby father was still around. Wherever she was, she'd say that the baby father was just around the corner, and would they like to meet him. She did not tell Robin of these approaches.)

In the early morning sunlight, Femi turning four years old; four years old and soon for school. The last birthday to be theirs and theirs alone; their last birthday of play, of swimming pool and picnic, of movie time in the late afternoon before Robin made it home from work, on time once in the year. Cake then. The smell of candles; the singing of the song; the reminder of his insistent, firm-lunged screech.

Femi in the sunlight, stirring, then suddenly bolt upright in the bed, as though winched to sitting.

'Mummy,' he said.

'Hello, Beauty,' she said.

'It's my birthday!' he said.

'Yes,' she said. 'It's your birthday.'

'Happy birthday,' Robin said, as though he'd been awake the whole time, and perhaps had. He smelled malty, beery, the previous night escaping through pores. He put his arm over hers and cuddled them to him, to his smell. She liked it; Femi giggled.

'A boy sandwich,' she said.

'Presents!' Femi said.

'Presents!' Robin said.

At the foot of the bed, Femi's birthday presents were wrapped and bagged, a half-year of saving and planning, all changed after a visit to Callum's house and a viewing of *Toy Story*. Femi soon becoming obsessed, two instalments of the franchise bought from a charity shop and watched every weekend; the boy able to impersonate all the characters. She enjoyed the films, the sadness behind the primary colours. The single mother, the packed-up house, the boy and his toys oblivious to the reason for the elaborate birthday present and the downsizing move to a cheaper, smaller place.

Robin dragged the sack to the bed, held out something small, a packet of *Toy Story* pencils wrapped in *Toy Story* wrapping paper. Femi hurtled through the presents, was appreciative, said thank you for each one, moved on to the next, hoping for a bigger box, the one shaped like a spaceship. He wouldn't find one.

The toy he wanted was expensive, too expensive. She'd argued with Robin over it; said that they should get a credit card, but Robin was adamant.

'We spoil him now and what happens later?' he'd said.

'It's just a toy,' she'd said.

'It's a fifty-quid fucking toy,' he'd said. 'It sends the wrong message.'

The message not the money. Robin was uneasy about the acquisitive nature of his boy. His need for *things*, for *possessions*. Like Femi was skidding, vaulting, away from him already.

Through a friend of Callum's mother, she'd found a Buzz Lightyear second-hand. The mother she'd bought it from had opened the door and behind her two grown boys fought over a video game. She handed over the toy and took Neka's ten pounds. A moment, then, between them. Would that one could swap a life the same you could swap a toy for cash.

Neka got the toy home and imagined it surveying the new surroundings, finding it wanting. She set about cleaning it up with nail polish remover, erasing as many stains and as much ludic history as she could. She spent a week trying to remove the name of Buzz's previous owner from the left foot of the toy; then started on the ANDY scribbled on the right before remembering that ANDY was the name of the boy from the film. She laid the toy to rest in a shoe box, the plastic spaceman judging her as she covered him in sliced ribbons of white and purple crepe paper. The inanimate face stared so long she cried as she put him at the back of the wardrobe.

Femi unwrapped a pair of Buzz Lightyear pyjamas, shucked off his own there and then, pulled on the spaceman nightwear. They were pristine white, the purple detailing deep and new.

'I am Buzz Lightyear,' Femi said. 'I come in peace.'

'Nice to meet you, Buzz,' Robin said. 'You've got a friend in me, pal.'

They sang then, her two boys, tuneless singing, full of joy. She got up as they sang, walked to the wardrobe and took out the wrapped box. The box not like in the film, not like the one from the toy shop. Robin had said it didn't matter, but she felt sure it did.

'Here you are, Femi,' Neka said. 'I must have forgotten about this one.'

Femi's eyes so wide and his mouth a perfect O. The little teeth, the first gap on the bottom row, the burst of love. Holding the wrapped shoe box, inside the off-white Space Ranger; the stickiness of the helmet's action; the felt-tip mark on the right wing she could not wipe away.

Femi picked the Sellotape from the box, the toy rattling inside. Do not break, Buzz. You have a new mission, Buzz. You must work for us, Lightyear. Femi fiddled with the last bit of tape and Robin tried to help, but Femi pushed him aside.

'I can do it myself,' he said.

And so he could. He unpicked the last of the tape, flapped open the lid and nestled there was Buzz. Good as new, Buzz. Nothing ever as good as new. A shriek then. Loud like the moment he was born. He hugged the toy to his chest, then looked it up and down, disbelieving.

Femi went for the buttons on the spaceman's breast, finger out and ready to press. She'd tested them; they worked roughly sixty per cent of the time. Femi pressed a button and Buzz spoke.

'The atmosphere here is toxic,' Buzz said.

Robin looked at Neka and, over the sound of an actor's sampled voice, they both laughed for the first time in weeks.

★

She took the stairs down from the flat, Femi smeared with suntan lotion, smelling like holidays, Buzz in hand. A hell to get him out of the Lightyear pyjamas, the scuffle making Robin late for work, only the enticement of the swimming pool finally getting Femi into proper clothes.

His hand in hers, they crossed the road, the sun already high, and the usual battle to keep a sun hat on Femi's head. In her pocket she carried the small stone Femi and Robin had painted for her, their initials and a heart on the flat underside. A birthday tradition, something small from Robin handed to her when they were alone, alms for the blessing bestowed upon them, upheld with a smile of conciliation.

There was a job; somewhere in the dour Midlands; away from friends, away from their life, far away from dead babies. A team of men had come for him, approached Robin directly, said they'd been observing his work and that he was the man they wanted for a new project. He would be in charge of implementation, strategy, the very ethos that ran the initiative. He would be able to hire a small number of staff and he would be paid the kind of money neither he nor Neka thought people like them could ever earn. Nothing ludicrous, but comfort money; saving-money money; university-fund money, money-to-not-worry-about-money money.

Robin had showed her on a map the place he thought they could live; not so far from his parents, a town she'd never heard of. Rob had done his research: the time it took to get to London, distance from shops and pubs, local places of interest, the best schools. She'd not seen him so giddy since the Poll Tax Riots. The move and the project. The fact they had come to him, directly and without asking anyone else. The kids he would be helping. And all she'd said was that she'd have to think about it.

'You have to think about it?' he'd said.

'It's not just your decision,' she'd said. 'You're asking me to give up everything.'

She could see what he wanted to say: that there was no *everything* to give up. The everything she talked of was him and Femi, who were both eminently portable. There was no job, so what else was there? A park around which to walk? A market at which to shop? Cafes in which to drink coffee and pubs in which to drink cider? Friends they saw rarely these days? A city they no longer took full advantage of?

'I'm sorry,' he'd said. 'I'm sorry. Of course you need time to think about it. It has to be a decision we all make together.'

A week of silence since, the simmer of it roiling as it had when they'd argued over adoption, neither of them even sure of their respective positions. A week of silence and thankful now, the both of them, for the Space Ranger and his comic timing. Perhaps, she wondered, as she pushed Femi higher and higher on the swing, the toys were alive after all.

★

At the swimming pool's reception it was busy, the assembled looking like they were trying to scale the desk. A woman dashed out clutching her phone, almost knocking the two of them to the ground. Neka heard the word bombs and wondered why everyone was still here if there were bombs in the swimming pool. She heard the tinny noise of a small television, the sound of sirens, the whump of helicopter.

'Mummy,' Femi said. 'What's going on?'

'Nothing, Beauty,' she said. 'Just something on the television.'

She heard the reporter repeat what was known at this time. She heard the reporter say the names of the London places that had been attacked. She told Femi to take Buzz and sit on the bench while she made a quick call. She called Robin and got his voicemail. She texted him and she called and got just the sound of his voice, and the sound of beeps, and the sound from the television.

★

Femi said she was a bad mother. That she had never loved him. He was making his body limp, refusing to be taken from the swimming pool, crying his eyes out, calling for his father. Women passed and they must have thought the boy's father was dead in the bombings, couldn't have avoided it. The kid with the Buzz Lightyear screaming for his daddy and her on the phone frantic, calling everyone she could think of. No one answering, and that being neither salve nor hope. She picked up Femi and Femi tried to wriggle from her, almost fell to the concrete below, slipped down her arms and started to run away. She grabbed him by the back of his T-shirt, yanked him back, slapped his legs. The first time she'd ever hit him, the only time, and now people thinking the boy's howls for his father were more for protection than grief.

'Now sit still,' she said. 'Sit still there and be quiet.'

He sat on the floor. She put her hand into her pocket and stroked the stone, its flat underside. Stroked it and felt the cool of it, the smooth of it. Her phone rang, a number she didn't recognize.

'Did you hear the news?' Robin said. 'I must have just missed it. They say Canary Wharf's been shut down. Gunmen got it under siege.'

'You're okay?' she said.

'Everyone all right here,' he said. 'All accounted for, thank God. Where are you?'

'At the pool,' she said. 'You're okay? Everyone's okay?'

'Yes,' he said. 'I'm coming home now, we're all going to walk back.'

'Stay safe,' she said. 'I love you.'

'I love you too,' he said. She looked down at the edible boy, melting with tears and snot.

'Tell Daddy you love him,' she said. She put the phone in front of Femi's mouth. 'Tell Daddy you love him right now.'

Femi pouted into the phone. He nodded his head.

'Love you, Daddy,' he said.

She took back the phone and the line had gone dead. She called back and he answered.

'Stay safe,' she said.

'I will,' he said. 'Now, go swim. Forget about all this.'

★

They ate their picnic and walked home, the streets still doleful with shock, the faces of everyone still, reflective. She had some hours to make the Buzz Lightyear cake, to get dinner on. The sun shone with indifference, some people cycled by as though they hadn't heard. Femi was laser blasting anything that moved with the arm of the Space Ranger, and she let him do that, though the sound was harsh in her ears.

They crossed the road and a man walked past them, tall man, good-looking, familiar-looking. Like someone from her past, someone she might once have worked with. He walked past them and then crossed the road. She heard the noise of a motorcycle and then the thunk of body on asphalt, the pock of the head hitting the ground.

The motorcyclist drove off, did not look back, and she did not get the licence plate, but ran to the man on the ground. She called for an ambulance and soon other mothers were around her, trying to help him, trying to stop the bleeding on his head.

'You get off, love,' a man said. 'Take the boy away. I know CPR.'

She looked down at the man, his half-opened eyes, and she felt sure he mouthed her name just once. Just once, him saying Anneka. She stayed there in his eyeline for a moment, thought that he might be about to die, but then he vomited, the spray catching the running shoes of a jogger.

When she later told Robin she wanted to move, she'd tell him it wasn't about the bombs. It would not be a lie. Not because of the bombs, but perhaps because of the man run down by the motorcycle. Life too short. You could be knocked down by a bus.

'Let's go home,' she said and took Femi by the hand. 'It's almost time for cake.'

The Thirteenth B'ak'tun

2012

Sunday 4 – Friday 9 March

Tuesday, 6 March 2012

Drum's primary carer had a slide-rule fringe and long red hair. Not strawberry blonde, auburn or ginger, but fire-engine red, red right down to its dark black roots. The colour looked strange on her, something perhaps leftover from her youth, clung to and now stuck with. It swished when she moved, even more than her scrubs. Swished now as she opened the curtains.

Since arriving at the hospice two days before, Drum had thought a lot more about Alina – Alina who dyed her hair and cared for the dying – than he had about anything else more pressing. He wondered whether this was deliberate. Whether her hair was designed as some kind of distraction, a diversion to keep her patients from looking too far into their own souls, into their own pasts, weighing them against what was to come.

'How are you feeling this morning?' she said, opening the window just a crack.

'Do people make sarcastic comments when you ask that?' he said. 'I imagine they do.'

'Yes,' she said, laughing. 'A lot of them do. You know, "How do you think I'm feeling?" or "Well I'm not dead yet!" It helps, I think. Humour's important. Reminds you you're still thinking.'

She rattled some pills into a paper cup, handed it to Drum with a cup of water.

'How's the pain?' she said.

'What pain?'

'That's good. It means the drugs are working as long as they're supposed to. You don't feel nauseous, do you?'

'No,' he said. 'Just a little away with the fairies.'

469

'That sounds like fun,' she said.

'Swap you any time,' he said.

Alina helped him from the bed to the commode, him sitting there until he'd performed a small shit; the crap hard, like passing a pebble. She wiped him up and down and set him on the easy chair by the bed. Quick and practised this; impressive. She had better English than the other Poles and Latvians in the hospice; she'd been here for almost twenty years, so she said, following in her grandfather's footsteps. He'd been stationed in the town during the Second World War and never shut up about it when he returned home.

'Your wife will be here in half an hour,' Alina said. 'She says she's been sleeping well.'

'That's good,' he said. 'I'm glad about that. She needs the rest.'

An understatement, that. Gwen had found it impossible to sleep with his groans and sudden wakings, the gasps of pain and the shat bedclothes. A respite this. His idea. A week in the hospice, just a week, to let her catch up; a week for him to get some care.

'I won't die there,' he'd told her. 'Don't worry about that. I won't allow it.'

He was still certain of that. Certain of the will of the mind over the body. Sure that a body could run on fumes far longer than any car.

*

In late 2011, the doctor had given him six months; doctors always erring on the side of half a year. Assuming the specialist was correct, Drum would be around for the London Olympics, but not for the end of the world. Drum had studied the date, the Mayan conception of the end of times – or the dawn of a new age of consciousness depending on who you believed – and had decided it wrong. The apocalypse was scheduled for 21 December, the end of the thirteenth b'ak'tun, but why not on the 20th? The symmetry was perfect for the end of the world. 20-12-2012. A day out, a day only. Let me live, so I can prove I'm right.

How often had Dr Ahmed said those words? How often had he

erred on the side of six months? Hundreds, thousands perhaps. Drum was now one of a group so large the doctor would not remember were any of them to beat the odds. Drum wanted to beat the prognosis. He wanted to see Dr Ahmed in the supermarket, the one on the ring-road, six or seven years hence and tell him he'd been wrong. He wanted that. He wanted to see the lack of recognition in the doctor's face. Wanted to leave the doctor confused, wracking brain for who the man was. Looking at the oncologist's face, Drum knew there was no chance of that. No hope of seeing 20 December. Drum could see it in the doctor's black and reddened eyes. Just go home, Mr Moore. Let me have the rest of my afternoon.

After the murmur, Drum had assumed it would be his heart to give out; that at least quick. The clutched chest, knowing this was the big one, the one from which you do not return. That, to him, felt the only way to die. In sleep seemed a cheat, too peaceful a passage. Do I want to go peaceful? No. I want to know. Better the pull in the chest, better the shoot and stab of pain, better the mid-conversational pause and the quick lift of the rug. Carter would not die in his sleep; Carter would not allow it. Were death to come to him, then death would need bigger balls, some proper *cojones*. Same for Drum. Same for him and double.

A triple bypass for Carter. Private care, in and out. Right as rain now, though he rarely saw rain these days. A year or so from death, that what the doctor had said, had they not caught it. Living each day now as if it were his last, chasing tail in Spain, fucking the wives of two of his friends. One a younger wife, no more than forty-five; the other in her sixties, depraved in her predilections, or so he said. Living the best life now.

When Drum came out of the consultation, Gwen was in the waiting room, checking her phone. She was looking intently at it, deliberating single-finger typing, so far away he wished she would stay there. It was one thing being told; quite another to tell. Would that he had the abundant hair of the doctor, his house to go to, to swap their lives over at that moment.

Gwen looked up from the phone, and too many years, too many days and nights in company to even come close to hiding it. Better to collapse there; better to die right there than have to speak.

The short steps from the consultation room to her, the small table stacked with magazines between them. Do they censor the magazines? Do they look them through for tales of cancer deaths, heart complaints, loved ones cut down in their prime? Do they screen them for stories that might send you over the edge?

Gwen stood and placed her hands upon him, her saying, let's go home, Drum. Let's talk at home. And he followed her, saying nothing, not a thing, trying not to cry. Walking to the car, her hand in his hand, and nothing now needing to be said. Her going to the driver's side and opening the car with the remote, and him getting in the passenger side – how much a humiliation that – and Gwen sitting behind the wheel and her crying. Trying not to, but crying.

The hardest thing that, the hardest thing he'd ever done. Knowing she was grieving for him. He'd never thought about it, never considered this was how it would be. The two of them, and her loving him. Loving him the way he loved her. He had always assumed it was a one-way sort of affair, assumed that over the years, she had become accustomed, rather than actively in love. No shame in that, no shame at all. Close and happy, what more could you ask?

They had been young, and then they had not. They'd had no children, then they'd had two, then one. He'd not expected her tears. He'd not expected anyone to mourn. But here the tears and here the grief. The deep feeling. Only ever suspected, never quite believing. On the television, years back, watching *Billy Liar*, all those old memories stirred and frothed, and him remembering the shock of hearing Julie Christie ask Tom Courtenay, 'Who do you love?' and her having no doubt as to the answer. A question he would not dare ask, even after fifty years of marriage. How could you be sure? What if the answer was 'someone else'? What if the answer had always been someone else? But the love, the love in those tears. Almost worth dying over, those tears.

'How long?' she said.

'Six months,' he said. 'It's always six months, isn't it?'

'No chance they're wrong?'

He shook his head. He handed her the literature, the prospectuses and catalogues, the palliative care options. How many glossy brochures handed out today? How many in the week?

'I want to be at home,' he said. 'But they say somewhere like that might help towards the end.'

She threw the booklets on the back seats; angry now, he could see it, the suppressed fury.

'We're not talking about that now,' she said.

As they pulled out of the car park, he remembered something he'd heard on the radio, one of the many quirky news stories that ended the bulletin on the pop station Nate always listened to. There was a man who was diagnosed with terminal cancer. The doctors gave him six months to live, so he decided to live it up. He sold off his house, maxed out his credit cards, and spends, spends, spends. For six months he lived like a king, but at the end, he didn't die. If anything he felt better than ever. He went back to the doctor and the doctor told him there must have been some mistake: he was A1, not terminal at all. He then sued the doctors for the false prognosis.

In the silent car home, Drum thought what he would want to do with his last six months. He could not think of a single thing, a single place he would like to go. Except Doom Town. That was where he wanted to go, just one last time. To walk the streets, walk them with Gwen. He would have preferred a four-minute warning. Four minutes fairer, four minutes enough time to say what was needed and leave no room for awkward pauses or doubts. Four minutes ideal. Six months so long to fill. And Doom Town long ago dismantled, built upon: a prison now.

*

He had spent his respite in bed or easy chair, sometimes thinking he was back in the bunker. There was something in the quality of the air, the scent from the kitchens, the stoic sense of worry, which took him back there. He took a sip of tea, looked up at the television set, and then heard hushed activity outside his room. Someone, he assumed, must have lately died, but who it was from the dayroom he could not guess.

Do they revive those who arrest here? Do they save them? Do they give them a few more days' respite? Or do they let them pass, ready for the next cadaver-in-waiting?

He would not die there. Not in that bunker, not within those closed walls. He would die above ground; die in his own bed. No, not his own bed. It would be unfair on Gwen. In the spare bedroom, in there, he would die. In Annie's room.

Gwen would be there, Nate would be there, Carter would be there, Annie would be there. Annie there, yes. Annie, come back and come home. She would be there and she would say goodbye. He would hear her soft voice and he would know then it was time. Time to welcome the ceasing of the heart, the stilling of the blood, the closing down of the mind. It would be then. Yes.

He opened his eyes and Gwen was in the room, though he did not recall her coming in. She was made-up and spruce, effort made, clothes pressed and jewellery he bought for her hanging from thin arms and pinked ears. She kissed him on the lips.

'You must have nodded off,' she said.

'Did you think I was dead?'

'No, you were making that godawful noise you make when you fall asleep on the sofa.'

'I knew it would come in handy one day,' he said.

She looked if not refreshed, then partially revived: colour to her cheeks, a spryness to her eyes. She made tea, talked of something he could not quite hear, the hallway commotion louder now. A death should be quiet; it should have solemnity, not crashes and bangs, the sneaker squeaks of wheels on polished floors.

The advantage of a retreated life was that with few close friends, there were fewer deaths. His friends were, so far, immortal. Joseph he had lost, but a worker more than a friend, and expected that on account of his age. Younger than I am now, mind. Is that you, Joseph, looking through that window? No, not you, Joseph.

On the wall in Carter's kitchen in Spain, there was a picture in a frame, a joke Carter must have found funny once and assumed would find funny for a long time after.

Why Worry?

There are only two things to worry about: either you are sick or you are well.

If you are well there is nothing to worry about, but if you are sick there are only two things to worry about: either you will live or you will die.

If you live there is nothing to worry about, but if you die you only have two things to worry about: either you are going to heaven or to hell.

If you are going to heaven there is nothing to worry about, but if you are going to hell you'll be so busy shaking hands with friends you won't have time to worry!

Though he'd found it mildly amusing in situ, the print's simplicity and suppositions now worried Drum deeply. The last line offered little in the way of comfort. It would be all right for Carter, who would be busy for eternity; but Drummond would be out of handshakes in little under a minute. It haunted, this piece of supposed amusement. He saw it in its frame and the *Why Worry?* seemed so flippant. What else was one to do but worry? There was only one question left, only one last thing to consider: if there is only down or up, which way am I headed?

In his life, he'd committed few sins. Cardinal sins at least. A keeper of secrets and his own counsel, yes; but this seemed unlikely to be a punishable offence; covering for a friend's infidelities, for his debts: deserving more of a rap on the knuckles than eternal damnation. A godless life, but a one lived with goodness.

From there, he warrened backwards into his choices, his decisions. So many binaries, all as simple as *Why Worry?* Either you married Gwen or you did not. Either you stayed in Dagenham or you did not. What lives could you have lived? You might have married another woman, one less bright, less starry, less interested than Gwen. That thought adulterous. Could not conceive of bedding down with another. There had been another woman, back before Gwen; a friend of Carter's, her name escaped him, but not her breasts, her nose, her buttocks. Needed and important, that memory. Important not to have been a virgin on meeting Gwen. He couldn't think why, but knew it was important.

'Nate'll be over later,' Gwen said. 'He wants to bring Molly.'

Gwen was talking and he was thinking of the birth of calves, the filling of quotas, the wearing of boots, on his fingers he could feel mud and pelt. A life on the factory line or that. No decision at all then, and no decision now. The fear that Gwen would say no. The fear that he would have to insist. But her happy to move; how much happier her here than there. His decision, the right one for them both.

'Did you hear me?' Gwen said. 'Nate'll be over later.'

'Not here,' he said. 'Not here. I don't want Molly seeing this.'

'Okay,' she said. 'Don't get excited.'

'I wasn't,' he said.

Another reminder of the bunker, the way emotions seeped out of innocuous phrasing, the way tensions displayed in small movements, the way they could not talk about the one thing that needed to be discussed. More dreams of the bunker, more daydreams of it now. Not just there, but back at home too. Dreams of the bunker, dreams of the bare streets of Doom Town, dreams of Annie. Annie up and down the times, up and down the country.

Annie lost and dirty-kneed sometimes; sometimes the mother from *Threads*, sometimes the scream-inducing infant. In dreams he said to Annie there's not a day goes by when I don't think of you, and this is a truth in the dream and a lie in the waking world.

If a life is a ledger, this was the biggest weight in the debit column. Her decision. Her betrayal, let us not forget that. What had he done wrong? Was he expected to track her down, though she did not want to be found? Anyway, he did his job; he played his part in her life. Raised her well. To be respectful, to be intellectually curious and practically careful. That she abandoned him, that was all on her. He will forgive her. When she comes, in the night, in the day, he will forgive her. He will forgive her and she will be thankful for his forgiveness.

'I forgot to say,' Gwen said. 'Carter sent this over.'

She held up a CD, and Drum motioned with his head to the small stereo on the dresser. She puts on the CD and he knew what it would be, the hornet sound amongst the space interference, 'Telstar', the murder song.

'He made it for you,' she said.

'I know,' he said. 'That's very kind of him.'

'They'll be back Thursday, I think.'

'It'll be good to see them,' he said. 'Might be the last time.'

'Don't say that,' she said.

'When it happens, after the funeral and all that, promise me you'll stay with them for a bit. A month or something.'

She laced her hand in his. She kissed him on the cheek, on the mouth.

'You could come home tonight, if you like,' she said. 'I'm feeling better.'

'A week, they said. They know what they're talking about. It's better for both of us, a little break.'

'I brought you some books,' she said, putting a bag on his lap. 'Old favourites.'

Old favourites. In amongst them, *Saturday Night and Sunday*

477

Morning. An old edition, like the one they had both read, bought for his sixtieth birthday.

'Ah yes,' he said. 'Now this I want to read.'

How foxed and old everything was, how slanted and bumped. He leaned over to kiss her. That old red lipstick, that open handbag, the book looking up at them both, the night they met. The way she smelled then, the tightness of her hair, the thinness of her smile. How simple his life, when looked at in those terms. How very straightforward. A pub, a girl, a book. Three things, and all came from then.

How many such moments were taking place at that exact time, as he sat and held the book and held his wife's hand? These moments are the miracles we wish to protect; these the miracles we defend with guns and tanks and bombs. These the moments the reasons for ordinance; these moments the reasons for fortification. He cried at the realization, the harmony and magic of the human world around him. Not broken, not spindled like a smashed pane, but intertwined and woven. The sear and yawn of his heart as he cried for the joy of that.

'Is he all right, nurse?' he heard Gwen, faraway Gwen, say.

'Yes, Mrs Moore,' Alina said, even further away. 'Just the medication. He'll be right in a little while.'

A straw was in his mouth. The straw cool, the water cold in his mouth. Either it would be the apocalypse or a new era of consciousness. A new evolution, a new era in civilization. On 20 December 2012. Maybe that. Yes, let it be that. Let me be around for that. Will it to happen. Mind over matter. No chance of death before then. No chance at all.

Sunday, 4 March 2012

Drum always drove the long distances; never a discussion about it. Could not remember the last time she'd driven on a motorway; how odd it was to have eyes on the lanes, on the cars cutting in front, the cars coming up at back, and not on the meridian or the roadmap, not on fellow passengers.

'Remember, do not die on the road.'

She'd said this aloud on entering the motorway. Keep vigilant, alert to the silver cars weaving without fear, makes you wonder, doesn't it, how there are not more fatalities, how the roads are not clogged with the dead; how, with the sheer danger of the roads – look at him now, undertaking, speeding back – we don't all just come to a complete stop?

There was a sign and she followed it, saw the service station glowing green under the bright sunlight, its glass eaves and a glass proboscis on a big glass tetrahedron, a big sign: WELCOME. All the same, these places. Pre-fabricated. Dropped with the coffee concessions already intact, the lavatories ready for plumbing, the ovens a supply of electric.

She got out of the car into the cool and light. The service station was warm inside, the gaming machines and tiled floors, the coffee and bakery waft, the drift of cigarette smoke from outside the automatic doors. She walked straight to the lavatories, deafened on entry by the blast of the hand dryers, their howl loud even inside the cubicle.

She sat down. On the door, two-thirds from its foot, someone had carved their name. Elise. The dedication to score the letters into the door. How long had it taken? And for what purpose? An act of love, or of vanity? She looked more closely. It was Elise herself, she decided. Elise declaring herself. Here I am. She wondered how many women had seen it. Thousands! Hundreds of thousands! How would it feel if Elise came back to see her name still there? A vindication? Or worse, to look for it expectantly and find the door had been replaced and her name erased. Would it haunt? She touched the letters, ran her finger across them. She wanted to remember Elise. Remember her as she no doubt wished to be remembered herself.

The coffee queue was long, the machines huffed and hissed, Elise faded into their steam. There were tables of families and couples, a few men reading newspapers, a few watching the subtitles stutter across the News24 television feed.

'All human life is here,' Drum had said once, taking the same table on which she was now setting down her tray. 'The service station, the great leveller. All races, creeds, ages, classes!'

A laugh and a smile. She looked around and she did not see the rich, or the famous, or the very old. No one as old as her, certainly. Mainly she saw kids lull between tantrums, couples drinking from coffee mugs, truckers eating fries. She took a bottle of water from her bag and drank from it as she watched the silent cars zip along, most of them silver now though once they'd mostly been red.

Two days after the respite, after moving him for a stay at the hospice, gathering up clothes and driving off, Nate over at Carlie's for the night. Enough time that, if she could face the drive. Now, the coffee cooling and wondering whether this the right thing, whether turning back would be a better use of time. Ray had not wanted her to go; he had given his express reservations.

'When was the last time you drove that far?' he'd said in their first phone call.

'It's not just the distance, it's the time.' On the second.

'I'd feel better if I drove you. I hate to think of you going all that way on your own.' The third. Her husband dying, and this the nub of his objections.

'I'll be fine,' she said. 'I've booked a hotel.'

'At least call me when you arrive.'

She'd agreed to this, though wondered what he would do if she didn't call. Send out the search parties, report it to the police. Good luck with that, Raymond.

She finished her coffee and went to the toilets again. Inside, against the whump of the dryers, she tried to remember which cubicle had been scored by Elise. She narrowed the choice to three, then two, then one. She entered the cubicle, closed the door expectantly, perhaps as Elise had once done. The door was unmarked. She put her hands on the door but there was nothing there. The hand dryers roared. She peed, left the cubicle and washed her hands. She avoided her face in the mirror, darted her eyes left and right. As she left the toilets, she thought of the song 'Stranger on the Shore', her lips moving but without any sound.

★

There were no crashes and no incidents, just a lowing sun and the radio playing. She drove miles with just one hand on the wheel, overtook HGVs and coaches, indicated at the correct turnoff without even thinking about it. It was a little after midday and she had made good time. Just over two hours with a stop. Through trading estates and housing estates until reaching the hotel.

After check-in, she slept on the single bed, sparked out, utterly exhausted and rinsed. To do the whole thing again tomorrow. Should have taken the train, got taxis; Ray's suggestion again. Nothing he could say though. Nothing that would change her mind.

'You're so stubborn!' Ray had said.

'You've only just noticed, Ray?' she said. 'Really?'

Just a laugh from Ray, caught out and familiar.

She woke and checked the clock, panicked she was late, too late and the whole thing a vainglorious bust. She had enough time, though, just enough. In the mirror she looked like a seventy-year-old woman who had just woken, hair in place, low maintenance. She slipped on her fleece; drank a glass of water. She had an address and in the car typed it into the satnav.

The playing fields were a short drive from the hotel; she wished it further, another two hours away. Preparation time, time enough to set herself, remind herself of what to say, what not to say. No time for that, a roundabout and junction, a left and a right, the woman satnav voice, Sally Satnav, taking her through the turns. At the destination, Sally so happy to have delivered Gwen there, into a rammed car park, cars double lined, blocking each other in.

There were many football pitches, all of them with a game going on. When watching Nate there had been only one, or at the most two; but here there were ten or twenty. Once, she'd seen Nate headbutt an opponent. He'd professed his innocence, escaped censure, but she'd seen it: the leap for the ball, his eyes on the nose of the opponent. She never watched another match, never talked to him about football again. And when later, when everything with Carlie came out, she saw him at that same moment, arms waving wide, appalled that anyone would think he'd done anything wrong.

She walked the pitches, thin netting behind the goals, the bright kits and brighter boots. The teams playing in yellow and blue were too old; those in red and gold too young. Towards the back, there were three pitches, the players the right kind of age, more fans at the touchlines, louder roars from fathers. She looked to the pitches and to the supporters, hoping to spot her, to spot him. She saw Femi first, running up the wing, taking the ball, passing it backwards. As if that were normal, as if that was what he did all the time. Collecting the ball, laying it back to a teammate. She did not know if this were a good thing, but it looked right. It looked like something he should be doing.

There were spectators on both sides of the pitch, those wearing the colours of Femi's team on the right-hand touchline. Her daughter there. Clutching a paper cup of coffee, watching the game intently. Her daughter, same as in the photographs, older now than she thought herself. Her daughter pointing, her husband laughing, some man beside them screaming at the children, telling them to pull their fingers out of their arseholes.

She walked the touchline, settled behind Anneka. Gwen thought she'd be able to smell her, to know she was in her orbit, but there was nothing, no forcefield or traction to put her off. Not seen, unnoticed, but there, yes. With her daughter, the first time since forever, her grandchild on the pitch, missing a tackle, getting up from the sodden turf, running back to try and cover.

'It's not our turn for the kit this week, is it?' Anneka said to Robin.

'No,' he said. 'Pritchard's.'

'Good,' she said. 'More mud than shirts this afternoon.'

The two of them laughed, happy people. How best to break them up, how to wade in between them. She wanted to leave. Leaving was the best idea for all. Turning away, walking back to the car, taking off the muddied shoes, driving to the hotel in socks and nothing else. She stood back from Anneka, a knight's move away from her, just a lift and turn of the head and she would see her face.

A goal was scored; Anneka raised her fists, raised her arms, turned slightly, narrowed her eyes, fixed her eyes, fixed on Gwen. Gwen watched her daughter juggle the coffee cup, it not falling, then falling to the ground. Her daughter said something to Robin and he shook his head and went back to watching the game, shouting something onto the pitch as Anneka walked towards her.

'There's a cafe,' Anneka said. 'Follow me.'

There was steel to her voice, it was flat and trammelled, all trace of accent gone, evened out to generic south. She wore denims and a North Face raincoat, her hair short like Gwen's, almost the same cut, feathered and cropped. Gwen gave her a head start, followed in her wake, past goal celebrations, fouls and injuries, past insults and encouragements. Not like in Nate's day. Surprisingly quiet then. She did not recall Drum shouting, could not remember her or any other mother shouting Man On. She remembered washing the kit though; the slog of that twice a season.

On the other side of the dressing rooms there was a low-slung brick building, its steps strewn with mud and energy drink bottles, a small coffee concession, large windowed, room for about ten tables. It was sticky warm inside, condensation on some of the windows, steam from the espresso machine released in relieved waves.

'Would you like something?' Anneka said.

'No,' she said. 'But you get yourself whatever you like.'

Gwen went for her purse, but Anneka had already moved to the counter. Gwen sat down at a table as far from the other patrons as possible. Her hands shook, the way Drum's did all the time now, that low tremor, sign of the old. She watched her daughter pay, the casual way she spoke to the woman behind the counter, clearly a regular exchange. She watched her put the change in the tip jar.

Her daughter sat down at the table, as though they often did this, a slightly stilted Sunday morning ritual, daughter to talk of this and that; mother to complain of ailments. Perhaps still time for that. For get-togethers, chinwags, getting to know one another again.

'Was it the Internet?' Anneka said.

'What?'

'How you found me.'

No, love. Through a journalist who remains in love with me, who has been surveilling you for decades, perhaps in the hope that I'll fuck him. No love, it was not the Internet, it was analogue, old-fashioned.

'Something like that, yes,' she said. 'You can find anyone these days.'

That what Ray had said, sadly and with nostalgia. The process so much quicker now, so much less rewarding. She had not called him. The search parties would be out.

Anneka stirred her coffee. She had holes in her ears where once there had been rings or studs. She had not changed significantly; those who do not add weight seem to stay the same as they get older. Daphne said she knew about as much about her daughter as Gwen knew of hers.

'You think there will be an impermeable bond,' she'd said. 'You believe that, but it's a mirage. It's a one-way passage: you only get what they're willing to give, and Natasha wouldn't give me the steam from her kid's piss.'

Anneka took a sip from her mug and looked up at Gwen. Cold in the eyes, so blue her eyes, so blue and cold.

'I expected it'd be him, not you,' Anneka said. 'All these years, I thought I'd be standing somewhere and then he'd be beside me. Telling me to come home. That kind of thing. I never thought it'd be you.'

Gwen put her hand out to touch her daughter. Anneka moved away. Gwen was unsure whether coincidence or natural reflex, or whether simply revolted by the thought.

'I told my husband you were dead,' Anneka said. 'Both of you actually.'

She laughed, scratched her temple. 'It was a car accident, if you're interested. So convenient, a car accident, they're such easy ways to kill two birds with one stone.'

Gwen should have got a coffee, should have had something to shift to, to look down on. But there was just the inquisitor eyes.

'You know about him?' Anneka said.

'And Femi,' Gwen said. Anneka pursed her lips. Gwen had wanted to get that one out of the way. Annie wanted to weaponize them, her husband and child. Especially Femi. What a warhead that one; but one now neutralized.

'You've done your research,' Anneka said. 'Saves me having to precis thirty-odd years in a few minutes. Thanks for the reprieve.'

In those words, the memory of her teenage daughter, the firing back, the anger and resentment. The things we do not lose, the tics that do not desert us, no matter what else we change. Anneka looked out over the playing fields, would not look at Gwen.

'Is he dead?' Anneka said. 'Is that it?'

The slack body and the screams in the night, the drugs, the bone-set pain, the agony of it, the discomfort of it all. And her daughter sitting there, with her coffee. Is that it? Is that the thing you've come to say? The dismissal set her teeth. The calculation, the intended effect. A memory of calling her a little bitch, calling her that when there was no one around to hear.

'No, Anneka, he's not dead. But he's dying. The doctors have given him a few months, but it could be any time, really. He's in a tremendous amount of pain . . .'

Do not say, good. Do not say, I'm glad. Do not say, he had it coming. Do not say that to me. Do not. I will slap you, I will tear you apart if you say anything of the kind. Daughter or no, I will rip you clean if you say any such thing.

Anneka stared right back at her, took up her coffee cup.

'My husband, Robin, he says that we're all born into politics,' Anneka said. 'That without realizing it, we experience right from the day of birth a political system. Some will live with an enlightened despot, some get an illusion of democracy, others they get something between the two. But it's a political system nonetheless.'

Anneka leaned in closer to Gwen.

'He talks like that all that time. He's very clever is Robin.'

Gwen had no idea what she was talking about, but this bragging interlude was unbearable. For a moment a mother–daughter exchange, the kind of offhand comment intimates make with one another. Anneka's voice changed at its end, though. As though she knew she had strayed from the course she had plotted.

'Robin asked me about my home. What kind of system I'd grown up under. I said that I'd been raised in a dictatorship. That home had been a banana state, a military junta. He ruled us all. You, me, Nate. A tyrant in his tower. Never to be questioned, never to be challenged, never to be contradicted. The all-seeing—'

'Oh, Annie,' she said, 'that's just not—'

'No one calls me Annie. Don't call me that.'

'I'm sorry,' Gwen said. 'Of course, I'm sorry. But he loved you so dearly, Anneka. He *loves* you so dearly. There isn't a day goes by he doesn't talk of you.'

Where this lie coming from, where this deliberate falsehood? Demonstrably untrue, demonstrably wrong. It felt like the right thing to say, the kind of thing that would stop someone in tracks, give them pause. Emotive and manipulative, how low to sink.

'I don't expect you to understand,' Anneka said. 'I don't expect you to even realize. After what is it now, almost sixty years? You don't have eyes left to see it.'

'He's dying, love. He's going to die.'

Don't say, please don't say. Please keep decorum, please keep civil.

'I didn't come here to argue,' Gwen said, going again for her arm and getting no purchase. 'I just came here to tell you—'

'No, *Mother*, you came here to lay on the guilt. You came here to give him, what, absolution? His deathbed wish? Some kind of last rites? You think telling me he's dying changes anything? You thought you'd come here and I'd just collapse under the weight of the news? He's been dead a long time to me. So many years dead.'

Anneka was shaking, anger ripping through her. Should have seen this coming. In the book she'd read, *On Death and Dying*, one of the stages, anger.

'Look, Annie—'

'I told you don't call me that. Call me that again I'll leave right away.'

'Look, Anneka—'

'No, you look, *Mother*. You look and you listen. I will not see him, not now, not ever. Do you understand that? I don't want to know when he dies, and I won't be there at the funeral. I won't be a hypocrite and I certainly won't be a liar. I'll leave that to him and I'll leave it to you.'

Anneka stood, looking down on Gwen, then bent down her

head. As though about to bestow on her a kiss. Her lips stopped short, rested an inch from her ears.

'You know,' she whispered. 'You look like him now. Like you've both become the same person.'

She stayed there for a beat, Gwen could hear her breath in her ear.

'Such a shame,' she said. 'You used to be such a good-looking woman.'

Anneka stayed there for a moment, just standing there, her daughter. She shook her head, bent down again. She kissed Gwen on the cheek.

'I'm sorry,' she said. 'I'm so sorry.'

And then gone, the automatic doors parting, her quick steps, almost a run, back to the game. Back to her son and her husband; Gwen looking at an empty coffee mug; Gwen staying like that until someone took it away, a ring where it had sat, a faint circle on the Formica.

Tuesday, 6 March 2012

'It's beautiful,' his mother said. 'Look at this, Drum.'

Nate could see his father was furious with him, but Molly had not taken no for an answer, never took no for an answer; and even were she to do so, Nate rarely said no. Molly had drawn Grandpa Dum a get-well-soon card and Nate didn't have the heart to deny her. She was quite the artist: the cows perfectly drawn, the surprisingly detailed likeness of his father, capturing something of him, though quite what Nate didn't know. Too much to say an essence, just something elemental of him.

'Oh that's a bobby-dazzler, that,' his father said. 'You're good at drawing, aren't you, Molly?'

She was eleven, smaller than most in her class, confident, but already with the dark clouds of adolescence knitting. There had been tears, there had been meltdowns about friends, about the prospect of Big School; shouting matches and slammed doors.

'I'm glad you like it, Grandpa Dum,' she said.

'I love it,' he said. 'I'm going to put it up on my wall when I get home.'

The week had been Nate's idea, one he was sure his father would nix, but surprisingly he'd seemed happy for the change of scenery. 'It'll give your mother a week off,' he'd said, but did not mention Nate, him working the farm as well as helping his father at night. The nights of hearing him cry, with pain and with fear, hearing him talk of the Mayan prophecy and how it had been a good life, a good life but a terribly slow death.

His mother was making tea, and he went to her and held her,

the smaller frame, the smaller breadth of shoulder, the bones tight against the skin.

'Carter sent Dad a CD. All old tunes. Nice thing to do, I thought.'

'When are they coming back?'

'Thursday, I think.'

'Does Dad know?'

'I told him, but I don't know if he remembers. Either he knows or he doesn't. Either way is fine.'

'How was Patsy?' he said.

'Patsy?' she said.

'Your friend Patsy. You went to stay with her on Sunday night.'

She looked confused, then relieved.

'You mean *Patty*. It was good to see her. It's been a long time. She hasn't changed much.'

'Did she keep you up?' he said. 'You look exhausted.'

'Why thank you, Nathan. What a gentlemanly thing to say.'

She laughed and he laughed and they stayed like that, in each other's arms, in each other's exhaustion, then resumed their roles: wife and mother, son and father.

Sunday, 4 March 2012

Cold, those last words to her mother. So unnecessary, not even true. Vile to have said such a thing. Not her fault, not her fault. What it would be to nurse her father to death, to look on him vacating his body, to peek with terror on the world to come without him. Her mother was always dependent on him, always nothing without him.

'What's wrong?' Robin said as she took her place beside him.

'Nothing,' Neka said.

'You've been gone ages.'

'Bumped into Lucy in the cafe. What did I miss?'

'Nothing of note,' he said.

'You okay?' he said again.

'I'm fine,' she said. 'Just cold all of a sudden.'

Her mother wouldn't last without him. There'd be nothing for her to live for, nothing to prop herself up with. Like the wailing women in North Korea, distraught at the death of their beloved leader, but without the hope of a successor.

She should not have apologized though. It was weak to have apologized.

Robin put his arms around her, warming her, rubbing her back. She looked for Femi on the left wing, his hands on his hips, looking around, deciding on position, where to run to. She watched him and not the ball, watched him jog then sprint, challenge for the ball. She hadn't asked about Nate. The ball came to Femi and he shot it at goal. The keeper saved it, touching the ball over the bar. It missed and she hadn't asked about Nate. Not one question. Cold again. Cruel.

Wednesday, 7 March 2012

Something by the door, something breathing, human-shaped, but with no scythe in sight, just shallow breath and the sad scrape of a chair, the light dark, and the breath closer, coming to the bed, coming close to him, loud the breath beside him.

'Hello, Dad,' it said.

'Annie,' he said. 'Is that you, Annie?'

'Don't call me Annie,' she said.

'Sorry,' he said. 'I forget. I forget you don't like that name. There's another name. Another one you don't like, isn't there?'

'Fish,' she said. 'You used to call me that, but I didn't like it.'

'You were such a good swimmer,' he said. 'Like a fish in the water, you were.'

'Does it hurt?' she said. 'Are you in pain, Dad?'

'Yes,' he said. 'It hurts. It's agony.'

She made a noise, rearranged herself. He couldn't quite see her, but he could smell her, almost touch her.

'I knew you'd come back,' he said. 'I always knew you'd come back to me.'

'You knew?' she said.

'I said to your mother you'd come back. Eventually. In your own good time. No point in chasing you. No point sending out search parties. You're my daughter. Stubborn runs through you like Brighton rock.'

He laughed, coughed, a machine blinked.

'Did you think of me?' she said.

'Oh my love, I thought of you every day. Not a day went past when I didn't think of you. No matter what they've done, you always love your children. Even if they're killers or terrorists, you can't help but love them. Can't help but forgive them.'

'You're comparing me to a murderer? To a terrorist?'

'They're just examples,' he said. 'Don't overreact. It's the drugs, they make me say things I'm not sure of.'

'But you forgive me, that's what you're saying?'

'Tell me it wasn't the making of you.'

'The making of me?'

'Yes. Had we come for you, had we marched you home, what would have happened then? Would you have respected that? Would you have been happy? We knew you were with Lissa in Liverpool. We went there and we knew she'd tell you. We gave you an option. But you ignored us. You punished us for nothing. And that was so hard on us, so very hard. But we let you live your life, even though we were not part of it.'

'So you forgive me?' she said. She laughed.

'Why do you laugh?' he said.

'You know why,' she said.

'You think I should be asking for your forgiveness?'

'Do you think you should?'

'You left *us*,' he said.

'You should have believed me,' she said.

'What was there to believe?' he said. 'You'd done it before, there was no reason to think—'

'I told you what happened,' she said. 'You should have believed me.'

'So you keep saying,' he said. 'But you ran. You defied me.'

'That's the crux of it? That I disobeyed you?'

'I forgive you,' he said.

She put her head next to his head. He could not see her, but could smell her. His Annie, his little Annie.

'I forgive you too,' she said. 'I just wanted to say that, I just wanted to let you know that you're right. It made me who I am. And I forgive you. I absolve you.'

'I'm dying,' he said.

'I know,' she said. 'I have to go now.'

'You'll be back?'

'No,' she said. 'Not again. This is the last time.'

'But you forgive me?'

'Yes,' she said. 'I forgive you.'

'Now I can die?' he said.

'Yes,' she said. 'Yes, you can die.'

Friday, 9 March 2012

The medics carry him into the farmhouse, upstairs to the spare room, two of them, though one would be enough to haul his bones. Carter and Daphne are waiting downstairs, Nate is making them tea. This is the last round, the last goodbyes. He gibbers sometimes, sometimes he is lucid. Gwen has never been one for organizing parties, but this has fallen to her, to let each of them have their last time with him. Surrounded by friends and family, what they say in the papers when someone famous dies. Somehow a comfort that, as though softening death; death not so bad when done in good company.

The medics leave and Gwen plumps up the pillows. He feels drool at the corner of his mouth.

'Bath,' he says.

'What?' she says.

'Bath,' he says. 'I want to go in clean.'

'Hush now,' she says. 'I can't carry you that far.'

'A shave?' he says.

'I don't know how,' she says. 'Wouldn't know what to do.'

'Carter,' he says. 'Carter do it?'

She puts her hand on his arm.

'I'll ask him,' she says. 'Are you comfortable?'

'She came to me,' he says. 'Did I say?'

'Yes,' she says. 'You told me she came.'

'My Annie came back,' he says. 'Tell me when she gets here, Gwen. Tell me when she's here.'

'I'll go and get Carter,' she says.

★

He's always envied the way Carter shaves, always so neat, so exact, the upward stroke, the downward stroke, watching him of a morning in their berth, the bristles collecting in the small sink.

'Keep still,' Carter says. 'Don't want to cut you now, do I?'

The blade is warm from the water, it glides along his face, the foam comes off in a thick pile, drops to the water in the bowl below his chin.

The two of them alone again, the two of them old and young, always both. Safe in his hands, always safe in his hands. Safe in each other's. Ready to catch if they should fall. Feeling small in his arms, Carter towering over, scraping away the beard, saying nothing. Tears in his eyes, wipes his nose on a handkerchief before recommencing the shave.

'It's been a good life,' Drum says. 'Hasn't it?'

'The best,' Carter says. 'The best with you in it.'

'I saw they were cheating you, didn't I? The skates with their cards.'

'Yes,' Carter says, 'You stood up and you were counted. And you saved me on our One.'

'We did our best, didn't we?'

'Yes, Drum, we did our best. In difficult circumstances, we did our best.'

'Without you,' Drum says. 'Nothing. No life without you.'

'You would have done fine without me, Drum, don't you worry there.'

'Annie came to me,' he says. 'Did I say?'

'Yes,' he says.

'We forgave each other.'

'I'm glad,' he says.

'Can die now,' he says. 'Easy to die now.'

'Well don't do it yet,' he says. 'I've not finished the shave. Don't want you arriving at the pearly gates with foam all over your neck.'

'You're always thinking of me,' Drum says.

'Always,' he says. Carter cries then, the real tears, the proper tears, no faking that. No faking them, not those tears, real ones, for love those tears.

'Don't die,' he says. 'Not now, not here, Drum. Don't die now.'

'Not yet, no,' he says.

'We always keep our promises, don't we, Drum. Always keep the promises we make.'

'Always,' Drum says. 'You can depend on me.'

'Yes,' he says. 'Always.'

Carter finishes the shave, wipes the foam from Drum's face, holds up the mirror so he can see the result. In the mirror there are the two of them. He wants to see their younger faces. He wants to see their hair cut *en brosse*, their eyes shining. He wants to see them in their uniforms, their lives ahead of them. But he just sees two old men. Two old men, one of whom has shaving foam on his earlobe. They look into the mirror. The two old men look back at them. Caught, the two of them there, in the mirror, in their age, never to be younger, never again to make the choices they made.

★

They are alone, again, for the last time, she knows, alone. Still him. Still not Montgomery Clift, still just Drum. She holds his hand tight, but the hand is slack in hers. She strokes the side of his face, familiar after all the years, altered in the closeness to his passing. She hears the first rattle and can feel it inside her, as though she is dying right there with him.

'I love you,' she says. 'Know that I always loved you.'

'I love you,' he says. 'Know that I always loved you too.'

'Best thing I ever did,' his voice is close and weak, but there remains will. Remains the last of fight.

'What?' she says.

'Waking up and seeing you there. In the hunters' lodge.'

'A long time ago now,' she says.

'That's how it'll be,' he says. 'I'll open my eyes and you'll be there. Looking at me.'

'Yes,' she says.

'I'll wake and you'll be there. Always be there.'

'Yes,' she says.

There are so many things to say, but she cannot speak. She is alone with her husband in her daughter's room and he is inching away. Another rattle. Another. Another.

'Come quickly,' she says loudly. As loud as she can. They come into the room, all of them. She will not let go the hand. She strokes his arm as though she can revive him. His eyes open and close, open and close. And he smiles, a wide smile with teeth and lips. His eyes open and he looks astonished at what he sees.

★

They are all around him, all of them, he can see them, though they are dim and hazed. They are trying not to cry and he is high on the drugs, away with them, and he sees them all, and can feel the laying on of hands. He can no longer speak. He has tried but they tell him not to speak, just to rest, and that is good advice, he's happy to receive it, happy to receive what is coming to him, what is starting low in his gut, to the left-hand side, coming up that side, warming that, like hands caressing, how warm and cosy the hands, and Gwen is holding his hand, her cool hand clasped around him, a soft cooing, still her face the most beautiful, his girl, Gwen, you can take the girl from the pub, but not the Gwen from his life, and his son there, Nate, how old he looks now, Natey my boy, the milkers needing fixing, do right by her, Nate, for Molly, Nate, and the warm on the right-hand side now, the warm hands, toasted the hands, and the spangles in his chest and in his arms, like fireworks, and no fear now, no fear of what coming, already coming, the buttons already pressed, already primed the bombs, and he survived did he not, he walked Doom Town and came out the other side, surrounded by friends and family now, surrounded and the sirens inside, the sirens in the stammer of leg and the quiet hurry in the guts and here, never more present, the bombs in the neck, the bombs in the head, and Annie, where Annie, Annie there, somewhere, sure, Annie there, standing at back, crying now, Annie, all the years lost, but all forgiven and all forgotten, and feeling he can hold it back, stave off death, silence the bombs, can hold it off forever, just let it come close, then shut it down, a rehearsal and a drill, that's all, but the feeling too warm, too drowsy, not wanting it to end, wanting it to be there forever, between states, that glorious slip between waking and sleeping.

Surrounded by friends and family, all the years between them, Carter's hand on his knee, attending to him as though injured, needing to be taken to the field hospital, and suddenly in Spain at Carter's house, the warmth of the sun on his face, walking the fields and pastures, a heifer born and a baby in swaddling, her mother screaming, Annie screaming and the rush of it now, the warm and the coming cold, the cold coming over the warm, the pins and needles of the cold, and a catch in the throat, a catch and the cold coming strong, coming thick, coming with spite, the warm gone and the cold blasting and the hands on his hands and the hands on his legs and them all waving, waving goodbye, no, not waving, him waving perhaps, and the light changing, the image of them, like a photograph burning, white the light, white the flame and the blind light coming, the blindest of blind lights, clouding the light, brilliant the light, blind the light, and beautiful as bombs, the light. My God, oh my God, the light.

Wildboarclough

2019

Sunday, 18 August

I

The house was cold stone and silence; no trace of Nate in the empty rooms, presumably out with the cows, the Sunday milking to be done. Neka made herself instant coffee; turned on the radio, turned it off again. The news never-ending, always going on, no matter if listened to or not. She no longer followed the news. To get old was to whittle, to pare life back to essentials. And so little seemed essential. Her son, her husband, her job, the quiet satisfaction of an orderly house, her mind no longer teeming, no longer racing. Leave that to Robin; leave that to Femi.

They talked, the two of them, animatedly, persuasively, of the world around them, the world and its descent. Conversations she was invited to join, but ones she could not in good conscience enter into. She made the right noises; she said the right things, but didn't feel them the way they did. In those deep, conspiratorial conversations, they became other versions of themselves, no less true, no less real, but altered, as though they were the superheroes Femi worshipped as a child, the two of them living double identities, neither guise the full story.

There had been a reawakening in Robin, a resurgence of the activism, the anger, even some of the language of their early days together. It was thrilling, magnetic, exhausting. He had lost weight, gained momentum, began receiving death threats on social media.

'Everyone gets them,' he'd said. 'Makes you nostalgic for when death threats actually meant something. The letters cut out of newspapers and all that.'

He was happy-angry, delighted-dismayed, optimistic-livid. But unlike before, back before they were married, lovers even, he did not mention the fact of her skin. Decades together, she'd seen it close at hand, he said, which gave her 'insight'. She did not feel insightful, though; she just felt swept into a battle she thought long-ago won.

This for him, and this for Femi. The whole thing, for them. What she told herself. What she told Robin. Femi would be the first of his family, the first of hers, to go to university. He'd been pushed for Oxford, pushed for Cambridge, but fancied neither. Not real enough. *Not real* the worst of all insults. Off to Manchester for now. London, he promised, for later.

She listened to him with his friends, the words she didn't understand; their alien argot. At home though, he was the same little boy, grown big, grown gangly, grown hairs on chest, on legs, on cheek, but still the same delighted boy, the same longed-for child. It had been hard not to spoil him, hard not to express to him every day how the world seemed to be waiting for him. Hard not to smile when, as a younger teen, he'd shouted he wished he'd never been born, as the ghosts of his dead and unborn siblings laughed at him.

She called home, sipped her coffee, waited for Robin to pick up. He'd wanted to come. He'd demanded to come, at least in his own little way.

'We could make a weekend of it,' he'd said over a pub lunch. 'We don't even need to drive. We could stay in a hotel. There must be nice hotels there.'

In bed, the television on: 'You don't know him, not really. Wouldn't you feel safer if I were there?'

The previous morning, the last of it. Sitting at the kitchen table, the car key pushed between his middle and ring fingers, the way she'd once held door keys while walking home. She'd heard what he'd said, but had not listened. It was his final appeal.

He was going over the hotel options again. From the iPad he read the names of places they could visit, the places they could stay: spas and lodges; old staging posts and thatched-roof inns. She did not recognize any of them.

She disconnected her charging phone and put it in her handbag. Their coffee mugs were still on the table, the crusts from his toast scattered on top of two stacked plates. A normal, lazy weekend morning, late waking, Femi still in bed, and soon to drive to the supermarket, to start on the garden, to visit family.

'Look, here's one,' he said. 'Pool and a spa, a few miles from your brother's.'

She didn't look at the screen. She put her hand on his shoulder and lightly kissed his cheek.

'I told you,' she said. 'Nate said to come alone.'

'He wouldn't need to know. Look, it's got a golf course,' he said.

'You hate golf.'

At this he smiled. Then didn't. The dark under his eyes. The slight bloodshot to their whites, the creeping hoods of his eyelids. She saw the frustration he failed to conceal, his quick movements and swallowed annoyances. Her brother had not told her to come alone; Nate lacked the wit to have even suggested it. It was an easy deception, simple to execute after years of Robin believing he knew when she was lying.

She'd left the room, taken the stairs quickly. In the bedroom, she packed the small trolley suitcase, the one that matched his, the pair that fitted snug in the boot, side by side. She opened drawers and threw in underwear, a pair of jeans, some soft trousers, some thin summer T-shirts, a fleece: a job Robin usually did, the clothes neatly folded, avoiding all wrinkles.

Someone – who was that? – once told her he was fascinated by the act of dressing. To think, he'd said, everyone gives the world such signifiers, such insight into their lives, and each day such a decision taken without due thought or consideration. Before Robin and her, this man. Tony. No, Toby. From Brighton, but moored up in the North, stranded there, so he said. Always wore the same suit jacket, the buttons hanging off, clacking at the cuffs. If I gave a fuck about how I presented, he'd said, looking with disdain at her carefully worn Mod dress, I'd never leave the house.

Presenting now in pyjamas, the tartan ones bought for her birthday, sitting in the empty farmhouse, leaving a message for Robin. As though the years having not passed, or passed in an altogether different fashion: the farmer's wife, a toiler of the land. She went upstairs, showered, dressed, sat in her old room, the space angling back, reforming to its old appointment, the light adjusting. Scrubbed of memory; the room, and herself. Hard to recall what was real and what imagined; the depths of the passions and the thresh of hormones. In one of Lissa's pieces Neka had read, she'd written that she distrusted anyone who harked back to their teenage years, anyone who would gladly repeat them. A bullseye that. Bad enough they existed at all, without the threat of them happening again.

She would see Thomas, she would see Carter. This was the deal Nate had brokered with her. Long emails over which they had formulated a plan; emails in which she noticed the colour of therapy, its ripeness rising up from the screen. Nate had not used the word closure but it was close at hand. She could not imagine him on the same relaxed chairs she'd sat in, sometime late in her twenties. The long sessions. She wondered if Nate had used the same obscurantism, the same evasion with his therapist as she had. Those hours of terror. No one to tell that to. No one to ever know. Not wanting to talk of it, not wanting ever to think of it. There were dreams. Of course. Event dreams. But coped with, expected, easily displaced. Dreams of Thomas too, of Kate Bush and Cathy and Heathcliff chanting liar, chanting fantasist as Thomas put his hand into his unzipped slacks.

Outside, a mobility taxi arrived, the backend bulbous, an oversized estate. She watched Nate dash from the passenger side, the rear door opening on its own, a ramp extending out to the ground. He bent himself inside the space, came out backwards, pulling the chair down the ramp. The wheelchair bumped and fluked on the pitted ground, spat stones out from under the tyres. Nate held open the door, kept it open with his leg, contorting himself to push her through. Neka stood and took quick steps down to the kitchen, filled a kettle as she heard the struggle through the door. I should get a ramp, she heard Nate say, next time I'll fit a ramp, and Neka set the kettle on the stove, sat down at the table as he pushed the chair into the kitchen.

In emails, Nate had warned her about their mother, but Neka was wary of elaboration, of sickness-inflation. When Nate had written that she looked like a skeleton dripping skin, she thought Nate might have read that somewhere; but that was how she looked: cadaverous, pumpkin-carved skin, the shade of pistachio ice cream, gobble-gobble folds of skin beneath her chin. Her eyes liquid light now, like a blue rinse grown out to a dove grey. The stroke had given her face a slant, her mouth hanging open on one side, drool below some angry hairs, unplucked and defiantly dark.

Not drool but tears, Neka saw that now. A beckon of the hand, and Neka knelt by the chair, a hand grabbing hers, surprising strength and rapidity, a pulling in close. A kiss from the unplucked lip, a kiss on the cheek, on any flesh she could find.

'You're here,' her mother said. Not clearly, not without a certain amount of translation, but understandable enough. Face tooth and twist, but something not quite undimmed.

'Never thought it,' she said. '*Merch hardd.*'

Crying without effort now, just a stream of tears, another incontinence.

'I missed you,' her mother said. '*Wedi dy golli ers Cymaint.*'

And somehow a laugh, a stutter of the mouth. A certain laugh though, gaiety, levity. Hand gripping tight on her arm, keeping hold, as though she might spring up and fly the coop.

'She's been speaking a lot of Welsh,' Nate said. 'Sometimes it goes on all day.'

'He used to understand,' her mother said, nodding to Nate. 'Do you understand, *cariad?*'

Neka nodded.

'*Da,*' her mother said. '*Da iawn.*'

'Tea?' Neka said.

'Yes,' Nate said. 'Tea.'

2

First the grief and then the rush; the rush turning to stumbles, and then to falls. It was too much for Nate, she knew that. Too much for Nate, the farm and everything, as well as looking after his mother. He tried his best, but there was no choice. She got lost once in the field, was looking for Harris, his long-dead dog. She burned her hand taking a roast from the oven. A residential home. Safe for them both.

She'd kissed Ray. Just once, and just quickly. She blamed that. She was sure that was it. Never the same after that kiss. A spell broken and not in the right way. Cursed from the pit, after that. She began to see God. He looked like her father. She saw the devil. He looked like Old Nick. The nightmares starting then. At Daphne's funeral, wearing an old gown of hers, a long black number, Carter there and Carter broken, almost as broken as she. Nate holding her up, fetching her drinks, the champagne Daph reserved for apocalypse. Looking out for her in the big house, waiting for her to whisk her away, take some time just the two of them.

Not the kiss, but the death of Daphne. Knew it was something. One of two. Which the more likely? In the night, Old Nick talked of books, of sex; in the mirror she saw the young Drum and Carter, dressed in their fatigues, drinking black and tan, her pouring the drinks, her father there, hale and gin-soused; her mother scolding Old Nick for his questions. The bite of Annie at her breast, the nip of Nate as he pinched her in anger.

None of this today. Today, coast clear, skies cloudless, waking at the home and refreshed, a good sleep, unmet with dreams and the tea in the beaker, the little sippy cup, the woman who looked like Bridget from Dagenham some days and some days not, handing her the cup and saying Nate would be there soon. A day out today, a day out, always saying things twice, this sometime Bridget, a repeat just to be certain she understood, which Gwen always did, even if she liked to reply in Welsh to keep her father happy.

Oh, Annie. There now, old Annie, young Annie, unchanged and changed. In the kitchen taking a cup of tea from Nate, stirring a cup of tea in the kitchen. The times she'd thought of that, always over tea, over coffee, the normalcy of that. No grand meeting, no fatted calf, just Typhoo or Mellow Birds. You think of things for so long, and bury those things, they have the texture of reality, the crumb of real biscuit.

'How's she been?' her daughter asked Nate, not asking her. Why not ask me? I can speak, can say what needs to be said. Already said all that needs to say, done all that needs to be done. Signed it all over. Power of attorney to them both. And gave them blessing. Gave Annie blessing. To see them together again, sitting at the table, talking amongst themselves. No time having passed, apart from the years in their grey hairs.

The tears again. Crying again. They were talking of Molly, of Femi. Photographs on telephone screens, a library of lockets, those little devices. Molly wanting to go study in Birmingham, or maybe Leeds. There to study, now what now? Something technical, something scientific. Not from our genes, as if we didn't know it. Femi to study politics and something else. Something international or something. To change the world that boy. Not knowing himself part-Welsh, part of a part-Scot, a stock of complex ingredients. They passed her the phones, the photographs of Molly, of Femi, those of Femi new to her, Ray having taken few over the last years, his interest waning after the kiss.

How longed-for that kiss, how quick it over. Had forgotten almost what a kiss of passion tasted like, how it presented in the mouth. Odd and greasy, it turned out. The years had dulled the senses, depopulated the synapses. And that had felt like a deeper transgression, the sudden knowledge this should have happened when they still had some fire in the blood, some heyday left. She could see that in Ray's face, in the tenderness of the kiss, flagging back the past, the moments he'd not lifted his head and just kissed her, taken her to his bed.

The kiss was underwhelming, but with the sure sense that, had the years rolled back, the bodies become harder, taller, straighter, the kiss would have undone them both. And so, proved her right; proved that the spell would have been a noxious one. But afterwards, again, what would that matter? She hadn't needed to elope. She hadn't needed to leave the children. She could just have done what she wanted and kept it a secret. What harm would have been done? Had Drum found out, he would have taken her back. He would have punished her every day for it, but she would not have lost him.

'When was the last time you saw Thomas?' Gwen said.

The two of them looked at her. Ah, still the capacity to stop them both still. A mother's knack; a barmaid's knack. One of the two.

'I saw him once in London,' Annie said. 'Walking up the road, on his mobile phone. One of the big ones. I wanted to kill him.'

Gwen nodded.

'He was good to Daphne,' Gwen said. 'Always there, no matter what.'

Oh, the unintended needle, the spite of that. I haven't forgotten what you said, Anneka. The last time. It still stings, that, apology or no.

'He's got a young family now,' Gwen said. 'Must be six and ten, something like that.'

'I know,' Annie said. 'Nate told me. Wife's the same age as his eldest.'

'You exaggerate,' she said. 'In her forties, isn't she, Ray?'

'Something like that,' Nate said, ignoring that she'd called him by the wrong name. The slips sometimes, the slips and the downward spirals. They might not have noticed. How much has she given away already? How loose her lips?

Annie looked at her phone. Her daughter in that cocked head, that expression, it all comes back, the tics, the smirks, the smiles. Nothing lost, nothing gone; all still there. The same despite it all, the same person beneath the aged skin and the grey-haired crown. Nothing changing.

'We should go,' Annie said.

No response to this; from Nate, from Gwen: nothing. In charge now, Annie, and Gwen glad of that. Glad it would soon be over, glad it was coming to a head. She saw Ray sometimes, sometimes Drum, mostly Drum, always really Drum. To love and love so long and to not know how that love could be surmised, how it could be expressed, how it could follow a natural course of action. Somehow they'd been together that whole time, and not yet together, but bound, snared somehow, a lash around the legs, pulled tight. How it felt now to be unyoked. To be able to do what he was unable to do. It was not a betrayal. No, it was not that.

She'd signed over the power of attorney. She trusted Nate, she trusted Annie. What they wanted was more important than Drum's promise to Carter. Femi was more important. Molly was more important. The farm was theirs. It did not belong to a promise that had nothing in writing; it did not belong to them. It belonged to Nate, and to Annie, and to their children. I'm sorry, Drum, my love. I know you promised, but such promises are no longer contracts.

3

They did not use the side door, the back door, the usual entrances and exits. Anneka walked ahead as Nate pushed Gwen in her chair, the heat up and sweat on his back; Anneka wearing sunglasses, large-rimmed with gold at the hinges and temples. They were delegation and welcome party, a tote bag over Anneka's shoulder containing a bottle of wine and a collection of papers. Advancing with smiles, with casual, mid-morning, amble.

There were three possibilities: Thomas would answer the door; Thomas's wife would answer the door or Carter would be there to greet them. Anneka pressed the doorbell. A choice of three. Whoever opened the door, Anneka in charge from that moment.

Nate set the brake on Gwen's chair, looked up to the gables, the fresh paintwork. Once, Nate had imagined himself living there, renting it from the Carters, moving in with Molly and Carlie. Had never even asked the price, Nate knowing he could never afford it. Contented with doing the odd jobs there, taking the work from the management company, Carter having recommended him. Job over now. Thomas come to take the big house back, to settle in the seat of his ancestors, 'There to semi-retire, to look once again on the land-scape of his youth –' this in the email to Nate terminating his employ – 'to show that landscape to my children who have only ever gazed on the cast-iron of New York's SoHo. I'm coming home to begin again, to survey the lands my forebears have cultivated over centuries.'

Nate felt bilious, shaken, as though on comedown, a strange memory that, the shivers, the run and hammer of the heart, the sense of death coming then retreating, pulling out at last moment. You put your faith in people, this what happens.

4

Neka rang the doorbell, the sound deep and long in the echoing hall. She'd seen him on the street, yes; she thought she'd seen him on the street. What were the chances of that? How long the odds? Not so long, walking in the financial district around lunchtime, meeting up with a friend who had promised some help for the children's centre, always a chance of seeing him. Had not wanted to kill him, had not even considered it, whatever it was she told her mother. You learn to blot, to blank.

Seeing him had not summoned up the past, had not raised ghosts. She'd thought instead how foolish the new mobile phones were, the size and weight of them. Thinking they would never catch on, who would want to be constantly found? That what she remembered. A glance in his direction, a lowering of the eyes, thinking the word Yuppie; though she did not know, exactly, what it meant.

Scrabbling sounds down the hallway, a dog sound, claws on stone, on parquet. So many locks unlocked, the pulling back of bolts, the releasing of chains. The door opened and a woman there. Long black hair, ironed straight, an NYU sweatshirt, skinny denims.

'Can I help you?' she said, looking beyond Neka, to Nate, to her mother. The accent American, pure television, pure the movies. Looked something like her at the same age, Neka thought. Like an American actor playing her for the US market.

'You must be Kim,' Neka said. 'Lovely to meet you. We're here to see Tommy and Uncle Jim.'

'Oh,' she said. 'They're in the kitchen. I'll go—'

'It's all right,' Neka said. 'We know where the kitchen is.'

Neka walked over the threshold, the times she'd done so in dreams. The walls as they were then, not as they were now. Spaces where portraits and landscapes had once hung, test swatches of paint over the wallpaper. Coats on the newel of the staircase, shoes by the door, but nothing else, everything removed, even the stair-runner carpet, ripped out, bare boards below.

'We've got the designers coming next week,' Kim said to Nate and to Gwen. 'Sorry for all the mess. You must be Nathan and Gwen.'

'Yes,' Nate said. 'We said to Thomas we'd stop by.'

'Yes,' Kim said. 'Tom did say you'd pop in. Again, sorry for all the mess.'

Just a friendly pop round. Just a welcome back, Tommy. Just a hello to Carter. No mention of her. She had insisted Nate say nothing of her coming.

5

Gwen watched Annie walk the hallway, looking up, looking down. Daphne disappeared in the hallway, all of her gone. Carter and Daphne, erased now, colour schemes Daph would never have countenanced bringing the house mewling into a century already older than anyone ever expected.

How many years ago, standing where she was sitting now, on the welcome mat, not daring to move from its pitch. Not a different life, a different world.

'I used to love this hallway,' Gwen said. 'It was Daphne's favourite part of the house.'

'It's so dramatic, isn't it?' Kim said. 'I just love it. When Tom showed me the pictures, I couldn't quite believe it. Like something out of *Downton Abbey*.'

Kim laughed and in the laugh, Gwen heard the jangle of excitement, of a world newly opened; some wayward dream of freedom and a different kind of life. Something away from what she knew, something safe and permanent and with the weight of history behind it.

'Where are all the pictures?' Gwen said.

'In storage,' she said. 'We're going to see what works and what doesn't.'

'Very wise,' Gwen said.

6

Carter's voice was old now, funny how the voice ages, becomes more querulous through the years, less sonorous. He was talking politics with Tommy; everyone at the time talking politics, everyone talking with the same level of knowledge and prejudice, the same level of biased prediction. At home, Robin and Femi perhaps doing the same thing, working through the same issues, saying variants on the same theme, from opposed positions. Country supposedly divided, but brought together in constant argument.

Neka waited before coming in, waited until flanked by Nate and her mother. You get one entrance. You get one go around. The house was cool but she felt clammy, dirt-streaked, stinking; her as the ill-wind, wafting in, turning filth. No matter the preparation, no matter how calm then, now pulsed with nerves, a slow slip of sweat running down from her armpit. She sneaked past Nate and entered the kitchen. The two men looked up from their coffee cups.

That face. Those faces.

'Annie?' Carter said. 'Is that you?'

'Last I looked, yes,' she said. 'How are you, Uncle Jim?'

'I'm . . . well, I'm . . .' Lost for fucking words and right to be so. Lost for words and looking around the room for some kind of help, some kind of assistance, and instead his mute son, standing up, scraping back the chair, composing himself, a hand on the kitchen table.

'You look well,' Neka said. 'I'm so sorry to hear about Daphne. She was such a wonderful woman.'

'You remember—'

'Tommy, yes,' she said. 'Hello, Tommy. It's been a long time.'

'Yes,' he said. 'A long time.'

'I hear you've been in America,' she said.

'Yes,' he said.

'Looks like you've brought back some souvenirs.' She laughed and they all laughed and Kim put her arms around her husband, in defence, not propriety. Clever enough to know this was dangerous; smart enough to know that whatever this was, this was not good.

7

'Oh, Gwen,' Carter said. 'Lovely to see you. I was going to stop by next week.'

He fussed and kissed her, bent down to meet her in the chair. Carter, a foot shorter or so it seemed. Hair all but gone, white banks between a sea of pate, flapping earlobes, a nose gone alarming red. How had he survived so long? Not just luck in the genes: money too.

Gwen watched Thomas shake Nate's hand, the tightness of the shake, the firmness of it.

'Nate, how good to see you,' Thomas said. 'Kim, this is Nate who's been keeping the house shipshape for us. And this is his sister, Anneka. It's been a long time since . . . well, it's been a long time since we were all in one room.'

'Yes,' Annie said. 'Must be thirty-eight years, give or take a few months. Probably before you were even born, Kim.'

Laughter all round. All round laughter.

'Well, I think this deserves a celebration,' Thomas said. 'Let's open some bubbles. It must be six o'clock somewhere, right, Dad?'

'It's very early,' Kim said. 'It's only just eleven o'clock.'

'Lighten up,' he said. 'This is how we do things in England, did I not explain? Drinks to celebrate, drinks to commiserate, drinks while you decide which is which.'

'I'm just thinking of—'

'It's just today,' he said. 'To celebrate. I wish Tash were here, she'd be so thrilled.'

'Where is Tash?' Anneka asked.

'Sweden these days,' Carter said.

Thomas took a bottle from the fridge.

'Get the glasses, Dad,' he said.

'He's man of the house, now,' Carter said, laughing. 'I know my place.'

Shuffled, only word to describe it, he shuffled over to the cabinet and took from it the flutes they used for second best. Must have known she would realize. You forget. All the time, things drip, spin, alter. Not today, though, seemingly.

The familiar corking pop and a slight issue from the bottle, clumsily opened. Pour of the glasses and the shake of the hands, and the noises made, deferring the moment, perhaps postponing it. Her daughter's calm, her smiles and the clink of the glasses. Overplaying the hand.

'How are the kids, Tommy?' Annie said.

'Well Luca's six and Joy is ten, they're joining us next week. They're so excited to come to England. I think they think they'll be going to Hogwarts.'

'I meant your other kids,' Annie said. 'Must be in their thirties now?'

Careful now, Annie. Put away the claws.

'I'm afraid we don't see them all too often,' he said. 'They're so busy these days. Josie's a lawyer in London and Jamie works in venture capital. He was in the US for a time, but now he's in Canada. Do you—'

'I have a son called Femi, he's just off to university.'

'What a lovely name,' Kim said.

'It's Nigerian,' she said. 'Like his father.'

'Oh, have you been to Lagos?' Kim said. 'We were there for a few months, weren't we Tom?'

'No,' Anneka said. 'We've not managed to go yet. But soon, I think. Soon, I'm sure we will.'

A stone-cold lie, a mother knows. Something in the quick smile afterwards. I did not play on the silos. I have not smoked a cigarette.

'How about you, Nate?' Kim said. 'Do you have any children?'

'One,' he said. 'Her name's Molly. She's the same age as Femi.'

'Oh how lovely,' Kim said. 'It's a shame, I don't have any siblings so there's no cousins for Luca and Joy.'

'Well, there's Tash's two,' Carter said.

'Yes,' she said. 'But they're so much older. It's not the same, is it?'

A beat there, a beat and no one looking at each other.

'So, you're moving back,' Annie said. 'For good?'

'Yes,' Thomas said. 'Time to finally take the family seat.'

'It's so peaceful here,' Kim said. 'I've lived in New York all my life, but I always dreamed of settling down somewhere peaceful, somewhere . . . beautiful. And is there anything more beautiful than this? It feels like we're alone in the world, alone save for the cows and the birds and so on.'

Gwen watched her daughter drain her drink. Watched her set the glass down on table. She'd decided to go. Gwen could see it. Carter looked out of the window. Kim looked at her husband. Thomas made his excuses, headed for the bathroom. A sound like the detuning of a guitar string, a sound from Nate. He was looking at Carter. Carter looked like he could feel it, fending it off like a tramp at the roadside.

They said nothing, waiting for Thomas to return, the long silence, followed by the rush of water along the hall. Sorry, my love. For the best this, my love.

She saw her daughter, young Annie, young Annie-moo walk towards the hallway, saying she knew where the bathroom was, thank you all the same.

8

'What the fuck are you doing here?' Thomas said as they passed in the hallway. He had Neka by the arm, loosely, but enough to arrest her.

'Just thought I'd stop by,' she said. 'Catch up on old times.'

'If you're here to—'

'Relax,' she said. 'I'm not going to bring all that up.'

And he did not believe it, but then seemed to believe it, then weighed it again and could not decide, the scales whirring, like a compass near a magnet. She walked past him into the toilet. It stank, even below the bleach and the air freshener.

9

When nervous, Nate could talk farm for hours, boring himself and anyone else who would listen. People think they want to know about how a farm works, the battles with supermarkets, the privations of the modern dairy farmer, but they don't. They want to hear about the birth of calves, about the funny things the cows do, but nothing so detailed. It must be great to work with your hands – this the kind of thing people said – it must be great to do something that matters. Weasel words, these, weasel justifications; the easiest way to stop the conversation.

He was boring Kim, he knew that, and she looked relieved as she spied an out, her telling him of a farm she'd visited on a school trip to upstate New York. Talk of horses and such. Well extricated. They talked now of horses, the one she planned to buy and ride once they were settled.

Neka came back and stood beside him, between him and their mother. She put a hand on the shoulder of their mother, and looked at Carter. Carter seemed to condense further, as though sinking deep into the ground beneath.

'Uncle Jim,' she said. 'Tommy, Kim. We thought it best that we let you know that, collectively, we've reached a decision.'

'On what?' Thomas said. 'Is everything okay?'

'Yes,' she said. 'It was a very tough decision, but we've made it together, and we are all in agreement.'

Neka looked at their mother, and she looked to Nate. Nate's heart gone all to the carnival show, juggling, acrobatic.

'We've been approached by a property developer. They would

like to buy the farm and the land. It's a very attractive offer, and after long consideration, we've decided to accept.'

That face. Those faces. Carter looking away, then looking directly at Gwen.

'I'm sorry, you've lost me,' said Thomas. 'You can't sell the farm. It's isn't yours to sell.'

'Aren't you going to tell him, Uncle Jim?' Anneka said.

Carter said nothing. Not a word.

'What your father wants to say is that we do own it, actually,' Anneka said. 'We have the deeds here. It's all above board.'

That face. Those faces.

'Dad?' Thomas said.

Carter shook his head, his body shaking before and after.

'It's your fault,' Carter said. 'Don't come *Dad* with me, it's your fault in the first bloody place.'

'What is?' Thomas said. 'What on earth is going on here?'

'You always know best, don't you?' Carter said. 'You never listened to me, never once listened to me. I told you what would happen. I said it would have repercussions.'

'Will someone please tell me what is going on?' Thomas said.

'You father gave the farm to Drum,' Gwen said. 'He needed money and in return for us mortgaging the farm, he gave Drum the deeds.'

'He said he'd sell it back to you,' Carter said to Thomas. 'He promised. He said he'd only ever sell to you.'

'There's no evidence of that,' Anneka said. 'Just a deed with Drum's name on it, and now with Mother's name there. He never left any instructions.'

'But he promised,' Carter said. 'He always kept his word.'

'You sold the farm, Dad?' Tom said.

Those faces. That face. Better than Nate could have hoped. Better than he could have ever expected.

'I had no option!' Carter said. 'We had nothing left. It was that or the house. Trust me, you said. You can't lose, you said. You ruined us!'

'You gave the farm to Drum? What were you thinking?'

'There was no more *thinking*. We had debts, I had to do something.'

'So you took my inheritance? You sat here and you listened to our plans and you let us believe that it would be okay? You let us think there was no problem.'

'There *was* no problem. He promised he'd sell it back to us at some point. How did I know you were going to move back here to set up some organic farm or something? And he promised. He gave me his word!'

That boom voice from youth, the shrunken mess of man. Like Rumpelstiltskin, hopping, incensed at being caught out. Anneka laughed. That laugh.

'Treacherous times indeed,' Anneka said. 'You can't even rely on the dead.'

'You stay out of this,' Carter said. 'The hell you made of his life and now you're even fouling up his death. What he wanted. What he promised.'

'He always said he wanted me to be safe and happy,' Anneka said. 'This is making me and my family safe and happy, so I think it's consonant with his wishes.'

Thomas didn't seem to know where to aim artillery, whether towards his father or to a smiling Anneka. Nate hadn't known what to expect, but Anneka seemed to have seen it all, how the scene would play out. Down into the bunker, the only place left now. From the light of summer to the dark of winter, from the upstairs to the downstairs.

'You're still holding this against me?' Thomas said. 'Nearly forty years later and you're holding something I didn't even do against me? You're delusional, you know that? You're insane. You come here, you upset my family, you come here and you disrespect your own father's memory and his good name and you stand there, smirking. Don't you fucking smirk at me, you cunt.'

The word settled, all eyes on Kim, all knowing the effect of that word on Americans. Unshocked by high-school shootings, but riven by a single cunt.

'We thought it would be a good idea to tell you in person,' Anneka said. 'But clearly this was a mistake. You'll see the notices about planning permission soon enough. I didn't think you could get over a hundred houses on the farm, but the developers seem more than confident.'

How much enjoyment, how much in her face, like the bug eyes when allowed to lick cake mixture from a bowl, like when she swam in the sea.

'We'll fight it,' Carter said. 'I still know people, you know. Tom knows people. There's no way you'll get the permission. Not while I've—'

'It's a formality,' Anneka said. 'We're in the middle of a housing crisis, do you not read the papers? They're crying out for land like ours. Desperate for it.'

He watched as Kim sat down, head bowed slightly, the rub and skirmish of the thoughts. Her husband called another woman a cunt. A dream, or something, dashed. She looked young there, young and a long way from NYU and asphalt and ironwork.

'Well, we'll see about that,' Carter said, but saw his son sit down next to his wife, put his hands on hers, her not looking at him, but down at her lap.

'How much?' Thomas said to the table.

'What's that?' Anneka said, 'I didn't catch that.'

'How much?' he said. 'To buy it outright. The farm I mean.'

Anneka joined him at the table, pulled up a chair. Light from the windows, refracted from copper pans, on the sheen of the tabletop.

'You want to negotiate?' Anneka said. 'What on earth makes you think I'd negotiate with you?'

How different would it have been had she stayed? How Nate's

life might have been altered, a few choice words from her. Another voice, a different voice in his ear, one not his father's. He could have left the farm a long time before, might not have fucked it all up with Carlie. It could have been all he needed. It could have been the difference. Not standing here, mute, like a personal guard next to his soft muttering mother, who, he realized, had just pissed herself.

IO

In Doom Town the lights are off and the wind is cold and there are dead dogs in the street. In Doom Town there is the distant sound of trains and of air-raid sirens, and there is Drummond in the distance, sitting cross-legged, in his shirtsleeves despite the chill. She walks carefully to him, does not run, does not trust her heels on the battered roadway. It is the first time she's been there and Gwen walks to him and he is crying and she puts her arms around him, feels the muscles under his shirt.

'Promise me,' he says.

'I promise,' she says, but does not know what she is promising. He kisses her then, a kiss she remembers, better than any kiss, better than any stolen or taken as right. She stands and holds out her hand, pulls him up and leads him to a small cottage. It is warm inside, there is a bed made up, a double, with downy sheets. She takes off his clothes. She kisses his chest, she puts her mouth on his penis. It grows inside her mouth. Soon he is inside her. Inside her, the firing damp, so much of it. They lie on the bed as semen slips down her leg, so much of it, so much liquid.

He says, promise me.

She says, I promise.

II

'Is she okay?' Carter said.

'Yes,' Nate said. 'Nothing to worry about.'

'She looks awful grey.'

'That's how she looks now.'

Neka looked across at Tommy, at his wife. Like poker, like three-card brag. She felt kinetic, able to move things, move people, fire bolts from her fingers. Come on. Lay it on. Show me your cards, Tommy boy. Show me their whites.

'Make me an offer,' she said. 'You have one opportunity. You have five minutes. Make me an offer, and if it's good enough, we promise to accept.'

'I'll have to—'

'You have the time it takes for us to change my mother's trousers to decide.'

Thomas laughed. 'You're loving this, aren't you? It's like a gameshow to you, isn't it? We have plans, you know, and you're sitting there laughing while your mother pisses herself.'

'He's always been a charmer,' Neka said to Kim, standing up. 'Some things never change.'

She followed Nate as he wheeled their mother into the dining room, the grand room bare, only the floor finished, everything else removed. Nate bent down and removed the trousers. From a bag he took wet wipes and cleaned her up as best he could, then dried her with a small towel. Wiped her up, threw the wipes in a lilac scented bag. She tried not to look at it and failed. Future and past.

'Is she okay?' Neka said.

'Yes,' he said. 'It happens from time to time.'

'Is she sleeping?' she said.

'Something like that. Sometimes she just zones out. Nothing to worry about though, is there, Mam?'

He plucked her from the seat, leaned her against his chest.

'Mop the seat for me, Anneka?' he said. 'There's a cloth in the bag.'

She wiped up with the cloth, the black vinyl seat quick drying.

'You don't have to be so harsh,' he said. 'It's too much.'

'It's done now,' she said. 'As planned. As you expected.'

'We're going to accept, aren't we?'

'I don't know,' she said. 'I really don't know.'

Nate turned his mother around.

'Now, put on the trousers. Not the jogging bottoms but the proper trousers.'

Neka found them in the bag, and inched the slacks up the just-dry legs, over thighs and hips.

'All set, Mam,' he said. 'All set.'

He placed her back in the chair, kissed her on the sleeping cheek.

'Ready?' she said.

'Are you sure?' he said. 'About all of this?'

'Think of Molly,' she said. 'Think of her. You can do this. I trust you, Nate.'

'Molly's not mine,' he said. 'Not really. Not really my daughter, biologically at least.'

'She's your screensaver on your phone,' she said. 'She's yours all right.'

She kissed his cheek, surprising, cementing. Knew that would be enough. Sure it would be enough. Certainty the great modern curse, as Robin had it. To be sure and certain the perfect kind of stupidity, the last trait of the idiot.

But sure, yes. Saw in Kim and saw in Thomas a plan, a series of dreams she could scupper. Power requires certainty; those who rarely have it are doomed to prevaricate. Fated to worry of outcome, of what the consequence. Give me the power. Let me hold it, just this once. Let me feel it, revel in it. Let me make the right choice.

Carter had poured his son and himself a Scotch; Kim was standing by the window, caught in thought and trapped in house. Nate wheeled his mother through and sat her at the table as though able to join the consultation. Happy, he saw that. The thought of Annie back, the two of them, enough. Now at drool, muttering with closed eyes.

'So?' Anneka said.

'Final offer,' Carter said. 'You take it and you leave within a week. I mean everything out. Gone.'

He passed a small square of paper across the table, folded over though there was no one there who did not already know, or wouldn't soon know, the amount on the paper.

Anneka let Nate open it. He examined it, passed it to her. To be able to write that many zeros. To write them and mean it. The zeros angled, slanting right. So many of them, neat and straight, perfectly judged.

'I'm sorry,' Anneka said. 'That isn't enough.'

'What?' Tom said. 'What?'

'It's not enough. Not nearly enough.'

'Anneka, we should at least discuss it,' Nate said.

'No,' she said. 'No, it's not enough and they know it.'

'Final offer,' Thomas said. 'Not to be repeated. One-time shot. Think of what you could do with the money, Nate. Think of that.'

'This is between me and my sister,' Nate said. 'Nothing to do with you.'

Nate looked at her. Could see the permutations whirring. Almost twice what the developers were offering. How much overage for the sweetness of revenge.

'Anneka, are you sure?' Nate said to her. 'It's a lot of—'

'It's not, and we won't accept this offer,' Anneka said. 'It's an insult.'

'An insult?' Nate said. He stood and knew how he looked. Same as he had looked before. A look like coming violence, a losing of control. The things he could say. The insult of her leaving. The insult of her not coming back. Wanting to say it all and knowing it futile.

He kicked the chair, which kicked the wheelchair, their mother jolting, looking up, looking round.

'Sorry, Mam,' he said. 'You okay?'

'Must have dozed off,' she said. 'Where are we?'

'Still at the Carters'.'

'Is Daphne here?' she said.

'No, Mam.'

'In Spain, I expect.'

'Yes,' he said. 'We're just talking about the farm. You remember?'

'Have you sold it yet, Drum?'

'Not yet, Mam.'

'Well sell it,' she said. 'And get a move on.'

13

From her bag, Anneka took a pen and changed one of the digits on the paper-fold. She looked at it for a moment, the scruff added to the clean numbers. A strange digit to add, on a whim. She passed the fold back to Carter and to Thomas.

'This we will accept,' she said. 'No less.'

They opened the fold. The two men huddled over it, a shared hand of cards. They muttered to each other. They looked to be doing sums.

Not what she wanted. Not the plan. Knew they would make an offer, knew it would be good. Knew that turning it down would be worth any amount of zeros. But Nate there. Her mother there. And something better than the plan. A line under it. All done. The victory of it, even if not the utter destruction she'd envisaged. Look at Nate. Do not regret. Do not look back and wish for the bomb. Do not wish for revenge. Do not look back and think you had him. You had him and you let him go. Do not think that. Think of the future, not the past.

Her offer was ratified with a nod. Simple and short, practised even. Just the nod. She stood and she shook hands with Carter. She did not shake the hand of Thomas, nor was it offered.

In Doom Town there is a jazz band playing. Gwen and Drum are getting dressed. Drum looks like Montgomery Clift and a writer she knows called Ray. He takes her hand and they dance through the terrorized cottage, dance on the pavements, the music lifting on the wind, the trumpets and trombones. They walk hand in hand, and head into a house. He is wearing overalls and two children are monkeying up his chest, there's oil on his hands and face, and Gwen is saying please, off you two, and the kids come back from the brook, all muddy and wet, and later she and Drum share a bath, lit by candles, and descend into the earth and only ever partially return, coming up to an old farmhouse, cold of stone and with a stout door, and through that door, a bump and jive and her two children, old and young, young and old, jump like frogs, up and down, they jump, the two of them, right there, joy on their faces, jumping like frogs.

They are in the farmhouse kitchen, the three of them, Gwen and her two children. Her children are holding a piece of paper in the air and they are jumping up and down. She watches them jump and holler and whoop. She wishes she could join them, could join in their victory dance. Her children are dancing together, laughing together, holding up the piece of paper. They are together.

She is looking at her children and she sees them together, both safe, both free. They are their most together here, at their most together now.

She is joined by Drum. He is smiling. They are safe, my love, she says. They are safe and free, my love. We are all of us safe and free.

Acknowledgements

I am indebted to a number of people for their help, encouragement and wisdom over the course of writing *The Blind Light*.

My agent, Lucy Luck, who knows what to say and when to say it. Thank you for always going above and beyond.

My editor, Kris Doyle, whose belief, enthusiasm, perseverance and attention to detail made this the book that it is. I can't thank you enough.

Jessica Cuthbert-Smith for her diligent and intelligent copy-edit.

Stuart Wilson for the UK cover; Lindsay Nash for the text design. Grace Harrison, Chloe May and all at Picador.

Tom Mayer, Nneoma Amadi-Obi and all at W. W. Norton in the US.

Harris the dog appears courtesy of Joe Cooney, who won the Authors for Grenfell auction to name a pet in *The Blind Light*. Thank you, Joe, for supporting such an important cause.

Kit Caless and Gary Budden from Influx Press for agreeing to publish fictional books.

Rowena Willard-Wright at Dover Castle gave me some wonderful insights into Cold War nuclear planning; while the staff at the Millom Discovery Centre provided wider understanding of the surrounding area.

Thank you to everyone at the Eccles British Library Writers Award, especially Catherine Eccles, Phil Hatfield and Jean Petrovitch.

Tom Cosson for his help with the Welsh. *Diolch.*

Kristina Radke, Natalie Fox, Lindsey Lochner, Tarah Theoret, Fran Toolan and all at NetGalley.

Oliver Shepherd for first-reading/best-friend duties.

William Atkins for advice, good humour, support, and appearing when needed.

Dawn Price for being there for everyone.

Gareth Evers and Megan Bond; Matthew Baker, Anna Herman and Pearl Baker.

My mother and father, Joyce and John Evers; Barbara Callender and Eugene Sorokin; Simon Baker and Hilda Breakspear for their incredible support over some difficult years.

Caleb and Max Evers. Lighting the years.

Lisa Baker. To the ends of the earth. Again and always.